Outside Looking In

Michael Wood is a freelance journalist and proofreader living in Sheffield. As a journalist he has covered many crime stories throughout Sheffield, gaining first-hand knowledge of police procedure. He also reviews books for CrimeSquad, a website dedicated to crime fiction. *Outside Looking In* is his second novel.

@MichaelWood
/MichaelWoodBooks

D1499847

Also by Michael Wood

For Reasons Unknown

MICHAEL WOOD

Outside Looking In

an imprint of HarperCollins*Publishers*
www.harpercollins.co.uk

Killer Reads
An imprint of HarperCollins*Publishers*
1 London Bridge Street
London SE1 9GF

www.harpercollins.co.uk

This paperback edition 2016
1

First published in Great Britain by
HarperCollins*Publishers* 2016

A catalogue record for this book is
available from the British Library

ISBN: 978-0-00-819047-7

Set in Minion by Palimpsest Book Production Ltd, Falkirk, Stirlingshire

Find out more about HarperCollins and the environment at
www.harpercollins.co.uk/green

To Jonas Alexander.

For the friendship, the laughter, and the coffee.

ONE

George and Mary Rainsford had the same night-time routine for over thirty years. As soon as the music marking the end of the ten o'clock news began it was time to go to bed. Mary would go straight upstairs while George put the kettle on. Waiting for the kettle to boil George would go around the ground floor of the cottage making sure all the windows and doors were locked, the cushions were neat on the sofa, plugs turned off, and say goodnight to his guppies in their tank. He made two cups of tea and headed for the stairs. Tonight, their routine would be shattered beyond repair. Tomorrow, there would be no routine. There would be no half an hour of reading before turning the light out, no goodnight kiss, nothing. Just a void where their previous life was replaced by an empty feeling of fear.

As George made the tea he listened to the sounds from the outside: a few sheep bleating from a nearby farm, a dog barking, and a car horn beeping. It was comforting; everyday life still going on outside the confines of their small cosy cottage.

He walked up the stairs carefully, a mug of tea in each hand.

'Can you hear that?' he asked upon entering the bedroom.

'What?' Mary was already in bed, a closed Colin Dexter paperback on her lap. She was rubbing cream vigorously into her hands.

1

She took her usual mug from George and cupped her hands around it. 'Blimey George, you've squeezed the bag a bit too hard. I'm not a builder.'

'There's a car beeping outside.'

'Well, there would be.'

'It's been going on for a while.'

'Maybe it's an impatient taxi driver waiting for a fare. You know what they're like.'

George placed his mug on his bedside table and went to the window. He parted the thick blackout curtains and poked his head through the gap.

'Can you see anything?' Mary asked, only half interested.

'No. Those new solar powered lamp-posts are bloody useless aren't they?'

'Ignore it and come to bed.'

'I can't ignore it. It's in my head now.'

'Put Radio 4 on low. That'll cover it.'

'Wait. Listen.' He was silent for a moment. He pulled his head out of the gap in the curtains and looked at his wife. 'Do you hear that?'

'I hear the beeping, yes. That's because you've drawn my attention to it.'

'No. Listen. It's rhythmic.'

'It's what?'

'Rhythmic. There's a pattern to the noise. That's not just beeping. Someone's signalling. It's Morse.'

'What?'

'Morse code. Listen. The beeps are dots and the silences are dashes. Sshh, listen.'

A long minute of silence passed while they both concentrated on the sound of the car horn in the distance.

'I can just hear beeping.'

'No. It's SOS.'

'What?'

'SOS in Morse code: three dots, three dashes, and three dots. Listen, beep, beep, beep, quiet, beep, beep, beep. Then a gap, then it starts again. Someone's in trouble.'

George turned on his heels and headed for the bedroom door.

'George, where do you think you're going?'

'To have a look. Someone could be injured.'

'Then call the police.' She followed him down the stairs, struggling into her dressing gown.

'You don't call the police over a car beeping.'

'Call the non-emergency number. What is it, 111?'

'101. Anyway, it's always busy. You can never get through. I may as well go and have a look myself.'

Fear was growing in Mary's voice. It was already etched on her face. 'George, don't go. It's dark. You said yourself those lamp-posts are no good. You won't be able to see anything.'

He opened a drawer in the hall table and took out a torch. He flicked it on and off to check it worked. It did.

'You don't know who's out there, George. It could be a trap.' Her voice had risen an octave. She was scared.

'I can't just ignore it, Mary.'

'Yes you can. It's nothing to do with us.'

'It's people saying things like that why this country's in the state it's in. People don't take an interest in others anymore.'

'It's called being safe.'

'It's called being ignorant. Where are my walking boots?'

'Oh God, George. Please don't go.'

'I won't be long. I promise.'

'Then put your heavy coat on, at least. It's cold. Wait.' She ran upstairs and quickly came back down. She was out of breath. It was years since she had run anywhere. 'Take your mobile. You see anything you don't like the look of call 999 straightaway. Do you hear me, George Rainsford?'

'Loud and clear.'

He unbolted the door, took the chain off, and unlocked it.

'Lock this door behind me. Don't open it until I come back.'

'I love you George, you silly sod.'

'I'll be right back.'

As George reached the end of the garden path he turned around. Mary was watching through a gap in the living room curtains. He gave her a little wave and she waved back. He hated seeing her frightened, but he couldn't stand by and leave a distress call go unanswered.

The beeping was louder outside, and George was more convinced than ever that it was Morse code for SOS.

From the end of the garden path he looked left and right wondering which direction the noise was coming from. He opted for left but only went a few paces before he changed his mind and headed right.

Quiet Lane didn't have any pavements. It was a steep winding road where drivers should travel with caution, but the national speed limit signs did not promote a safety-first action.

He zipped his coat up fully. The sky was clear and the moon full; an infinite number of stars helped to brighten the dark sky. It was cold. George could see his breath forming as his breathing became more erratic with nerves. With each step, the beeping grew louder. He was heading in the right direction.

Where Quiet Lane turned into Wood Cliffe Cottage Lane there was a junction. Clough Lane was a very narrow road full of cavernous potholes and broken tarmac. The beeping was coming from down this road.

Surrounded by empty fields and leafless trees, Clough Lane was in complete darkness. He took the small torch from the pocket of his coat and turned it on. Pointing it at the ground, he edged along the road into the unknown.

The sound of the car horn was definitely coming from down here. He rounded a bend and aimed the torch upwards. The weak beam hit something; a car, a silver car. He knew the make straightaway, a Citroen Xsara. His son had one in white. This was the offending car whose horn was shattering the silence.

He picked up the pace and was about to call out a greeting when he stopped dead in his tracks. The torch beam had picked up something from the side of the road. Slumped against a tree was a man; or a close approximation of a man. It was difficult to make out any features as he had been severely beaten; the nose had erupted at some point, the left eye was swollen shut, and the right side of his face was a mangled mess from where a bullet had exploded in him.

George put a shaking cold hand to his mouth. He could smell the metallic tang of blood. He could taste it. The sight was shocking, yet he could not tear his eyes away from it. This was once a person, a living human being, and someone had inflicted an unimaginable amount of pain and torture upon his body.

The loud beeping brought George out of his reverie. He pointed the torch to the side of the car. It was covered in smeared blood. The passenger door window was shattered. Slowly, he walked around the front of the car towards the driver's side. He could see the door was open but could not see anyone in the driver's seat; yet the SOS beeping continued.

'Oh, dear God.' He gasped.

Half hanging out of the car was the stricken body of a woman. Her face was a mess of sticky drying blood; her long hair was tangled and matted. She was naked from the waist down and was literally drenched in blood. One hand held on to her stomach where blood pumped out between her fingers. The other hand was rhythmically banging on the horn. She was half in, half out of the car, her body at an uncomfortable angle. She looked up and saw George through swollen eyes. She stopped the beeping and slumped to the ground. There was a brief smile on her face before her body gave up and she lost consciousness.

George dug the phone out of his coat pocket and dialled 999. He gave his location and tried to say what had happened but he

TWO

CARL MEAGAN: ONE YEAR ON
By Andrea Fullerton

Tomorrow marks the first anniversary of the disappearance of seven-year-old Carl Meagan.

Exactly twelve months ago, Annabel Meagan, Carl's grandmother, was looking after him at his parents' luxury home in Dore, Sheffield, when she was bludgeoned to death. Carl was kidnapped and a ransom was demanded. However, a catalogue of errors by South Yorkshire Police led to the kidnappers breaking contact with the Meagan family and Carl has not been heard of since.

Carl's parents – Philip 37, and Sally, 34 – have spent the past year in limbo as they desperately search for their only child.

'It's not knowing that is the most difficult part. He could be anywhere in the world. I'm his mother. I should know exactly where he is day and night and I haven't a clue. I've failed him,' Sally said. 'I never left him alone. I never let him out of my sight. He was my world and now I just feel empty.'

The Meagan family believe they were being watched for several days in the run-up to the kidnapping. On the night in question, Philip and Sally were attending an award ceremony for Yorkshire Businessman of the Year in Leeds. They were not due back until the following day and Philip's mother, Annabel, was looking after Carl.

'We had nothing to worry about. We knew he was safe with his grandmother. She doted on him and he loved her to pieces. As far as we knew he was safe. They both were. When we got back the next day it was pure hell.'

Philip Meagan, owner of Nature's Dinner, a chain of organic restaurants in South Yorkshire, says the blame is entirely on South Yorkshire Police. 'The whole investigation was badly handled from day one. From Carl going missing to the ransom demand it was two days. Those 48 hours were a nightmare and we had no support from the police at all. They just left us.'

Leading the investigation was Detective Chief Inspector Matilda Darke, who, following the botched ransom drop, was suspended from the force. She has since returned to work to continue leading the Murder Investigation Team.

'The ransom was for a quarter of a million pounds. It wasn't easy but we managed to get the money together. For some reason the kidnappers kept changing the location of the drop. I think the amount of press attention was too much for them. They eventually decided on Graves Park.

'It was DCI Darke who organized it all. She had the parameters covered and everything was in place. We had no reason to doubt we wouldn't be getting our Carl home. She came back to the house an hour later saying it had all blown up. We waited and waited but we heard nothing from the kidnappers.'

It was later revealed that the kidnappers had called DCI Darke demanding the whereabouts of the ransom money.

However, they were at a different entrance to the park, and in panic, they fled. That was the last anyone heard from the kidnappers and Carl.

'It is absolutely disgusting that that woman has been allowed to return to duty. She shouldn't have been suspended, she should have been sacked. She's not fit to do the job,' Philip continued.

DCI Darke was unavailable for comment yesterday, but South Yorkshire Police issued a short statement: 'While every effort was made to communicate with the kidnappers to ensure Carl's safe return, events beyond our control occurred and we were unable to succeed. However, the Meagan case is still ongoing and continuously being investigated. We will keep looking for Carl until he is found.'

Philip Meagan issued a direct plea to the people holding Carl. 'If you still have Carl, please take very good care of him. If you're worried about handing him back, just leave him in a public place and make an anonymous call to us telling us where he is and we will collect him. There will be no more action taken against you. We just want him back home so much.'

Sally continued: 'If Carl is reading this I just want you to know that your mummy and daddy love you very much and we always will. It may take us a while, but we'll come and find you.'

To mark the anniversary of Carl's disappearance there will be a special service at Sheffield Cathedral. Players at Sheffield United, who the Meagan family support, will wear special messages on their shirts at this weekend's fixture at Bramall Lane.

Matilda Darke, having read the article for the third time, threw the newspaper onto the floor and slumped back into the sofa, releasing a heavy sigh. She hadn't been 'unavailable for comment' yesterday; the reporter hadn't even tried to contact her. To the reading public, it would look like DCI Matilda Darke had washed her hands of the whole Carl Meagan case and his family, who were, in essence, grieving for the loss of their only child.

She closed her eyes and took a deep breath. It was at times like these when she wished she had alcohol in the house. However, after a year of heavy drinking, passing out in drunken stupors, only functioning with the aid of a bottle of vodka in her hand, she had made a promise not to touch a single drop again.

Realistically, that was never going to happen. Of course Matilda would have another drink at some point, but if she could learn to live without having to depend on alcohol then it would be an achievement.

Matilda had been saved by her close friend, Adele Kean. Adele had seen the slippery slope Matilda had been on and managed to drag her back before she descended into alcoholism. The disappearance of Carl Meagan was just the starting point in a year-long nightmare that snowballed into a cataclysm of self-destruction.

She opened her eyes, which immediately fell onto the silver framed wedding photograph on the mantelpiece. Five years ago, the happiest day of her life, she and James Darke had married. Three years later he was diagnosed with an inoperable brain tumour and within twelve months he was gone. His death coincided with the ransom drop for the Meagan kidnappers but Matilda's mind was on other things. She should have handed the case over to a more competent detective, taken some time off to grieve, but she couldn't. The devastation she left in her wake would stay with her for the rest of her life. She had to live with the consequences of her actions.

When it came to Carl Meagan, there would never be any redemption.

The picture frame was smeared with dried tears where Matilda had spent many a night curled up in bed, clutching her smiling husband and crying. Saying she loved him sounded hollow. She didn't just love him, she ached for him, and sometimes stopped breathing when she thought of him. Her body, mind, and soul wanted to be with James more than it wanted life itself.

There was a knock on the door. She looked at the clock on the mantelpiece: 22.50. A solid knock at this time of night could only mean one thing.

'Sorry to bother you, ma'am, there's been a shooting.'

DC Scott Andrews stood on the doorstep in a crumpled suit. His blond hair was windswept and it was evident from his red cheeks that he had been standing out in the cold for a while. There was no greeting. Sometimes, there wasn't time for one.

'Where?'

'Clough Lane. Ringinglow.'

'I'll get my things. Come in.'

Scott stepped into the hallway and closed the door behind him. He looked down at the three bulging black bags in the corner.

'Having a clear out? I keep meaning to do that. I buy new shirts for work and never think about getting rid of the old ones. I can hardly close my wardrobe door.'

'Those are my dead husband's clothes. I'm giving them to charity.'

'Oh,' he almost choked, his face reddening. 'Sorry. I didn't … well … I mean …'

Matilda smiled. 'I love how you blush at the slightest thing, Scott. Come on, let's go before you start trying to dig yourself out and make things worse.'

There was a strong breeze as Matilda stepped out of the house. She set the alarm and locked the door behind her. She looked up. The sky was cloudless and there was a large full moon beaming down on the steel city. It made the night brighter, bathing everything in an ethereal glow. They walked up the drive to where Scott had parked the pool car.

'So how serious is this shooting?'

'One dead and one critical.'

'Jesus! I hate guns.'

'Good evening.'

Matilda almost jumped out of her skin and quickly turned to see where the greeting was coming from.

'Oh God, I'm sorry. I didn't mean to scare you.' Jill Carmichael, Matilda's next-door neighbour, was unloading her car. She was struggling under the weight of a newborn baby in one arm and trying to safely put several bags on her opposite shoulder.

'You didn't.'

'How are things?'

Matilda frowned. Jill never asked that. Why, all of a sudden, was she showing an interest in . . . the newspaper article. She'd seen the story about Carl Meagan, read about how much of a failure Matilda was, and wanted the inside scoop. 'Things are fine,' she lied unconvincingly. 'Bloody hell, what's happened to you?'

'Sorry?'

'The black eye.' It was the first time Matilda had looked up at her neighbour. Usually she wasn't one for chatting with a neighbour but while this awkward exchange was going on she'd rather the attention be on Jill than herself.

'Oh, it's nothing,' she giggled. 'I'm having a few problems shaking off these last few pregnancy pounds so I've started kickboxing again. I think I'm a bit rusty to tell the truth.'

'I think I'd stick with the extra few pounds.'

'You're probably right.'

'Jill!' An angry shout called out to her from inside the house.

'That'll be Sebastian wondering where his takeaway is. I'll chat to you some other time.' With that, Jill kicked the car door closed and hurried into the house, struggling under the weight of the shopping, baby, and takeaway.

'That your neighbour?' Scott asked as they climbed into the car.

'Spot on as ever, Scott. Yes, that's my neighbour. Look, she's going into the house next door to mine,' she smiled.

'I never got a black eye when I tried kick-boxing.'

'I'm sure it wasn't for lack of trying on your opponent's part.' Scott's frown told Matilda he didn't understand her little dig. Her smile widened.

Matilda wished all she had to contend with was a few extra pounds. She looked down at the ripples in her shirt caused by the rolls of fat underneath. Adele had tried to coax her into joining a spinning class. Matilda went along once. She sweated to the point of serious dehydration and felt the effects on her bum for more than a week afterwards every time she tried to sit down. Never again. In the end she just went out and bought bigger clothes. She was content with being a size twelve on a good day (fourteen on a bad one), but still yearned for the gorgeous size ten Armani suit in her wardrobe. Maybe one day.

As Scott pulled away Matilda looked back at her house, which was now in complete darkness. Next door Jill Carmichael and her husband would be sitting down to a nice takeaway, a newborn baby fast asleep: a happy couple curled up together on the sofa watching television. She envied them so much. She hoped they appreciated the happiness they had.

THREE

To get to Clough Lane, Scott had to traverse Quiet Lane – a long, meandering road that belonged in the middle of the countryside. With tall trees on both sides and inadequate lighting you took the perilous corners and bends with caution. Scott slowed down to thirty miles per hour, and even then he felt like he was speeding.

The scene laid out before them was like a location set for a sci-fi film. Looking down Matilda could see the intense brilliance of white spotlights and a cast of white-suited police and forensic officers going about their work.

Scott pulled up at the roadblock, a sensible distance away from the crime scene.

Matilda hated this part: entering a crime scene for the first time. Scott had filled her in on the basics during the journey but it was nothing compared to experiencing it for herself. She was stepping into the unknown and had no idea how it would make her feel.

She opened the door and stepped out. The stiff breeze in the built-up area of Sheffield had been upgraded to a strong wind on the border of the Peak District National Park.

From the outset, the scene didn't give anything away. The white tent was covering the main stage. Inside, a brilliant light was glowing, casting shadows of forensic officers going about their grisly business.

'Ma'am.'

She jumped and turned to see DS Aaron Connolly standing beside her. He proffered a white forensic suit for her to try and squeeze into. She looked for Scott but he had disappeared. How long had she zoned out for?

Aaron was a tall, well-built man in his mid-thirties. Unfortunately for him, forensic suits weren't designed as a fashion item, nor did they come in an array of sizes. It was first come, first served, and judging by the difficulty Aaron was having breathing in his, he was obviously late to the scene.

'Sorry we had to call you out, ma'am. Any news on a new DI yet?'

'Not yet. The one who was joining us from Middlesbrough changed his mind.'

'Really? Why?'

'No idea. He probably saw the Park Hill flats from the train station and decided to head back north. What's happening here then?' she asked, quickly wanting to get off the subject of a new DI. Her involvement with the last one was still a very sore subject.

Aaron dug around in his pocket for a notebook. 'George Rainsford, an old bloke who lives in one of the cottages, hears a car beeping just after going to bed. It carries on and he realizes there's a pattern to the beeping. He listens and he says it's rhythmic; the beeps are SOS in Morse code. He decides to investigate and discovers a woman, barely conscious, sounding the horn, and a dead man at the side of the road. They've both been badly beaten and shot several times. The woman's gone to the Northern General Hospital and the man was already dead when we arrived.'

Matilda was sure that was the most she had ever heard Aaron say in one go. 'I'd better take a look then. Who's here?'

'We've got a full forensic team. They've not been here long

and it looks like they'll be here all night. Dr Kean and her assistant have arrived and the Crime Scene Manager is knocking around somewhere.'

Matilda stopped. She had a heavy frown on her face, thinking about what steps to take next. 'I want a full statement from the man who found her. What did you say he was called again?'

'George Rainsford,' he replied, checking his notebook. 'Sian's taken him back to the station. He was in a right state. I doubt she'll get anything out of him tonight.'

'OK. Give Sian a ring, ask how he's doing. If he's not capable of giving a statement tonight get her to send him home with a uniformed officer to stay with him and we'll interview tomorrow morning. Any other witnesses?'

'No.'

'I see I'm here before the gawkers; didn't anyone hear the gunshots, screams?'

'It doesn't look like it. It's pretty isolated around here.'

'Door-to-door?'

'There aren't many houses around here as you can see but I've got a small team together and they're going to knock on a couple of doors.'

Matilda was beginning to feel surplus to requirements. 'Do we know who our victims are?'

Aaron checked his notebook again. 'I've run the car through the ANPR. I'm still waiting to get information on where it's been in the run-up to it arriving here. However, the PNC says it's registered to Kevin Hardaker at Broad Elms Lane in Bents Green.'

'Not far away.'

'No.'

'And the woman?'

'I've no idea. There's nothing in the car to identify her; no bag, purse, nothing. I'm guessing she's his wife.'

'Are you thinking robbery then?'

'I'm not sure. Mr Hardaker is wearing a very expensive-looking watch, his wallet is in the glove compartment with cash and cards, and Mrs Hardaker still has a ring on her wedding finger.'

'How is she?'

'She was unconscious by the time we arrived. According to Mr Rainsford she was using all her energy to signal for help. The second he arrived she just collapsed. PC … blonde woman, Polish, can't pronounce her surname … she went with her in the ambulance; she called me a few minutes before you arrived. She has a collapsed lung, internal bleeding, and several broken ribs, and that's just what the paramedics mentioned. God knows what they'll discover when they fully examine her. It's not looking good.'

'Bloody hell. OK. Good work Aaron.' She reached up and patted him on the shoulder and headed towards the white tent protecting the area.

As Matilda entered she was presented with a scene of utter destruction. The body of Kevin Hardaker was lying in a painful-looking position. He no longer resembled a person. He was badly beaten and heavily bloodied; his limbs at unnatural angles. Not even his own mother would be able to identify him. His face had no recognizable features.

Photographs had already been taken of the body in situ, and bags had been placed over each hand and his head to collect any evidence that may have fallen off when transporting him from the crime scene to the mortuary.

Matilda was surprised to see pathologist Adele Kean bent over the body. Usually it was left to forensics to gather everything and Adele would wait in the relative warmth of the mortuary. During the more disturbing crime scenes Matilda would request that Adele attend.

'What are you doing here?'

'Sian called and told me how bad it was. I thought I'd put in an appearance.'

Matilda looked at the broken body of Kevin Hardaker. 'What can you tell me about this poor chap?'

17

Adele shook her head in disbelief. 'Where do I begin? Until I get him back to the mortuary I'm not going to make any snap judgements. Firstly, I can only describe the beating as savage. The majority of the blows are to the trunk of the body and head. If you look around, you'll see sprays of blood; this was a prolonged attack which covered a great deal of ground. It looks like he was kicked around like a football.'

'Bloody hell!' Matilda muttered.

'He was shot twice. One shot to the chest, the second to the head, which practically blew it open at the back.' She spoke with such nonchalance she could have been reading a children's story book.

'Was it the gunshots that killed him?'

'At this stage I'll say yes. Although judging by the blows to the face and head I'm guessing he was unconscious before the first shot.'

'Let's hope so.' Matilda was rooted rigid to the spot. She was surrounded by death on a daily basis but the level of violence people seemed able to inflict on others never failed to shock her. Adele's cool, calm presence was astonishing.

'His left eye is swollen shut. There's nothing left of his right. My guess is he didn't even see the gun being pointed at him. I'll try and get the PM done first thing and you'll know more then.'

'Thanks Adele.'

'You're welcome,' she said, placing a friendly, comforting arm on her best friend's shoulder. 'What's all this about an SOS call?'

'The woman was beeping SOS in Morse code; that's how the man who found her came to discover her.'

'Blimey, I didn't think people used Morse anymore. The last time I saw it was on *Titanic*.'

'Ah, Adele, you're not that old, surely,' Matilda said with a hint of a smile.

'The film, you cheeky cow. Come over to the car; I want to show you something.'

Both front doors of the silver Citroen Xsara were wide open. As Matilda approached she took a long look at it. There were specks of blood on both sides of the bodywork. On the back, full sprays of blood adorned the boot.

Matilda stopped in her tracks. On what was left of the window in the back of the car was a sticker that read 'cheeky monkey on board'. Kevin Hardaker obviously had a young child, maybe more than one. She closed her eyes tight to banish the image of a small boy in torment over the loss of his father at a young age: a father who called him his cheeky monkey.

'Right then, Kevin Hardaker was driving—'

'How do you know that?'

'Well, for a start I have a wonderful Assistant Technical Officer who spotted what I'm about to show you. He was forcibly pulled out of the car and was still wearing his seat belt at the time. If you look at the body, you can see where the belt cut into his neck and there's blood on the driver's side.'

'OK.'

'Judging by the spatter patterns of blood on the car he's punched, kicked, whatever, towards the back of the car; the attack getting more frenzied as he gets to the back, as you can see. If I were you I'd get forensics to get good detailed photos and film of these patterns—'

'We already have.' The interrupting call came from one of the forensic officers currently with their head in the back of the car.

Adele shrugged her shoulders and continued. 'Once he's behind the car the beating becomes more intense. I mean, look at the state of the car; the bodywork is knackered. When the attacker has finished he throws him to the ground – where he is now – and finishes him off with two bullets at point-blank range.'

'What about the blood on the other side of the car?'

'I'm guessing they belong to the wife. Forensics have taken samples.'

'Do you know what type of gun was used?'

'No. We've found some shells and I can't see any exit wounds so I think the bullets are still in him. I'm not too hot on guns so I'll need to do some research.'

'How long do you reckon the attack on Kevin Hardaker lasted?'

She blew out her cheeks. 'I've no idea. Anything from a few minutes to ten minutes to much longer. If there was a conversation between the attacker and victim it could have gone on for a very long time.'

'So while he was being beaten, what was Mrs Hardaker doing at the time? Even if the attacker took the key and locked it she could have still got out. A second attacker maybe?' Matilda was thinking aloud.

'So far we've found no foreign prints or anything on Mr Hardaker, but I may do once I get him back to base. There's a partial footprint on his chest though. I may be able to work out a shoe size from that, but I'm not hopeful.'

'So there was either a second attacker keeping her hostage while Mr Hardaker was beaten or she just sat there awaiting her fate.'

'That's your department DCI Darke, not mine, thank goodness.' Adele turned on her heels and headed back to the dead body of Kevin Hardaker leaving Matilda in deep thought.

'Ma'am?' DC Rory Fleming interrupted her.

'Good evening Rory, what … bloody hell, are you sponsored by Calvin Klein or something?' she asked, wafting away the strong smell of fragrance coming from him.

'Sorry?'

'You don't need to drown yourself in the stuff.'

'It's Paco Rabanne, actually.'

'Is that Spanish for sewer water?'

He pulled out his collar and sniffed himself. 'I think it smells nice; very sexy.'

'Since when was attending a crime scene sexy? Look, Rory, do me a favour, go to the Northern General and find out how Mrs Hardaker is.'

'Will do. I thought you'd want to look at this.' He handed her a wallet sealed in a forensic bag. It was open and the driving licence was showing.

Matilda studied the photograph. He didn't look familiar. 'A good-looking guy.' There was a trace of sadness in her voice.

'He used to be.'

'Where's Scott disappeared to?'

'He's over with forensics.'

'OK. Tell him to get a car and an FLO. I want to go to the Hardaker home. If they do have kids they'll be worried out of their minds.'

They were both interrupted by a bright white flash coming from further up the road. They looked up to see a man with a camera pointing at them, obviously a journalist.

'Shit,' Matilda said under her voice and turning her back on him. 'How do they find out so quickly?'

'I saw the story about you in *The Star* tonight,' Rory said.

'You and everyone else judging by the stares I've been getting.'

'I shouldn't worry about it. Nobody believes the crap they write anyway. Do you know what my mum always says?'

'That today's newspaper is tomorrow's chip paper?'

'How did you know that? Do you know my mum?' Rory asked, a shocked look on his face.

'No. I just knew one of you was going to say it at some point. I'd have put money on it being you, too.' She smiled. 'Now bugger off to the hospital.'

Matilda took out her phone and looked for a number in her contacts list. She had one eye on the journalist, wanting to make sure he wasn't trying to get closer to the crime scene.

'Ma'am, I'm sorry to call so late,' Matilda said when the call was eventually answered.

'Who is this?' The sleepy, gravelly voice of Assistant Chief

Constable Valerie Masterson. Obviously she had answered the call as a matter of urgency, not looking at the display to see who was interrupting her much valued sleep.

'It's DCI Darke, ma'am. There's been a shooting.'

That statement was better than a bucket of cold water thrown in the face. She suddenly sounded wide awake.

'Shooting? Where? Who?'

'I'm on Clough Lane – it's Ringinglow.'

'I know where Clough Lane is,' she snapped.

'As you know I'm a few detectives down and I'm going to need all hands on deck. I was wondering—'

'Let me stop you right there Matilda. I was going to talk to you first thing in the morning. I'm afraid the Murder Investigation Team no longer exists.'

FOUR

The scream woke Martin Craven with a start. His eyes wide and his heart thumping in his chest, he wondered where he was.

A second scream and he jumped up. He must have fallen asleep on the sofa. The cry was coming from upstairs. He left the living room and ran upstairs, taking them two at a time. He knew where the offending noise was coming from.

He burst into the small box room and turned on the light. Sitting up in the single bed was his youngest son, Thomas, aged eight.

Thomas was glistening with sweat, his face red, and tears streaming down his face. 'I had a bad dream,' he said loudly, too frightened to sign.

Martin ran towards him, sat on the edge of the bed and put his arms around him. He pulled him close and tight and tried to hush him from waking everyone else in the house.

He released him so Thomas could read his father's lips. 'It's all right, Thomas, calm down. It was just a dream. There's nothing to worry about,' he enunciated.

'Someone was chasing me ...'

'Now, come on Thomas. We've talked about this before. They're just dreams. They're not real. You're perfectly safe.'

Thomas sniffed and wiped his nose with the sleeve of his Batman pyjamas. 'I've had an accident,' he said, almost under his breath.

Martin carefully pushed back the Avengers duvet and saw the wet patches on his pyjama trousers and the fitted sheet. 'Don't worry about it. Come on, hop out and we'll clean it up.' He signed and spoke at the same time.

'Are you mad at me?'

'Of course I'm not mad.' He gave him a kiss on the top of his head. 'You go and have a wash and put on a new pair of pyjamas. I'll change your bedding and we'll meet in the kitchen and have a glass of milk and a few Oreos.'

Thomas's eyes lit up. 'Just us two?'

'Just us two.'

Thomas jumped out of bed. The prospect of milk and cookies brightened him up. He picked up the two hearing aids from his bedside table and placed them in as he trotted to the bathroom.

Martin took off the duvet cover and carefully lifted off the fitted sheet. Before he took them downstairs to the utility room he looked into his own room expecting to see his wife fast asleep in bed. She wasn't. The bed hadn't been slept in. He looked at his watch. It was almost midnight.

His wife should have been home more than four hours ago.

It took less than five minutes for Matilda, DC Scott Andrews, and DC Joseph Glass to get to Broad Elms Lane from the crime scene.

Matilda had been hoping for a female Family Liaison Officer, especially if the Hardakers had young children; a six-foot tall, stick thin, geeky looking bloke with stubble and thick-rimmed glasses may not have the natural ability to offer succour to petrified kids wanting their parents. It didn't help that the quickly drafted-in DC Glass reeked of the local pub.

'When did you complete the FLO course, Glass?'

'A couple of weeks ago ma'am.'

'Is this your first assignment?'

'It certainly is,' he replied with a smile. 'You don't need to worry though. I've done plenty of courses since joining the police. I'm on the fast-track scheme too. I know what I'm doing.'

'Do you have any kids of your own, Glass?'

'No. It's just me and a tortoise.'

DC Andrews sniggered from the driver's seat while Matilda could feel the oncoming tension of a stress headache creeping up the back of her neck.

Since hearing of the fate of the Murder Room, Matilda had been a mass of seething rage. She had helped to set up the Murder Investigation Team (South Yorkshire), to give it its formal title, five years ago, and now it was being axed, closed, deleted.

It was no secret that the future of the department was in doubt, but Matilda had been silently confident that ACC Masterson could save it, if she worked hard on the decision makers.

The national press had not been good to South Yorkshire Police; their part in the Hillsborough disaster and the unprecedented levels of sexual abuse in Rotherham had placed the force under intense scrutiny. Budgets had been slashed and non-essential projects and departments shelved or dropped. Even police dogs weren't immune; several were facing early retirement. It would appear that the Murder Room was also one such department. What did that mean for Matilda's future?

She thought of her team: Aaron and Sian were two very dedicated sergeants. They had been with the MIT from day one. It would be a waste of their talents to go back to investigating burglaries and druggies with egos from the sink estates. Matilda decided not to say anything to anyone yet. She would have a more detailed word with the ACC in the morning and go from there.

Broad Elms Lane was picturesque. Residents seemed to take care of their properties; neatly trimmed lawns and hedges, well-kept driveways, swept pavements, gleaming windows and doors, and not a single item of litter in sight. It was like they were anticipating a royal visit.

Matilda stepped out of the car and looked around her. Most of the houses were in darkness. It was rapidly approaching midnight, after all. The breeze had picked up and she felt a chill run through her; it may have been the task ahead, the breach into the unknown of what lay behind the front door of the Hardaker house; young children, teenagers, a baby? This was not going to be easy.

Everything about the front door was symmetrical: a small potted fern tree either side of the door, the pattern in the stained glass, even the door number, 101, was symmetrical. The gravel driveway was neatly swept too, not a stone out of place. A perfectly designed entrance to what appeared to be, from the outside, an orderly family home.

The property was in darkness save for the faint glow from the edge of the closed curtains in a downstairs front room. The sound of the doorbell echoed through the house and down most of the street. Matilda wondered how many curtains on the opposite side of the road were twitching right now. A caller in the middle of the night was rare; three people, smartly dressed with grim faces, screamed plain-clothes police delivering bad news.

The door opened and Matilda was surprised to see a tall woman around her own age, early forties. For a second she was side-tracked, and temporarily blinded by the hallway light. A thought suddenly struck Matilda. Was this Kevin Hardaker's wife? Of course she could be a neighbour or a relative, but something told Matilda this wasn't the case. Which begged the question: who the hell was the woman he was parked with on a quiet country lane?

She broached the question cautiously. 'Mrs Hardaker?'

'Yes.'

Behind Matilda, Scott and Joseph exchanged nervous glances. She held up her warrant card. 'I'm DCI Matilda Darke from

South Yorkshire Police ...' Was there a flash of recognition on the woman's face at the mention of her name? Had she read tonight's copy of *The Star*? 'This is DC Andrews and DC Glass. May we have a word?'

'Oh God,' the greeting smile fell from the woman's face. 'Has something happened?'

'Perhaps we could come inside.'

Alice Hardaker stepped to one side and allowed the three detectives to enter. She closed the door firmly, even putting the security chain on, and led them into a very large living room. The decoration was minimalistic; two large sofas, a large-screen TV with various consoles attached, and a solitary bookcase housing DVDs, games, the odd ornament, but strangely, no books.

'Mrs Hardaker, your husband ...?'

'Kevin.'

Again Scott and Joseph Glass exchanged nervous glances. They could have conducted this entire interview with their facial expressions alone.

'Does he drive a silver Citroen Xsara with the registration number ...?' She looked at Scott who rapidly flicked through his notebook.

'YP52 XPD.'

'Yes that's right,' Alice said. A heavy frown appeared on her forehead and she started to play with the loose collar on her shirt to give her hands something to do. 'Has there been an accident?' Her hands were shaking, fearing the worst.

'Mrs Hardaker, a short time ago this car was found on Clough Lane, just off Quiet Lane ...'

'Oh. He's had an accident hasn't he? I hate that road. Is he OK?'

'Mrs Hardaker—'

'Alice, please.'

'Alice, I'm afraid an incident has taken place involving your husband. As a result, he received a number of gunshot wounds.'

Alice stumbled and held out an arm to grab on to something. She found the flowery sofa and gently eased herself into it. Upon hearing the words gunshot wounds, Alice's face lost all colour. 'What? He's been shot?'

'I'm afraid so.'

'But he's going to be all right isn't he?'

'Alice, he didn't make it. He was dead when we got to the scene.'

Alice thought for a while. It was as if she hadn't heard what Matilda had said. She swallowed hard. Her bottom lip quivered and tears formed in the corners of her eyes. 'No. That's not possible. He wouldn't need to go on Quiet Lane this evening.' She fought hard to keep control of her emotions but she was fighting a losing battle. 'He was going to play tennis straight from work. He wouldn't come home that way. Maybe … maybe he's had his keys stolen from the locker room or something. Kevin mentioned about some things being stolen from lockers a few months ago. That's what's happened hasn't it? Someone's stolen his car and they've been killed. Oh my God, I should call him.'

With shaking fingers, she picked up her mobile and frantically looked for her husband's number. She held the phone tight, her knuckles turning white. She waited for her call to be answered.

'I can see why you think it's Kevin. It's definitely his car, but it won't be him.' Her nervous laugh was loud and forced. 'You had me worried for a while there thinking he was dead, blimey. He's not picking up. Strange.' She looked at the phone and disconnected the call. 'They sometimes go for a drink afterwards. I'll give Jeremy a call; his phone is practically glued to his hand.' While waiting for the call to be connected she ran her free hand frantically through her thick, dark red mane of hair.

Alice's denial made the atmosphere uncomfortable. Matilda stood back and watched until realization dawned. There was very little else she could do. Scott was interested in the framed photographs on the mantelpiece and Joseph Glass looked almost as upset as Alice; as if it were him receiving the bad news.

It had been a while since Matilda had had to deliver the death message. The last time she'd heard it she'd been on the receiving end; a shattered-looking nurse stated the obvious 'he's gone, Mrs Darke,' as she held the cold hand of her husband.

'Jeremy, it's Alice. Is Kevin with you? ... No? OK. What time did he leave you? ... Oh ... Don't you? ... No, nothing's wrong. I'll talk to you later, Jeremy.' She hung up and slumped further into the sofa. She held the phone to her chest. 'Jeremy hasn't seen Kevin for weeks. They stopped playing tennis together ages ago. What's going on?' She looked up at Matilda. A single tear fell from her right eye.

Joseph stepped forward and sat down on the sofa next to Alice.

'Is there anybody you'd like me to call?'

'Erm, no I don't think so. There's my sister but she's away. I could call her, I suppose.'

'I see you have children, Mrs Hardaker,' he said, nodding to the school photographs on the wall. 'Are they in the house?'

She nodded a reply. 'Oh my God, the kids. What am I going to say to them? They love their dad. Warren dotes on him. They're supposed to be going to the Wednesday match this weekend.'

'Alice, I'm going to leave DC Glass with you,' Matilda interrupted, wanting to get out of the house. The dark atmosphere was unbearable. She could feel the walls closing in. 'I'm going to find out what's happening. I will definitely keep you informed. If there's anything you need, let Joseph know and he'll get on to me.' She looked down at the weeping Alice who hadn't taken in a single word of what she'd said. 'I'll see myself out.'

Matilda nodded to Scott to follow her. She mouthed 'call me' to Joseph. He replied with a small sympathetic smile.

Matilda couldn't get out of the house fast enough. The blast of cold air was like a slap. She took a deep breath to regain her composure. She could tell Scott was going to ask her how she was feeling so she dug her phone out of her pocket and quickly made a call.

'Aaron it's me. Are you still at the crime scene?'

'Yes. Why? What's wrong?'

'I'm at Kevin Hardaker's home and just broke the news of his death to his wife. The woman he was with is not his wife.'

'Bloody hell. Who is she then?'

'I've no idea. That's what I want you to find out.'

'Rory's at the hospital.'

'Right I'll give him a ring. Is Dr Kean still there?'

'No. She got a call. There's been a suicide on London Road; she's gone to attend.'

Bloody hell, it's all go tonight. 'Is there anything there at all that can identify who the woman is?'

'Nothing at all. There are no mobiles, no purse, no bag. It's like she's never been in the car before.'

'Oh God.'

'What?'

'They were parked in a quiet lay-by. Why would a married man have a woman who isn't his wife with him while they're parked in a tree-lined lay-by?'

'You think she's a prostitute?' Aaron asked his voice louder with surprise.

'It's a possibility.'

At the Northern General Hospital DC Rory Fleming wasn't having any luck trying to find out who the mystery woman was. She was in theatre with a team of surgeons battling to save her life. With massive internal bleeding, a punctured lung, swelling on her brain, and two gunshot wounds, it was a miracle she had survived so far. It wasn't just the next few hours that were critical – the following minutes were touch and go.

Rory paced up and down the corridor waiting for somebody, anybody, to remember he was still there and bring him some kind of information as to the condition of the woman. He looked at his watch. It was rapidly approaching one o'clock in the morning but the hospital was still a hive of activity or maybe it was just the heaviness of the footfalls against a backdrop of silence that echoed louder in the small hours. Surely Sheffield's emergency surgery wasn't in such high demand all the time?

After twenty minutes of pacing and two chocolate bars from a vending machine he left the hospital and called his boss.

'Any news?' Matilda didn't bother with a greeting.

'Nothing so far, ma'am. She's in theatre.' He relayed the information he had been given by a duty nurse. 'To be honest, I doubt she'll survive the night.'

'Bloody hell. Look, go back in and try and get her clothes from the nurses before they're destroyed. Then get them straight to forensics. After that go home. Back at the station first thing for a briefing.'

He was just about to reply when he realized he would have been talking to dead air.

Matilda looked down at her mobile and watched as the display faded before going back into standby mode.

'I think we may have a double murder on our hands.'

She was in the front passenger seat of a pool car with DC Scott Andrews behind the wheel. They were parked up at the side of the road halfway between the crime scene and Kevin Hardaker's home.

'Do we know who she is yet?'

'Not a clue.'

'You really think she could be a prostitute?'

'I've no idea, Scott. It's too early to say.'

'So … what now?' he asked after a full minute of contemplative silence.

'There's not much more we can do tonight. Drive me home then you get off home yourself. We'll make a proper start of it first thing.'

Scott turned the key in the ignition and headed the wrong

31

way to Matilda's house. She quickly informed him of his error and he made an illegal three point turn before heading in the right direction. There was very little traffic around at this time of night; nobody noticed.

That wasn't technically true. One person did witness the traffic violation. The driver of a black BMW, several yards back so as to avoid detection, was watching very carefully and had to make the same illegal move in order to keep the pool car in their sights.

FIVE

The next morning started very early for Matilda. When she woke her duvet was half off the bed and the fitted sheet was not living up to its name; evidence of a bad night tossing and turning. Her dreams had been unsettling and disturbed; her mind unable to rest. She constantly thought of the dead woman, who she might be and if anyone was missing her; the impending closure of the Murder Room and what that meant for her job and her team. Eventually at five o'clock she decided to get up.

When she went into the living room her eyes fell on the framed photograph of her and James at their wedding. She could not believe it was almost the first anniversary of his death. How did that happen so quickly?

Whenever she thought of the death of her husband she immediately thought of the disappearance of Carl Meagan. Even if Carl was eventually found safe and well she would always think of him whenever she grieved for her husband. The two would be forever entwined. Like James, Carl would constantly be in her thoughts; he was engraved on her memory and nothing would erase it.

It was too early to go to work but Matilda knew one person who would definitely be up and ready to face the world at this time.

'Perfect timing! There's coffee in the pot and bread waiting to be burnt.'

As always, Adele Kean was bright and cheerful. How it was possible so early in the morning was way beyond Matilda's reckoning. Should a pathologist, who spends her days up to the elbows in dead bodies, have such a bubbly personality?

Adele was neatly dressed in well-fitted clothes. Her hair was tidy with not a split end in sight, and she was wearing just enough make-up to be professional with a glamorous edge. Matilda couldn't remember the last time she'd applied make-up or when she had her hair professionally styled; probably around the time of James's funeral.

'So what brings you around here so early?' Adele asked, feeding bread into the toaster.

'I couldn't sleep.' She slumped on the stool at the breakfast counter and released a loud, wide yawn that would make a Labrador jealous. 'What time did you get in last night?'

'It was almost two o'clock. An elderly man had jumped from a tower block on London Road.'

'So you've only had about two or three hours sleep?'

'About that, yes.'

'You've no right to look that good on three hours' sleep. If you weren't my best friend I'd be scratching your eyes out.'

Adele gave a sweet smile. 'I'm just a naturally beautiful woman. L'Oréal are testing my skin to find out why I'm so youthful and good-looking.'

Matilda rolled her eyes. Adele's personality was warm and infectious. She didn't have an ounce of malice or bitterness in her, despite all she had gone through. It was refreshing. Matilda would love to be more like Adele.

'Any news on your double shooting?' Adele asked, interrupting Matilda's thoughts.

'Not yet. We've still no idea who the woman is. She certainly isn't his wife; I delivered the death message to her myself last night. I called the station on the way over here but there have been no reports of a missing person.'

'You're wondering if she's a prostitute, aren't you?'

'Yes. God only knows how many of them go missing every year. I find it unbelievable how someone can disappear and not one person misses them. Don't you find that sad?'

'I do. How is she by the way?'

'I haven't called the hospital yet. I'll do it later.'

Adele poured coffee into a large mug and handed it to Matilda. Conversation over, Matilda's mind drifted off again. She gave a small sigh and looked into the distance, through the wall, out of the house and into another world.

'What else is on your mind?'

'Sorry?'

'Something else is stopping you from sleeping. Is it James's anniversary? Eight days away isn't it?'

'Yes. 28th March. But no, it's not that. I called Masterson last night. She told me the Murder Room is closing.'

'What?' Adele asked, stopping midway through buttering a slice of toast.

'Budget cuts apparently. Last week the police dogs, this week us.'

'What's going to happen to the team?'

'I've no idea. I'm working with a reduced team anyway. Faith Easter has transferred back to CID, I'm down a DI, and I've got two DCs who still behave like students. Honestly, Adele, it would be funny if people's lives weren't at risk.'

Matilda got up from the breakfast bar. She could feel her legs starting to shudder and she was seconds away from remembering her old anxiety exercises. She walked to the back of the kitchen and leaned against the patio doors. She looked out at the well-kept garden.

'Why can't my garden look as good as yours?'

'Because I have a son to blackmail. Can I ask you a question?'

She turned to face Adele. 'Oh God. Why do I get the feeling I'm not going to like this? Go on.'

'Are you drinking again?'

'What? Where did that come from? No I'm not drinking again. New Year's resolution, remember? I don't have a drop in the house and I haven't had a drink since New Year's Eve. What made you ask that?'

'You seem anxious; more than usual. The anniversaries, this case, it's bound to cause some stress. I don't want you falling backwards.'

Adele's son, Chris, could be heard getting up. His size eleven flat feet slapping on the hardwood floor travelled down the stairs. Matilda lowered her voice and walked back to the breakfast bar, helping herself to a slice of toast.

'Adele, in the past year I think I've drunk more than most people do in a lifetime. Just thinking about everything I went through, how I was feeling when I was drinking, makes me feel sick.'

They looked at each other for a long few seconds. Matilda could tell Adele wasn't convinced. 'You don't have to worry about me, Adele. I'm fine. I'm smiling. I'm happy. You find me a bloke called Larry and I bet you a month's wages I'll be happier than he is.'

Adele smiled. 'You are a lot brighter than you were a few months ago. I just wish you wouldn't end your visits to the therapist. At least not until the anniversaries have passed.'

'I don't need therapy anymore. I'm coping very well without it. Dr Warminster said I would know when the time was right to end the sessions, and I do.'

'But …'

'Adele, I'm fine. Look, if I feel like I can't cope you'll be the first to know. I promise you.'

Adele visibly sighed, relieved. 'Thank you.'

'You're a good friend, Adele.'

'I know I am. The best.'

Right on cue Chris entered the kitchen. He was gangly; a skinny frame and neck-achingly tall. He had a wild abandon of unruly hair; a rival for Matilda's back garden.

'Bloody hell, it's Sideshow Bob,' Adele said, laughing.

He sat next to Matilda at the breakfast bar and slumped forward, his head in the crook of his arm.

'Why do students make tiredness an art form?' Matilda asked.

'What are you doing up so early?'

'I kept hearing two crazy women with no volume control.'

'This crazy woman is paying your tuition fees, so mind your manners.'

'And this crazy woman knows where your nude baby photos are kept. If you don't want them posted on Facebook, you'll watch your mouth,' Matilda said, winking at Adele.

Both women laughed while Chris slammed his head against the table, admitting defeat.

'You can't win against us two. We're experts in cunning and manipulation. Isn't that right DCI Darke?'

'It certainly is Dr Kean. Don't worry Chris, when you have kids of your own you'll be able to play mind games with them. Right, I'd better be off. Thanks for the breakfast and chat.'

'Not a problem. Leave your tip at the door.'

Matilda smiled. She always felt better after just half an hour in Adele's company. 'Have a good day, Christopher.'

A grunt came from under his hair. Matilda left the house a different woman from when she entered. Her head was held high, shoulders back and she felt ready to take on anything, even the ACC. Adele must have healing powers; she was wasted on the dead.

SIX

The reduced Murder Investigation Team comprised DSs Sian Mills and Aaron Connolly, DCs Rory Fleming and Scott Andrews, a smattering of uniformed officers and a couple of support staff. It was pathetic. They were originally spread out around the room but Matilda called for them all to group together.

Matilda stood in front of a wall of whiteboards. Presently, very little information was written down as the case was in its infancy.

'Good morning everyone. We seem to be very few in number but you're all professional and know your job. Following the events of last night, we're going to be working long and hard; however, we can do this. I believe in you all and have faith in your abilities.' She wondered if she sounded convincing enough. She hoped so. 'Right after this briefing I'm going to the ACC to ask for more support so hopefully we will shortly have a larger team. Now, last night's double shooting ... who did door-to-door?'

'I did ma'am,' Rory said putting his hand up. Rory Fleming was like a male version of Adele Kean. It didn't seem to matter how little sleep he had, he always turned up for work looking fresh and clean in a sharp, fitted suit, perfectly ironed shirt, understated tie and a messy hairstyle that probably took hours to perfect. Was it just Matilda who looked like she'd had five minutes' sleep in a skip?

Rory continued. 'There aren't many houses around there; just a few cottages. I knocked on them all, although I don't think they were happy to be woken up. I don't have anything to report I'm afraid. Nobody heard a thing.'

'How can they not have heard anything? Kevin Hardaker was beaten to a pulp. Surely he screamed. And gunshots aren't exactly quiet.'

Sian interrupted. 'Mr Rainsford said his wife has the TV turned up more loudly than is necessary. She refuses to accept she's losing her hearing.'

'Mrs Foster next door was at a wedding and didn't get back home until after we were on the scene,' Rory read from his notebook. 'Another cottage is home to Mrs Cliff. She's recently come out of hospital following hip replacement surgery. She's on sleeping tablets and slept through the whole thing.'

'Maybe the gunman used a silencer?' Scott Andrews suggested.

'Oh God, I hope not. A silencer suggests a professional job, a hitman. Let's not go down that road until we have to. What about Clough Lane itself? Where does it lead?'

Aaron had stuck a map of the area onto one of the whiteboards. He followed the road with his finger. 'Well it's quite a long road, passes a few farms then out into the Peak District.'

'So it's not the type of road you'd go down if you lived in Sheffield?' Matilda said, thinking aloud.

'I wouldn't have thought so.'

'So why would you pull up on Clough Lane late at night?'

'For a shag,' Rory said unwrapping a KitKat he'd taken out of Sian's snack drawer.

'Precisely. Help yourself to a KitKat, Rory,' the rest of the officers sniggered. 'So, Kevin Hardaker, cheating on his wife, is with his girlfriend, or whoever she is, and they park up on a quiet lane, for what Rory so romantically calls a shag. What happens next?'

'A bloke comes along and kills them?' Aaron said.

'No. That's not what happens. If this was a random killing, a drive-by shooting, then that would have happened, but this is more personal. Our killer comes along, drags Kevin Hardaker out of the car, beats him senseless then shoots him. Then he drags our mystery woman out from the front passenger seat and does the same to her. Thinking she's dead, he leaves. What does this tell us?'

Matilda looked out at the sea of blank faces staring back at her. To be more accurate, with a reduced team, it was more like a river of blank faces.

'It wasn't a random killing,' said Rory, licking melted chocolate from his fingers.

'Go on,' prompted Matilda.

'Like you said, if this was a drive-by shooting they would have been shot dead where they sat. They weren't. They were pulled from the car and subjected to a right beating. This was personal. Someone knew they were going to be there, or maybe followed them there, then attacked.'

'Exactly my thinking, Rory.'

Rory was still only young and had the fresh-face of a skin-cream commercial actor. He also had a vacant expression that wasn't always comforting while trying to have an in-depth conversation. However, he was an intelligent young man and would make an excellent detective. He just needed to do a bit of growing up.

'So, in a personal attack such as this,' Matilda continued, 'who are our most likely suspects?'

'The man's wife or the woman's husband,' Scott spoke up.

'Thank you, Scott. We need to talk to Kevin Hardaker's wife and the second we find out who our mystery woman is we need to talk to her husband – if she has one.'

'That reminds me,' Aaron spoke up. 'I had a call from forensics first thing. They've found a mobile phone at the crime scene. It could belong to the woman.'

A phone rang. Rory answered it, talking quietly.

'Excellent. Give forensics a call and have them do their usual routine on it. I want a copy of all the contacts and text messages, photos, emails, apps used, and whatever else is on there. Now, Scott, what was the name of the FLO last night?'

'Joseph Glass.'

'Right. Give him a call. Ask him to bring Alice in. She needs to make a statement and I want to know everything about their marriage, any money problems, Kevin's work – the usual. Also, talk to the neighbours, Kevin's work colleagues, friends. Aaron, can you sort that out?'

'Sure.'

'Sian, what's happening with Mr Rainsford?'

Sian looked up from her notebook where she had been making extensive notes. 'PC Grabowski stayed with them overnight. I called her first thing and he's actually feeling a lot better after a good night's sleep. She's bringing him in after he's showered.'

'OK. Sian will you interview him and keep me informed?'

'No problem.'

'Thanks. Right, I'm going to have a word with the ACC about getting more people in this room to make it look less like a gathering of the Nick Clegg fan club.'

'Boss,' Rory called out, putting the phone down, 'that was a nurse from the hospital I got chatting to last night. The woman is stable, but still critical. There's evidence she was raped.'

ACC Valerie Masterson was enjoying breakfast at her desk. Like Matilda, she also had trouble sleeping. Once the phone call had come through about the double shooting the logistics of the case weighed heavily on her mind; this could possibly be the Murder Room's final investigation.

Much to the annoyance of her retired husband, Valerie decided to come to work early. She wanted to prepare for the battle with Matilda. Valerie believed her still to be a fragile individual; she had only been back at work four months and in that time she had faced a fight for leadership of the Murder Room, and internal scrutiny of her ability to carry out her duties. There could have been better resumptions to her career.

The loud knock on the door did not surprise Valerie – she had actually expected it sooner than this. She was tempted to say 'Come in Matilda,' but decided against flippancy.

Matilda burst into the room with all the grace and determination of a charging bull.

'Good morning, Matilda. Coffee?'

'Please.'

'I know why you're here,' Valerie began, her back to Matilda as she prepared the coffees, 'I need you to listen to what I have to say first before you erupt.'

'I have no intention of erupting.' Matilda's tense white lips told a different story.

Valerie handed over the cup and saucer remembering that Matilda took her coffee black with no sugar. It was very hot and very strong. Matilda took a sip; it was good coffee. She placed it carefully on the desk.

The silence in the room was crippling; it was like a Mexican stand-off – who would blink first. Valerie sat behind her large desk, which looked bigger than it was due to her small stature.

'I want you to know that I fought long and hard for the Murder Room to be kept open. You've done a brilliant job in building up an impressive reputation, and figures have proven its success.'

'So why is it closing?' Despite wanting to remain calm, the firmly folded arms across Matilda's chest suggested otherwise.

'It's mostly budgetary reasons. South Yorkshire Police is under intense scrutiny, as you're aware; we're still under the microscope with the Hillsborough inquiry and the level of sexual abuse that has emerged in Rotherham has taken its toll. We've got representatives from the National Crime Agency looking into this sex abuse scandal. They've uncovered more than three hundred potential abusers. I'm lucky to still be sitting here. As we've been underperforming, so they say, we're having our budget cut. Another reason is that the levels of murder within South Yorkshire have dropped. The Chief Constable believes that a dedicated murder unit is no longer necessary.'

'I'm guessing he hasn't heard about the double shooting last night,' Matilda said with a hint of sarcasm.

Valerie gave a half-smile. 'That has come with unfortunate timing. However, the Murder Room still exists at present and you have the full backing of the force.'

'Just not the resources.'

'Whatever you need to help you solve this case you will have.'

'I want more detectives.'

Valerie sighed. 'I will do the best I can for you; however, with these aggravated burglaries occurring left, right, and centre, CID are stretched as it is. Besides, you have Mills and Connolly, Fleming and … what's his name, blond hair?'

'Scott Andrews. I need a replacement DI.'

'And you're getting one. I have several candidates to interview in the coming days.' That was a lie. Valerie had one person left to interview. It appeared that South Yorkshire Police's reputation was not favourable with people seeking to improve their position. It would appear nobody wanted to be associated with the force.

'Can't I have one from CID? What about Brady?

'DI Brady is working round the clock on these burglaries.'

'Brady has been in this job longer than I have and you've got him working on burglaries. It's not using him to his full potential.' Matilda's frustration was mounting. 'With the Murder Room closing you're sending dedicated detectives back to menial tasks. They won't stand for it and they'll leave. You'll end up with a force like a ghost town and below-par coppers out of their depth when a serious crime occurs.'

Matilda paused for breath. 'If the Murder Room closes the inevitable is bound to happen – the more experienced detectives will apply for a transfer to a force with dedicated units and South Yorkshire will be left with the dregs, and before the Chief Constable can polish his buttons crime will rise and the region will be crying out for a dedicated Murder Investigation Team, but there'll be nobody skilled enough to run it.'

Valerie didn't seem to be listening as she looked for a folder on her desk. 'A warehouse in Snig Hill was broken into; £15,000 of computer equipment stolen, the whole place trashed and a security guard with a fractured skull. A house on Dore Road was broken into; elderly man and woman tied up while their house was ransacked. The woman was threatened with rape if she didn't take off her wedding ring. A man was severely beaten in Heeley and had expensive watches and computer equipment taken. He was tied up with duct tape and doused in petrol. Need I go on? These are not just teenagers pissing about, Matilda.'

'I'm sorry,' she said quietly, her head bowed. 'I had no idea of the level of violence involved. Christian Brady is a fine detective. He'll do well on the burglaries. I just feel like I'm fighting a war single-handed. There's no way I can win so why bother with the battle?'

'Matilda, I understand your frustration, and your anger. I will do everything in my power to help you but I'm limited in what I can do. What you did with the Harkness case before Christmas was beyond excellent. I'm not going to placate you but I do believe you can work this case with the minimum of officers and still get a result.'

'Why should I, though? Why should I work my arse off and get a result when it's not appreciated? The Chief Constable is closing us down; I'm guessing there will be redundancies and I'm guessing I'll be one of them. Why should I sweat blood just to be given my cards in a few weeks' time?'

'I've been assured there will not be any redundancies. It's about having a CID and an MIT running side by side when it isn't necessary. Combined you can have pockets of teams working individual cases with one or two senior officers overlooking the whole department.'

Those words may have been spoken by ACC Masterson but they were written by the Chief Constable, and, judging by the look on Matilda's face, she knew that too. Matilda stood up to leave.

'Before you go, did you see *The Star* last night?'

'I'm afraid I did, yes.'

Valerie pulled out her dog-eared copy and laid it flat on her desk. It was open at page seven: '**CARL MEAGAN: ONE YEAR ON**'. Her stomach began performing somersaults.

Robert Walpole, Spencer Compton, Henry Pelham, Thomas Pelham-Holles, William Cavendish.

It had been a long time since Matilda had recited the names of the British Prime Ministers as an aid to relaxing. She hadn't needed them since she'd given up drinking and learned to channel her grief. It seemed it only took the mere mention of Carl Meagan's name and she was plunged back into her paranoiac nightmare.

'We don't come out very well I'm afraid. Were you contacted yesterday to contribute to this travesty?'

'No.'

'I thought not. It says you were unavailable for comment.'

'I know,' Matilda said, looking away from the paper. She didn't need to see it; it was imprinted on her memory. 'Why do they have to keep raking it up?'

'It's been a year. The parents want to keep the story alive. It's understandable. He's their son.'

'I know,' she said, bowing her head. 'But I can't keep doing this if I'm smacked in the face with Carl Meagan every time I'm working on a case.'

'Matilda, leave the press to me. Do your job, a job you do incredibly well, and defy them all. I know you don't believe this Matilda, but I'm with you 100 per cent,' Valerie said when the expression on her DCI's face remained hollow and drawn.

'You're right, I don't believe it. I don't believe it at all.' She turned and left the room, not caring if there was more to the meeting.

Matilda didn't have the energy to storm out and make a scene. What was the point in shouting and screaming from the rooftops if nothing was going to change? As Matilda walked away from the door and headed to the nearest toilets she was reminded of the saying 'no man is an island'. Maybe not, but a high-ranking woman in the police force certainly was.

SEVEN

Matilda entered the pathology suite and was met immediately by a team of police officers milling around. It was imperative the body of Kevin Hardaker was not left alone at any time for fear of evidence tampering.

'Morning Adele,' Matilda said. 'I see you've got a full house.'

'We certainly have. The coroner has given the go-ahead for the Digital Autopsy.'

'I've never seen one before. What are they like?'

'It's just looking at scans on a computer screen,' she said, folding her arms.

'You don't seem impressed. Worried it might make you redundant?'

Three years before, Sheffield had become the first city in the country to open a state-of-the-art, non-invasive Digital Autopsy Facility. Its aim was to establish the cause of an unnatural death using sophisticated visualization software and a scanner rather than a scalpel. With the results available almost immediately, it was a huge step forward for the Sheffield police force, but Matilda could see why Adele might be concerned.

'No, of course not. It actually makes my job a whole lot easier.

You can rotate a body 360° without getting your hands dirty. I'm all for that.'

The doors opened and the radiologist, Claire Alexander, stepped out. She was a small woman in her mid-thirties, with long brown hair, tied back in a severe ponytail. She was wearing hospital scrubs that were a size too big for her.

'Morning Claire, happy birthday,' Adele said.

'Thank you. I see you've got me a present.' She nodded towards the black body bag containing Kevin Hardaker.

'I certainly have. No peeking.'

'We're all set next door if you are.'

Victoria Pinder, Adele's Assistant Technical Officer, led the way with the trolley. It was a short narrow corridor leading into the Digital Autopsy suite and the trolley banged loudly against the walls and door.

'Mind my paintwork. It's just been redone,' Claire said.

The mood as everyone entered the suite quickly changed from one of levity to sombre professionalism. They were all here because of a dead man: a person whose life had been brutally cut short. He deserved respect and dignity.

The machine was simple in design. It reminded Matilda of the many times she accompanied her husband to the hospital in the early days of his diagnosis and the many scans he had to endure. This scanner didn't seem as bulky as the one at the Northern General; it was obviously a newer model. It looked less daunting and not as claustrophobic.

Victoria and Claire lifted Kevin, still in the bag, onto the scanner and secured him in place using Velcro straps. Everyone then made their way into the control room.

The small room, with a bank of five large computer screens, was packed with police officers and technical staff. Claire squeezed her way through and seated herself behind a computer in front of the window looking out into the main room. She clicked a few buttons and the scan began.

'What's happening now?' Matilda whispered to Adele.

'You know those annoying Slinky things that go down stairs on their own?'

'Yes.'

'Well, imagine you're standing in the middle of a large Slinky. The scan circles around the body from top to toe. Claire can adjust the thickness of the spirals to get a more detailed view of the body. The smaller the gap, the more detail we can pick up.'

'So why is Claire doing this and not you, if you're a pathologist?'

'The scan works like an X-ray and you have radiographers for that. That's what Claire is. All I do is interpret the results.'

'It's not noisy is it?' Matilda whispered. 'I remember going to an MRI with James and I could have done with earplugs.'

'Everything is less noisy these days; with the exception of a Dyson vacuum cleaner.'

A ghost image of Kevin's body appeared on the screen and looked like an X-ray. Leaning forward, Matilda frowned at the bright white objects on the body, but didn't ask any questions. She'd save that for later.

Claire singled out the head and rescanned to get a better image. A full 3D picture of Kevin's head filled the screen. She rotated it several times to get a good look at it from all angles; something that wouldn't be possible in a traditional post-mortem without physically turning the body over.

'The entry wound of the bullet was just below the left eye. You can see the bevelling of the bone as it enters. The exit wound,' Claire said as she tilted the 3D image to view the back of the head, 'is here. Just above the base of the skull. Those white specks are metal fragments from the bullet.'

Matilda's question was answered.

'What about the second bullet?'

Going back to the full body scan, Claire selected a second region of interest, the chest, and looked closer. The impact the bullet had on the body was shocking to see in glorious technicolour. The ribs and organs were easily identifiable but were in a condition Matilda had never seen before.

'The bullet entered the chest just below the heart.' Claire pointed to a bright white object the exact shape of a bullet, which was firmly lodged in Kevin Hardaker's body. 'It shattered the ribs, as you can see. The rib fragment has punctured his left lung, which is why it's deflated. He suffered a pneumothorax.'

'Is that what killed him?'

'It depends which bullet came first. Either one was enough to kill him.'

'What about the beating he received? Would that have led to his death?'

'It's not easy to pick up bruising on these scans but we can see where blood has settled. Look here,' she said, pointing to the screen, 'on the right side of his ribcage there are several fractures in the ribs. This doesn't follow the trajectory of the bullet in his chest, so must have come from where he was kicked or beaten with something.'

'So the killer was standing over Kevin while he was on the ground, and shot him?'

'It wasn't at point-blank range,' Adele said. 'There were no burns on the skin.'

'My point is the beating came first. He's given a kicking, fractured ribs, bruising, the works. Then, when he's down, the killer fires into his chest and face, finishing him off.'

'That's about the shape and size of it, yes,' Claire said.

Matilda gave the nod to Adele and they left the room. The scanner room was hot and Matilda had a sheen of sweat on her face. Neither of them said a word until they were in Adele's office.

'Bloody hell, how do you stand it in there?' She picked up some tissues from Adele's desk and wiped her face.

'It does get a tad warm. Are you OK? You look flushed.'

'I'm fine. Poor bloke. He wasn't shown an ounce of mercy was he?'

'Not in the slightest. I don't envy your job at all. Whoever did it sounds like a nasty piece of work. What do you think of our new equipment?'

'It's very impressive. It's a bit ghoulish watching a floating head rotate a full three-sixty but I can't believe how clear everything is. You can actually see the path the bullet takes in the body. Frightening, but fascinating.'

'I'm pleased you think so.'

'So you won't have to cut him open now?'

'No. Well, not for a post-mortem. We'll need to get the bullet out of him, obviously, so your forensic people can find out what kind of gun was used. We'll get a report and I'll read it and the coroner will read it but I think it's pretty self-explanatory how he died. There should be no need to go in with a scalpel.'

'It's a bit more dignified isn't it?'

'Absolutely. It's not nice for the family knowing their loved ones are naked on a slab having their insides removed.'

'It depends if you like them or not,' Matilda laughed. 'Is anyone working on developing a scan that will reveal the name of the killer?'

'I think for that you'll need a doctor more qualified than I am. Preferably one with a sonic screwdriver.'

EIGHT

Martin Craven approached the front desk of the police station like a member of the walking dead. His eyes were circled red and bloodshot, his hair a tangled mess, and his face was grey and sallow. His suit, one he had worn for work the previous day, was creased and stained.

'I want to report my wife missing,' he said in a voice affected by lack of sleep and too much caffeine.

The uniformed sergeant behind the desk didn't even blink. He had seen it all over the years; people came to the counter with all kinds of stories ranging from the bland to the bizarre. A missing person was banal in comparison.

'When did you last see your wife, sir?'

He swallowed hard and took a deep breath. Holding on to the counter for balance he spoke slowly with determination. 'She left for work yesterday morning. She was due home about eight o'clock last night, but never arrived. Her mobile was going straight to voicemail. By ten o'clock I started phoning around her friends but they hadn't heard from her. This morning I called her work but she hasn't turned up. They said she was there until five o'clock yesterday and left as normal. Nothing out of the ordinary had happened at work either. She's disappeared. I need you to find her.'

DC Joseph Glass hoped training as a Family Liaison Officer would impress the bosses when it came to promotion time. He had been on several health and safety and first aid courses and was even a fire officer at South Yorkshire HQ. What he hadn't expected was how unbelievably boring being an FLO was.

He had spent most of the night wondering what to say to a tearful and desperate Alice Hardaker.

'Should I wake the kids and tell them or wait until morning?'

'Only you can answer that, Alice. I'll provide you with whatever support I can though.'

'How sure are you that it's really Kevin?'

'As sure as we can be at the moment.'

'Do you think he suffered?'

'I honestly don't know, Alice.'

This went on until the small hours of the morning until, physically and mentally drained, she had fallen asleep sitting up on the sofa. He had taken the eighth undrunk cup of tea from her hands and placed a throw over her to keep her warm. He returned to the armchair and waited. He managed an hour's sleep at about three o'clock but woke with a start; his subconscious telling him he was in unfamiliar surroundings. He made another cup of tea, something he was becoming an expert in, and waited for Alice to wake up.

At four o'clock, knowing his sister would have come off the late shift at the Children's Hospital, he gave her a call.'

'Morning, you'll never guess what's happened,' he spoke quietly into his phone from the kitchen so as not to wake the snoring Alice. 'There's been a shooting on Quiet Lane.'

'I know. We've heard. Tom's girlfriend works at the Northern. She phoned earlier.'

Feeling downhearted at not getting in first with the gossip, Joseph added, 'Yes, well, guess who's FLO for one of the victim's family?'

'You're not!'

'I bloody am.'

'Good for you. How is it?'

'Boring. I've lost count of the amount of cups of tea I've had and they've only got plain biscuits. Two kids and not a single bit of chocolate in the house.'

'Sod the biscuits, Joe. Let's have some juicy details.'

'I haven't got any. Like I said, it's boring. Hang on, I think I can hear movement upstairs. I'll call you later.'

He hung up without saying goodbye and listened intently to the noise from upstairs. He heard the sound of feet padding lightly along the hallway, a toilet flushed and then more footsteps. One of the children going to the toilet. He sighed and returned to the living room.

When the children, Warren aged ten and Milly aged seven, came down for breakfast, they looked with heavy frowns at the gangly detective. Who was this man and why had he spent the night on their recliner?

Alice had no idea what to say to them and stumbled her way through a statement of silences, um's and ah's. In the end, Joseph stepped forward and took over. Surprisingly, Alice allowed it.

Joseph bent down in front of the two frightened children who looked vulnerable and innocent in their pyjamas and dressing gowns. He lowered his voice and tried to sound soothing and calm. 'At the moment, we don't know what's happening but we think your dad has been involved in some kind of accident. The reason why I'm here is to look after you all while the main police officers find out what's going on. If there's anything you need or anything you want to know, come and ask me and I'll do what I can to help. Is that OK?'

The children nodded in unison. They looked to their mother who nodded and gave a painful smile, doing all she could to stop the tears from falling.

'Right then Warren, your mum tells me you're a very good boy and always help at mealtimes. I bet you know where all the breakfast things are don't you?'

'Yes,' he nodded.

'OK. Now, you look like a Coco Pops man to me. Am I right?' He knew one of them would like Coco Pops having seen two boxes of them in the cupboard while looking around during the hours of darkness.

'Milly likes Coco Pops. I prefer Frosties.'

'Cool. I like those too. Have you ever mixed them together?'

He ushered the kids into the kitchen and Alice mouthed her thanks as her emotions took over. She turned her back so nobody would see her cry.

As Alice made her way towards the hallway the front doorbell rang. She quickly wiped her eyes and turned round to look at Joseph in the doorway to the kitchen.

'Would you like me to answer it?'

'No, it's OK,' she sniffled. She looked through the spyhole. 'It's my sister.' She had barely opened the solid front door before her younger sister burst into the house and grabbed Alice in a bear hug.

'Oh my God, Alice,' Jenny was younger, shorter, fatter, and plainer than her sister.

Alice had called Jenny last night, before she had fallen asleep, and told her the tragic news. Jenny, who was away at a wedding in Skegness, had come straight back to Sheffield.

'I didn't think you were coming straight back,' said Alice. 'What about Geraldine's wedding?'

'She's got another three bridesmaids; I won't be missed. Alice, what happened?'

Alice put her arm around her sister and led her into the living room where they could talk in private.

Joseph was torn. He wanted to listen in on the conversation. Would Alice say something to her sister she wouldn't say to him? However, there were two children in the room behind him and it sounded like they were making a mess.

As Alice closed the door to the living room, Joseph heard her say 'you'll never believe what's happened'. Joseph had started the conversation with his sister the same way a few hours earlier. But he'd just been gossiping then. He never would have said that had he been talking about the brutal murder of a close relative.

NINE

Matilda's office was a small cubicle in the corner of the Murder Room. She liked to keep her door open so her team knew they could step in at any time to talk to her, and also so she could keep an eye on them. Usually at the start of a major investigation the Murder Room would be a hive of activity – unfortunately, being able to hear the clock ticking was not a good sign.

Through the open doorway, Matilda looked out at her team. Aaron looked strained and brooding like he had the entire world's worries on his shoulders. She had heard Sian refer to him as John Luther but without the cool coat. This was an accurate description of Aaron Connolly. If he won the lottery he'd still have the dour face of a basset hound. Scott was on the phone, held in the crook of his shoulder while tapping away at the computer. He was a quiet man, almost monosyllabic. She wondered what it would take to bring him out of his shell. Despite him being an excellent DC he was the hardest of the team to try and get to know. Rory Fleming was his polar opposite; confident, brash, smiling, bounding around like a puppy. Matilda was surprised that Rory and Scott liked each other, yet they often went to the gym together after work. She wondered what they found to talk about, if anything.

Sian popped her head around the door. 'Have you got a few minutes?'

'Sure. Come on in.'

'You looked lost for a moment there.'

'Just thinking. What can I do for you?'

'I've had forensics on the phone. They've not been able to get anything from the partial footprint on Kevin Hardaker's chest.'

'Adele said as much last night.'

'The bullet from his chest is from a semi-automatic handgun, similar to the kind our armed officers use.'

'A Heckler & Koch?' Sian nodded. 'Do we have any reports of guns being stolen or missing?'

'None at all. I've run through the list of local gun owners and we've contacted the majority of them. They all know where their guns are.'

'So an illegal weapon bought on the black market then?'

'It would appear so.'

'Anything else?'

'Yes. Uniform were called out to an RTC in the small hours of this morning off Psalter Lane. A nurse going home from the late shift was driving her Nissan and was run off the road by a man driving a black BMW. She crashed into a tree.'

'Is she OK?'

'Yes, she's fine. The car was being driven way over the speed limit and the driver didn't stop. She said it all happened rather quickly but she was sure the car didn't have a registration plate. I've been in with traffic for the last hour; I've looked at the cameras close to Psalter Lane and a black BMW is seen speeding at the roundabout at Hunter's Bar. It didn't have any plates.'

'Can the ANPR track it back?'

'I've got someone working on that for me.'

'Could you make out the driver?'

'No. It was dark.'

'Have any BMW's been reported stolen?'

'No.' Sian shook her head. 'What do you think – same guy?'

'Could be.'

Sian whistled. 'So a black market semi-automatic handgun and potentially stolen BMW. This guy means business.'

'He certainly does.' Matilda's expression darkened. 'Excellent work, Sian. Well done.'

'You're welcome. I'll keep you up to date.'

Matilda's mobile phone burst into life as Sian was leaving the office.'

'DCI Darke,' she answered. There was no reply but she could definitely hear breathing. 'Hello,' she waited, listening to the background noise. 'Hello, is anyone there? I can hear you, you know.' The line went dead. She was just about to pull away when the phone rang a second time. Once more, no number was displayed.

'Yes!' she snapped.

'DCI Darke?'

'Yes!'

'Hello, I'm Alex Winstanley, the new crime reporter on the *Sheffield Star*. I was wondering if I could have a word.'

Matilda visibly relaxed. 'How did you get my number?'

'From my predecessor. Is this a good time to talk to you about the murder on Clough Lane last night?'

'How do you know about that?'

'Pure chance I'm afraid,' his accent wasn't local so Matilda guessed he'd moved to Sheffield purely for the job. That meant he would be ambitious and ruthless about getting his hands on the juiciest story, and the Clough Lane murder was certainly juicy. She had an eerie feeling they would not get on. 'I was in A&E last night and happened to see all the commotion. Is it true you have no idea who the victims are yet?'

'A statement will be released in good time.' She gave the standard reply.

'I heard several shots were fired. Adding to this the recent spate of aggravated burglaries, in which a gun was used in at least one incident, should the people of Sheffield be worried about the rise in gun crime in the city?'

'There is no rise in gun crime Mr Winstanley.'

'Really? Official figures seem to show otherwise. Are you aware of an eight-year-old boy found waving a replica gun in Gleadless Valley last weekend?'

Matilda had not heard of this, not that she could let Winstanley know that. Maybe having a dedicated MIT was isolating them from the rest of CID; bringing the two back together would mean information would be passed around more freely. *Bloody hell, I'm justifying the scrapping of my own department.*

'Mr Winstanley, allow me to be frank: South Yorkshire Police work very hard to keep the people of Sheffield safe. These minor incidents are being investigated by the best detectives we have. The public are under no threat from gun crime. As for the incident last night, like I said, a statement will be released in due course. Good day Mr Winstanley.'

Matilda didn't realize it, but that statement would return to haunt her when the local paper hit the shops that evening. Before she had time to think, however, Rory burst into her office.

'I think we may have found our mystery woman.'

TEN

Martin Craven, a short man with rapidly receding brown hair, fingernails bitten down to the quick and displaying all the tension of a bomb disposal expert on his first day on the job, paced anxiously inside interview room one. The door opening made him jump.

'What's going on? Why have I been left in here like this?'

Matilda and Rory entered and sat down.

'Mr Craven, I'm DCI Matilda Darke—'

'DCI? That's a high rank, what's happened? What's happened to my wife?'

'Mr Craven, please, sit down.'

If it was possible his face looked graver. Reluctantly he pulled out the hard plastic chair, scraping it on the floor, and sat down, straight backed and uncomfortable.

'Would you like a tea or coffee?'

'I don't want a bloody drink.' He almost exploded but managed to hold himself back. 'I just want to know what the hell is going on.'

'Sir, your missing person report has coincided with an anonymous woman being admitted to the Northern General last night.'

'The Northern? Oh my God. Is she OK? What happened?'

'I can't tell you how she is as I don't know yet. However, I would like to ask you a few questions. When was the last time you saw your wife?'

'I've been through all this once already,' he said, deflating in his seat. 'Yesterday morning. I had to leave for work early so I left about 7.30. She didn't need to be in work until later so she was still in her dressing gown at the table with the kids. I said goodbye to her and the kids and that was it.'

'Did she arrive at work?'

'Of course she did. I've already checked on that. She arrived on time, had lunch at the same time, and left at the same time. It was just an ordinary day.'

'Was she going anywhere after work?'

Martin Craven sighed at having to repeat himself. 'Yes. She plays tennis. She was going straight to the club from work. I was expecting her home at about 8 p.m.'

At the mention of tennis Matilda and Rory exchanged a quick glance with each other. Martin didn't appear to notice.

'But she didn't come home?'

'Well obviously not.'

'Did you call her?'

'Many times.'

'No reply?'

'None.'

'When did you suspect she might be missing?'

'This morning. I waited up for her. I must have nodded off in the chair. Our youngest came down at six and woke me up. Lois hadn't come home so that's when I realized something must have happened.' He looked at the blank expressions on the officer's faces in front of him, hoping to find anything there that might explain the disappearance of his wife. 'Something has happened hasn't it?'

'Mr Craven, is there any reason why your wife might have been on Clough Lane last night?'

'Clough Lane? No,' he frowned. 'There's no reason at all for her to go that way. Hang on; there was something on the radio this morning about a shooting at Ringinglow. It's her isn't it? She's been shot.' Tears started to fall from his eyes.

'Do you have a photograph of your wife?'

'Shit,' he said. 'I should have brought one with me, sorry.'

'That's OK. Mr Craven, a woman, who we have not yet been able to identify, was attacked and shot last night on Clough Lane. She's currently in Intensive Care. It could – and I stress could – be your wife.'

He fell forward onto the desk, buried his head into the crook of his arm and gave out a loud sob. He looked up at Matilda. 'I want to see her.'

'Of course. If you'll wait here I'll make a call to the hospital.'

'Thank you. Look, would it be possible for me to have a drink of water or something.'

'Certainly.'

Matilda and Rory left the room. They waited until they were out of hearing range before they began talking.

'What do you think?' Rory asked looking across at his perplexed boss.

'It's possible. We need to get him to ID her. Get a car sorted. What did you think of him?'

'He genuinely seems concerned for his wife. He obviously cares for her.'

'So what was she doing in a car with a married man?'

'I hate these domestic cases. We always end up in the middle of some kind of marital dispute.'

With the amount of work she had to do Matilda should have sent Rory to the hospital alone with Martin but she wanted to go herself. Rory was right, this was a domestic case and if the mystery woman was Lois Craven then the question of what she was doing with a married man would arise. If she was having an affair, who knew about it? Did Martin know? Did he commit the attack? His reaction to seeing his wife unconscious in a hospital bed could be pivotal. She needed to see this for herself.

On the drive to the Northern General Hospital, Matilda allowed Rory to take the wheel while she sat in the front passenger seat and Martin Craven in the back. She had angled the rear-view and side mirrors so she could glance at his expressions. He sat poised in the centre of the back seat, his hands firmly clasped in his lap, fingers twitching. He looked worried; his eyes were wide and staring and he was biting down on his bottom lip. It was clear he was nervous about what he was going to find.

The doctors in Intensive Care were not happy about the intrusion from the police. Their main duty was to the well-being of their patient. A nurse with a frosty attitude led them to the private room but would not allow them to enter.

'She is unconscious and in a critical condition. She's lost a great deal of blood and is at a high risk of infection. Until she is assessed later by a consultant I cannot allow anyone unauthorized to enter. I'm sorry,' she added as an afterthought when she saw the tears in Martin's eyes.

The woman in the bed was hooked up to all kinds of machines. Wires and tubes were coming out of her nose, mouth and hands. Her head was heavily bandaged and there was thick padding to the left side of her neck. Matilda looked through the window at her without emotion. She looked as if she was sleeping and Matilda guessed she was not feeling any pain. At this stage it would be best if she remained in this condition.

Martin Craven banged on the window with fists squeezed so tight together they were almost blue. He let out an unnatural sound like a wild animal caught in a trap. Rory caught him just in time as he fell to the floor while several nurses ran to attend to him. Matilda stepped back. On the night she returned home from the hospital after her husband died she had made exactly the same noise. Almost one year ago to the day.

ELEVEN

By the time of the evening briefing at 6.30 the backgrounds of Kevin Hardaker and Lois Craven had been established. Matilda stood at the top of the room in front of the whiteboards and looked at the half dozen officers assembled.

Matilda opened the briefing and quickly handed over to Aaron while she sat back and took it all in. She needed to know what everyone had been working on.

'Kevin Hardaker is forty-three-years-old, married to Alice who is forty,' Aaron began, pointing to their respective photographs on the boards. 'They've been married for thirteen years and have two kids, Warren is ten and Milly is seven. Kevin worked for Currys as a sales manager. Supposedly, he's been playing tennis several times a week after work for many years. However, according to his tennis partner, Jeremy somebody, can't remember his surname, they stopped about six months ago. Kevin has been having an affair with Lois Craven, also a member of the same tennis club, for a little over a year. Six months ago is when it started getting serious and the tennis stopped.'

'Did Alice know about the affair?' Matilda asked.

'No.'

'Are we sure?'

'DC Glass is pretty convinced and I thought the same when I spoke to her,' Scott said, looking up from his pad.

'Is DC Glass still there?'

'Yes, I think so.'

'If Alice Hardaker doesn't need him, get him back here. We need all the help we can muster.' Scott nodded. 'What about this Jeremy somebody? Did he know about the affair?'

'Yes he did. He didn't know Alice very well, he only met her a couple of times, but he felt guilty about keeping Kevin's secret.'

'Not guilty enough though,' Matilda said to herself. 'What's his alibi for the attack?'

'He was in a restaurant with his wife. I've seen the receipt,' Aaron said. 'Two hundred quid on one meal.'

'Blimey, they had more than a Big Mac then,' Rory said.

'OK. Has anyone spoken to Kevin's colleagues at Currys?'

'Not yet.'

'That's the next job. Let's move on to Lois Craven.'

'Lois Craven is forty-one-years-old. She's married to Martin. They celebrate their twentieth wedding anniversary later this year. They've got three children; Jack is eighteen, Anna is fifteen, and Thomas is eight. Lois is an office administrator at the Sheffield College and Martin is a medical rep. He frequently works away. Now, according to her colleagues Lois started the affair with Kevin because she was bored. Martin's always away and two of the kids look after themselves, she only had Thomas to contend with. She was bored with playing the happy housewife and mother and wanted some excitement while she was still able.'

'Well, she sounds like a lovely woman,' Matilda said with a hint of anger. She immediately thought of James. Matilda would have relished the opportunity to find out what a bored housewife was like. Lois should have been content with what she had. 'What's Martin's alibi for the attacks?'

'He was at home. All three kids can corroborate that. So can a neighbour, a Mrs Blanchford,' Scott said.

'How does she know?'

'She went round about half past eight to borrow some foil. Apparently her son is making a robot for school and she'd run out. She went next door, stayed for a few minutes then went back home. She said everything was as it always is. Nice robot too.'

'What are the neighbours saying about them as a couple? Are they well liked?'

Scott flicked a few pages in his notepad. 'The Hardakers' neighbours were shocked by Kevin's death. I didn't mention the affair but just asked about what they were like as a family. Apparently they were very happy. They often went out together, weekends away, etcetera, and they always invited the neighbours around for the kids' parties. They seem like the perfect couple.'

'There's no such thing as the perfect couple,' Rory said while rummaging through Sian's snack drawer. As usual, Sian was keeping her eyes firmly glued on the young DC; making sure he didn't take advantage.

'What about you and Amelia?'

'Like I said, there's no such thing as a perfect couple.'

Matilda looked at Rory with a frown.

'OK, what about the Cravens' neighbours?' she asked, bringing the conversation back to topic.

'They keep themselves pretty much to themselves,' said Rory flicking through his notebook. 'One neighbour said they heard arguing a few times but nothing too serious.'

'When was the last argument?'

'He didn't say.'

'Go back and find out. Try and find out as much as you can. How private are we talking here? Do they mingle with their neighbours, exchange Christmas cards, or do they pull up the drawbridge at night? How did you get on with the ANPR?'

Rory turned on the laptop and asked Aaron to turn off the lights. He then asked Scott to pull down the white screen covering the whiteboards. His laptop now acted as a projector.

'OK, so, the ANPR has picked up eight images of Kevin Hardaker's car as it travels from his place of work at Heeley to where he ends up on Clough Lane. As you can see, the first picture shows Mr Hardaker sitting behind the wheel of his car. He is alone.'

Rory flicked through the next three images as they only showed the rear of the car at various junctions and traffic lights. It was impossible to say if he was still alone in the car.

'Here is picture number five; next to him in the passenger seat is Lois Craven.'

The photograph showed them both smiling, obviously in the middle of a conversation. They looked happy and relaxed. If only they knew what horrors were in store for them.

'Number six is only half the car; he's blocked by a bus. Number seven shows them on Bents Road, and just as they turn off onto Common Lane they're snapped once again.'

The final picture showed a front image of the car. Their smiles had gone. They had finished their conversation and were both looking straight ahead. There was a sense of foreboding about the picture. In the few minutes after it was taken they would both be subjected to a violent attack, which would leave one of them dead and the other fighting for their life.

'Thanks for that Rory. Any other cars picked up in front or behind them that could be of interest?'

'I'm afraid not.'

'No problem. Sian, how's our Mr Rainsford doing?'

'Poor bloke. He's in bits. He keeps blaming himself, saying he should have noticed the beeping sooner. I tried to comfort him but it wasn't helping. His wife seems like a pretty strong woman; she'll soon bring him round.'

'No chance it's a guilty conscience is it?' Matilda asked with a hopeful half-smile.

'I'm afraid not. He's definitely just a witness. I've told him to pop in if he remembers anything else or if he wants to chat but I doubt he will.'

I bloody hope not. That's all we need, hysterical witnesses cluttering up the investigation.

Scott's desk phone rang. He answered, said a few words then hung up. 'Ma'am that was the ACC's secretary. She was wondering if you could pop upstairs for a moment.'

'OK, thanks Scott. Look, wrap up what you're doing here then we'll call it a day. Until we can have a word with Lois Craven there's very little we can go on.'

ACC Valerie Masterson only ever called down for Matilda when something serious had occurred. She could feel the prickly sensation of tension slowly creeping up her back.

TWELVE

HIGH-RANKING COP RIDICULES 'MINOR' GUN CRIME

By Alex Winstanley

A top detective within South Yorkshire Police has ridiculed the spate of gun crimes in Sheffield as 'minor incidents'.

Detective Chief Inspector Matilda Darke, head of South Yorkshire's prestigious Murder Investigation Team, said the people of Sheffield had nothing to worry about despite a double shooting in Clough Lane last night, killing a man and leaving a woman in Intensive Care.

This comes a week after an 8-year-old boy was found playing with a replica handgun in Rollestone Wood, Gleadless Valley.

This year alone, there have been a number of burglaries in the city, many of which have involved the use of guns.

In February, two Co-op stores were held at gunpoint, and earlier this month three young women on a night out in the city centre were mugged by a masked man they believe had a handgun in his pocket.

DCI Matilda Darke said, 'These are minor incidents. The public are under no threat from gun crime.'

Cheryl Glover, 19, one of the three mugged said, 'If DCI Darke thinks having a gun pointed at you and having your possessions stolen is a minor incident she's obviously in the wrong job.'

DCI Darke has recently returned to leading the Murder Investigation Team following her suspension over the Carl Meagan kidnapping. Carl was taken from his home last March and his grandmother killed in a robbery, again involving guns.

DCI Darke's comments will come as a blow to the Meagan family, who, next week, will commemorate a year since their son was kidnapped. Sally Meagan, Carl's mother, has been particularly critical of DCI Darke's return to work and once again calls for her to be removed from South Yorkshire Police.

'I have no idea why she was allowed back to work,' Mrs Meagan said in a recent interview. 'My mother-in-law was murdered and my son kidnapped. She botched the ransom drop, which led to the kidnappers fleeing with him. She's not fit to work for the police and I sympathize with any family of victims of crime she is involved in.'

Assistant Chief Constable Valerie Masterson was unavailable for comment.

Matilda felt like she was taking the long, slow walk to the gallows as she ascended the stairs to the ACCs office. By the time she reached the top (two floors up) she was breathless. Maybe she should rejoin Adele at her spinning class, get in shape, and back down to a size ten.

Robert Walpole, Spencer Compton, Henry Pelham, Thomas Pelham-Holles, William Cavendish.

She knew the stress was becoming too much when the Prime

Ministers turned up. An exercise suggested by Dr Warminster. She had told her to concentrate on naming the British Prime Ministers during times of stress to help her regain control of her breathing and settle her thoughts. It worked. However, Matilda had thought now she could cope with life and its many hurdles without their appearance. It would seem not.

Through her jacket she could feel her shirt sticking to her back, damp with sweat. She hoped it wasn't noticeable. She knocked on the door and was called in almost immediately. Masterson had obviously been waiting. This did not look good.

'Matilda, come on it. Have a seat,' Masterson was all smiles, her voice friendly. A very bad sign.

As Matilda stepped fully into the room she saw the heavily pregnant Karen Sweetland from Media Support standing beside a seated ACC.

'You wanted to see me?' Matilda asked once she was as comfortable as she could be while visibly sweating. Her lungs seemed to have shrunken down to the size of a pound coin. Her breathing was laboured and her vision began to blur. She hated not being in control of her own mind. Panic attacks were crippling, and just when she thought she had a handle on them she was floored by another.

'Yes I did. The evening edition of *The Star* has just been delivered to me.'

Matilda had a sinking feeling. Her heart practically plummeted through the floor. She was beginning to loathe this paper.

The newspaper was neatly in front of Val Masterson on the desk. Matilda tilted her head slightly to read the front page, which was upside down from her point of view, but she couldn't quite make it out.

'I believe they have a new crime correspondent,' Val continued. 'You've spoken to him.'

'Yes. He called me this morning trying to get something out of me about the shooting last night. I just told him a statement would be released in due course.' She looked at the grave faces of her boss and the press officer. She quickly went over the very short conversation with Alex Winstanley but could not think of anything controversial she may have said. 'Is something wrong?'

'You tell me.' Val opened the newspaper to page five, folded it back and slapped it down hard in front of Matilda. The headline screamed out at her: '**HIGH-RANKING COP RIDICULES "MINOR" GUN CRIME**'.

'What the hell?' Matilda snapped up the newspaper.

'My words exactly.'

Matilda scanned the article. Her hands were shaking, rattling the pages. She stopped reading as soon as she found Carl Meagan's name. 'Where did he get this crap from?'

'You.'

'What? I didn't say gun crime was a minor incident.'

'I think you'll find you did.' The ACC turned to Karen Sweetland who was now sitting down uncomfortably to take the weight off her back.

'Alex Winstanley sent me, via email, a recording of the conversation you had. You definitely said minor crime.'

'I honestly don't remember,' Matilda said, taken aback. 'I didn't mean minor. I'm sure I said isolated. I meant to say isolated. I would never deride gun crime.'

'Isolate and minor do not sound similar. I'm not sure how you could have mixed up those two words, Matilda.'

Matilda sat forward in her seat. 'Ma'am, I am truly sorry for this article and I will apologize to anyone you want me to but I honestly, hand on heart, did not mean to call gun crime a minor incident. I wouldn't.' She placed her shaking right hand firmly on her erratically beating heart.

There was a heavy silence before ACC Masterson spoke again. 'I do believe you Matilda, I really do; however, this is not what we need right now.'

'I know. Look I'll talk to this Alex Winstanley—'

'No you bloody won't,' Val interrupted. 'I'll be speaking to him myself. If you look at the bottom it says I was unavailable for comment. I've not had a call from anyone at *The Star* all day. I'll be having a few words with this Mr Winstanley and Karen here will be putting together a placating statement for you.'

'Thank you,' Matilda said to both Karen and Val before looking down at the floor in shame.

'I do not want you speaking to Alex Winstanley or anyone else from the press again. Do you understand?'

'Yes, ma'am.'

'If they do happen to call you be polite, but firm, give no comment, then hang up.'

'Yes, ma'am.'

'Karen, would you leave us alone for a while?'

Karen agreed and struggled to get up out of her seat. She said she would start work on the statement and would email it through when she had finished. Val Masterson waited until the door closed and Karen was out of earshot before she began.

'What's going on with you, Mat?' Her voice was all concern, giving the impression of two friends chatting over coffee. Matilda wouldn't dare call her Val.

'Nothing's wrong. I'm fine. Understaffed, but fine.'

'Then why do you look like shit?'

'I wasn't aware that I did.' She tried to scoff but it wasn't working.

'I'm not completely heartless you know. I'm aware the anniversary of James's death is looming, but you need to talk to me, Matilda. You can't allow things to bottle up.'

'I'm not bottling anything up.'

Val Masterson rose from behind her desk; five foot nothing tall and wafer thin, she came to the front and sat on the edge of the desk. Matilda had to hide a small smile when her boss had to jump up.

'We've known each other for a very long time; let's forget rank for the next few minutes. We're just two middle-aged women having a chat. So, what's on your mind?'

Has she been taking lessons from Dr Warminster?

It took a while for Matilda to find the courage to open her mouth to speak without a flood of tears pouring out. The moment the first word came out, the rest followed in an almost incomprehensible tumble. 'James is on my mind twenty-four hours a day. Carl is constantly vying for attention. I want to look for him. I want to search every inch of this country to try and find him. I'm losing my team. Sian and Aaron are doing their best but I need a DI I can leave in charge when I'm not here. I'm down countless support staff and a DC.'

The large clock on the far wall ticked loudly. Matilda sniffed hard to try and rein in the tears. She managed it just in time. It was never a good idea to cry in front of your boss.

Val looked down at her most trusted detective. The silence grew.

'What happened to James was devastating. I cannot begin to imagine what you're going through and I won't even try. If you want to take time off, you just have to let me know ...'

'I don't want ...'

Val held up a hand. 'I know. I was about to say I know that you won't want to take time off work, but the offer is there for you whenever you need it.'

'Thank you.'

'As for Carl Meagan,' she shrugged her shoulders. 'Well, I've no idea what happened there. The kidnappers knew the money was there to be dropped off. They got spooked and did a runner but they could have contacted the Meagan family again. Why they didn't is anybody's guess. There hasn't been a sighting, a phone call, a letter, nothing. There is nothing we can do about that now.' She spoke slowly and with determination as if she was drilling every single syllable into Matilda's head. 'It's easy for me to say, I know, but until we receive any more information about

Carl Meagan there is nothing else we can do to locate him. You need to keep telling yourself that.'

'I know. I keep thinking of his parents; what they must be going through, not knowing where their son is. It must be torture.'

'The case will be reviewed on a regular basis, you know that. However, you need to move on. Your job is to solve murders. You can't do that if you're constantly harking over an unsolved case. As for your team, you're right and I'm sorry. It's wrong of me to expect you to solve a murder case with a couple of DSs. I'll get some drafted over to you from CID.'

Matilda looked up. Val's face looked softer and there was a genuine sincerity in her voice. It was the first time in a long time Matilda actually believed in what Valerie was saying.

'Now I want you to go home—'

'But—'

Again, Val held a hand up to silence her. 'This is not negotiable. I want you to go home.'

'I can't leave—'

'My grandfather used to always say there's no such word as "can't". It annoyed me when he said that but it's true. You can leave and you are leaving. I will arrest you if I have to.' She smiled.

Matilda was about to thank her boss but, once again, the hand came up. Matilda took this as her cue to leave.

Matilda should not have driven home. Her mind was a maelstrom of activity. Not only did she have James and Carl battling for attention in her head, she had the Meagan parents judging her, ACC Masterson offering comforting words, which wouldn't last if she continued with her erratic behaviour, and now, Alex Winstanley was throwing her to the dogs. There was very little room in her mind for anything else.

The doormat was covered with the usual array of white and brown envelopes, junk mail, and fast-food menus. She stepped over them and made her way to the kitchen. At the back of the drawer she used for items that didn't have a place to live, she found an emergency supply of the Venlafaxine tablets she used to take. It had been her decision to stop taking them, but she still collected the prescriptions from her GP. With shaking fingers, she took three tablets, two more than prescribed.

Her head pounded and weighed heavy on her shoulders. As she went into the living room, she picked the post up from the front door and threw it onto the coffee table.

James was looking down on her from the mantelpiece. His gorgeous smile, his bright blue eyes, his broad shoulders; he wasn't judging, he had love in his eyes. He cared for Matilda and he wanted her to be happy. The only way she would be happy again would be for James to enter the living room and wrap his strong arms around her.

Through teary eyes she looked at the post on the coffee table. One envelope stood out among the bills and offers of credit cards; it was a brilliant white and didn't have a stamp on it. A hand-delivered letter. Matilda ripped open the envelope and pulled out the single sheet of paper and a cutting from a newspaper. She didn't notice the tears fall down her face as she saw the scathing article written by Alex Winstanley in today's edition of *The Star*. She threw it down and looked at the letter:

You're a murdering bitch! There's blood on your hands Detective Chief Inspector Matilda Darke.

THIRTEEN

Dr Adele Kean pulled open the glass doors to the Murder Room and stepped inside. She immediately noticed the lack of activity and the lack of officers. 'It's like a closing-down sale in here,' she remarked without thinking. Matilda had told her she wasn't telling the rest of the team the Murder Room was closing.

'Morning Sian, where is everyone?'

Sian looked up from her computer, probably for the first time that morning. She breathed out and answered Adele, glad at the chance of a break. She leaned back as far as she could in her chair, stretched her aching muscles and enjoyed a very wide yawn.

'Well, Rory's with forensics, Scott's ... I've no idea where he is actually. I think Aaron's in ... Do you know what, I don't know where anyone is. I didn't realize I was on my own in here.'

'You're busy then I take it?'

'You could say that. I've been here since six and I haven't shifted from this desk yet. Anyway, what can I do for you?'

'Well, I came to see Matilda.' Adele noticed a tray of muffins next to the kettle. 'Ooh, are they to share?'

'They were. Nobody's had time for a break yet. Help yourself.'

'Thanks. What's the occasion?'

'It's my wedding anniversary today.'

'Oh congratulations. How many years?'

'Thirteen. We've been together about twenty years though. It took him six years to propose, bless him.'

'A bit slow on the uptake?' Adele asked, still trying to choose a muffin.

'You could say that. I gave up hinting in the end and just came out with it. I said, "Stuart Mills, are you ever going to propose or should I start making eyes at your brother?"'

Adele laughed. 'What did he say to that?'

'After he finished choking on his beer he asked me to marry him. I told him I'd have to think about it.'

'These are gorgeous, Sian,' Adele said, her mouth full of chocolate sponge. 'Did you make these?'

'Yes. They're Mary Berry's.'

'Well next time you speak to Mary tell her thank you. Are you doing anything special tonight?'

'You're joking! By the time Stuart remembers it's our anniversary it'll be time for the next one. Do you think you'll get married one day?'

Adele almost choked on her muffin. 'God no. Men are only useful for one thing and half the time they're no use at that. Anyway, I won't keep you. I'm actually looking for Matilda. Is she in yet?'

'I haven't seen her. Mind you, a marching brass band could have walked through and I wouldn't have noticed.'

'Well, I've got some information about your double shooting. You couldn't tell her for me could you?'

'Sure.'

'Now, let me show you something.' In the folder she had been cradling in her arms she produced some close-up photographs taken by the scene of crime officers. 'This is a photo of fibres taken from under Lois Craven's right hand. They're black and man-made.' She took another photograph out of the file. 'Now, on the night of the shooting I was called out to a suicide on

London Road. This is a photograph of the jumper's right hand. Under the forefinger and middle fingernails there are identical fibres.'

'So, what are you saying? The bloke committed a double shooting then went to London Road to kill himself? Why not just shoot himself in the head?'

'No. I'm not saying that. Look at these,' Adele took out the remaining photographs from the suicide. 'These are photos of Gerald Arthur Beecham aged 80. Apparently he jumped off the roof of a high-rise block of flats and landed face down on the paving slabs below.'

'Why apparently?'

'Look at this one; there's blood on the back of his jacket.'

'So?'

'If he jumped, why would he have blood on the back of his jacket?'

'Good question. Is it definitely his blood?'

'Another good question. I'll answer that in a bit. When we got him back to the mortuary and removed his clothes we found him covered in very fresh bruises. He didn't jump. He was either pushed or thrown.'

There was silence while Adele allowed Sian to take in what she had just said.

'Why would anyone want to throw an 80-year-old man from the roof of a block of flats?'

'I've no idea. Fortunately, I don't have to find the answer to that question, that's your job.'

'So, tell me whose blood it is then.'

'Are you ready for this?'

'If you decide to cut to a commercial break I'll slap the make-up off your face.'

'The blood belongs to Lois Craven.'

'What? How?'

'My best guess is that whoever committed the shooting in

Ringinglow went to London Road, for whatever reason, got into a bit of a tussle with poor old Mr Beecham, and pushed him over the edge,' Adele said. She sat back in her seat and folded her arms. She had a slight smug look on her face, a look she always had when she delivered ground-breaking news.

'This is very … I don't understand this at all,' Sian readily admitted. 'You need to speak to Matilda.'

'Well I've called her mobile but she's not answering. I think I've filled up her voicemail.'

'What about her landline?'

'Straight to answer machine. I didn't see her much yesterday after the post-mortem. How was she?'

'I hardly spoke to her.'

Aaron stormed in and kicked the door closed behind him. 'Thirty minutes I've just spent on the phone, twenty of them on hold, only to be told that Kevin Hardaker's manager is off sick and the relief was from a store in Derby and didn't know him. Why couldn't the bloke who picked up the phone tell me that? No wonder their sales are falling. Gormless pillocks.'

'Good morning to you too, Aaron,' Sian said over the top of her computer.

'Yes, whatever.'

'You haven't seen Matilda on your travels have you?'

'No.'

'How was she last night before you left?' Sian asked.

'What do you mean?'

'Was she happy, sad, fed up, excited, what?'

'Well she was a bit low. There was an article in *The Star* about the Carl Meagan anniversary the other day. I saw her reading the story a couple of times in her office. Then there was something in last night's edition about a conversation she'd had with the new crime reporter. The ACC called her in towards the end of the day but I didn't see her after that.'

'How was she when she went to the ACC?'

'A bit stressed.'

'Right. OK. Cheers, Aaron.'

When Aaron was out of earshot Adele turned back to Sian and said, 'I think I'm going to pop round to her house, see if she's OK.'

'Do you want me to come with you?'

'No. Look, hold the fort here and cover for her. If anyone asks, tell them she's come to see me about this development. I'll let you know as soon as I find anything out.'

At exactly 9.30, Matilda's landline began to ring. As she knew it would. She took a deep breath and answered the phone.

'Matilda?'

'Yes.'

It's Doctor Sheila Warminster.'

As usual, Dr Warminster called Matilda on the morning of her appointment for a quick chat about how she had been coping since her last therapy session and if there was anything in particular she wanted to discuss once she was in the hot seat later that day.

Sheila Warminster found this helped with the majority of her clients. Usually, once they were sitting face-to-face, many people clammed up and gave unresponsive answers to probing questions, a shrug or a monosyllabic reply. In a pre-arranged phone call, the client could be in their own environment, comfortable, and not feel under any stress or embarrassment about answering questions on their behaviour.

'How are you feeling?'

'I'm OK, thanks,' Matilda said. She was in the kitchen sitting at the breakfast bar. She was picking the label off a bottle of water, just to give her hands something to do.

I saw the article in *The Star* about Carl Meagan. It must have brought back some shocking memories.'

'It did.'

'How did it make you feel?'

'I was upset. It should have been an article about Carl, one year on, etcetera, but they had to put me in there and twist it. They can't seem to leave that part alone.'

'What did you do after you'd read it?'

'Well, as you know, I've allocated time to sit with my wedding album and have a bit of a weep, which I did. That helps a great deal. I always feel better afterwards. Then I was called out to a shooting so everything else was put on the back-burner.'

'I heard about that on the radio. I'm guessing you're heading the investigation.'

'That's right.'

'The last time we met you mentioned the lack of detectives in your team and you were feeling a little overwhelmed. Is that still the case?'

'Well, I am short of detectives, yes, and … I suppose I am a little overwhelmed.' Matilda surprised herself by admitting the truth. She was annoyed with the state of the Murder Room but it certainly wasn't causing her the personal distress it would have done a few months ago. 'I have an excellent team. We're small in number but we're dedicated. I trust them to do their job and do it well.'

'The anniversaries of James's death and Carl's disappearance are coming up. Are they weighing on your mind?'

Matilda sighed and sank back into her chair. 'Yes they are. I'm trying my best not to let them but it's not easy. I think if I keep myself busy then I'll be fine.'

'You need to take some personal time though too, Matilda. It can't all be about work.'

'It won't. I've got the *Hannibal* box set to work through,' she said with a smile.

It felt strange having a light-hearted moment with her therapist. In the beginning she loathed the woman on sight. The sound of her voice, so sickly sweet and hushed, made her want to smother

her with one of her handmade throw pillows she had in her office. However, over the weeks and months, Matilda had warmed to her and she found herself opening up and gaining something from their sessions.

'It's good you have outside interests, even if they are programmes about a cannibal,' there was a smile to Sheila's voice. 'I'm pleased you're feeling a tad more positive too. You sound brighter. Is there anything in particular you would like to talk about this evening?'

'No, I don't think so. I think I'd like to just have a chat if that's all right?'

'That's perfectly fine. These are your sessions, Matilda. It's entirely up to you what we talk about. I'll let you get on with your work.'

'Thank you. Thanks for calling.'

Matilda hung up. She took a deep breath and relaxed. She felt better. It seemed therapists were good for something after all.

The drive from South Yorkshire Police Headquarters to Matilda's house on Millhouses Lane took thirty minutes thanks to Sheffield's never-ending road works, road closures, and detours.

Adele was worried for Matilda's state of mind. Her return to work last December seemed to have given her best friend a new lease of life. She thought Matilda had moved on from the fallout of the Carl Meagan investigation and was learning to manage the grief for her husband. However, with the first anniversaries of both less than one week away it would appear that the black dog had returned to torture her.

Matilda's car wasn't in the driveway. Adele couldn't decide if this was a good sign, or not. It could simply have been in the garage but Matilda rarely used it in case she needed to leave the house quickly.

Adele pulled up in her Vauxhall Astra and ran to the front door. She pressed the bell and knocked several times. Impatiently, she stepped back and looked up at the house. The curtains were open in all the rooms but it seemed to be enshrined in silence. She knocked again.

'Matilda, it's me, Adele. Are you home?' She called through the letterbox. She knocked and rang the bell another few times, the knocks becoming louder.

When Matilda's husband was in the final throes of his illness, she had given a key to Adele to let herself in whenever Matilda was working so someone could always be with James. After his death, Adele kept hold of the key so she could keep an eye on Matilda. Fortunately, she still had it.

Racing back to her car, she tipped the contents of her handbag on the passenger seat and rummaged around the mound of rubbish for her keys. She found them and was about to go back up the drive when she was interrupted by a neighbour.

'Is everything all right?' asked a young woman cradling a baby.

'Jesus, you scared the life out of me,' Adele said, stopping in her tracks, hand on heart. 'You haven't seen Matilda today have you?'

'No, I haven't.'

'When was the last time you saw her?'

'A couple of nights ago. She was going out as I was coming in. Is something wrong?'

'No, probably not,' Adele said with a fake smile and a nonchalant shrug.

She waited until the neighbour turned away before letting herself in and locking the door behind her. If Matilda was somewhere in the house, potentially lying in a drunken stupor, she wouldn't want a nosy neighbour creeping in and seeing her.

'Matilda?'

'Adele? Is that you?'

'Yes. Where are you?'

'I'm in the shower.'

Adele visibly relaxed and sat on the padded seat in the corner of the hallway. She looked down at the three black bin bags, which had been there for the past few weeks. Matilda had made a step

85

forward in clearing out James's wardrobe, but not gone as far as taking them to a charity shop. A few seconds later Matilda stumbled out of one of the bedrooms, tying a dressing gown around her waist.

'What are you doing here?'

'Looking for you.'

'Why? What's happened?'

'Nothing. I went to the station and you weren't there.'

Matilda frowned. 'You look flustered. What's really going on?'

'I'm sorry.'

'For what?'

'Aaron said you looked a bit down yesterday and he mentioned the article in the newspaper and as you weren't there this morning and not answering your phone, I thought—'

'You thought I might have topped myself?'

'No,' she lied unconvincingly.

'And the truth would be?'

'Yes,' she looked at the ground. 'I'm so sorry, Mat.'

'Adele, you need to be able to trust me. I'm not going to fall to pieces just because a journalist reports lies about me.'

'I know. I'm sorry. I don't know what I was thinking.'

'Look, why don't you make me a coffee while I go and get dressed?'

Adele walked into the kitchen and set about making coffee. She filled the kettle and put it on to boil. While waiting she looked around. Her eyes fell on the dresser, on the note delivered last night:

You're a murdering bitch! There's blood on your hands, Detective Chief Inspector Matilda Darke.

'Who sent you this?' Adele asked when she heard Matilda walk into the room.

'I've no idea. I've been getting phone calls too. Silent ones. I can hear someone breathing but they don't say anything. Then they hang up.'

'You don't seem overly worried.'

'I'm not. It's just someone messing about. You know what some people are like; they read the paper, they pick someone out they don't like and target them. They'll move on when 'Wednesday are relegated at the end of the season.' She smiled.

'So how come you're not in work yet?'

'I had a phone therapy session with Dr Warminster this morning. I'd rather have it at home than in my office.'

'Phone therapy?'

'Yes. Don't snigger.'

'I'm not. Does it work?'

'Yes it does. I know I didn't take to Dr Warminster very well in the beginning, but she's very insightful. When we finish chatting I actually feel better.'

'That's because she's impartial. It's good to talk to someone on the outside rather than a friend.'

'I suppose that's true,' Matilda said, realizing for the first time she appreciated talking to someone who didn't know her on a personal level and who wasn't going to judge her. 'Look, pour that coffee into travel mugs, we'll take it with us.'

Outside, Matilda and Adele chatted for a few minutes. It was light-hearted and they were both smiling. Adele caught the eye of the neighbour next door.

'What's wrong with her?' Adele asked, nodding towards the living room window where Jill Carmichael was looking at them while cradling a baby.

'Jill? Nothing why?'

'She's having a right gawp at us.'

'She's been trying to chat to me quite a bit lately. I think she's feeling a bit down since the baby was born, you know, lack of adult contact, that kind of thing. She's harmless enough.'

'She's got a black eye.'

'Kick-boxing.'

'Ouch. She should take up spinning.'

'And swap a black eye for a black arse?'

They both laughed.

Adele kissed Matilda on the cheek and headed for her car. A few seconds later Matilda opened the garage door and reversed her car up the drive before closing the door with a remote. She gave an awkward wave to Jill Carmichael who didn't respond and drove off in the direction of the police station.

As Matilda pulled away she passed a black BMW parked a few houses down. The driver was slumped down behind the wheel to avoid being seen. Matilda seemed to be happy, smiling, joking; getting on with life as if nothing had happened. It was time to raise the stakes.

FOURTEEN

Driving an unfamiliar pool car with an unrecognizable smell, Rory Fleming pulled up outside the Craven home on Williamson Road. Sian suggested someone should try and talk to Jack Craven, the oldest son, and preferably alone. He was eighteen-years-old, an adult, and wouldn't need supervision during any interview. The question was, who would talk to him? Who was on the same wavelength as a teenager? Rory hoped it was down to his youthful looks that he'd been chosen and not his child-like behaviour.

He managed to find a parking space close to the detached house, though it was a tight squeeze; he'd have difficulty getting out. As he climbed out of the car he saw a young man heading in his direction. He was tall and skinny and had the gait of a typical student; head down, shoulders slumped, and dragging his feet. He was wearing painfully tight jeans that made his feet look huge, and an over-sized Disney jumper. Charity shop chic. His hair was in an out-of-bed style, or maybe it hadn't been brushed in days.

'Jack Craven?' Rory called out.

The skinny student, though on closer inspection skinny could be downgraded to gangly, stopped and turned. 'Yeah?'

Rory whipped his ID out of his inside jacket pocket. 'DC Rory Fleming, South Yorkshire Police. Could I have a word?'

'Is this about my mum?'

'Yes.'

He nodded. 'I suppose.' He headed towards the house.

'How about I buy you a coffee?'

The student, facial expression unchanged, nodded and headed back up the driveway. Rory had been a student; college then university – was he ever like that? He couldn't remember ever dressing like he'd landed naked in a skip and put on whatever people had thrown out. Jack Craven had the dour expression of the permanently miserable. Rory expected him to look upset given what had happened to his mother, but something told him Jack always looked like a man taking the long walk to the guillotine.

In a nearby coffee shop Rory had asked Jack to choose his poison. He opted for a large cappuccino and cheekily asked if he could have something to eat too. Rory consented, but was surprised when Jack picked up a tuna melt Panini and asked the barista for a slice of gluten-free carrot cake. Rory wondered if he could claim this back on expenses.

'How are you doing?' Rory asked once they were comfortable. Jack with his banquet, he with his medium white coffee.

'I'm fine.'

'What about your brother and sister?'

'They're fine.'

'Your dad?'

'He's OK.'

'Have you been to see your mum?'

'Dad won't let us.'

'Why not?'

'He says we'd be too upset.'

'Has your dad told you everything that's happened?'

'He's told us she was attacked.'

'Has he said anything else?'

'No. He doesn't need to though. I'm not thick.'

'What do you mean?'

'She was in a car with a man. She was having an affair.'

'Do you know that for sure?'

'No. Like I said, I'm not thick.'

'Why would she have an affair?'

'It's what she does.'

'She's done this before?'

'Yeah. More than once.'

'How many times?'

'Dunno,' he shrugged. He had managed to polish off the Panini in four large bites. Judging by his skeletal frame, Rory wondered if he ever had a decent meal.

'Why does your mum have affairs?'

'She gets bored.'

'With what?'

'Dunno. Life, Dad, work, us. She keeps talking about doing some charity work, going out to Africa or joining Greenpeace or something but that's as far as it goes. She's too selfish to do charity work.'

'Are you close to your mum and dad?'

'Not really. Dad more than Mum.'

'What about your brother and sister?'

'What about them?'

'Are they close to your mum and dad?'

'Anna's closer to Dad than Mum too. Thomas isn't even Dad's.'

Rory's eyes widened. He tried to hide his sudden interest but it wasn't easy. Just when he thought this one-sided conversation was going nowhere out came this nugget of gold. 'What?'

'Mum had a one-night stand with someone from work,' he held the large coffee cup in both hands, breathing in the strong fumes. 'She found out she was pregnant too late to do anything about it.'

'How did she know it wasn't your dad's?'

'Dad had a vasectomy about a year after Anna was born. He only wanted one of each.'

'How did he take it?'

'He was fuming. He threw Mum out. He took her back after a few months of her begging. His name's on the birth certificate too.'

'Really? He's bringing Thomas up as his own child?'

'Yeah.'

'Does Thomas know?'

'No. I only found out by accident.'

'How?'

'I overheard Mum and Dad arguing once.'

'How do you feel about that?'

'Dunno. I suppose I should respect Dad for taking on another man's child. Not many would. Thomas was born deaf and Dad was the first of us to learn sign language. He loves him like he does me and Anna.'

'What's your home life like?'

'What home life? It's bloody depressing. Dad tries his best but Mum may as well not be there. It's bad to say, I know, but since she's been in hospital, it's been lighter.'

Rory sat in silence, trying to take it all in. Did he hear correctly or did an eighteen-year-old actually say life was better with his mother critically ill in hospital?

'Cheers for the food and drink, Detective. I've got to get back.'

Jack wiped his face on the napkin, and left.

Rory, his face a massive question mark, walked slowly from the coffee shop to the car. He pulled his phone out and dialled. 'Sian, it's Rory. You've got children, right?'

'So that's what those four people in my house are. I did wonder.'

'Is it possible for a man to have the snip and still have a child?'

'Well it's not impossible. There have been examples of it happening. Do I dare ask why you want to know?'

'I've just been talking to Jack Craven. He says the youngest child, Thomas, isn't his father's. He'd had the snip before he was born, yet his name is on the birth certificate.'

'Do you believe him?'

'That's the thing, I don't know. He sounded convincing but how can we find out?'

'Without asking for a DNA test I don't think there is a way. I suppose we could ask a doctor how successful they are these days. How long ago was it when he had it done?'

'I'm not sure. About fifteen, sixteen years ago I guess.'

'Right, OK, leave it with me.'

Before ringing off Rory filled Sian in on everything else Jack had revealed; his mother's affairs and how the atmosphere was bleak whenever she was home.

'Well that's just given us a few more suspects,' Sian said. 'Martin, at a push, the son, and everyone who Lois has had an affair with. Just when we thought this case couldn't get more complicated.'

FIFTEEN

MYSTERY DEEPENS AS SHOOTING VICTIMS ARE NAMED

By Alex Winstanley

The identities of the victims of the double shooting at Clough Lane have been revealed. They are Kevin Hardaker, 43, of Broad Elms Lane, and Lois Craven, 41, from Williamson Road.

Mr Hardaker was killed after being beaten and shot twice. Mrs Craven is still in a critical condition in hospital following several operations to remove three bullets and reduce swelling from her brain.

Close friends of Lois Craven have revealed that she and Kevin Hardaker had been having an affair for more than a year. Kevin, a regional sales manager for Currys is married with two children while Lois, a college administrator, is married with three children.

As of the incident taking place, the spouses of both victims had no knowledge of an affair, both believing themselves to be in a stable and loving marriage. Neither Alice Hardaker, nor Martin Craven were available for comment.

A neighbour of the Hardaker family, who wished to remain anonymous, said: 'I'm finding all this incredibly hard to believe. They're a lovely family. You couldn't wish for two nicer kids. It was their son, Warren's, tenth birthday last November and they had a wonderful party. The whole neighbourhood was invited. We thought they were all very happy.'

Giles Mitchell, a retired civil servant, lives on Psalter Lane and knows the Craven family well: 'This is heart-breaking news. It's the kids I feel sorry for. Lois always did her duty with those three.'

Police are still appealing for witnesses to the shooting and are pursuing many lines of inquiry.

'Have you seen this?'

DC Scott Andrews entered the desolate Murder Room. Someone, probably Rory, had stuck a handmade sign reading 'Marie Celeste' over the top of the door. He showed Sian the latest edition of the local newspaper that named the victims of the shooting.

'I wondered why the phones had been busy,' she said, scanning the article. 'Who is this Alex Winstanley? Should we be worried about him?'

'I've no idea. I haven't met him. He's new so it sounds like he's trying to make a name for himself.'

'Could be dangerous. Did you get anywhere with the door-to-door statements?'

'I did.'

For the past hour Scott had been through every statement given by the neighbours of the Craven and Hardaker family.

'The Cravens are a quiet family. They like to keep themselves to themselves apparently. A couple of the neighbours have said how polite and well behaved the kids are. Most of them tend to talk more about Martin Craven than they do Lois. He's always with the children, taking them out, driving them wherever they want to go. Lois is usually spotted on her own.'

'Not the motherly type then?'

'It would appear not. One of the neighbours, Eva Charles, said she got the impression Martin and Lois were living separate lives.'

'What gave her that impression?'

'You never see them together. Lois goes to work, goes out with her mates, and comes home at any time. Martin has a routine and deals with the kids. She says you could set your watch by him.'

'I wonder if Martin knew about Lois's affair with Kevin Hardaker then.'

'It's possible.'

'Rory has just been speaking to Jack Craven. According to him, Lois has had affairs in the past. Either Martin knew about Kevin, and the others, and just let her get on with it, or—'

'He finally snapped.'

'Exactly. Something to think about. I'll let Matilda know, see where she wants to go with this. What about the Hardakers?'

'This is more interesting. According to the woman who lives two doors down,' he looked in his notebook, 'a Mrs Monica Bryce-Owens, Alice has a brother and sister; the sister is all right, but the brother comes round at all hours of the day and night. He's often drunk and shouting. She says he's been in prison a few times. I've looked him up and Lucas Branning has been in the nick three times; twice for burglary and once for car theft and drink driving.

'Any history of violence?'

'Well he's not been charged with any violent behaviour, but if he's responsible for these latest burglaries then I'd say he has a short fuse to say the least.'

'I tell you what, go and see Faith in CID. She's working on these burglaries. They'll have been looking into everyone with a history of burglary, and that means Lucas Branning will have come up. Get a background on him and we'll take it from there.'

'Will do.'

As he was leaving the room Sian called out, 'Good work Scott, well done.'

That brightened up his young face. He smiled and there was a spring in his step as he left the room.

DC Faith Easter had once been a part of the Murder Investigation Team. She was brought in by Acting DCI Ben Hales who was filling in while Matilda was away. At first she enjoyed being part of an elite team and she was happy to be eased in gently. Her first case was a suspicious death at an eighteenth birthday party. After a short investigation, a young man admitted to spiking the drink of a girl he allegedly loved and that was that. He handed himself in, answered every question put to him and was sent to court. Case closed.

It was the Harkness case last winter that had been the real shocker for Faith: a twenty-year-old cold case and a current murder case; tensions in the office on Matilda's return, and the Acting DCI changing personality overnight. He had been a mild-mannered, hard-working boss until Matilda came back. He was dedicated; commanded respect and he'd received it, especially from Faith. But the threat of Matilda retaking her position as the head of the Murder Room had turned him into a tyrant and a bully.

Faith made errors during the investigation and had questioned her position in the team. She didn't make any rash decisions and made sure she pulled her weight until the case was solved. Then she had asked to be transferred back to CID.

Now she was back in CID, a small fish in a very large pond, and she was content with her work.

Scott entered the open-plan office and headed over to her. Her desk was a mess of paperwork and files. She was engrossed in something on her computer screen and didn't notice her former teammate standing by her. Scott, who had taken a chocolate bar from Sian's snack drawer, dropped it from a height in front of her. It made her jump.

'Bloody hell, Scott.'

'I've brought you a present.'

She picked up the chocolate bar. 'Please thank Sian for me,' she said with a smile.

'How do you know I didn't buy this myself?'

'Because as sweet as you are you're very – what's the right word? – economical with your money.'

'OK you got me, but it's the thought that counts.'

'It certainly is. I shall enjoy this with a coffee later. Now, what can I do for you?'

'I need to pick your brain.'

'I don't think there's much left to pick. I'm knackered.'

'These burglaries you're working on—'

'Aggravated burglaries,' she interrupted.

'Sorry, aggravated burglaries. Has the name Lucas Branning come up at all?'

'It sounds familiar, let me have a look.'

Faith, a slim woman, despite the amount of chocolate she ate, had silky dark brown hair which, today, she had neatly tied back in a loose ponytail. Her coffee-coloured skin was unblemished but did look a little dry under the fluorescent lighting. She rummaged around on her desk for a file of suspects and opened it up.

'Here we go, Lucas Branning. Thirty-seven-years-old, five foot five inches tall, stocky, cropped hair, works as a part-time mechanic, foul-mouthed and a massive attitude problem.'

'He sounds lovely.'

'Yes. I'm hoping he's single,' she said, grinning. 'Why do you want to know about him?'

'He is the brother of Alice Hardaker who is the wife of Kevin who was shot dead in our double shooting.'

'I heard about that. Sounds nasty,' she shuddered, pleased that she wasn't on this particular investigation.

'Is he a potential suspect in your aggravated burglaries?' Scott asked.

'No. He has an alibi for all of them. He said he's going straight, and, actually, it sounds like he's managing it too. He drinks a lot so spends most of his evenings in his local pub playing pool. As he's a regular the landlord and staff know him, as do the other regulars, so they were able to confirm his alibis.'

'Bugger.'

'Do you really think the person responsible for these aggravated burglaries is the same one who committed the double shooting?'

'I've no idea. Guns have been used in both. Just how bad are these burglaries?' Scott asked, his interest piqued.

Faith slapped her hand down on top of a pile of more than twenty files, all of various thickness. 'These are all the burglaries that have taken place in the past six months involving weapons or menaces.'

'Bloody hell.'

'Exactly,' she opened the top file. 'Mr and Mrs Harrison, both eighty-six and living on Shirecliffe Road. They were forced to watch while a masked man rifled through their home. When he tried to take the rings off Mrs Harrison's wedding finger Mr Harrison lunged at him. He's currently in the Northern General with a broken nose, jaw and cheek bone. He may need facial reconstruction surgery.'

'Oh my God.'

'He's very lucky he's still alive. Mrs Harrison is in bits and permanently at his bedside. They've been married for over sixty years, bless them.'

She picked up another file. 'A family of four in Darnall were tied up as a masked man robbed their home. When he didn't find much worth stealing he took the teenage daughter, at gunpoint, to cash machines and withdrew as much money from the parents' bank accounts as he was able. He threatened to rape her and slit her throat on more than one occasion. He returned her home unharmed. The father's left leg was broken in three places and the five-year-old son suffered a head injury when the burglar hit him with a baseball bat.'

'Jesus. He's a real nasty piece of work.'

'That's one way of putting it. We're lucky nobody has actually been killed yet.'

'Unless he is responsible for the double shooting. He's got a gun, he's threatened rape. Who's to say he didn't stumble across Kevin Hardaker's car and decided to rob them and it went too far? Do you have a description of him?'

'Tall, well built, strong, dressed in black and masked. He's got a strong Sheffield accent and he smokes. Not much to go on is it?' Faith said, shaking her head.

'So it definitely rules out Lucas Branning?'

'Definitely. Lucas is shorter than me and fat. It's not him.'

'So maybe these are two separate incidents then.'

'Maybe. Sorry I couldn't be more helpful.'

'No you've been very helpful, thank you. Will you keep me informed if there are anymore, or you get a more detailed description?'

'Of course I will.'

'Thanks Faith. Enjoy the Double Decker.'

SIXTEEN

Adele Kean pulled back the white sheet covering a man, face down, on a drawer she had just pulled out of the fridges in her mortuary. 'Matilda, I'd like you to meet Gerald Beecham.'

'I appreciate you trying to help Adele, but he's a bit old for me.'

Adele tried not to smile. She failed. 'On the night of the shooting, Mr Beecham, who lives in a tower block on London Road, was found dead at the bottom of the block of flats.'

'He jumped?'

'Pushed. Or thrown.'

'OK. I don't quite understand where you're going with this …'

'The bruises on his back show that he was attacked before plunging to his death. There is a partial footprint in the small of his back too, if you look closely, which has been photographed and scanned. Anyway,' she covered him up with the sheet and pushed him back into the fridge, 'on his clothing there was some blood which doesn't belong to him.'

'Would you like me to ask who it belongs to?'

'Yes please,' Adele gave a smug smile.

'Dr Kean, to whom does the blood belong?'

'Lois Craven.'

'What?' Matilda's smile dropped. The time for playing was over. 'Is this my killer?'

'I doubt it.'

'I don't get it then.'

'Whoever performed the double shooting came across Mr Beecham; they somehow ended up on the roof together, and over he went.'

'This is making no sense whatsoever.' Matilda walked away shaking her head. She tried to get things into perspective but nothing was fitting. It was like she had all the pieces of the jigsaw but they were from different boxes. 'For a start why kill a man then throw him off the roof of a tall building? He could have left him up there and he could have remained undetected for weeks, months maybe.'

'According to the police report a scream was heard around the time of death.'

'Bloody hell, he was still alive when he was thrown?'

'It would appear so.'

'Why would anyone throw an old man off the roof of a building?'

'No idea. I don't really want to think about the kind of person who would gladly hurl another person off a roof.'

'So, Kevin Hardaker and Lois Craven are beaten and shot. About an hour later, Gerald Beecham is beaten and thrown off a roof. The connection in both scenes is that Gerald Beecham has Lois Craven's blood on him.'

'Also, Lois and Gerald both have black man-made fibres under their fingernails, which are identical. Whoever attacked them, they both managed to get hold of whatever he was wearing in the struggle.'

'Is there any of Gerald's DNA at the scene on Clough Lane?'

'No.'

'Jesus. So this means Kevin and Lois's attacker also killed Gerald.'

'Your killer certainly had a busy night.'

'Let's just hope he's finished,' Matilda replied, scared by the thought.

SEVENTEEN

In the matter of: GERALD ARTHUR BEECHAM
Place: SHEFFIELD, SOUTH YORKSHIRE
Date: MARCH twenty-second, 2015
Name: REBECCA BEECHAM

I am Rebecca Beecham, 47, of Meadow Head, Sheffield, South Yorkshire. I am the daughter of Gerald Arthur Beecham, 80, of London Road, Sheffield, South Yorkshire. This statement made by me accurately sets out the evidence that I would be prepared, if necessary, to give in court as a witness. The statement is true to the best of my knowledge and belief and I make it knowing that, if it is tendered in evidence, I will be liable to prosecution if I have wilfully stated in it anything that I know to be false, or do not believe to be true.

I last spoke to my father on the 18th of March in the morning by telephone. I had to be at Manchester airport by noon and I called him just before I left home.

I was travelling to Stockholm on business. I work as a freelance magazine photographer.

My father seemed to be in good spirits. He had recently suffered a chest infection that took some time to clear up but the tablets were working and he was feeling a lot better. He took medication for a heart condition he had had since he was a child and medication for arthritis. Apart from that he was in good health.

My mother died in August last year after a long battle with cancer. My parents had been married for more than fifty years and were inseparable. Her death hit my dad very hard. She had been ill for a very long time and we all had time to get used to her not being around anymore. However, when she died my father did become depressed. There was a time I thought he might have taken his own life but we had a long conversation in October of last year and he stated that he would never put me through that. He knew he wasn't going to be around forever and said that he could wait to be reunited with my mum.

I did worry about my dad living in a high-rise flat but he and mum had lived there for the best part of twenty years and loved it. The whole block had been renovated in the past five years or so and they really did enjoy living there. It wasn't ideal when my mum became ill but the lifts always worked and they were happy. They lived a happy and simple life.

At Christmas I had my dad stay with me for a few days. I live in a bungalow at Meadow Head and asked Dad if he would like to move in with me. At first he said a categorical no. He said he refused to be a burden. However, I managed to win him over and he eventually agreed. I had a lot of work at the beginning of this year but was taking some time off over Easter so we were going to move all his things into my home then. The closer we got to the moving day the more excited he became. I think he was looking forward to having a garden.

I know 100 per cent that my father did not take his own life. He had no reason to. Somebody did this to him. Somebody lured him up to the roof and killed him.

'Sian have you eaten yet?' Matilda spoke into her phone as she left the Autopsy Facility.

'I haven't moved from my desk all morning. I haven't had time to pee yet.'

'Fancy discussing a dead body over lunch?'

'Spooky, that was my husband's opening line when he first asked me out,' Sian laughed.

Fifteen minutes later they were sitting opposite each other in the Lloyd's pub on Division Street looking out onto Charter Square at the war memorial and the City Hall.

Suddenly, Matilda no longer felt hungry, so she ordered a tuna salad. Sian, who was looking forward to a big meal to celebrate her wedding anniversary, asked for the same.

'What links an 80-year-old widow and a couple in their 40s having an illicit affair?' Matilda asked.

'That sounds like the beginning of a really bad joke.'

'I think this entire case is a really bad joke.'

'I've spoken to Rebecca Beecham again since her original state- ment,' Sian said. 'She's pleased her father's death is being investigated seriously. I asked her about Kevin Hardaker and Lois Craven but she's never heard of them and her father never mentioned them either.'

'Is there anything linking them? Do they belong to the same club or gym or library?'

'Gerald Beecham didn't go out at all without his daughter. She didn't like the idea of him being out on his own so always took him shopping and wherever else he wanted to go. They were quite close.'

Matilda did not enjoy hearing this. 'There's no way Gerald Beecham could be Kevin's long lost father. Or maybe he was having a secret affair with Lois?'

Sian sniggered. 'I'm afraid not. Sorry.'

'Anything from the SOCOs from the roof of the high-rise?'

'There was evidence of a small fire recently but nothing to get excited about. I was looking into something when you called; does the name Nathaniel Glover mean anything to you?'

'It rings a bell.'

'Back in 2000, Nathaniel Glover was sentenced to eleven years for attacking a couple in a car at Endcliffe Park. He robbed them and beat the bloke up pretty bad. He slapped the woman a few times and tried it on with her too. When he couldn't get an erection, he thumped her in the stomach and fled.'

'Was he armed?'

'No.'

'So why was his sentence so high for a robbery?'

'The woman was about four months pregnant at the time and she lost it. The couple were only in their late teens, both still lived at home, they often went for a drive and parked up somewhere quiet to have some privacy.'

'Poor kids. I'm guessing this Nathaniel Glover is out now?'

'Yes. He only served five years and was let out on good behaviour.'

'Where is he now?'

'No idea. I'm going to look him up this afternoon.'

'Good. Bring him in and question him. I want every minute of where he was on the night of the attack accounted for.'

A young barman literally dropped their meals onto the table and walked away. No smile, no 'enjoy your meal', nothing.

'Now there's a bloke who enjoys his job,' Matilda smiled.

'He could be Aaron's younger brother.'

Matilda picked at her salad. It didn't look appetizing but she guessed she would have to eat something. In her head she could hear Adele chastising her for missing meals. 'OK. Ignoring the actual crimes for a second, why would someone commit a double shooting then go to a high-rise block of flats?'

'Maybe he lived there,' Sian shrugged, shovelling a forkful of lettuce into her mouth.

'You've got a point there. I never thought of that. Maybe the killer does live there. OK, say he does, why did he go up to the roof?'

A thought suddenly came to Sian. Her eyes lit up. 'To hide something.'

'Like what?'

'I'm not sure. Maybe hide the gun he used.'

'And was disturbed by Gerald Beecham,' Matilda finished the thought. 'Does that sound credible?'

'So far it's the most credible thing about this.'

'Good point. Get Rory and Scott to look into it. I want every member of that block of flats identified.'

Sian laughed. 'I shall look forward to telling them. They'll love that job. Not eating?'

'I'm not that hungry anymore. I've got a headache.'

'I'll be using that line tonight.'

'Sorry?'

'It's mine and Stuart's thirteenth wedding anniversary today. He seems to think that's a green light for him getting sex. I love messing with his head.'

'Congratulations.'

Matilda's mind wandered. She had only managed five wedding anniversaries with James. They celebrated their fifth with a long weekend in an isolated cottage on one of the islands in the Outer Hebrides. Thursday to Tuesday, just the two of them. They didn't leave the cottage once. Actually, that wasn't true. They did leave it once. They went for a long walk with a picnic, found a nice spot overlooking the sea, and forgot all about the picnic.

'I can't believe we've been married for thirteen years. I remember when we first met. My mum told me it wouldn't last. She thought Stuart was a flake and wouldn't make anything of himself. Typical Mum, I suppose—' Sian suddenly stopped when she saw the faraway look on her boss's face. 'Oh my God, I'm so sorry, I didn't think.'

'What?'

'It's coming up to a year since James … isn't it?'

'Yes it is.'

'I'm sorry. I didn't mean to go spouting off about my wedding anniversary like that.'

'Don't be silly. You can't stop talking about things because of me.'

'How are you coping?'

'I'm OK. I'll be better when the anniversary's been and gone.'

'I saw the story in the newspaper about Carl Meagan. They're bastards aren't they? They haven't got a clue what we have to do on a day-to-day basis. Look, I know it's easy for me to say but don't take it to heart. The readers will have completely forgotten it by the time they buy the paper again tomorrow night.'

'I know.'

Sian smiled. 'Would you like to come over for dinner tonight; join me and Stuart?'

Matilda laughed out loud. 'I don't think Stuart would be too happy to see me at the dinner table when he's hoping for some fun.'

'Stuart's always hoping for fun. He's used to the rejection. You must come over for dinner at some point though.'

'I will,' she lied. 'Look, I have an appointment to go to, would you set Rory and Scott on identifying the high-rise residents and just—'

'Cover for you?'

'Would you mind?'

'Of course not.'

'Matilda?'

She stopped, half-rising from her chair. It was never good when her colleague used her first name. It was obviously going to be a personal comment.

'Are you all right?'

'Yes. I'm fine. Why?'

'You look tired.'

'I'm fine. I just want to have a think about this case; get my head around it.'

Matilda left the pub. She avoided looking up into the window as she passed as she knew Sian would be looking out at her. She wasn't on the brink of tears yet, which was an improvement, but she was feeling emotional and she had no idea why.

She stepped up the pace as she entered the multistorey car park where she had left her car. Once behind the wheel, she locked the door and bowed her head. Whenever she thought of James it was never long before the tears started to flow. When Matilda first met James she had, more or less, given up on finding someone to fall in love with. Like the majority of people, she had had her fair share of failed relationships, doomed from the start, dead-end romances, and never came close to 'the one'. It didn't bother her if she never married. She had never been maternal and children didn't feature in her life plan. So she'd be single: who cared?

Then she met James and her life was turned upside down and inside out. She was shown happiness for seven years and then it had been ripped from her in the cruellest of ways. The symmetry of Carl Meagan's life was not lost on her. He was seven when he disappeared. His family had seven years of happiness and now, like her, they were living in limbo. They didn't know what to do without their little boy and she didn't know what to do without her husband.

Matilda wiped her eyes and looked up into the darkness of the car park. It was cold and there was a lingering smell of damp.

In the parking bay opposite the headlights of a dark-coloured BMW were turned on and lit up Matilda's face. Her red eyes and tears were visible. She squinted into the brilliant whiteness and waited for the car to pull out. It didn't move. It didn't even have its engine on.

A paranoid fear gripped her. Was there someone watching her? It wasn't the first time she had noticed a dark BMW lingering. Who would do that? Panic set in as she tried to turn the key in the ignition and stalled the engine a couple of times. She selected the wrong gear and juddered to a halt. She looked up. The car opposite had started its engine.

'Shit,' Matilda cursed herself. She turned the ignition key again. It took three attempts but the engine eventually came to life. A deep breath and ten Prime Ministers later she exited the car park. Once out in the open she checked her rear-view mirror. There was no sign of the black BMW.

EIGHTEEN

The armchair looked comfortable but once Matilda sat down she was squirming, kept crossing and uncrossing her legs, moving from side to side, sitting up, slouching, sitting up again, and generally wishing she was anywhere but in a converted house on Manchester Road sitting opposite a psychotherapist with split ends and a ladder in her tights.

It had been at the insistence of South Yorkshire Police that Matilda had sought professional help. Following the death of her husband and the collapse of the Carl Meagan case, it was no secret that Matilda had a breakdown. She rarely left the house and spent her days crying and drinking alcohol. Occasionally she went through stages where she would binge on junk food, but this was followed by periods of vomiting and more alcohol.

Before she had been allowed to return to work last December, she'd had to be psychologically evaluated, and Dr Sheila Warminster was her appointed therapist. Matilda loathed her. Before they even met Matilda knew she would hate her on sight. As the weeks and months went by Matilda slowly warmed to her. It was difficult to admit, but Sheila Warminster really knew her stuff and her advice and exercises often helped.

Matilda had intended for this afternoon's session to be the

final one. However, the anonymous note, the current, baffling, case, and the thought of being followed had made her change her mind. She would continue with the sessions.

As she approached the converted house, Matilda felt different. It was like she was here for the first time. This time, she wasn't dreading the unknown, but determined to get well. She was prepared to listen.

'Matilda, I would be lying if I said I wasn't happy you've come to this decision. It's been a few weeks since your boss said you could quit these sessions if you wished and I expected you to do so. The fact you are deciding to continue with your therapy of your own free will really is a huge step in your recovery.'

Matilda found herself smiling back at her. 'I thought that once I'd returned to work I'd be able to pick up where I left off and everything would go back to the way it was. I was wrong. That doesn't happen does it?'

'No it doesn't. Matilda, I can't begin to imagine the torment you've been through. You are an incredibly strong person. A weaker person would have given in but you haven't. The fact you're here is testament to your strength.'

'I don't feel very strong.'

'You won't. You'll feel like the entire world is against you. I'm here to show you that it isn't.'

'If I'm such a strong person, why do I feel like a complete mess?'

'Because you haven't come to terms with everything that has happened. James died and Carl Meagan disappeared at the same time. Both events were huge blows to you and your brain didn't know which one to cope with first so it just shut down. You need to make sense of them, question why they happened, but you can't as every time you think of James, Carl jumps up and vice versa.

'It was Adele's idea for me to arrange a time to sit down with my wedding album and grieve. For example, say at six o'clock

113

every evening, sit down and have a good cry for an hour or so then go back to being me in the present.'

'That's a very good idea. You should be paying Adele,' Sheila said with a smile.

That was the first time Matilda had ever known Sheila to make a light-hearted comment. She found herself relaxing and smiling in return.

'I can't keep relying on Adele though, can I?'

'No you can't. Adele sounds like a wonderful woman and she's perfect for you to have as an ally, but not as someone to cling to when you go through a bad patch. By all means, ring her up and moan about having a bad day, etcetera, but don't use her as a crutch. She's a friend, not a counsellor.'

'Well she is a doctor,' Matilda quipped.

'A pathologist. If you want her to cut you open, then let her, but I doubt it will help.'

Another light-hearted comment. She was a long way off being called funny, but it was an improvement. Like she said, the first step to recovery is actually wanting to get better in the first place. Maybe Sheila was lighter because she knew her advice would be heeded now.

'If I'd been more receptive to therapy from day one, would I have been better than I am now?'

'Definitely,' Sheila said without hesitation. 'But I can understand why you weren't receptive. Like I said, you're a strong woman; to be told to seek help is not what you wanted to hear from your boss. You thought you were coping with it in your own way but you weren't and you couldn't see it. Now you can.'

'So where do we go from here?'

'You tell me what's wrong?'

Matilda let out a heavy sigh. 'If I said everything was wrong what would you say?'

'I wouldn't believe you. Can you go to the shop to buy a newspaper?'

'Yes,' Matilda shrugged.

'Can you drive to work in the morning?'

'Yes.'

'Can you cook a meal?'

'Yes.'

'Can you make a cup of coffee?'

'Yes.'

'Good. White, no sugar, thanks.'

OK, now that was funny.

'Seriously,' Sheila continued. 'You can do all of those things and so many others. You are stronger than you think. We need to reprogramme your mind so that you believe you're more worthwhile than you currently think you are. You can get out of bed in a morning, get dressed, put in a full day at work, come home, have a meal and go to bed, and do it all again the following day. On that level, there is absolutely nothing wrong with you.'

'So what is wrong with me?'

'Your thought process. You're going through a period of mourning and you've become stuck. We need to get you out of that funk.'

'And how do we alter that?'

'One step at a time.'

'One step at a time,' Matilda repeated. 'Thank you,' she nodded.

NINETEEN

'Dad, what does rape mean?'

The question was powerful enough to stop time itself. The entire room descended into silence as all heads turned to look at Thomas Craven. He hadn't used sign language. His muffled voice resounded around the silent room.

The whole Craven family, minus Lois but including her mother, Margaret, were sitting around the dinner table eating a meal prepared by Martin. He was famous for his home-made spaghetti meatballs and the kids always enjoyed it. Tonight, though, everyone seemed to have lost their appetite as meatballs were pushed around the plates and pasta slowly twirled around forks to give them something to do.

Margaret was eating little. She constantly felt sick since the attack on her daughter, especially since she'd been to the hospital and seen the condition Lois was in. It was heartbreaking. Martin had been picking at bits of food all day so was no longer hungry. Jack and Anna were just going through the motions. Only Thomas was eating with any gusto.

'Where did you hear that word?' Martin was shocked. He spoke loud and clearly so Thomas could lip-read. He didn't dare release his grip on his cutlery to expose his shaking hands.

'Molly at school said that Mum was raped; that's why she's gone away. What does it mean?' This, he signed.

Anna's lip quivered. She pushed back her plate, and ran out of the room and up the stairs. Margaret quickly followed, eager to comfort her granddaughter.

'Thomas, rape is a very nasty word. You shouldn't know words like that. Now, your mum has had a bit of an accident and she is in hospital until she gets better.'

'Can I see her?'

'Not at the moment. Soon, though.'

'What happened?'

Martin looked up at Jack. Their eyes met and they both saw a look of grief, sadness, and horror in each other. This was eating away at the entire family. Anna had hardly spoken since Martin told her what had happened, Jack was his usual quiet self, Margaret was full of questions and Martin was just trying hard to keep it all together for the sake of his children.

'Thomas, your mum was in a car accident. She wasn't badly hurt but she just needs to spend a bit of time in hospital until she's better. Then she can come home.'

'Will she be home in time for my birthday?'

'Of course she will,' he lied convincingly.

'If I waste my meatballs do I still get afters?'

Martin laughed. He wished life was so simple: to move from the horror of his wife being raped, beaten, and shot to worrying about dessert in a single heartbeat. The innocence of children was beguiling. He wondered what age it was lost – when do people lose it and become cynical, harsh, and cold.

'Of course you can have afters. Just this once.'

Thomas gave a grin that exposed the gap where his two front teeth should have been and pushed his plate to one side.

Alice Hardaker was alone in the family home on Broad Elms Lane. Her sister Jenny had taken Warren and Milly out for the evening to the cinema to give them a treat and a break from the heavy atmosphere at home. It also gave Alice some alone time to have a bath, something to eat, and maybe have a think about what to do next.

She could not come to terms with Kevin's betrayal. Apparently the affair had been going on for almost a year. How could she not know? There were no changes in his behaviour, he didn't spend any extra time at work, no additional meetings, no late nights. The obvious signs of adultery had not appeared at all.

Or had they? Since being made redundant eight months ago she had been spending every day looking for new work as an estate agent. She had contacts who she called and emailed on a regular basis, she posted her CV on recruitment websites and drove round Sheffield going into every estate agent office offering them her expertise. After eight months she was getting desperate. Had being so self-absorbed blinded her from what was happening around her? Had the signs been there? Had Kevin been spending extra time at work and Alice just didn't notice?

These are the questions she asked herself as she tried to relax in a hot deep bath. By the time the water started to cool her mind was still going over the past few days, weeks, and months seeking answers but not finding them.

Alice was beginning to get yet another headache. Paracetamol was no longer working. Maybe if she had something to eat she would feel better, but she couldn't stomach anything.

Wrapping herself in a towelling dressing gown she placed her feet in a pair of novelty slippers her children had bought her for Christmas and went downstairs to find something to eat.

It felt strange being in the house alone. Usually it was busy with some form of noise; the television tuned in to a children's channel where the programmes were loud even at low volume, a music channel with incoherent beats vibrating through the floor boards, or, if her husband was watching television, the news channel would be on, again at a volume loud enough to drown out the playful sounds of the children.

Now, the house was silent: just the hum of the fridge, the distant sound of a clock ticking, and the filter from the fish tank evidence that life was continuing.

Suddenly, Alice felt incredibly alone. The kids were gone, and although they were only ten and seven-years-old, it wouldn't be all that long until they were grown up and had left for university. What would happen to her then? She'd be left to rattle around a five-bedroom house by herself. Would she re-marry? No, definitely not. She loved Kevin, had trusted him, and he had betrayed her in the worst possible way. How could she trust another man after all the lies and manipulation?

Alice always thought her relationship was a perfect one. Jenny, and her brother, Lucas, had hopped from partner to partner without a care; as if it was their duty to sample as many different people as possible. Every time she met Lucas he seemed to have a different woman in tow, but all Alice had ever wanted was one man, and she had found him. She assumed.

The door to the stainless-steel fridge showed evidence of the sham happy family Alice believed she was a part of. Photographs of Kevin with his arm around his children: all smiles and toothy grins, happy times on holiday, playing in the back garden on the rare occasion it was sunny and dry in Sheffield. Pictures of Kevin and Alice taken at parties: a glass in one hand, the other draped around her waist or over her shoulder. They looked happy, in love; there was no sign of Kevin's betrayal. He looked genuinely happy. The bastard.

She opened the fridge door and looked inside. She didn't feel hungry but knew she had to eat something. Her energy levels were dropping and she needed to be strong for the kids, for herself. She picked up some cheese and put it back, did the same with a packet of ham and a salami before going back to the cheese. A cheese toastie – comfort food.

She closed the fridge door and was given the fright of her life. Standing behind it was a figure dressed in black. A tall menacing figure, only the eyes visible through a black mask. He took three huge strides until he loomed over her. She froze in terror and didn't move a muscle.

'I've come for my money,' his voice, thick Sheffield accent, was low and deep, scratchy and terrifying.

'What?' Alice gasped.

'My money. Where is it?'

'I don't know what you're talking about.'

He rolled his eyes. 'You rich bitches are always the same. You're all talk until it comes to paying up.'

'Honestly, I think you must have the wrong house or something. I don't owe anyone any money.'

He plucked a photograph of Kevin with the kids off the fridge and looked at it. 'Cute kids. You know, some people won't hurt kids. They say they have to draw the line somewhere. Me? I don't give a fuck who I hurt. I'll make them watch while I rape you then slit their throats.'

'No. Please don't hurt my children. They're all I have left.' Tears streamed down her face.

Slowly, he pulled at the belt of her dressing gown and let it fall open revealing her shaking naked body. 'Nice tits, decent body. I could enjoy myself with you. I'd fuck you better than that tosser husband of yours.'

Alice closed her eyes tight and squeezed more tears out. 'Please,' she begged, her voice barely a whisper.

He stepped back. 'It's a nice place you've got here. Mind if I have a look around?'

He started to leave the room then turned back. He pulled a gun out of his waistband and rammed it hard between Alice's legs. She let out a muffled cry and almost doubled over in pain. 'You even try to phone the police and I'll put a bullet in you. You understand?'

She nodded. Alice was shaking, every muscle in her body tensed. As soon as the masked intruder left the room it was as if her spine had been ripped out. She fell to the floor in agony as the tears rained down.

TWENTY

Matilda felt positive when she left Dr Warminster's office. That was a first. Usually she wanted to put a couple of bricks in her pockets and jump into the River Don. Before tonight, therapy had been a chore, something she had to endure. Now it was her choice and she found she had a new respect for Sheila.

Sheila? I'll be inviting her over for dinner next.

She hadn't told her therapist everything, though. Matilda still wasn't at the stage where she completely opened up. The anonymous note, the feeling of being followed – until Matilda could make sense of what was going on she was going to keep those to herself.

While Matilda was still feeling positive she gave Adele a call and invited her and Chris over for dinner. Chris was out with the lads but Adele was never one to turn down a free meal. She was waiting outside Matilda's house by the time she pulled up in the drive. A bottle of wine in each hand.

'Bloody hell, I only phoned you about five minutes ago.'

'I'm hungry.'

'I thought you didn't approve of me drinking,' Matilda said noticing the bottles.

'You can drink under adult supervision.'

'When's the adult getting here?'

Matilda had been hoping for a good thirty minutes before Adele turned up to get a head start on the meal but instead they prepared it together, enjoying the wine with Matilda filling Adele in on her therapy session.

'So it was helpful then?'

'I hate to admit it, but yes it was. It was like starting all over again.'

'Well you seem brighter, just after one session. Are you sure she didn't slip you something?'

'Yes, we had a few snorts before I left.'

'Are you going to be OK?'

'I think so. It's not going to be easy, obviously, but I'm going to be fine. I know it.'

'Well don't forget you've got me and Chris too.'

'I know. I really do appreciate everything you've done for me, Adele.'

'I should hope so too. Bloody hell, have we polished off a full bottle already?'

'Well you have. I've only had two glasses.'

'What is this anyway? All I seem to be doing is chopping. It's like being at work.'

'It's Carbonnade a la Flamande,' Matilda said, reading from a recipe book.

'It looks like beef stew.'

'It is beef stew.'

The doorbell rang. Matilda wiped her hands on a tea towel and went to answer the door.

'If that's Aiden Turner, tell him I'm busy,' Adele called out.

A few seconds later Matilda returned to the kitchen with her neighbour, Jill Carmichael, in tow.

'Oh I'm sorry, I didn't realize you had company,' Jill said. She was playing with the sleeves of her sweater and backed out of the doorway. She looked tired. Her hair was lank and lifeless, her skin blotchy and dry.

'Don't be silly, come on in. Adele isn't company, are you?'

'No. I'm practically furniture. Glass of wine?' Adele proffered the bottle.

'I better not, thanks. I just came over to beg an onion. I could have sworn I put them in my trolley but I couldn't have done.' She ran her fingers through her hair, or she tried to at least. They became caught up in the knots.

Matilda handed her a large onion from the fridge. 'Anything else?'

Jill remained rooted to the spot, staring straight ahead.

'Jill?' Matilda prompted.

'Sorry?'

'Is there anything else you'd like?'

'I … No that's it, thank you. I'll buy you a replacement when I next go to the shops.'

'Don't be silly. It's only an onion.'

'Thanks. I appreciate it. I'd better get back. Sebastian will start wondering where I am. Nice to have met you,' she said to Adele.

Matilda showed her out while Adele poured two more glasses of wine.

'She looked rough,' Adele said when Matilda returned.

'I think she's having a hard time with the baby. Her husband works a lot of hours so she's looking after her on her own practically.'

'Poor cow. She was a bundle of nerves. Mind you, if she's not sleeping properly she will be. Wine?' She handed a glass out for Matilda.

'You're a bad influence on me, do you know that?'

'That's really sweet of you to say, thank you.'

While the beef stew cooked Matilda and Adele sat in the living room. A fire was lit and the curtains were drawn. It was starting to go dark.

'How's it going with the shooting?' Adele asked.

'Slowly. I had an email from Sian when I came out from therapy. The tech guys have finished with Lois's phone. Seems she deletes everything on it at the end of every day but nothing is permanently deleted, as we know. There are some steamy conversations between Lois and Kevin.'

'Ooh, send them over to me. I could do with a bit of steam.'

Matilda was just about to reply when the doorbell rang again. She looked at her watch. 'I wonder who this is.'

'Maybe word has got out about your Carbonnade a la Flamande and people from all over Sheffield are flocking for a taste.'

'You're a sarcastic bugger, Adele.'

Matilda opened the front door to a bored-looking delivery driver in a dishevelled uniform.

'Matilda Drake?'

'Darke.'

'Sorry?'

'It's Matilda Darke.'

He squinted at his clipboard in the fading light. 'So it is. Got a delivery for you.'

'Oh right, thank you.'

He slouched to the large van and lifted up the back doors. 'I might need a hand,' he called out to her.

'Sorry?'

He looked back at his clipboard. 'You're not going to stand there while I bring thirty-seven boxes into your house are you?'

'What?'

Adele joined Matilda on the doorstep. 'What's going on?'

'Somebody seems to have sent me a few dozen parcels.'

The delivery man made his way up the pavement carrying one box. It looked heavy. 'This is the first one. There's a letter attached.'

Matilda took the box from him. It was heavy. She carried it into the living room and placed it carefully on the table. She tore off the envelope with her name handwritten on it. She scanned the two-sheet letter before stopping at the end to read the sender's name.

'Oh my God.'

'Who's it from?'

'Jonathan Harkness.'

'But he's dead.'

'I know.'

'So this is a letter from the other side.' Adele teased.

Jonathan Harkness would always occupy a place in Matilda's head. He was the first case Matilda had worked on following her husband's death. She had grown fond of Jonathan, seeing something of herself in the emotionally fragile young man. The fact that she head read him all wrong did not change how she thought of him.

Dear Matilda,

I never thought about making a will before. I didn't think I'd ever have anything worth leaving to anyone. I've just realized how fragile life actually is. Stephen Egan died tonight. As I'm writing this letter to you I'm grieving for a man I guess I didn't really know. He wanted to make me happy but fate got in the way. I told you at the hospital people who come into my life don't last long and it's true.

I'm making myself out to be some kind of saint aren't I? We both know I'm not. I've killed three people and I'm not sorry in the least. They deserved to die for the pain and torment they inflicted upon me. All I'm sorry for is that Stephen became involved. He is on my conscience and he always will be.

Now, to business. I have employed a solicitor to take care of the sale of my flat and my bank accounts. I hardly touched the money I inherited from my Aunt Clara and with the sale of her house in Newcastle and caravan in Whitby it came to a tidy sum. I've spread the money out over a number of children's charities. Children deserve a good start in life and we don't all get one. I hope I can help. I know it won't make up for what I've done but I'm not doing it for that.

I don't have many possessions to leave and I don't have anyone to leave them to. I've instructed my solicitor to sort out a house clearance. However, I wanted you to have my books. You showed a great interest in them on the occasions you came to my flat and I know you'll give them a good home. I am aware there are a lot of them but I get the feeling you'll look after them like I did. They meant a lot to me and they helped me through the difficult times. I know you've been through a great trauma too so I hope you can get some pleasure out of them.

You're a good woman Matilda and I'm pleased I met you. I hope you manage to overcome your demons and be a force to be reckoned with.

Kind regards,
Jonathan Harkness.

'He's left me his books.'

'What?' Adele asked carrying in a second box.

'Jonathan Harkness has left me his entire book collection in his will.'

'But didn't you say he had thousands of them?'

'Yes.'

'Oh my God,' she laughed.

'Adele, it's not funny. Where am I going to put them all?'

'I've no idea. You may want to think about that later though. You have a very disgruntled delivery driver out there.'

Between the three of them it took just under forty-five minutes to bring all the boxes into the house. Matilda offered the driver a cup of tea, but he declined. Adele offered him the Carbonnade a la Flamande. He looked at her with astonishment as if she'd said something dirty.

'Well, the British Library would be jealous if they came in here,' Adele said as they surveyed the living room.

The room, usually a cosy yet minimalist environment, now resembled a warehouse with boxes piled high.

'What am I going to do with all these?' Matilda asked, shocked by the state of her home.

'Change your surname to Waterstones?'

'I mean, what was he thinking of?'

'Well it's your own fault for showing an interest in the first place.'

'I must admit, it is a very impressive collection. I haven't got room for it though.'

'Mat, you live alone in a five-bedroom house, you've got plenty of room.'

'You think I should keep them, then?'

'It's entirely up to you. He left them to you though. He could have easily have donated them to Oxfam or a library but he didn't. He cared about his collection. It was the only thing in his life he did care about and he wants you to act as caretaker.'

'I suppose if I did give them away or split the collection up it would seem a bit disrespectful.' She suddenly remembered who she was talking about. 'Hang on, respect? The guy was a murderer. He killed three people for crying out loud.'

'You liked him though, didn't you?'

Matilda thought for a second. She nodded. 'I did. I did like him. He was tormented, tortured, lost. He reminded me so much of myself. We even took the same medication.'

'So what are you going to do?'

'In his suicide note to me, Jonathan told me not to think of his parents as being the victims. He didn't want the whole world remembering Jonathan Harkness as being a sadistic, cold-blooded murderer. I don't think he was. He didn't kill for the enjoyment. He killed for … well, I still don't know the reason for it. However, this collection represents the real Jonathan Harkness.'

'You're going to keep them aren't you?'

Matilda took a deep breath. 'Do you know a carpenter who can build me a few dozen shelves?'

With their appetite gone and the Carbonnade a la Flamande dried up, they both picked at their food in silence, eating very little.

'I always find a stew tastes better the day after. Warm it up tomorrow night and have it for your tea,' Adele said, looking on the bright side as always.

They moved into the living room with the second bottle of wine and a box of chocolates Matilda had in a cupboard. Sian at work had a snack drawer for people to help themselves to (providing they replaced it with something equally tasty); at home, Matilda had a spare cupboard full of junk for when she was hungry but couldn't find the energy to cook for one. Crisps, chocolate, biscuits, cakes – all stacked neatly, waiting for when a sugar rush was needed.

'Are they all crime fiction?' Adele asked opening the first couple of boxes she came across.

'Yes. That's all he read. I'm telling you, Adele, his flat was like the crime fiction section of a bookshop. The way it was set up and organized.'

'Didn't he work in Waterstones as well?'

'Yes, the one in Orchard Square.'

'I bet they've noticed a drop in sales since he died. Look at this, *Messiah*, by Boris Starling. I remember seeing that on TV. It was brilliant. Very chilling. I might have to borrow this,' she said reading the back of the paperback.

'Providing you don't break the spines, fold over the corners or rest your coffee on it.'

'Yes Jonathan,' she joked.

'This one is full of Lee Child novels. James loved reading him. He had a few but I don't think he read them all. I read one once on holiday, can't remember which one. Jack Reacher is a very attractive man.'

'Tom Cruise?' Adele asked, pulling a face.

'No. The Jack Reacher in the books is well over six foot. He's all manly and rugged and sexy.'

'Blimey, Tom Cruise was definitely miscast there.'

'I haven't seen it. Look at these; Mark Billingham, Ruth Rendell, Val McDermid, Michael Robotham, Peter Robinson, Peter James. He must have spent thousands over the years,' Adele said carefully unloading them. 'Reginald Hill, Chris Simms, Stephen Booth. Oh look, *The Sculptress*, by Minette Walters. I remember watching that on TV too. Now that really was chilling.'

Adele looked up and saw Matilda staring into space clutching a couple of hardbacks to her chest.

'Mat, what is it?'

There were tears in Matilda's eyes. 'James would have loved these,' her voice was breaking with emotion. 'He wasn't a massive reader, but he loved a good thriller, especially on holiday. I can almost see him going through these boxes wondering which one to read next.'

Adele stumbled over the mounds of books and boxes and found a gap to squeeze into next to Matilda. She put her arm around her and pulled her close.

'I can't believe it's been a year, Adele,' Matilda continued. 'A year and I still miss him like he died yesterday.'

'It takes a long time to get over something like this. If he'd been old, it would have been different but he wasn't. He had a full life ahead of him. That's what's so hard to comprehend and that's why it's taking a long time for you to come to terms with it.'

'I just miss him so much. Sometimes it physically hurts how much I miss him.'

Adele comforted Matilda and stayed with her for another hour. They left the books until Matilda could decide which room to renovate to house them in. When the second bottle of wine was empty and Adele made sure Matilda was fine on her own, she said her goodbyes.

Sitting among the boxes, she took in the collection she had inherited. It was almost surreal. She remembered standing in front of the shelves in Jonathan's apartment, which ran from floor to ceiling. She hadn't heard of the majority of authors but she had been genuinely impressed, and slightly jealous too. Matilda always wished she had more time for reading.

Opening up the box nearest to her she pulled out a hardback copy of an early Ruth Rendell; *Wolf to the Slaughter*, from 1967. She saw it was a first edition. This must have cost Jonathan a fortune. Reaching further into the box she discovered they were all hardback copies of Ruth Rendell novels, not all first editions, but all in excellent condition. He must have really cherished his favourite authors to have amassed such a collection.

She picked up one book that took her back to her childhood: *An Unkindness of Ravens* from 1985. Matilda remembered her grandmother having the exact same copy. It was the first grown-up novel she'd read and she had loved every page. She closed her eyes and smiled at the memory; a summer holiday spent in her grandmother's home on the south coast, sitting in the back garden with a book, a jug of orange juice, and a rapidly melting Tunnock's teacake under the sun's rays.

The phone rang, bringing her back from her reminisces of her halcyon youth. She reached across a pile of boxes, picked up the handset from the coffee table, and looked at the display. There was no number; probably a sales call.

'Hello,' she answered half-heartedly.

'Are you enjoying your books?'

This woke Matilda up. 'I'm sorry?'

'Which are you going to read first? I've heard James Oswald is quite good.'

'Who is this?'

'You'll want to hang on to those books. You're going to have

131

plenty of free time on your hands soon. You're not fit to work in the police. There's blood on your hands.'

The caller hung up.

Matilda went around the house closing the curtains. Since James had died she felt more vulnerable living alone. Was a five-bedroom house too big for one person? Of course it was. But James had designed this house from the rafters to the basement. There was no way she was going to leave it. However, during the hours of darkness, she felt nervous at the slightest noise, and even questioned a car as it drove past the house.

She looked out of the spare bedroom onto the main road. There was nobody about, nobody watching the house. Or was there? The caller could have been a neighbour; one of the local children playing a sick joke.

Matilda's phone rang again. She didn't look at the display.

'What?' she snapped.

'Boss?'

Now she looked at the display. 'Rory, sorry, I thought you were someone else.'

'Are you plagued by companies wanting you to claim for PPI too?'

'Something like that. What's up?'

'I know it's late but I thought you might want to know – Lois Craven is conscious.'

Matilda breathed a sigh of relief. Finally, she could get somewhere with this case.

TWENTY-ONE

Martin Craven had taken a leave of absence from CJS Pharmaceuticals to look after his three children. They were all at a delicate age where they needed stability and with their mother in hospital for God knows how long, Martin was going to have to be a single parent.

At eighteen, Jack was studying for his A-levels. He was a naturally bright young man but he didn't need the horror of what had happened to prey on his mind. Fifteen-year-old Anna was studying for her GCSE exams next year. Anna was not as clever as her brother and she struggled academically. She had also taken the attack on her mother very hard. Both teenagers needed reassurance, Anna more than Jack, so Martin made sure they received it. Eight-year-old Thomas was gradually finding out what happened to his mother, but he didn't need to know all the gory details.

Lois's mother had insisted on coming to stay with Martin. She was adamant he wouldn't be able to look after himself, three children, and a house. She had been wrong. The house was neat and tidy, and the kids well fed. Anna and Thomas arrived at school on time and on their return home there was a parent waiting for them with a hot meal. Lois wasn't a domesticated person and the evening meal often came out of a packet. Martin, a talented chef, when he put his mind to it, whipped up something hearty with plenty of vegetables and red meat. The children needed stability at a time like this and Martin was determined they get it.

'Do you want me to take Thomas to school today?' Margaret asked.

'That's OK. I'll do it,' Martin replied. He was busy preparing Thomas's packed lunch. Since he had been creating excellent sandwiches and snacks for Thomas, Anna had asked for a packed lunch too; doubling his morning routine. Jack was jealous but taking a packed lunch to college would seriously damage his reputation.

'Won't you be late for the hospital?'

'No. The police aren't coming until eleven.'

'I'd have thought you'd want to get there before eleven.'

'I do. And I will.'

'Do you want me to come to the hospital with you?'

'No thank you.'

'She is my daughter, Martin,' Margaret sounded put out, struggling to maintain a grip on her emotions.

'I'm aware of that Margaret but it's not going to be easy to listen to. She was beaten half to death, raped, and shot. Do you really want to hear the details?'

Margaret closed her eyes and looked away. She flinched at the word 'rape'. 'No I don't.'

'There you go then. Look, I don't want to hear it either but I need to be there for Lois. I need to … understand.' He returned to concentrating on the sandwiches. His face was a picture of doubt.

'She does love you, Martin,' Margaret said quietly after allowing a silence to build.

'Then why was she having an affair?' he snapped.

'I don't know. I've asked myself that question a thousand times since it happened. All I keep coming up with was maybe she was bored.'

'Bored? She's a woman in her forties, not an eight-year-old

134

child. She has a job, three kids, friends, me. She shouldn't have had time to be bored.'

'We all get bored, Martin.'

'I don't. You were married to Brian for over thirty years. Did you ever get bored?'

'Well no but then I—'

'What? But then you loved Brian. Is that what you were going to say?' He raised his voice loud enough to sound angry but not so loud that the kids upstairs could hear him.

'I didn't mean—'

'How could she do this to us? I can understand couples splitting up but there are three children involved here. Did she honestly think she would get away with it again; that we wouldn't have found out about it eventually?'

'Martin, the kids don't know do they?'

'Of course they know.'

'Oh Martin, you didn't tell them, surely.'

'I had to tell them something. You've read the newspapers. They're not stupid, Margaret. They knew something was going on. Besides, their mother has been lying to them for over a year. I'm damned if I'm going to lie to them too.'

The silence grew once more. Margaret knew Martin was right. Lois may be her daughter but she had behaved incredibly selfishly, putting her own needs before those of her children.

'Are you going to leave Lois?'

'I haven't even thought about that yet. To be honest, I don't know what I'm going to do. The kids need support right now. They're my main priority. I'll worry about me and Lois when she's back home.'

It had rained heavily overnight and was almost dawn before it stopped but the sky still remained threatening. Despite it being warm for the time of year the oppressive clouds hung over Sheffield as a reminder: winter was far from over.

Scott Andrews drove with Joseph Glass in the front passenger seat. The newest member of the team was yawning loudly.

'Didn't you sleep much last night?' Scott asked.

'No. I was out until just gone one, got piss-wet through going home.'

'Where did you go?'

'Just to a few pubs with a couple of mates, then a club. What did you get up to?'

'Not much. I was in bed by ten,' he said.

'Ten? Why?' Joseph sniggered.

'Nothing to do.'

'You should have come out with me.'

'I'm not really into clubs anymore,' he lied. Scott had never been into the club scene. On the rare occasion he did go out socially it was for a meal or the cinema.

'Next time we go out, you've got to come with us. We'll have a laugh.'

'Thanks Joe, but like I said, I'm not into clubbing.'

'Come to the pubs then; have a few drinks, game of pool.'

'I'll think about it,' he was already trying to think of an excuse to get out of it.

'Just you and me then. We'll have a couple of drinks after work one night.'

'Really?'

'Yes, sure.'

'OK,' Scott could cope with a one-on-one night out. It was groups, especially groups of people he didn't know, that scared him.

'On Friday, The Showroom are showing *The Towering Inferno*. It's one of my favourite films. Have you seen it?'

'Of course. It's a classic.'

'Fancy going? We could go for a curry afterwards, have a discussion about disaster films. Sorry, I'm a bit of a film geek, especially when it comes to the classics.'

'So am I,' Scott's face lit up. 'I'm a huge Hitchcock fan. Is there anything creepier than *The Birds*?'

'I've seen that film hundreds of times and it still scares the crap out of me. You up for it then; Friday night?'

'Yes. Definitely.' Scott genuinely meant it, too.

They pulled up outside Anderson's Garage. Scott looked at his watch; it was almost nine o'clock.

Lucas Branning was the closest person to Alice Hardaker yet to provide an alibi for his whereabouts on the night of the shooting. The PNC confirmed his address and registered place of work. They had tried his grubby flat above a long since closed shop but there had been no reply. Fingers crossed he was at work.

'They're obviously open; the shutters are up,' Joseph said, stifling a yawn.

'No sign of life though. Come on, the fresh air might wake you up.'

The air was extremely fresh. A strong breeze had picked up bringing in an easterly wind. They both closed their jackets tight and made their way over to the garage. There was still no sign of life.

'Hello?' Scott called out. His voice echoed around the empty yard.

'Hang on a minute,' came the eventual reply followed by the sound of a flushing toilet.

Scott and Joseph exchanged glances and smiled.

'Typical. I can't even have a shite in peace.' The man came through the doors fastening the belt on his jeans. He was short and stocky and had a shaved head.

Scott put his hand in his inside pocket for his warrant card. 'Lucas Branning?'

'The one and only.'

'I'm DC Scott Andrews and this is—'

He didn't get time to finish his introduction before Lucas

Branning turned heel and headed back through the door. Joseph followed with Scott bringing up the rear.

The inside of the garage was dark, cold, wet, and filthy. They couldn't see much but they could certainly hear the overweight Branning making his way through the maze. He came out into a yard with abandoned cars and mounds of tyres. There was an eight-foot fence at the back, which would slow him down as he struggled to heave his heavy frame over. Joseph was well over six foot and lean. He'd be on him in no time.

At the fence, Branning turned around. He picked up a discarded carjack and hurled it at Joseph without a second thought. It caught him a glancing blow on his head and the young DC dropped like a stone. Using the piles of tyres as steps Branning hopped up and over the fence, jumped the eight feet to the ground on the other side, and away into the distance without looking back.

Scott stopped to tend to his colleague. The head wound looked bad and the whole left side of his face was covered in blood. Joseph Glass was unconscious.

TWENTY-TWO

'Rory, with me.'

Matilda didn't even enter the Murder Room. She opened the door just wide enough to stick her head through, gave her command, then left again.

Matilda hadn't slept much last night. The phone call had been repeating itself over and over in her mind, refusing her sleep. Earlier in the car park near John Lewis she thought it was strange – the dark-coloured BMW opposite her own, not moving. The bright headlights were focused on her, blinding her, so she couldn't see into the car and identify the driver. At the time she thought it was a potential mugger waiting to pounce. However, in the depths of night, as she lay in the dark, her mind tormenting her, she remembered the car from before. It had been following her for days. But who would follow her and why? Was it the same person who had sent the newspaper clipping and the cruel note? Was it the same person who made the phone call? If so, why were they doing this? Who was targeting her?

She wondered if she should report it. The sensible answer was yes but with the way she had been acting lately would anyone believe her? Valerie might do, but then she might think Matilda's paranoid mind was in overdrive and force her to take some time off, or at least hand the case over to someone else. Matilda couldn't have that. For now, she would keep it to herself.

Matilda eventually fell asleep around three o'clock. It wasn't a natural sleep; it was mere exhaustion. Her mind had worn itself out and it needed a couple of hours to rest. Over a forced breakfast of toasted stale bread and a black coffee strong enough to sit up and smack her in the mouth she received a text message from Sian telling her Lois Craven was well enough to be interviewed. She sent a reply asking Sian to make the arrangements for late morning, giving herself time to inject plenty of caffeine inside her.

As she left the house she had a good look around before getting into the car. The caller last night had known about the books being delivered. When they had arrived it had been dark. Whoever had called had obviously been watching her, watching the house. Were they watching now? Looking around she saw an elderly woman walking an elderly dog, a sullen teenager dragging his feet as he delivered newspapers, two young women in their early twenties chatting and laughing as they made their way to the bus stop. Who were these people? Matilda hadn't seen them before, hadn't acknowledged their existence, but she could have passed them every morning. Suddenly, they were all threats and possible intruders.

Rory came out of the Murder Room. As usual he was dressed in an immaculate suit, matching tie and crisp shirt. His hair was perfectly styled; the dark curls beautifully sculptured. And not a blemish on his skin.

Matilda looked him up and down. Why did he always have to look like clothes were tailor-made for him? He could make a potato sack look like a designer suit. Matilda's shape made designer suits look like a bag of marbles.

'I've got something for you,' Rory began. A smug smile on his face.

'It can wait. We're going to the hospital to interview Lois. We need to be there for eleven.'

Matilda saw Rory examine her. He had obviously noticed the

dark circles under her eyes, and guessed she'd had a rough night. Would he wonder if she was back on the drink? Usually Rory enjoyed a good gossip among his colleagues in the Murder Room but recently he had been uncharacteristically quiet. She hoped his moody spell would continue and he wouldn't say anything about her appearance.

'I had a phone call from forensics this morning. They apologized but they've been snowed under with all these burglaries. They emailed me what was on Lois Craven's phone.'

'Go on.'

'Well she's a crafty woman. She'd deleted all her texts. They've managed to obtain them but the majority were all mushy crap between her and Kevin Hardaker. There was only one conversation left on her phone. It was from the day of the shooting and it was between her and Kevin.'

'Anything interesting?'

'You could say that. She was planning to leave her husband and set up home with Kevin.'

This stopped Matilda. 'Seriously?'

'Take a look for yourself,' he handed her the printout he'd been carrying since leaving the Murder Room.

Hello. Are we still on for meeting later?

Yes. 5.30. Usual place.

Excellent. I've got some great news for you.

Can u tell me now?

I wanted it to be a surprise but I don't think I can wait until tonight.

Go on then.

We've got the flat!!!

You're JOKING!?

I wouldn't joke about something like this. The contract was emailed to me this morning. I signed it and sent it straight back.

OMG! This is really happening then isn't it?

It certainly is. No backing out now.

So when do we do it?

Absolutely no pressure. Whenever you want to tell Martin, you go for it.

When r u telling Alice?

This weekend. She's out on Saturday morning with her sister. I'll pack my things, tell her when she gets back and then go straight to the flat.

Right. Blimey, I can't believe this is happening.

You're not going off the idea are you?

Of course not. I want this. I love u.

Love you too. I'm going into a meeting now. We can discuss this more tonight. See you later, xxx.

Bye, xxx

'Bloody hell,' Matilda said when she'd read it twice.

'They've bought a flat together and everything.'

'Do we know where this flat is?'

'No. I've got someone in tech going through Kevin's phone and email account. As soon as they've found something they're going to let me know.'

'Something to question Lois about. That and why a woman in her 40s is using OMG. Excellent work Rory. I'd kiss you if it wasn't inappropriate.'

Despite all his bravado Rory found himself blushing.

TWENTY-THREE

Thanks to the never-ending roadworks around the Northern General Hospital, Matilda and Rory were ten minutes late arriving. Matilda gently knocked on the door to the private room and walked in.

Lois Craven was sitting up in bed. She had a thick bandage wrapped around her head and her face was a mass of bruises and cuts. She looked frightened and timid. There was a cannula sticking out of her right hand leading to a drip, and her heart rate and blood pressure were constantly being monitored. She smiled at her visitors but it looked painful. On the bedside cabinet and windowsill there were cards from family and friends, a hand-drawn one from Thomas stood out, and several teddy bears were dotted around the room, each of them offering a sweet smile to aid the patient in her recovery.

Next to the bed was a drawn and pale looking Martin Craven. He appeared to have lost weight since the last time Matilda had seen him. His eyes were heavy and his lips a thin white line of pent-up aggression. It was obvious he didn't want to be here. Matilda couldn't blame him. Surely he wouldn't want to hear what had happened to his wife, the ordeal she went through or what the man she was with meant to her. He probably wished he was anywhere else in the world other than in this small oppressive hospital room.

'Mrs Craven, I'm Detective Chief Inspector Matilda Darke. This is Detective Constable Rory Fleming. How are you feeling?'

'Battered. Bruised. Tired.' Her voice was broken and she took long pauses between each word.

'If you're in too much pain to do this we can come back another time.'

She shook her head, or tried to at least.

'I think we'd like to get this over with as soon as possible,' Martin said. He stood up and brought two chairs forward from the back of the room.

Matilda took her chair and put it beside Lois so she could be close to her. Rory maintained his distance.

'Do you mind if I record this interview? DC Fleming will be making notes but I'd like to make sure I don't miss anything.'

'Just do what you have to do,' Martin said; his attitude was frosty. The way he bit his lip and his eyes darted rapidly from his wife to Matilda and back again was evidence of his patience reaching breaking point.

Matilda brought a digital recorder out of her inside pocket and placed it on the bed next to Lois.

'First of all Lois, do you want your husband present while we have this conversation?'

'What kind of a question is that?' Martin jumped up out of his seat. 'Of course she wants me present. I'm her husband for fuck's sake.'

'Mr Craven, please, this isn't helping. Your wife has been through a terrible ordeal. What she is going to say is not going to be easy to listen to. She may not want to put you through it.'

'We've been through a lot as husband and wife as it is. Trust me, there's nothing she can say that will shock me.' He sat back down and folded his arms in defiance.

'Lois?' Matilda asked.

Lois refused to look at her husband but gave a brief nod to Matilda.

'Right. Let's begin. First of all, I want you to tell me what you were doing on Clough Lane at that time of night.'

It was a while before Lois answered. She swallowed a couple of times as if trying to stop the words from coming out. Eventually, she took a deep breath and began: 'I've been having an affair …'

The words resounded off the walls like a ball in a game of squash. Matilda could see Martin's reaction out of the corner of her eye. She had angled her chair in the perfect position to gauge their responses to the questions answered. Martin closed his eyes tight and took a deep breath. Knowing about his wife's betrayal was one thing, having it confirmed was difficult to hear.

She continued. 'I've known Kevin a while. We went to the same tennis club. We met in the bar. Swapped stories about matches and tournaments on TV. We started playing doubles together.'

She paused to have a drink of water, just a few sips. It was difficult for her to talk, both mentally and physically.

'We had so much in common. Not just the tennis but other things too. Favourite foods, holiday destinations, films, books. I started going to the club more than twice a week. It was about three weeks after we met that I realized we weren't playing tennis anymore. We'd meet in the bar, get a drink and just talk. Eventually I even stopped getting my gear out of the car. It was Kevin who brought this up. He said, instead of meeting at the club why not go for a meal or to a gallery.

'I've had an affair before. More than one. Martin has always taken me back. I don't know why. I love him. I really do, but I'm a terrible wife. I love my husband and I love my kids, but I just keep hurting them all and I honestly don't know why.'

I'm sure Dr Warminster would know why.

Lois looked in a great deal of discomfort. Matilda wondered how much of this was due to her injuries and how much was recounting her story in front of her husband.

Matilda could see anger rising on Martin's face. How could he sit and listen to this without wanting to scream or throw something?

'So why Clough Lane?'

'It's out of the way. We'd been there a few times. It's so sordid isn't it? Two people in their forties parking on a quiet country road for … well … It's just, we had nowhere else to go.'

'Oh, I'm sorry, you should have said. I'd have taken the kids to the cinema twice a week,' Martin chimed up. It was obvious he had been struggling to hold his tongue.

Three pairs of eyes quickly turned to him. He apologized and looked down at the floor, ashamed of his outburst.

'What happened on that night?'

'We parked up. We weren't doing anything. We were chatting. Then, the driver's door opened and Kevin was literally ripped out of the car. It was like some kind of animal just grabbed him and pulled him out.'

'What did you do?'

'I don't know. I think I screamed. I leaned over to where Kevin was to see what was happening but the door was slammed closed and the car was locked.'

'Who locked it?'

'I don't know. I'm guessing the attacker took the key out of the ignition. It all happened so quickly.'

'Did you try and open the doors?'

'Yes, but they wouldn't open.'

'What happened then?'

'I was looking out of the window to see what was happening but I couldn't see anything. It was dark.'

'Did you hear anything?'

A tear fell down Lois's face, which she quickly wiped away. She nodded. 'I could hear Kevin. He was being beaten. He was begging for the attacker to stop, to just take whatever he wanted and leave us alone.'

147

'Where was the attack taking place? Was it right outside the car or a bit further up the Lane?'

'It was right outside. The car was rocking.'

'Could you hear what was being said?'

'No. Just Kevin begging for him to stop.'

'How long did it go on for?'

'I'm not sure.'

'Two minutes? Five? Ten?'

'I don't know. It seemed like forever, but was probably only about five minutes or so.'

'Didn't you try and get out of the car during that time?'

'I already said. I tried the door handle.'

'Where was your bag?'

'I'm sorry?'

'Your bag. Did you have it with you in the car?'

'Yes. It was on the floor in front of me.'

'Did you have your mobile with you?'

'Yes I did. I'd turned it off late afternoon to save the battery; me and Kevin had been texting quite a bit that day. I turned it on but I couldn't remember the PIN to unlock the phone. I just froze. Then the door opened and the attacker grabbed my phone and pushed me away. I fell and knocked my head on the dashboard.'

'Did you lose consciousness?'

'I don't know. I don't think so. I remember sitting back up.'

'How many attackers were there?'

'One.'

'Are you sure?'

'Yes. I think so. I only saw one.' She thought for a while, as if going through it all in her mind. 'No, there was definitely only one.'

'So after the attack on Kevin finished, what happened next?'

'It all went very quiet. I thought he'd gone.'

'Did you try and get out of the car again?'

'I was about to when the door opened.'

'Who opened the door?'

'The attacker.'

'Did you get a good look at him?'

'Yes.'

'What did he look like?'

'I mean, no. I saw him but he was wearing a mask.'

'What kind of mask?'

'I don't know. It reminded me of one of those masks you see cyclists wear when they're cycling through smog but it was more … I'm not sure … more elaborate.'

'Did you see his eyes?'

'No. He was wearing tinted glasses.'

'Sunglasses?'

'Not really. They sort of wrapped around his head. A bit like goggles, but not. With the mask, his whole face was covered.'

'What about his hair?'

'He had a hat on.'

'Baseball cap?'

'No. One of those woollen ones. He was literally dressed from head to toe in black. It was dark too so that didn't help.'

'Did he talk to you? What was his accent like?'

Lois looked down at her shaking hands. 'He called me a few names. They were horrible. He sounded local. He had a Sheffield accent. I could smell cigarettes too. It was strong, like he was a heavy smoker.'

'So what happened then?'

'He just stood there, looking at me. Then he grabbed me and pulled me out of the car.'

'Where did he grab you?'

'He grabbed my collar,' she said, gripping her own throat.

'Then what?'

'He threw me on to the ground. I looked up and I saw Kevin.'

'Where was he?'

'He was on the ground at the back of the car, close to the kerb,' the tears were flowing down her face as she remembered the ordeal. This time she didn't try to wipe them away.

'Was he alive?'

Lois nodded. 'He was covered in blood. I could hardly see his face. He looked like he was in so much pain. I tried to go to him but I was pulled back.'

The room fell silent. The atmosphere was heavy. Rory was making sporadic notes. At times he forgot to write down things at all as he was caught up in Lois's story. At other times, he couldn't write fast enough. On the other side of the bed Martin looked ashen. He looked like he was living through the same ordeal as his wife.

'Would you like to take a break, Lois?'

'No,' she replied. 'Just give me a minute.'

Martin stood up to stretch his legs. He paced around the room and took several deep breaths. He looked at the posters on the wall giving tips on how to wash your hands correctly, how to combat MRSA, and the importance of healthy eating. He looked everywhere except at his wife.

Rory and Matilda exchanged glances. She raised an eyebrow and nodded towards the DC, asking him if he was all right. He nodded back and blew out his cheeks. This was the most difficult interview any of them had endured.

'He shot Kevin,' Lois said suddenly. They all resumed their positions.

'What happened?'

'I tried to go to Kevin but he pulled me back. He lifted me up and slammed me against the car. I hit my head. I couldn't take my eyes off Kevin. He looked like he was in so much pain. The man had a gun. He took it out of the back of his trousers and he pointed it in my face. I … I …'

'Go on.'

'I wet myself,' Lois confessed through the tears. She helped herself to more water and wiped her mouth with the back of her hand. 'I'd never seen a gun before. I could see right down the barrel. I looked away, towards Kevin. I didn't want to see the gun going off but he didn't shoot me. He shot Kevin.'

'Where?'

'The first shot hit him in the chest. I screamed. I wanted to turn away but I couldn't take my eyes off him. Then he shot him again. This time in the head and it was like his whole head exploded. He dropped to the ground and that was it. I knew he was dead.'

Matilda waited until this latest outburst of tears subsided before continuing. 'Tell me what happened next.'

'He pointed the gun in my face. It was hot. I could feel it burning into my skin. I asked him to leave us alone.'

'Did he say anything back?'

'No. He punched me in the stomach. I've never been hit before in my life. I thought I was going to vomit. I bent over to be sick but he pulled me back up and then hit me in the face. He started hitting me, harder and harder. I could feel his hands on me. I could hear him grunting but I couldn't feel the pain. It was like I'd gone numb or something.'

Lois fell silent, and so did the entire room. The sounds of the ward outside went on as normal; nurses chatting, trolleys rattling, machines beeping, but inside the confines of this small private room, time seemed to stand still.

'I'm not sure if I blacked out but it felt like one minute I was on the ground and the next I was back on my feet and against the car and he was ... he was unbuttoning his trousers. Martin!'

Lois called out to her husband and held out her hand for him to hold. It was shaking. He looked up and his eyes were full of tears. At first he didn't move and for a minute Matilda thought he was going to deny his wife comfort in her time of need. Yes, she had betrayed him, but she had paid the ultimate price. Right now, she needed his support more than ever. Surely he couldn't sit there and watch her go through this alone?

He moved his chair closer to the bed, took her hand in both of his and kissed it. She smiled a painful smile and more tears fell.

'I don't know whether it was because I'd been so badly beaten or what I'd seen happen to Kevin but I don't remember reacting when I saw him unbutton his trousers. It seemed inevitable that this was going to happen. He held me by the throat, pinning me to the car, and he just did his thing. It was like I knew what was happening but I wasn't a part of it. Does that make sense?'

'Like an out-of-body experience?' Matilda guessed.

'Yes. That's exactly it. It's like I was watching it happen to myself but it wasn't me. When he finished he let go of my throat and I just dropped to the ground. I thought maybe it was all over. I just lay there.'

'How long was it before you were shot?'

'I've no idea. It could have been minutes; it could have been months. I was just lying on the ground and I've no idea what was going through my mind. I heard the gunfire and I felt my body jerk but I didn't feel any pain.'

'Did you scream?'

'I don't think so. I think I accepted that I was going to die there.'

'You were shot two more times. What happened after that?'

'I waited. I could hear footsteps. I think he was walking around the car. I was looking over to where Kevin was, the car was behind me. I've no idea what he was doing. After a while, his feet came into view. He stopped right in front of me.'

'What did you do?'

'I pretended I was dead.'

'How did you do that?'

'I kept my eyes open and I held my breath for as long as I could. He must have been convinced because I saw him walk away. I heard the sound of him walking through the grass in the field. He was leaving and he thought I was dead.'

'How long did you stay in that position?'

'Long after I stopped hearing his footsteps.'

'Then you decided to call for help?'

'I looked down and I saw that I'd lost so much blood. I tried to stand up but I couldn't so I dragged myself around to the car.'

'Did you think you could drive away?'

'No I don't think so. It took me ages. I was dragging myself with my arms and my legs weren't helping at all. When I got to the car I thought that if I kept pressing the horn someone would hear me and come running.'

'Did you know you were beeping the SOS distress signal in Morse code?'

'Yes,' she gave a half-smile. 'I remembered it from the film *Titanic*. It's my favourite film. At least, it used to be.'

Matilda smiled. Adele had said the same thing. Who would have thought a James Cameron film would come in handy for people under attack?

'I just beeped, and beeped, and beeped, and hoped someone would help me.'

'Did you see the person who came to help you?'

'No. Did someone come?'

'Yes. A man who lives close by.'

'Did he save me?'

'Yes he did.'

'Will you thank him for me?'

Matilda nodded. 'I think we should leave it there for now. Can you remember anything else about the man who attacked you?'

Lois closed her eyes tightly shut, as if straining hard to conjure up an image. 'He was tall. About six foot, maybe an inch or two taller. He was very well built, not fat, but solid. He had broad shoulders. He was … powerful.' Her bottom lip quivered but there were no more tears left for her to cry. 'Wait. He had a tattoo. While he was … his neck was close to me. I could see he had a tattoo. It looked like a snake or something on the side of his neck.'

Matilda turned off the digital recorder and put it back in her pocket. Rory closed his notebook and quickly stood up. He obviously couldn't get out of this room fast enough.

'Thank you, Lois. I'm sorry to put you through this but we need to know all the details if we're going to catch this man. We will need to speak to you again at some point. If there's anything you remember in the meantime, please let me know. No matter how small the detail, it could all help. I'll see if someone can bring you both a cup of tea.'

Lois turned her head on the pillow to face the wall. Martin, who'd had his head leaning on the bed since his wife asked for his hand, finally looked up and smiled at Matilda. The sheet was stained with his tears and his face was red.

Matilda stood in the doorway of the hospital room and looked back at the couple. 'I swear I will find the man responsible for this.' She knew she shouldn't promise, but she felt she needed to add something.

TWENTY-FOUR

Matilda and Rory walked slowly down the corridor. They felt physically drained by what they had heard. The oppressive heat in the hospital didn't help either. They only just made it to the door when Matilda heard her name being called. She turned to see Martin Craven heading towards her.

'I'm sorry,' he said quietly. 'For what I said in there. I'm trying to be supportive but at the end of the day she's betrayed me and the children. It's hard to get past that.'

'I do understand, Mr Craven,' Matilda said.

'You will catch the person who did this won't you?'

'We will. I promise.'

'My children mean the world to me, Inspector. I'd do absolutely anything for them.' He turned and headed back into the room to his wife.

Matilda wondered what the atmosphere was like in there now the truth had finally been revealed. She shook the thought from her head. She didn't envy either of them right now. She doubted any couple would be able to survive such an ordeal, no matter how stable their marriage.

*

They didn't make it to the car. Matilda suggested they have a coffee at the café just inside the hospital's main entrance. Rory sat and waited, staring into space, while Matilda went for the drinks. She returned with two very strong coffees in polystyrene cups and a Mars Bar each.

They sat in complete silence.

'Is it my imagination or are Mars Bars smaller than they used to be?' Matilda said to fill the silence between them.

'They're smaller,' Rory replied without looking up. He was staring into his coffee cup.

'And more expensive too. I remember when a KitKat used to cost 25p. You can't get anything for 25p these days. Bloody hell, I sound like my mother. Rory, are you going to say something?'

He eventually looked up. His face was pale, his eyes drawn, and his usual sparkle and smile had disappeared.

'What kind of man are we dealing with here?'

'I don't know, Rory.'

'I can never get my head round how someone can inflict so much pain on another person and not think anything of it.'

Matilda said nothing. She took a sip of her coffee, winced at the bitter taste and sat back. She looked at Rory and waited for him to continue.

'Whatever the circumstances, they were happy. A couple who loved each other. But he was prepared to destroy all that. He forced her to watch while he shot the man she loved then raped her. Why? Why would you do that?'

'Until we know who this person is it's best not to dwell on the why. We need to work out the who first. Don't allow yourself to be consumed by your horror at the crime. Take the facts one by one and analyse them – that's how we'll find who did this.'

He took a deep breath and had a bite of Mars Bar. 'Lois Craven said she had had an affair before, more than one. Do you think it could be one of her exes?'

'It could be. Maybe she broke up with him, said she wasn't

going to leave her husband for him. Then he sees her with a different man, thinks it should be him and snaps. It's worth looking into. Let's hope Lois has kept a list of the men she's been with.'

'I don't know how Martin has stuck by her all these years. I mean, Thomas isn't even his son, yet he just carried on with the marriage like nothing happened.'

'Maybe this will be the final straw.'

'Do you think he'll leave her?'

'I wouldn't be surprised. He looked like he was sitting on a knife edge in that room. You could almost see his blood boiling. Wait a minute—' A thought suddenly came to Matilda.

'What?'

'When Martin came out to us just now. Did he say his children were the most important thing in his life?'

'Yes. Why?'

'He definitely said children, not family?'

'Yes. Is that significant?'

'Shouldn't he have said family? His family includes his wife. He just said children meaning that he doesn't consider her to be an important part of his life anymore.'

'Not to sound too disrespectful, but can you really blame him? She admitted that she's had more than one affair. I think he's been patient enough with her as it is. I mean, would you have left your husband if—' Rory stopped, suddenly aware of what he had said. His mouth was agape. 'Oh my God. I'm so sorry. I didn't mean to—'

'Rory,' Matilda gave a half-smile. 'It's fine, don't worry about it. In answer to your question I would have torn his bollocks off with my bare hands.' *I probably would have forgiven him anything and everything.*

'Can I ask a question?' Rory asked, his mouth full of Mars Bar.

'Go on.'

'Lois said that after she was shot she played dead. Is that normal?'

Matilda thought for a while. 'I don't know. You read about people playing dead after an attack. Practically every time there's a shooting in America you get a survivor saying how they played dead to avoid more gunfire. Personally I always thought people went into one of two modes: fight or flight. You either fight back or run away. Lois did neither – not that she could after she'd be shot,' Matilda added. 'If a bloke tried to rape me I'd kick him so hard between his legs he'd need surgery to have his balls removed from his throat.'

Rory smiled. 'Maybe we could ask a psychologist.'

Dr Warminster came into Matilda's mind. She may feel differently about her now, but did she really want to involve her in her police work?

'Leave it with me,' she said, hiding her fear behind a small smile. 'Come on, let's go into town. I'll treat us to a proper coffee.'

Still feeling the effects of the interview, they both rose slowly from their hard plastic seats and staggered out of the hospital. As they made their way to the car Rory turned on his mobile. Several text messages and voicemail messages came through.

'Jesus Christ,' he said, looking down at the screen. He'd stopped dead in his tracks.

'What's wrong?'

'DC Joseph Glass has been attacked. He's in Intensive Care.'

They looked at each other for a few seconds before turning back towards the hospital and running inside.

Matilda and Rory burst onto the ICU ward, slamming the double doors hard against the wall. Scott was standing outside a room waiting for them. He looked drawn and scared.

'Scott, what's happened?' Matilda said. She genuinely cared for all of the members on her team and although DC Glass hadn't been with her for long, a matter of days, he was still someone worth caring for.

'We went to interview Lucas Branning. When we identified

ourselves he did a runner through the garage where he works. We gave chase. Joe was in front. Branning got to a fence. He wasn't tall enough to climb over so he picked up a carjack and lobbed it at Joe. It got him right on the side of the head. He just … I can't describe it … he just dropped to the ground.' The words fell out of Scott's mouth in a torrent of panic and emotion.

'Bloody hell,' Matilda looked through the small window in the door at the stricken DC. Like Lois Craven his head was heavily bandaged and he was hooked up to several machines. 'How is he?'

'They don't know. He's been unconscious since he fell.'

'What have the doctors said?'

'They've stopped the bleeding and are waiting for the results of the CT scan. I got on to HR and they've contacted his parents. They're on their way in.'

'How are you?' she asked, placing a hand on his shoulder.

'I'm fine. Branning turned and climbed over the fence after he'd thrown the jack.'

'I didn't mean physically.'

'I'm fine, honestly. A bit shaken, but I'll be OK.' His smile didn't reach his eyes.

'Right.' Now Matilda had absorbed everything that was going on she was back in work mode. She was angry one of her officers had been assaulted and she wanted answers. She wanted someone to pay. 'Scott, wait here until his parents arrive. Tell them anything they need to give me a call. Then I want you and Rory to go round to Alice's house; find out everything you can about her bastard brother.'

'You want me to stay here?' Rory asked.

'No, come back with me. Scott, we'll meet you back at the station. Let me know the second you hear anything.'

'Will do,' Scott looked genuinely upset.

'Are you sure you're OK?' Matilda asked.

'Yes. Honestly.' The fake smile again.

Matilda made a mental note to have a quiet word with Scott later. He may not have been physically injured but seeing a colleague assaulted was bound to have an effect, especially on a quiet, reserved person like Scott Andrews.

They made their way back down the corridor. Matilda, thinking aloud, said. 'I'll need to inform the ACC. HR should be able to look after Glass and his family. I also want a search warrant to get into Lucas Branning's house and give it a good going over and I want him arrested by the end of the day. Nobody hurts a member of my team and gets away with it.'

Matilda's hands were shaking. This time it wasn't due to anxiety or stress. It was anger.

TWENTY-FIVE

Nathaniel Glover didn't relish being back in a police station after all this time. When he was convicted in 2000 he made a promise to himself that he would go straight upon his release. Only nineteen when he was sent to Doncaster Prison, he finished his education and by the time he came out he was twenty-four and had qualifications coming out of his ears. His probation officer had worked very hard for him and he was soon in gainful employment in the warehouse of a department store. It wasn't what he wanted to do with his life, but it was all about gaining experience in a work place.

Three years later, he left, and after a brief spell with British Gas, he set up his own business as an electrician.

Sian Mills entered interview room two with a female uniformed officer behind her. She had hoped to interview Glover with Scott but he hadn't returned from interviewing Lucas Branning yet.

'Mr Glover, thank you for coming.'

'I didn't feel like I had much of an option,' he replied. Nathaniel was a tall man in his late-thirties. He obviously worked out or played regular sports as he filled out his polo shirt nicely. His arms were covered in tattoos and his hair was neatly styled. 'The way your PCs came round banging on my door. I'm surprised they didn't spray me with that CS gas and handcuff me.'

'I apologize for the heavy handedness of our officers. You're more than welcome to make a complaint.'

'Yeah, like that'll get listened to.'

'The reason I want to talk to you is regarding an incident which happened a couple of nights ago on Clough Lane at Ringinglow …'

Nathaniel interrupted. 'I know all about it. I read the news. I wondered how long it would be before you called me in. A bloke attacked a man and a woman in their car while they were parked up in a quiet place. So obviously I'm your main suspect.'

'I didn't say that. There are similarities between your case and this one and I'd like to rule you out of our enquiries.'

'So rule me out then.' He sat back, folding his arms.

'Can you tell me your whereabouts between about seven o'clock and eleven o'clock on Tuesday night?'

Nathaniel's eyes widened. He didn't move and remained in stony silence. He looked to the floor then up to the ceiling. He looked over to the female officer standing by the door, back to Sian, then down at the floor again.

'I was out,' he eventually replied.

'I'm going to need more than that.'

'With some mates.'

'And their names?'

Nathaniel remained silent, looking straight ahead, not blinking.

'Come on Mr Glover, you know the score. I need names and where you were.'

'Erm … you see … the thing is …'

'Go on.'

'I'm married. I've got a kid.'

'Mr Glover, I don't care if you're a bigamist with a string of wives and kids all over the country. I just want confirmation of where you were on Tuesday night and who you were with.'

'I'm sorry. I can't tell you,' he said with defiance.

'In that case I'm going to keep you here in the cells until you feel you can tell me.'

'Wait. You can't do that,' he called out, jumping up.

'I think you'll find I can.'

Dr Sheila Warminster stepped out of her office and stopped in her tracks. Of all her patients to make an unannounced visit, she didn't expect Matilda to be one of them.

'Oh, Matilda, hello,' she was taken aback.

'I'm sorry Dr Warminster,' began the young receptionist. 'I did tell her you were busy but she insisted on waiting.'

'That's fine Stephanie. Matilda, would you like to come through?'

Matilda smiled, and with her head down, she passed the doctor and headed into the stifling office.

She decided not to sit in her usual chair. When she looked at it she could picture herself sitting there, sobbing. That chair would forever be known as the chair of tears. She wondered how many people had sat there and rendered themselves speechless with their blubbering and wailing.

She walked over to the window and looked out. Surprisingly, there was a good view of the city from here – if you enjoyed looking at soulless concrete shells.

'I must say I'm surprised to see you here Matilda. Is everything all right?' Dr Warminster asked, closing the door firmly behind her.

'Yes. I'm sorry to turn up like this. I'm not here for myself. I'm here in a professional capacity.'

'Oh?'

'Yes. I'm sure you've heard on the news about the double shooting at Ringinglow.'

'Yes I have.'

'Well, I was hoping you'd be able to give me some advice on psychology.'

'I'll try but I'm more of a therapist. I'd have thought the police would have a criminal psychologist to consult with.'

'We did have but we lost her in the first wave of budget cuts. I don't want anything too deep. I'm trying to get my head around something and want some clarification.'

'I'll try. Would you like to take a seat?'

Matilda looked at the brown leather armchair. 'I'm fine here, thanks. Great view.'

'Yes, I like it. So what do you want to know?'

'OK. This is in strictest confidence, however.'

'Of course.'

'The woman who was attacked; she was badly beaten, raped, and shot three times. When the attacker finished he left her for dead. Before he left she was conscious of him walking around the crime scene and she played dead so that he would leave her alone. Is that normal after such a vicious attack? I'd have thought she'd be in too much shock.'

'Not necessarily. From what I can gather from the newspapers, wasn't there a man killed at the scene?'

'That's right.'

'And I'm guessing the woman saw this happen?'

'Yes she did.'

'The thing is Matilda, and you know this better than most people, is that the mind is a powerful object. It's also very unpredictable. This woman has been through the worst horror imaginable – she's seen a man killed in front of her, she's been beaten, raped, and shot, all within the space of a very short period of time. Her mind has had to take all of this horror on board and it's been unable to cope, so it decided to shut down. This woman is protecting herself by switching off.'

'So she's not really playing dead, is she?'

'No. Her mind is looking after her. By switching off it's like it's decided not to take in any more information until it has processed what happened.'

Matilda frowned and returned to looking out of the window.

'Has the woman regained consciousness yet?'

'Yes she has.'

'Does she remember everything of what happened?'

'Yes.'

'I'm surprised.'

'Why?'

'Sometimes, when a person has been through a horrific ordeal, the mind blocks out some of what's happened to protect the person. You'll know this more than anyone else. Maybe she'll remember being beaten or raped but not necessarily the shooting or seeing the man get killed. It will only give her the amount of information it thinks she can cope with. The fact she remembers everything suggests she's a very strong individual indeed.'

'Well she did say she couldn't feel being shot. She was very vague about that part.'

'That's probably the case then. Do you remember the terrorist attack in Tunisia with the gunman on the beach shooting at the tourists?'

'Yes, of course.'

'Many of the people there played dead in order to escape the gunman. Put yourself in their position: you're relaxing on an idyllic beach, you're in paradise, having the holiday of a lifetime and then all of a sudden you're in the middle of hell. In the space of a second you've gone from one extreme to the other and the only way some people can make sense of it is by blocking it out. By closing your eyes and your mind to the event you're not taking in what is happening.'

Matilda thought back to the first few days when James died. She knew it was coming; she didn't want to imagine a life without him. When he finally died, she should have been relieved he was no longer in pain, but she wasn't. It was like he had been unexpectedly killed in a car crash. She was hit by a massive wall of shock and grief. The days between his death and his funeral were missing from her memory. She had no recollection of what occurred during those nine days; did she eat, sleep, take a bath, leave the house, go to work? Had she blocked out the torment because it was too much for her to process?

'Did you think the woman had staged the attack?' Dr Warminster asked.

'I don't know. No. Her attack is too severe. If she hadn't been shot and raped, I'd probably be considering her as a suspect. I can't conceive of anyone allowing themselves to be subjected to such a nightmare. It's too risky. I just wanted to know how a person can play dead after such an appalling attack.'

'The name is very misleading. We call it playing dead as if it's school children at playtimes but it's more deeply rooted. A lot of children who are abused block it out and genuinely believe it didn't happen, but it is the mind protecting them.' Dr Warminster let this sink in then turned her attention to Matilda.

'While you're here Matilda, I wanted to mention this at our session but didn't get around to it. I know you're no longer under restricted hours at work, but don't spend all your time there. You still need to make time to be on your own, relax, read a book maybe.'

Read a book? I've got plenty to choose from.

'I'm sorry,' Matilda said, fearing more advice coming on. 'I came here for your help professionally and I've turned it into a therapy session. I should go.' She hurried to the door. 'Look, thanks for the advice. Add it to my bill and I'll pay at the next session.' She closed the door firmly behind her before Dr Warminster could get another word in. It may have been a mistake including her therapist in her work: Matilda didn't want her personal and professional issues overlapping, but who else did she have to ask? *Bloody budget cuts.*

Sitting in her car she went over her conversation with Dr Warminster. She already knew how protective the mind was but she had no idea how it could hold a person hostage. If the mind hid certain pieces of information to protect the person from the horrors of reality, did that mean it could release them whenever it wanted to? If so, would the minutes between Kevin getting shot and Lois being raped come back to haunt her at some point in the future? Matilda shuddered at the thought.

Dear God, I hope not.

TWENTY-SIX

With no replacement for DI Ben Hales and DC Faith Easter, and DC Scott Andrews keeping a vigil at the hospital, the Murder Room resembled a party at the end of the night; only the stragglers remained. In this case, the stragglers were a couple of civilian support staff and DS Aaron Connolly and DC Rory Fleming.

Aaron sighed and pushed himself away from his desk. It had been a long day and he was feeling tired, yet the working day was far from over. 'Rory, get your coat.'

'Have I pulled?' He smiled.

'You wish. Come on, we're going to see Alice Hardaker.'

'Oh. Why?'

'Nobody seems to know where Lucas Branning is. We've had surveillance at his flat all day and he hasn't come back. If anyone knows where he hangs out, his sister will.'

'I was supposed to go with Scott earlier but he hasn't come back from the hospital yet.'

'This can't wait,' he said, picking up his car keys.

'Can I drive your car?' Rory asked with all the enthusiasm of a five-year-old on Christmas morning.

'There's no way I'm letting you behind the wheel of my Audi.

I don't even want you in the front passenger seat. I've seen the mess you make of the pool cars.'

'But …'

'There's a bus stop right outside the station,' Aaron smiled to himself as he left the Murder Room with Rory following, close at his heels.

It was dusk by the time Connolly and Fleming pulled up at Broad Elms Lane. It was as quiet as the night the police rolled up to inform Alice about her husband's murder. No cars drove by, no children playing in the street, no dogs barking, nothing.

'The town that dreaded sundown,' Rory said as he climbed out of the Audi.

The lights were all off in the Hardaker house. They slowly walked to the front door, both of them looking up at the house. There didn't seem to be any sign of life behind the façade of gaudy faux leaded double glazing and neatly trimmed hanging baskets.

Aaron rang the doorbell and leaned in to look for signs of movement behind the stained glass. He rang again.

He lifted the letterbox and called out. 'Mrs Hardaker, it's the police. Can you open the door please?'

Eventually, after a long minute, a blurred figure approached the door. It was opened by Alice who looked drawn, pale, tired, and hollow.

'What do you want?' she asked, poking her head out of the small gap she made in the doorway.

'I'd like to talk to you about your brother.'

'Lucas?'

'Yes.'

'Now isn't a good time.'

'Mrs Hardaker, I know you've been through—'

Her dramatic tears stopped Aaron in his tracks. She walked away from the door leaving it ajar. The two detectives looked at each other and followed her.

The large hallway was a mess. The table under the mirror had been overturned. The items on it spilled on the plush carpet and left there. The mirror was askew and a potted palm in the corner had fallen.

Alice headed for the living room but didn't make it. She stopped in the doorway and turned to face Aaron and Rory who were gazing at the destruction.

'I've been burgled.'

'You wanted to talk to me?'

Sian stood in the doorway to the cells and looked down at the tired and drawn-looking Nathaniel Glover. He had spent the whole day in a small space with only his mind and conscience to occupy him.

'If I tell you something, do you promise me it won't get back to my wife?'

'It depends on what you tell me.'

'It's not a criminal matter or anything like that.'

'In that case, yes, I promise.'

'I was out on Tuesday night, like I said. I wasn't with my mates though. I'm seeing someone ...'

'I'd worked that one out for myself,' Sian said, a hint of sarcasm in her voice. 'You're going to need to give me a name though if you want to get out of here tonight.'

Nathaniel sighed and shook his head. Whatever was weighing on his mind was obviously causing him some distress. It was clear to Sian he was dying to tell her but didn't know how.

'Ian Pritchard,' Nathaniel said the name like he was spitting out something foul.

'You're seeing another man?'

He nodded. 'I didn't mean for it to happen. I did some work for him a few months ago and we just hit it off—'

'Mr Glover, I'm really not interested in your personal life. However, if you give me Mr Pritchard's number, I can contact him, get your story verified and you can be home in time for your tea.' He looked up at her, his eyes shining. He looked on the verge of tears. 'I can be incredibly discreet. This will be between you and me. I promise you.'

'Thank you.'

Sian closed the cell door and went down the corridor to make the call to Ian Pritchard.

'Any joy?' the duty sergeant asked her.

'Joy wouldn't be the word I'd use. I'll never understand people, Tony. They seem perfectly happy to lie to their loved ones yet tell the truth to a complete stranger.'

'And that's what keeps the beer industry in this country thriving,' he replied with a smile.

TWENTY-SEVEN

Scott had been at the hospital all day. He hadn't left the small oppressive room Joseph Glass was laid up in. He hadn't eaten, had anything to drink, or been to the toilet. When Joseph's parents arrived he filled them in on what had happened, what the doctors said was happening to their stricken son, and had spoken about their work. However, the conversation soon dried up and then there were three awkward people with nothing to do, nowhere to go, and nothing to say.

It started to go dark early under the thick cloud and one of them stood up to turn on a light. Nurses came to check on Joseph's condition and quickly left, moving on to the next patient. All the while, the three visitors waited patiently for something, anything, to happen. Time ticked by at an excruciatingly slow pace. Scott stole a glance at his watch and saw it was well past eleven o'clock. He made his excuses to leave and promised someone from the police station would be in touch. He said goodbye, taking one last look at his comatose colleague, before he left. It had been a hell of a day.

'Boss, it's me,' he said sleepily into his phone as he made his way to the exit.

'Scott, hello. How's DC Glass?'

'Still unconscious. His parents have been with him since lunchtime. I don't think they've taken it in yet. They're just sat there like zombies.'

'That's understandable. How about you? You sound knackered.'

'I am. Hospitals are so tiring. And why do they have to be so bloody hot?'

'Look, go home, have a long shower and something to eat and get a good night's sleep. You can be late tomorrow too if you want a lie in.'

'Thanks boss.'

'You've done well today, Scott. Thank you.'

Matilda hung up the phone before Scott could say anything else. He pocketed the phone and dragged his feet along the scuffed flooring. The automatic doors yawned open noisily and a blast of cold air hit him full in the face. It woke him up instantly. He took a long deep breath and felt his entire body relax.

His battered Renault wasn't far from the entrance. He shouldn't really be driving, his eyelids were heavy with fatigue, but he didn't have the number for a taxi and the buses had stopped running for the night. All he wanted was to get home, kick off his shoes, and fall onto his bed. He didn't even care about changing out of his suit, and he only had two.

He pulled out of the car park and headed for home on the opposite side of the city. He opened the windows to allow in the stiff cool breeze, and kept well below the speed limit.

The traffic was steady but not busy, however, concentration was still called for. He headed up Barnsley Road, his hands firmly gripped in the ten and two position, his eyes on the road.

He was overtaken by cars, taxis, and vans, and was branded a wanker by a boy racer in a Subaru. He concentrated hard on the road and didn't notice the car on his tail. He looked in the rearview mirror but all he could see were the bright lights from the car's headlights. Some people had no manners.

The car started to overtake, sounding its horn at the same

time. The car took a sharp turn left, banged into Scott's Renault and forced him off the road into a ditch. Scott slammed down on the brakes but his tiredness had an effect on his reflexes. He hit his head on the steering wheel and heard something crack, he hoped it wasn't his skull.

Before he lost consciousness he looked up and saw a dark-coloured BMW heading off at speed over the hill.

TWENTY-EIGHT

Up early as usual, Matilda was tempted to call her mother for a chat. It had been a long time since she had called home and she really should make the effort. Last night when she had returned home there were four messages waiting for her on the answer machine, all of them from her family.

You have four new messages. Message one: 'Matilda, it's your mother. I haven't heard from you for a few days and you said you'd keep in touch. Do you still want me and your dad to come with you to the cemetery? I don't like these machines. Ring me when you can.'

Message two: 'Matilda, it's me again, your mother. I left a message for you this morning but you still haven't called. I've heard on the news about this double shooting business so I'm guessing you're busy with that but surely you're going home at some point. Just ring me. Please.'

Message three: 'Matilda, I'm not sure if you remember me, my name's Harriet; I'm your sister. I've had Mum on the phone night and day asking if I've heard from you, now stop being selfish and give her a call. I've enough on my plate as it is without Mum badgering me too. By the way, your youngest nephew has chickenpox; just thought you'd like to know in case you fancy playing at being an auntie from time to time.'

Message four: 'Matilda, it's your father. Will you call your bloody mother right now? She's getting on my sodding nerves.'

She was just about to pick up the receiver and dial the familiar number when her mobile burst into life. The display said ACC. It was a no-brainer. She couldn't ignore her boss.

'Matilda, bit of a problem,' no cheery greeting, no hello. This did not bode well. 'There was an incident late last night. DC Scott Andrews is in hospital.'

Matilda's heart hit the floor and her eyes darted straight to the photograph of her husband on the mantelpiece. 'What? What happened?'

'He was run off the road, probably a joy rider. He's in the Northern.'

'Right. I'll get over there now. Thanks for letting me know.'

She hung up the phone without waiting to hear if her boss had anything else to add. This was not the start to the day Matilda was hoping for. She picked up her keys from the coffee table, blew a kiss to James and headed for the front door. There was no time now to call her mother. It would have to wait. Before leaving the house she looked at her reflection in the mirror. She looked tired. She always seemed to look tired lately. She could sleep for a week and still look physically drained. She neatened her hair as best she could and left the house.

'Hello. Can I come in?'

Matilda peered around the door to the room Scott was recuperating in. He was out of bed and looking around for his clothes. Sitting on a chair in the corner of the room was a petite woman with a worried look on her face. She guessed she was his mother.

'Hello Boss. Yes, come in.'

'How are you?'

'I'm fine.'

'What happened?'

'Nothing. Some shit in a BMW ran me off the road.'

A BMW?

'Are you hurt?'

'No. I banged my head a bit. They just wanted to keep me in overnight for observation.'

There was a purple lump just above his left eye and his left wrist was bandaged. Apart from that he seemed physically fine.

'Have you been discharged?' Matilda asked.

'No he hasn't,' the stern-looking woman in the corner of the room said.

'Boss, this is my mum, Gillian. Mum, this is my boss, DCI Darke.'

'Nice to meet you,' Matilda said.

'Likewise. Scott has mentioned you many times.'

'Anything I should be worried about?' Matilda asked with a nervous smile.

'No,' the first hint of a smile appeared on Gillian Andrews' face. 'He speaks very highly of you. Now, would you tell him that he needs to stay in hospital at least until the doctors have been round?'

'Haven't you been seen this morning?'

'Not yet he hasn't.'

'I am still here you know,' Scott said, sitting on the edge of the bed. 'Look, I'm fine. It was just a bump on the head.'

'You have to be careful with bangs to the head,' Gillian said. 'Remember what happened to your Uncle Richard? He had a bang on the head, said he was fine. A week later he was dead.'

'Mum, Uncle Richard fell off a sixth floor balcony. It's hardly the same thing.' He looked at Matilda and rolled his eyes.

'I don't care. You're not leaving this hospital until you've seen the doctor.'

'I agree with your mum here, Scott. They'll be round in a bit anyway and they'll probably discharge you. Just give it another hour.'

'Exactly. I've got the car from your dad. When you're released I'll take you straight back home and make you a bacon sandwich. I've got your dad flipping your mattress so you'll be nice and comfy.'

Matilda looked from mother to son and saw Scott's face redden. He looked to the floor.

'Mum, would you go and get me a drink from the vending machine?'

'OK. I'll get you something fizzy. You need to keep your sugars up. Would you like anything?' Gillian asked Matilda as she rummaged in her bag for her purse.

'No. Thank you.'

'I won't be long. Make sure he doesn't leave.'

They waited until Gillian had left before either of them dared speak.

'Your mum seems nice.'

'She is.'

'She's sweet and obviously cares about you.'

'You won't tell anyone will you?' His frown looked as if it was causing him some pain.

'Tell anyone what?'

'That I still live at home.'

'Scott,' Matilda began, sitting on the edge of the bed. 'There's nothing wrong with still living at home. Besides, you're only twenty-six, there's plenty of time to move out. With the state of the house prices, you're not the only twenty-six-year-old still living with their parents.'

'I've told Rory and the others I live on my own.'

'I know you have. You shouldn't have done. There's nothing wrong with living at home,' she repeated.

'Rory's had his own place for four years.'

'No. Rory moved in with Amelia four years ago. Her father bought her that house for her twenty-first birthday. He'd still be living at home if he hadn't met her. There's no way he could

178

afford his own place, especially with the amount of money he spends on fragrances.' She smiled.

'I am saving up. It's not easy though.'

'I know it isn't. Look, I won't tell anyone. You know I don't go in for office gossip, but tell them yourself. Say you've moved back home because the rent kept increasing. Blame the government. Blame the police for not giving you a wage increase. If you keep secrets from your colleagues it will create a barrier and we all need to get on well together to be able to do the job we do.'

'Thanks, boss.'

'You're welcome. Now, seeing as you're on the mend I think I'll pop up to ICU and see how Joseph Glass is doing. There are more coppers in the hospital than there are at the station this morning. Say goodbye to your mum for me won't you?'

Scott nodded and smiled. He looked years younger in his hospital gown and his bed hair. Scott was a bit of an enigma. Rory and Sian always told the rest of the team what was going on in their lives. Aaron did too, though it often had to be dragged out of him. Scott was always on the outside, looking on but never participating. He needed bringing out of his shell and living at home with his parents wasn't helping.

As she climbed the stairs, rather than waiting for the lift, she thought of what Scott had said to her. He was run off the road by a BMW. She knew there was more than one BMW in the world, but surely it was too much of a coincidence. Now that the lives of her officers were being threatened, she felt duty bound to report her stalker to the ACC.

DC Joseph Glass's condition wasn't anywhere near as comfortable as his colleague's two floors down. He was still unconscious and hooked up to a plethora of machines. Keeping a bedside vigil were his parents; their faces ashen, their movements limited, their eyes firmly set on their comatose son.

Matilda knocked on the door and opened it slowly. 'Hello, I'm Joseph's boss. Am I all right to come in?'

'Oh, sure, of course. Please, come on in. I'm Sandra. This is Grahame.'

Both parents stood up to greet Matilda. Sandra was short and round. Her naturally curly hair was blonde streaked with grey and an unruly mess. Grahame was a carbon copy of his son: tall and lanky with similar hair and the same angled nose.

'I thought Joe's boss was a man,' Sandra snorted.

'He is but Joe was seconded to me on the case we're working on.'

'Oh right, I see. Well it's nice of you to come.'

'How's he doing?'

'We don't really know,' she slumped back down into the toughened plastic seat similar to the ones they had back at the station in the interview rooms. 'They've done a few scans and say there doesn't seem to be any permanent damage but he won't wake up.'

'They're going to do some motor tests on him later today,' Grahame chimed up. 'Apparently it could all be linked if his reflexes aren't working properly. It's all to do with the brain and what messages it's sending out.'

Matilda was reminded of what Dr Warminster had said about Lois Craven playing dead. It wasn't necessarily her decision to play dead but her mind was blocking out what had happened to her. Was this the same with Joseph? Was he not waking up because his brain didn't want him to know what was happening to him?

'Is there anything either of you need?' Matilda asked, not knowing what to say. She had hoped he would have been sitting up in bed laughing and joking. She could have handled that.

'No I don't think so,' Sandra said looking at her husband for confirmation. 'Everyone is being so helpful. I keep sending Grahame out for something to eat, with his diabetes, but we're fine.'

Matilda dug around in her pocket and produced a dog-eared card. 'My number is on here. If there's anything you need don't hesitate to give me a call.'

'That's very kind of you, thank you.'

'And if there's any change in his condition—'

'We'll let you know, definitely,' Sandra interrupted.

Matilda said her goodbyes and left the room.

Matilda's final stop in the Northern General was Lois Craven. Her interview yesterday was candid and Matilda had been surprised to see her revealing so much in front of her husband. However, she felt she was holding plenty back. There would be more she would divulge when she was alone. Fingers crossed.

'How are you feeling?' Matilda asked.

Lois was lying on her side, back to the door, and didn't notice Matilda enter. She turned around slowly to look at her visitor.

'I'm surprised it took you this long to come back.'

'I'm sorry?'

The pain of moving in the bed to sit up and be comfortable was etched on Lois's face as she slowly adjusted herself. 'I knew you'd be back. You'll want to know about all the men I've had affairs with but didn't want to ask me in front of Martin.'

'That would be helpful.'

'First of all, I want you to know that Martin is a wonderful man. He's a saint for what he's put up with over the years from me. I'm a terrible wife and he deserves so much better.'

'Why are you a terrible wife?'

'I'm not good with routine. I get bored very easily. When Martin and I first met we were fun, always going out, spontaneous weekends away. Then the children came along. Don't get me wrong, I love them to pieces, I really do, but they certainly cramp your style. Do you have kids?'

'No I don't.'

'I don't know whether to say you're lucky or not. I wouldn't

181

be without them at all. I love them. I genuinely love them, but I'm not a natural wife and I'm not a natural mother.' She leaned back in her bed against the mound of pillows. She closed her eyes and squeezed out a tear. 'I hate myself for that,' she added.

'I remember when I was a child,' she continued. 'All the others girls were playing with dolls and pretending to be mums and pushing prams around and I couldn't think of anything more boring. I wanted to play with Lego and play football in the park. When I was older and all my friends were getting married and having kids I wasn't jealous that it wasn't me. If it happened, it happened.'

'So what changed when you met Martin?'

'I fell in love. I truly loved Martin.'

'Past tense.'

Lois rolled her head to one side and looked at Matilda out of her one good eye. 'Yes. Past tense.' It seemed to cause her pain to say that.

'Why don't you love him anymore?'

'Because he took me back after the affair I had when I became pregnant with Thomas.'

'But you wanted to go back didn't you?'

'Yes I did. For completely selfish reasons. I wanted stability. I wanted a father for my child. You know, I would have respected him if he'd told me to piss off and thrown me out on the street but he didn't. He took me back. It showed how weak he was. He wanted an idyllic family unit and he was willing to sacrifice his own self-respect to have that.'

'So why have you stayed with him all these years?'

'I want my children to grow up in a stable environment. There's nothing wrong with that is there?'

'No. Nothing at all. Tell me about Kevin Hardaker.'

Lois's eyes lit up. She smiled. 'Kevin was the anti-Martin. He was fun, exciting, romantic. He touched me too.'

'I'm sorry?' Matilda frowned.

'Despite Martin and me sharing a bed he refused to touch me since Thomas was born. He was repelled by me but not enough to divorce me. Again, he showed his weakness. Kevin loved me. He wanted to be with me.'

'You were planning to leave Martin, weren't you? We've had the texts from your phone printed out.'

'Yes,' she replied, looking down, showing a modicum of shame for the first time. 'I didn't think Kevin was serious at first. I never thought he'd leave Alice and his kids. Even when he said he was looking for flats I didn't think he'd go through with it.'

'Did you go and view any flats with him?'

Lois laughed. 'Yes, several. I thought of it as a game. We went around them as man and wife; it was fun.'

'And then Kevin made an offer on one.'

'Yes. That completely threw me. All of a sudden it was happening. I had no idea what I was going to do.'

'Where was the flat – here in Sheffield?'

'No. We saw some here, a couple in Dronfield, but the one he finally settled on was in Stockport.'

'Stockport? That's far. You wouldn't have seen your children much.'

'I know,' she replied, looking down, sad.

'You talk like this was all Kevin's idea. You didn't want to move in with him did you?'

'I did. I really did. It was just escalating too quickly. I wanted to take things slower.'

'Yet he went and put a deposit on a flat without you knowing.'

'I know.'

'Would you have left Martin and the kids behind?'

'To be honest … I have absolutely no idea.'

Matilda watched as a wave of varying emotions played out on her bruised and battered face. 'Lois, who do you think could have carried out the attack on you and Kevin?'

'I don't know.' She shook her head and winced at the pain it caused her. 'I've been lying here thinking about it all and I didn't really know Kevin at all. I didn't know if he had any brothers and sisters, if his parents were still alive, if he was allergic to anything. I didn't even know if he had a middle name. We talked about moving in together but we knew absolutely sod all about each other.'

Lois looked ahead. Her troubled mind was etched all over her face. 'I told Kevin I loved him so many times. I told myself I loved him too. Sitting here I've had time to think. If I didn't know much about him, then did I really love him? I've made a complete mess out of everything.'

'Lois I'm going to need to know the names of the men you've had affairs with.'

'Why?'

'I'll need to know their alibis.'

Lois laughed. 'Look, I don't want to sound crude or anything but I was raped by this man. I would have known if it had been a man I had previously slept with.'

'I'll still need to know their names.'

She sighed. 'There were only three: Craig Monroe. He lives in Meersbrook. He's a teacher. Sean McCleary. He lives in Leeds and works on the council there. Owen Masak. There was some kind of line over the "s". I never knew how to pronounce it correctly. He lives in Dronfield. He's a plumber.'

Matilda was noting all these names down in her notebook. 'Thank you.'

'I suppose this is my retribution isn't it? I should have been happy with my lot: husband, three kids, a nice house, money in the bank, but I wasn't. I had three affairs, several one night stands and the odd grope and snog when out with the girls. This is some sort of karma isn't it?'

'I'm not sure if I believe in karma,' Matilda said. 'Who is Thomas's father?'

'Owen Masak. Although you wouldn't have needed to ask that

when you see him. He's the spitting image of his father.' She shook her head. 'I have no idea how Martin can look at him and pretend he's his son.' She looked at Matilda, 'I bet you think I'm a complete bitch don't you?'

'I don't think anything.' *Yes, actually, I do.*

'I wouldn't blame you. I am a bitch. I'm a horrible person. I've been horrible to Martin and the kids. They would have all been better off if I'd been killed the other night.'

'Your kids need you, Lois.'

Tears were freely flowing down her face. 'No they don't. What kind of example am I setting for them? Anna is fifteen. What am I teaching her about being a woman – that it's OK to be selfish? That it's fine to sleep with whoever you want and screw the consequences? I should be a role model for Anna, and I'm nothing but a slut.'

It was difficult for Matilda to sympathize with Lois. She wouldn't call her a slut to her face, but she was definitely not a role model to her three children. Why had Martin decided to take her back after her last affair which resulted in the birth of Thomas? He could have brought up Jack and Anna alone and still given them a stable environment.

Lois wiped her eyes. 'You know, while I was lying on the ground by the car after being shot I could feel the blood flowing out of me. I honestly thought it was my life slipping away. I was sorry for what I'd done. I hoped my children would forgive me, but most of all, I wished death would come quickly. I wanted all of this to end.'

TWENTY-NINE

A quick phone call from Matilda to Aaron as she was leaving the hospital set up the events for the next hour. If there was a connection between the aggravated burglaries, the double shooting, and the seemingly suspicious suicide on London Road then it needed to be established. She asked Aaron to organize a briefing and have everyone present in the Murder Room. By everyone, she meant her own team and DI Christian Brady from CID and his team investigating the burglaries. She then put in a call to the ACC and asked if she wanted to sit in on the briefing. She did. *Damn.*

It was the first time DC Faith Easter had been back in the Murder Room since her short-lived attachment to the Murder Investigation Team, and she wasn't looking forward to it. As Faith walked in, she tried to maintain a professional demeanour; her head was high, her dark shiny hair was severely pulled back into a tight ponytail, and her back was straight. She tried not to think of her time here in this room as a failure. She had tried her hand at a dedicated murder squad and it hadn't worked out. At least she'd tried. That was the most important thing to remember. She was still only twenty-four, a few more years in CID under her belt, a few more cases successfully solved and maybe she would be ready for a more specialized department.

Faith found a seat and looked around her. She recognized a few faces: Rory and Aaron, and gave them a smile and a wave. Did she look confident? She hoped so.

Matilda Darke entered the Murder Room, stopping briefly on the threshold. It was strange seeing it full to capacity once again. It gave her a buzz, the assurance to carry on. Despite her self-doubt and anxieties, she craved a full team.

She shook hands with DI Christian Brady, who, at six foot three, loomed over her. He was built with the erectness of a man in a position of power, the strong jaw of a man not to be messed with, and the stance of a no-nonsense copper. He probably exited the womb waving his ID badge.

'Christian, thanks for coming,' she said quietly while the rest of the room was still abuzz with chatter.

'No problem. These burglaries are getting out of hand. I'm kind of hoping your case and mine are connected; at least by pooling our resources we might actually get somewhere.'

He obviously hadn't heard the Murder Room was closing. Matilda decided not to tell Christian that her team didn't have any resources. All she was bringing to the table was an extra headache for them all to share.

Sitting at the side of the room away from the rest of the officers was the diminutive ACC Valerie Masterson. With her back straight and her legs crossed at the knee she seemed very business-like and authoritative. She nodded at Matilda when they made eye contact but her expression remained stony.

'Firstly,' she began as the room fell silent and all eyes fell on her. 'I'd like to update you on the condition of our colleagues. DC Scott Andrews is doing well and should be back in work tomorrow. He suffered a mild concussion and a sprained wrist—'

'That's his love life gone for a burton,' Rory interrupted to much laughter from the rest of the room.

'As for DC Joseph Glass, his condition is much worse. At

present there are no signs of any brain damage but he is in a coma. As soon as he wakes the doctors will run more tests to find out if there is any permanent damage. His parents are by his side and they're going to let me know the second there is any change.'

'Should we have a whip-round?' Aaron asked.

'I'd hold off for now, Aaron. Let's see how things go over the next couple of days.'

'Was what happened to Scott just an accident?' Rory asked.

'What do you mean?'

'Well, Joseph Glass gets coshed and then a few hours later Scott is run off the road. Is this a coincidence or is someone out there targeting police officers?'

There was a muttering around the room as officers suddenly started putting two and two together.

'I think you're reading far too much into this DC Fleming,' the ACC said. 'We know who attacked DC Glass and that is being investigated. What happened to DC Andrews was just one of those things. There's no evidence to assume police are being targeted in any way. I'd give the American cop shows a rest for a while if I were you.'

'Yes, ma'am,' he said, head down.

'Now, let's move on to the matter at hand,' Matilda quickly said wanting to move the subject to safer territory. 'Our main priority at present is to find Lucas Branning. We know he attacked DC Glass and I want him charged for assault. He also has a history of burglary so DI Brady and his team can question him about those too. No, he doesn't match the description given by the victims of the burglaries but I don't care about that. I want him questioned. Now what do we know about him, and where is he?'

DI Christian Brady stood up from the edge of the desk he was perched on. He moved over to a whiteboard where there was a very unflattering mug shot of Branning. 'Lucas Branning is thirty-seven-years-old, five foot five, stocky, and has cropped hair. He works part-time as a mechanic in the Wicker and lives at Wincobank. Officers have been to his home but there's no sign of him. They're currently camped outside waiting for him.'

'Not in a marked car I hope.'

'No,' he smiled. 'Two DCs.'

'Does anyone know where he hangs out?'

'We interviewed his co-workers yesterday. They named a few pubs he's likely to be found in but they're not open yet.'

'What about his sisters? Do they know where he's likely to be?'

Aaron stood up. 'Ma'am, Alice Hardaker was burgled the night before last.'

'What?' Another headache she didn't need.

'Me and Rory went round there last night. The house is a tip. She's been done over. She'd hardly talk to us.'

'Has she reported it?'

'No. She didn't want to give a statement either. We could hardly get two words out of her.'

'Was she in the house at the time?'

'Yes. She said she disturbed him by coming downstairs.'

'Did she give a description?'

'Very vague: tall and dressed in black.'

Matilda looked to DI Brady.

'The description given to us by the other victims of the burglaries have said he was tall and dressed in black.'

'It's not much to go on is it?' Matilda sighed. 'Put Rory in dark clothing and he could be your man. So could Aaron, so could you, Christian.'

Faith Easter raised her hand and spoke. 'I know Lucas Branning doesn't match the description but even he's not stupid enough to burgle his own sister, surely.'

'I think we can safely say Lucas Branning is out of the frame for the burglaries,' DI Brady said.

'So why run?'

There was no answer to that.

Thinking aloud, Matilda said, 'So are we saying that the man who committed these aggravated burglaries also committed the double shooting that killed Kevin Hardaker and nearly killed Lois Craven, and then just happens to choose Alice Hardaker as his next target for burgling?'

'You think he chose the Hardaker house deliberately?' Rory asked.

'Yes,' she said, almost with sarcasm. 'You've been to Broad Elms Lane; it's full of detached houses, away from the road, surrounded by high fences and tall trees. He could have chosen any one of them to burgle, but he goes right to the end and happens to come across Alice Hardaker? I don't think so.'

'If it is the same person, could he have been watching Alice Hardaker and waited to strike?' Brady asked.

'It would appear so.'

'Wait a minute,' the ACC put her hand up to halt the conversation. 'Assuming the killer and the burglar is the same person, why is he going back to the Hardaker family? What is in that family's background that makes him kill the husband, terrorize his girlfriend, then go on to terrorize his wife?'

If a pin had dropped it would have made everyone in the room jump.

Matilda walked over to the whiteboard where a basic history of the Hardaker family was written. 'There's nothing there. Kevin is a hard-working family man. Alice was recently made redundant. They've got two kids who are doing well at school. Kevin's an only child, and despite having an affair with Lois Craven, he's a model citizen. The neighbours love him; they say he's great with the kids, knows how to throw a good party and always smiling.

'What about any money worries, debts?'

'Just the usual; a mortgage and a couple of credit cards, but nothing they can't handle.'

'Could someone have an issue with Lucas Branning and be taking it out on his sister?' asked Aaron.

190

'If that's the case why target Kevin and Lois? Why inflict such violence on them? In what way would that hurt Lucas?'

'Because it would hurt his sister.'

'No. I don't buy that at all. If you wanted to get some form of revenge on Lucas, you'd target Lucas.'

Rory, flicking through his notebook, chimed up. 'According to the neighbours, Lucas only visited when he wanted something – usually money. When he came round it always ended up with voices being raised in their house.'

'OK,' Matilda stopped to think for a moment. 'So, Lucas is a selfish man. He only cares for himself. If, as Aaron said, someone wanted to hurt Lucas, they'd go directly to him. I doubt he'd give a toss if they hurt his sisters.'

Faith spoke up again. 'If the Hardaker family really are the intended targets here, why is the killer committing all these burglaries?'

'Good point, Faith.'

'Perhaps the two aren't connected,' the ACC said.

'The description Lois Craven gave of the man who attacked her matches the description we have of the burglar. That's the only link we have, but it's a good link.'

'The description is incredibly vague, and nobody else has mentioned a tattoo on his neck. You need to proceed with caution. Yes, they may be linked, but it's a tenuous link. Don't assume this is the same person.' The ACC pointed to a third whiteboard. 'Where does Gerald Beecham come into it?'

Matilda scratched her head hard, digging her nails into her scalp to try and stave off the rising tension. Her mouth was already drying and she could feel the prickle of heat creeping up her back.

Noticing Matilda's discomfort, Sian took the floor. 'Gerald Beecham lived in a tower block on London Road. On the night of the shootings he, apparently, threw himself off the roof and died when he hit the ground, fifteen floors below. The reason he's up there,' she said, pointing to a picture of the smiling elderly man, 'is because when Dr Kean arrived on the scene she found anomalies that were not consistent with a suicide.'

'Such as?'

'He was bruised and had blood on the back of his jacket that didn't belong to him.'

'Who did it belong to?'

'Lois Craven.'

'I'm guessing the description Lois Craven gave you of her attacker doesn't match Mr Beecham?'

'Not in the slightest.'

'How reliable is Lois?'

'As reliable as a woman can be after she's been beaten, raped, and shot three times,' Matilda said. She had sat down and was looking in the distance and out of the dirty windows at the dirty city beyond.

'You need to get a formal statement from her.'

'As soon as she is able to leave hospital I intend to bring her in. I also want Alice Hardaker in too. I don't care if she's grieving for her husband or upset by the burglary. I have a feeling she knows more than she's letting on.'

'So what about these burglaries then?' DI Brady asked.

The ACC answered before Matilda could. 'I think you need to keep investigating them as you are for the time being. However, liaise very closely with Matilda, just in case there is a connection. The shooting has all the hallmarks of bad blood, a revenge attack for something. I cannot see a career burglar turning his hand to rape and murder.'

'But the descriptions match.' DI Brady clearly wanted the cases to be linked. He wanted more people working on this to get it solved as soon as possible.

'What you need to do', said the ACC, 'is get a more detailed description of the burglar from the people who have been targeted, and CCTV footage. You also need a full description from Lois Craven when she's up to giving one. Compare and contrast, but never assume you're looking for the same person. And, you need to find a link between Gerald Beecham and both the Craven and Hardaker families.'

She makes it sound so simple.

The ACC stood up and addressed the whole room. 'This is not going to be an easy case to solve and it's going to take a lot of time and effort from you all. However, it needs solving quickly. Whether the burglar and the killer is the same person or not, whoever is doing this is extremely dangerous. Matilda, when you've finished, I'd like a word.'

With that, she left, leaving a room of worried expressions.

Matilda, slightly deflated, set everyone a task. Rory and a few of the other DCs she had borrowed from DI Brady were to locate the names of Lois Craven's lovers, and find out their alibis for the night of the shooting. They also needed to finish identifying everyone who lived in the same tower block as Gerald Beecham. Brady started to lead his officers out of the Murder Room. He too was feeling less invigorated by the ACC and the mammoth task that seemed to lie ahead.

'By the way,' Sian said quietly to Matilda, taking her to one side, 'I've had Nathaniel Glover in and he's in the clear.'

'It was a long shot I suppose. Thanks Sian.'

With the room slowly emptying and those remaining going about their business, Matilda made her way to her office. She closed the door behind her, something she rarely did, and sat in her chair behind the desk. She swivelled it around so her back was to the rest of the room and she was looking out of the grimy window at the view of the city laid out before her.

Under her breath, she said, 'David Cameron, Gordon Brown, Tony Blair, John Major, Margaret Thatcher ...'

Matilda hardly ever recited the names of the Prime Ministers in reverse order. It was too difficult. It was only when she needed maximum concentration to block out the whirlwind of thoughts in her head.

'James Callaghan, Harold Wilson, Edward Heath ...' Now she was stuck. Who came before Edward Heath? 'Fuck, fuck, fuck, fuck,' she whispered with as much venom as she could muster.

She bit down on her lip so hard she could taste blood. She bit harder still until she could feel blood freely flowing in her mouth. The relaxation was instant. She closed her eyes and could feel the tension slowly ebb away.

THIRTY

'When are you going to start tidying up?'

Jenny Evans stumbled as she made her way around the living room of Alice Hardaker's ransacked home. The sofa cushions were still scattered around the floor, tables overturned, and pictures smashed.

'I'll do it later,' Alice replied. Since the intruder had visited she had hardly done anything. She still wore the same tracksuit, hadn't showered, eaten very little, and barely moved from the leather recliner.

Her children were staying at Jenny's house for the time being; both sisters thinking this was the safer option, but it couldn't be a permanent one. They needed their mother now more than ever since the murder of their father. She needed to get a grip, and take control of her life.

'The kids are asking for you,' Jenny said. 'They're scared. They want to know what's going on.'

'I'd like to know what's going on myself.'

'Alice, you need to snap out of this. You need to get up, have a shower, have something to eat, sort your house out and get your kids back in their own bedrooms at night.'

'Jenny, I can't have them back here. Not yet.'

'Why not?'

'What if he comes back?'

'The burglar?'

Alice nodded.

'Why would he come back?'

'Oh for Christ's sake, look around you. Haven't you noticed yet?'

'Noticed what?'

'What's missing?'

Jenny looked around the large living room. The TV was still there, as was the DVD player and several games consoles. 'Nothing that I can think of.'

'Exactly.'

'What are you talking about?'

'He didn't steal anything. He trashed the place but he didn't take anything. He's coming back.'

'You don't know that.'

'Yes I do,' she said with stern determination.

'How?'

'He asked me for money. He said he'd come for his ten grand.'

'What?' Jenny asked, confusion written all over her face. 'Was he a loan shark?'

'No! He said he'd come for his money. He seemed pretty sure I owed him money. When I said I didn't know what he was talking about he kicked right off.'

'But you don't owe anyone any money, do you?'

'Of course not.'

'And Kevin didn't?'

'No.'

'Maybe he got the wrong house.'

'No. He knew my name. Jenny, do you think Lucas might owe someone money and they've come here for it?'

'Oh God. I don't know.'

'Have you seen him lately?'

'I've not seen him for ages. You?'

'No.'

'Oh shit. What's he got into?'

'I've no idea, but if it is to do with Lucas we'd both better watch our backs. This is a nasty piece of work. If he knows I'm related to Lucas, then he'll know you are too. He could be watching us.'

'Oh my God, Alice, don't say that.' She wiped a tear from her face before it could roll down her podgy cheek. 'What about your kids?'

'I don't know. I thought they'd be safer with you but now I've had time to think about it all I don't know if there's anywhere they'd be safe.'

'Maybe we should—'

The doorbell rang. Under the tension in the house it sounded louder than usual and both Jenny and Alice jumped. Jenny gave a yelp and clamped a clammy hand firmly over her mouth.

'Do you think that's him?' Jenny asked in a muffled whisper.

'I doubt he'd come to the front door and ring the bell.'

Alice leaned over to the window and angled her head slowly around the curtain. When she saw Aaron and Rory standing on the doorstep she visibly relaxed, then suddenly fear overtook her once more.

'Shit, it's the police. Look, Jenny, don't tell them anything about the burglar. Don't mention Lucas, the ten grand, or anything. Do you understand? He may be a pain in the backside but he's still our brother. We protect each other. Like Mum and Dad taught us.'

'But they could help. They could move you and the kids to a safe house or something.'

'It doesn't work like that, Jenny. Just say nothing, OK?'

'I don't like this.'

'Neither do I.' The doorbell rang again. 'I'd better answer it.'

Walking slowly to the front door, Alice smoothed down her

tracksuit and ran her fingers through her knotted hair. A brief glance in the hallway mirror told her she looked completely different to the glamorous Alice Hardaker she usually presented to the world. Right now though, a made-up face and designer clothes were the last thing on her mind.

'Mrs Hardaker, I'm DS Connolly and this is DC Fleming. Do you remember us from last night?'

'Of course I do. What can I do for you?'

'We need you to come with us to the station.'

'What for?'

'We need you to make a formal statement about your husband.'

'It's not really convenient right now,' she said, looking back over her shoulder.

'I'm afraid DCI Darke insists that you come with us right now.'

'Am I under arrest?'

'No you're not.'

'So I don't have to come if I don't want to.'

'DCI Darke could issue a warrant for your arrest if she believes you're obstructing an investigation.'

Alice stared into Aaron's eyes. She tried to remain stoic and icy but after everything that had happened over the past few days her emotions were all over the place. She blinked and turned away first.

'Fine. I'll get my coat.'

She slammed the door on the waiting officers and went back into the living room. Jenny looked a bundle of nerves. She'd obviously heard everything that had been said on the doorstep.

'Oh Jesus Christ, Alice. Do you think they've arrested Lucas? Maybe they think he's killed Kevin. Maybe he has. Shit, Alice, what if Lucas has actually killed someone?' Her voice was no louder than a whisper but she was in full panic mode.

'Jenny, you need to calm down. It's probably to do with Kevin. Look, take care of my kids and I'll come straight over to yours as soon as I'm finished.'

'What if they want to question me?'

'So what? You don't know anything.'

'Look at me though, I'm shaking. If they put me in one of those interview rooms, I'll break down. I'll probably say that Lucas is really Lord Lucan or something. You know what I'm like Alice.'

'There's no reason to interview you, Jenny. You told that DC Glass everything you know the other night.'

Alice took her younger sister by the shoulders and pulled her close. She kissed her on top of her head and released her. 'Tell Warren and Milly that I love them and they can come home tonight when I've tidied up. That's a promise.'

With that, she turned and left the room. She picked up her coat and bag from the hallway and opened the front door where Aaron and Rory were still in the same position she'd left them in.

'After you then, gentlemen,' she said, slamming the door firmly behind her.

Back in the house, Jenny helped herself to a small whisky from the decanter in the living room. She hated the stuff, the smell alone made her want to heave, but she needed something to settle her nerves. She threw the golden liquid to the back of her throat and quickly swallowed. It tasted nasty but she felt the effects immediately. She took a larger measure from the decanter and necked that too.

Taking a deep breath, Jenny looked around the room at the broken furniture and discarded cushions. It would be nice for Alice to return home to a neat and tidy house. Then the kids could come straight here from school. She had just begun when the landline started ringing.

It took a while for Jenny to locate the handset. 'Hello,' she answered, running her fingers through her hair.

'Alice Hardaker.' The voice was muffled and deep.

'She's not in at the moment. I'm her sister. Can I take a message?'

'Yes. You can tell her I'll be back for my money later. If she hasn't got it, then it'll go up to fifteen grand.'

Jenny hung up and threw the handset down on the floor. The tears came. What the hell had Lucas got them all mixed up in?

THIRTY-ONE

'I'm being watched. I know it sounds stupid and I know you'll think I'm being paranoid, at first I thought I was too, but when Scott was run off the road I knew that I was right.'

'Matilda, you're not making any sense. What are you talking about?' the ACC asked from behind her desk.

'I've noticed a black BMW following me lately. It's everywhere I go. The car that ran Scott off the road was also a black BMW. It can't be a coincidence.'

'You think someone is out there targeting the police?'

'I didn't want to think so but it seems like it.'

Matilda was determined to tell the ACC about her being followed, but with every step up to her office she went off the idea more and more, putting it down to her overactive imagination. If these incidents were solely aimed at her she would have dismissed them herself, but not with Scott being hurt.

When she entered the ACC's office she couldn't get the words out quickly enough. She had refused the offer of a seat and launched into her rehearsed tirade.

'Have you got the registration number of the one following you?'

Matilda looked to the floor. She felt guilty. 'No. To be honest, I wasn't taking it seriously.'

'OK. For now, let's not panic. If you see the car again, get the number and run a check. Also, try and get more information out of Scott about the type of BMW that ran him off the road.'

'Will do.'

'Keep me informed on this, Matilda. And for now, it's just between us, OK?'

When Matilda left the office she leaned against the wall and let out a massive sigh. At least now if anyone else was hurt she wouldn't feel as guilty. Who was she kidding? She'd feel guilty regardless. She was heading back to the Murder Room when Aaron accosted her.

'I've been looking for you. We've got Alice Hardaker in interview room two.'

'Good. Did she mind coming in?'

'Well she wasn't happy about it.'

Matilda had to walk faster to keep up with the lengthy strides of the towering Aaron Connolly. As they made their way to the interview room Aaron filled Matilda in on Alice's behaviour. She then informed Aaron of how she wanted the interview to go, what she wanted to know, and which roles they would both play. Before entering, Matilda stopped a passing uniformed officer and asked him to bring them three teas. She took a deep breath and opened the door.

Alice had transformed completely since the night Matilda first met her. She had answered the door looking neat and tidy, hair nicely combed back, skin freshly moisturized and looking elegant. Now, she was wearing old clothes that were covered in heavy creases and stains, her hair was knotted; there were bags under her eyes and her dehydrated skin gave the impression she had a slow puncture.

'Mrs Hardaker, thank you for coming in,' Matilda said, sitting down opposite her.

'It was hardly an invitation. I don't feel like I had much choice,' she replied, glaring at Aaron.

'We need to discover what happened to your husband. In order to do that we need to question everyone involved. Sometimes on more than one occasion.'

'I told DC Glass everything I know. Look, I had no idea Kevin was having an affair. Do you honestly think I would have put up with it if I had? He would have been out on his ear. My parents divorced when I was five. My dad cheated on my mum. It tore us all apart. I swore that I wouldn't put up with it when I married. Kevin knew all this too.'

'Did you know he had stopped playing tennis?'

'Not until you came to my house and shattered my world, no.' She sounded angry, as if all of this was Matilda's fault.

'Does the name Lois Craven mean anything to you?'

'Yes. She's the slag who stole my husband.'

'You know her then?'

'Only from what I've read about in the papers. No, I don't know the Craven family at all. I've been through everything of Kevin's in the house to try and find something about his secret life. He was obviously very careful because I've not turned up anything, the bastard.'

There was a knock on the door and Matilda was glad of the interruption. She needed Alice to calm down, to start thinking rationally about the questions she answered rather than saying the first thing that came into her head. The uniformed officer brought in three mugs on a tray and placed it down in the centre of the table. He left without making eye contact with anyone.

Matilda handed a cup to Alice. She looked at it and wrinkled her nose. Was it the colour of the tea or the fact it was a chipped mug and not a china cup that irked Alice? Matilda wondered.

She took a sip and a small smile appeared on her face. It obviously tasted better than it looked.

'Alice, how are the children coping with all this?'

'I've not told them,' she shrugged. 'They're too young. DC Glass helped me with that. He told them Kevin had been in a small car accident and that he was in hospital. They keep asking but I honestly don't know what to say to them.' She turned away to hide her tears. 'I'm sorry.'

'Don't be.'

'I've no idea why I'm crying. The man betrayed me. He lied to me and his children. I can't forgive that. I certainly can't forget it.'

'Alice, Detective Sergeant Connolly here tells me you were burgled.'

She nodded. 'That's right.'

'But we have no record of that.'

'That's because I didn't report it.'

'Why not?'

'Because there was no point. Nothing was taken. I disturbed him before he could steal anything. Besides, it was in the papers the other week that the police are too understaffed to always come out. South Yorkshire Police are fourth from bottom when it comes to solving burglaries. You only catch about nine per cent of them. What's the point in reporting it? You lot wouldn't have even bothered once you'd found out nothing was stolen.'

'You still should have called us.'

'Why? It would have been another unsolved crime on your statistics. I doubt you need anymore more of those.'

Was that a dig? Was she talking about Carl Meagan?

'Alice, don't you think it's a coincidence that you happen to be burgled around the same time your husband is murdered?'

'No. I read the papers. I watch the news. There's a whole spate of robberies going on in Sheffield at the moment. And what are you doing about them? Bugger all.'

'A dedicated unit has been set up to deal with those.' Matilda found herself defending DI Brady and his team.

Alice leaned back in her chair and folded her arms. 'Yes, you're good at that aren't you? Something happens so you form a unit or a team or a committee. Just like the government: a member of the cabinet gives himself a paper cut and the Prime Minister holds a COBRA meeting. God knows why, for all the good it does.'

'I think we're getting away from the matter in hand here,' Matilda said. 'Do you know where your brother is, Alice?'

'Oh here we go. I wondered how long it would be before you brought him into it. Yes, he's been in the nick for burglaries in the past but he's put it all behind him now. He's got himself a flat, he's got himself a legit job. Can't you lot just leave—?'

'Alice, your brother assaulted one of our police officers yesterday.'

'What?' That stopped her dead. Her eyes widened and she felt around her collar. 'No. I … no. Lucas isn't like that.'

'Two members of my team went to his place of work. As soon as he found out they were detectives he fled, not before throwing a carjack at one of them and hitting him on the head.'

Alice didn't say anything. She looked straight ahead, yet her eyes were moving from side to side.

'It was DC Joseph Glass who your brother injured.'

'Is he going to be all right?' She sounded genuinely concerned.

'We don't know yet. He's still unconscious. I need to know where he is, Alice.'

'I've no idea. Honestly, I don't. Look, if I knew, I'd tell you. I don't want a cop killer in my family.'

As soon as she mentioned a cop killer, Matilda and Aaron exchanged glances. It was the first time the possibility Joseph could die had been mentioned. The atmosphere in the room changed dramatically.

'Lucas only really comes round when he wants something. Months can go by without me seeing him.'

'What kind of things does he want?'

'Money usually.'

'What about a place to hide if the police were after him?'

'No. Well, I mean he might come round and ask but I wouldn't let him in. I don't want my kids seeing that. Look, I'm sorry about DC Glass I really am. He's a lovely young man. If I knew where Lucas was I'd tell you.'

'Let's get back to your husband,' Matilda said, swallowing the bile of grief that was slowly rising. 'Can you think of anyone who would want to kill him?'

'No. At the moment I hate him, that'll pass, I know that. However, he was a good man. He didn't have any enemies. He was hard-working, he provided for us, especially recently when I was made redundant. He looked after the kids, took them out. Every time Sheffield United played at home, or locally, he and Sam three doors down took the lads, whatever the weather. He was everything you'd want in a husband and father. The fact that he turned out to be a lying, cheating, waste of a fu—'

'Alice,' Matilda interrupted. 'Moving on to the burglary, can you describe the person who broke in?'

'No. It was dark. It happened so fast.'

'Surely you must have noticed something.'

'No. He was tall, broad shoulders, dressed in black. That's all I can say. I know it's not much but I was scared. You can hardly expect me to grab my mobile and ask him to pose for a selfie. Look, why are you asking me about a burglary where nothing was taken? It's not important. Someone is out there who killed the father of my children. I'm not bothered for me but they'll want to know who killed him and why. You should be looking for him not interrogating me.'

'Alice, we're not interrogating you. We just need to—'

'Am I under arrest? Can I leave?'

'Of course. You can leave whenever you want to.'

'Right,' she stood up quickly, pushing her chair back. 'I don't know why I should be surprised really – you're focusing on the wrong thing. You couldn't find Carl Meagan and you'll not be able to find my husband's killer either.'

Matilda could feel Aaron's eyes burning into her. She didn't dare to look at him in return. She didn't want him to see the look of dismay on her face. It was the first time anyone had thrown Carl Meagan at her, apart from former DI Ben Hales. From him she expected it. From Alice she didn't.

'Show her out,' Matilda said quietly to Aaron.

He jumped from his chair and led Alice out of the interview room leaving Matilda behind with her thoughts.

She pictured Carl in her head. From the many photographs she saw of the cute blond, blue-eyed boy with the cheeky smile, he was permanently etched on her mind. Whenever he was mentioned he came racing to the front. She saw him now, but she wasn't seeing him in his school uniform mugging to the camera, or playing in the back garden dressed as Batman, or on the sofa with his Labrador puppy. She was picturing him lying dead in a ditch somewhere; the life torn out of him, his face pale, bruised, and cold. The innocence in his young face and the cartoon pyjamas he had been wearing when he was snatched appearing in stark contrast to the horror of a murder scene.

Aaron re-entered the interview room, and startled her. She shuffled her papers and had a drink of her cold tea to make it look like she hadn't just been wallowing in his absence.

'Are you all right?' he asked quietly.

'Yes I'm fine. What did you think of her?'

'I don't like her,' he replied.

'Me neither. You go first.'

'She's avoiding the burglary. She says she interrupted him but when me and Rory went round we saw the state of the place: the hallway, kitchen, dining room, and living room were all a complete mess. You're not telling me the burglar couldn't have found something worth nicking in any of those rooms.'

Matilda thought about that. 'So, either the burglar did take something but Alice doesn't want us to know about it because it was already stolen or illegal or whatever, or, he came round for some other reason entirely.'

'Such as?'

'To scare her maybe?'

'Why would he want to scare her?'

'I'm not sure. There's something about that family that I don't quite understand. I can't put my finger on it. She refused to make eye contact either. Did you notice that?'

'I did. She looked everywhere but straight ahead. Do you think we should put a surveillance on her?'

'The ACC won't go for that on the basis of a funny feeling. We need to interview the sister and find her sodding brother.'

'I'll go and see where we're at with finding Lucas Branning then,' Aaron said. He seemed in a hurry to leave the room, not that Matilda could blame him.

He closed the door behind him leaving Matilda alone. The clock on the wall ticked loudly and she sat perfectly still. She went over the interview with Alice Hardaker in her head. When she brought up Carl Meagan she looked straight at Matilda; she looked directly into her. She knew exactly what she was saying. Was she really suffering from grief, lashing out at the police force as a whole, or was she personally attacking Matilda? What was it that she didn't want Matilda finding out?

THIRTY-TWO

'Hang on Rory, let me make a cuppa before you start.'

Sian trotted over to the mini kitchen the Murder Investigation Team had created at the back of the room and flicked the kettle on. Rory had come bounding in all smiles after locating and chatting to the three lovers that Lois Craven had cheated on her husband with. After a long and tiring day, Sian was ready for a bit of gossip.

She came back with two mugs and sat down. She even took out a full packet of Bourbon Creams from her snack drawer, opened them, and placed them on the edge of the table for Rory to help himself to. This was unprecedented.

'Right, I'm ready, let's hear all the juicy bits.'

At that point Aaron Connolly walked in, his face ashen. Although with his dour expression and permanently wrinkled brow it was difficult to tell whether he was tired, happy, scared, or angry.

'Aaron, you're just in time. Grab a drink and pull up a chair.'

'I'm ready for a pint actually. You'll never guess what that Alice Hardaker said to Matilda.'

'It can wait,' Sian said. 'Rory has been talking to Lois Craven's lovers.'

'I thought you were busy. Aren't you supposed to be working on identifying the residents in the block on London Road?'

'I'm sure we can all spare a few minutes. I've missed lunch again today,' Sian said. 'Come on then Rory, spill.'

'I think you're going to be disappointed, Sian,' Rory said. 'I'm not about to read you a chapter from *Fifty Shades of Grey*.'

'Oh come on, she was having an illicit affair; there's bound to be some juicy bits.'

Aaron pulled up a chair, coffee in hand, and settled in. They were like three kids around a camp fire.

'OK. Lois's first lover was Craig Monroe. He's a teacher and lives at Meersbrook. He dated Lois for three months about twelve years ago. He was single at the time but he's now married with triplets, poor bloke. He knew Lois was married but he was young and thought it was a bit of fun. He ended it when she started getting serious.'

'In what way serious?' Sian asked, perched on the edge of her seat.

'She wanted to move in with him.'

'What? But she had two young kids by then. Was she planning just to leave them?'

'I've no idea. Craig said as soon as she started talking about living together he backed off.'

'Wise man,' said Aaron, reaching across for a handful of Bourbon Creams.

'He's not heard from Lois since then and his alibi checks out so that's him off the list. Now then Sian, you'll love what I'm going to tell you about Sean McCleary.'

Sian's eyes lit up. She cupped her hands firmly around her coffee mug and eagerly waited. She was almost salivating.

'When Sean McCleary went out with Lois ten years ago he was working and living in Leeds as a council worker. They met when she went to Leeds on some kind of training course. He now works as a financial coordinator here in Sheffield. They dated for about six months. At the time he was also seeing someone else – a man.'

'No!' Sian shrieked. 'You're joking?'

'No I'm not. Sean's thirty-one now so at the time he was twenty-one and he was experimenting with his sexuality. He couldn't decide which way he swung so he had a crack at both. His relationship with Lois was mostly sexual. They'd often meet in car parks and do it in the back of his car or a cheap hotel. He even boasted about a threesome they had with the bloke he was seeing.'

'Oh my goodness,' Sian almost blushed. 'And I thought I was being adventurous when me and Stuart went on that boat to the Isle of Man and—' she stopped, suddenly realizing she was talking to two colleagues. 'Never mind. Carry on.'

'Anyway, to cut a long story short, Sean decided he preferred the company of men and gave Lois the elbow. He's been in a relationship with his current partner, Rufus Abbot, for seven years. They're getting married in September.'

'That's nice. I've never been to a gay wedding. I wonder how they differ,' Sian mused.

'They're probably just as long-winded and dull as straight weddings,' Rory commented.

'Does his alibi check out?' Aaron asked, clearly the only one interested in the topic at hand.

'Yes it does.'

'Are you saving the best until last?' Sian asked.

'I am. Owen Masak is originally from Poland but has been living in Dronfield for the last fifteen years. He met Lois about nine years ago, and, as we all know, it culminated in the birth of her son, Thomas. Owen is a plumber and met Lois when he did some work at the college where she works. They went for a drink together after an afternoon of flirting and then had sex in the back of his van.'

'Blimey, she's not backward about being forward our Lois Craven, is she?'

'What are you smiling at?' Rory asked Aaron when he noticed a smirk on his face.

'Just remembering the time me and Katrina did it in the back of a van. We'd bought something off eBay that was collection only. So we hired a van and drove overnight up to Glasgow. It added a bit of spice to our marriage. You should try it Sian,' he smirked.

'There's nothing wrong with my marriage, thank you very much. I've been married thirteen years to my Stuart.'

'But are you still passionate?'

'At times.'

'At times? You should be passionate all the time.'

'We're not rabbits, Aaron. Besides, it's not normal to still be at each other like that after thirteen years of marriage.'

'Excuse me you two,' Rory interrupted. 'When you've finished with the marriage guidance is there any chance of getting back to our Polish friend here?'

'Oh, yes. Sorry Rory. Go on.'

Rory looked down at his notes. 'It doesn't matter now, you've ruined it. Anyway, Owen didn't realize Lois had become pregnant. They only did it a couple of times before they lost touch.'

'Did you tell him about Thomas?'

'No. He's married with a child himself. I asked if she ever made contact with him again for any reason and he said no. I left it at that. His alibi checks out too.'

'So it's not a jealous lover out for revenge then,' Aaron said. 'Why do I get the feeling this case is never going to get solved?'

'Because it's one of those cases with several blind alleys. It doesn't help that everyone seems to be hiding something either,' Sian said. 'On paper the Hardakers and the Cravens are two normal, hard-working families. Their neighbours can't praise them highly enough, their friends and family love them, there is nothing that opens them up to being a target apart from the affair.'

'The only people affected by that are Alice Hardaker and Martin Craven, and they both have alibis.'

'So we have no suspects, no leads, and no evidence. Well I don't know about you two boys but I certainly feel proud of a job well done today,' Sian said heavy with sarcasm.

Rory stood up to leave when Sian stopped him.

'Rory, you said you saved the best until last. Lois's affair with Owen didn't sound too steamy to me.'

'Well you interrupted before I could get to the best bit. I was going to tell you about the time Owen and Lois were cautioned for dogging but I'll not bother now.'

He left the room with a smug smile on his face. Sian leaned back in her chair looking dejected.

'That's your fault,' she said to Aaron, taking back her Bourbon biscuits.

THIRTY-THREE

Trying to park on Williamson Road was almost impossible. It was a short, narrow road with cars on both sides. Matilda had to park around the corner and make her way to Martin Craven's house on foot. By the time she reached the front door she was cold; the spring breeze had increased to a stiff wind. Trees were still bare from the harsh winter and thick branches swayed and creaked as they waved.

The door was answered straightaway by fifteen-year-old Anna. She took one look at Matilda and knew that the mood for the rest of the evening would depend on what information she was about to reveal.

'We're just about to have tea,' Anna said with all the moody vigour of a typical teen.

'I'm sorry for the timing but I really need to speak to your father. Is he home?'

'Of course he's home. You'd better come in.'

Anna showed Matilda into the living room and went straight upstairs. She didn't need to be told this was going to be a private conversation. She obviously didn't want to hear about what was happening with her mother.

'Mr Craven, I'm sorry for calling so late but I was wondering if I could have a word?'

Martin was sitting on the sofa, his son next to him. Thomas was signing and saw Matilda first. He stopped and looked up at her, leaning into his father for safety at the sight of a stranger.

'Of course, come on in.' He turned to his son and signed, 'Thomas, go upstairs and play with your sister for five minutes. I'll let you know when tea is ready.'

Thomas smiled and left the room.

'Is it difficult to learn sign language?' Matilda asked, sitting down.

'It was at first but I soon picked it up.'

'Was he born deaf?'

'Yes he was. Lois had an infection while she was pregnant, they put it down to that. So, what do you want to talk about?'

'I wanted to talk to you on your own about Lois, your marriage.'

'I thought as much,' he gave a half-smile. 'Lois said you'd been to see her afterwards to talk in private. I knew she wouldn't have told you everything with me there. I'll not ask what she said. What do you want to know from me?'

'Lois has had more than one affair …' Matilda began. This was a very delicate subject. She wondered how much Martin knew of his wife's indiscretions and didn't want to jump in with both feet and be the cause of a scene, especially not with his kids upstairs.

'She's had four. That I know of.'

'How did you feel when you found out?'

'I was furious. I didn't think Lois was the type.'

'Did you separate?'

Martin looked away. 'No,' he said, almost in whisper. 'I should have done. I always put my kids first and believe they should have both parents to bring them up. We had many arguments, several nights of sleeping in different rooms but I forgave her.'

'And the second time?'

Martin gave a loud sigh. 'Are you married?'

Matilda's heart skipped a beat. 'No. I'm not,' was all she said.

She couldn't bring herself to refer to herself as a widow just yet.

'It's easy to sit there and judge but until it happens you never know what you're going to do. I never thought I'd put up with a wife who cheated and slept around, but when it came out I just thought of my kids. I couldn't put Jack and Anna through a divorce. It would have destroyed them.'

'I'm not judging you Martin. What about when Lois became pregnant with Thomas?'

'When she first told me she was pregnant I almost fell through the floor. I thought that was the end. It was the final slap in the face. I threw her out. I was outraged.'

'How did the children react?'

'They were upset that their mother had left, but I explained that we couldn't live together anymore but that we both loved them and they would always come first. I shouldn't really have said that. I had no idea how Lois felt but I could hardly tell them their mother was a slag who slept with any man who smiled at her.'

'If that's how you felt, why did you take her back?'

Martin suddenly exploded. 'Because I'm weak and pathetic, that's why. She slept with three other men, got pregnant by one of them and I still loved her. I'm a doormat. I let her walk all over me, wipe her feet on me, and I still loved her and wanted her living in my house.' Angry tears fell down his face.

'What you did was very brave,' she placated. 'You took on another man's child as your own. Not many would have done that.'

'Brave or gullible? Once again she's got me where she wants me. She knows now that she can do anything she wants and I'll take her back because that's what I do.'

Matilda left it at that. She allowed the silence to grow while Martin composed himself. He was angry, but who with? His wife for her constant betrayals or himself for allowing her to get away with it?

216

'Did you know about Kevin Hardaker?'

'No. I honestly thought she was playing tennis. Naive aren't I?'

'Did you know him?'

'No.'

'Does the name Gerald Beecham mean anything to you?'

'No. Who's he? Another one of Lois's lovers to come out of the woodwork?'

'No. It's not important. I'm sorry to have brought up painful memories for you.'

'You haven't. They're always there. Sometimes they're hidden, like when I'm playing with Thomas or when I'm at work, but they're always there just waiting to come out and slap me in the face.'

I know that feeling.

Matilda dug in her inside pocket for a business card and handed it to him. 'If you think of anything about who you might think is responsible, or if you just want to talk, give me a ring.' She smiled at him warmly.

'Thank you. I will,' he said, looking her in the eye and smiling back.

Matilda stood up and headed for the door to leave but stopped and turned back. 'I was married. My husband died.'

'I'm sorry.'

'To be honest with you, if my husband had cheated, I probably would have forgiven him too. I loved him so much that I sometimes ached when we weren't together. I'll see myself out.'

THIRTY-FOUR

While Alice Hardaker had been at the police station her sister Jenny had been tidying up the house as best she could. The threatening phone call had been preying on her mind. She had told Alice the second she walked back through the door. Although Alice told her not to worry, it was obvious she was scared for her life and those of her children.

As darkness fell, Jenny went around the rooms closing the curtains while Alice settled the children in front of the television for the hour before it was time for them to go to bed. After that it would be their turn to play with the remote.

It seemed strange for Alice to be in the house with the knowledge that her husband wouldn't be coming home. It was usually around this time – 6.30 – when she'd hear him pull up on the drive, his key in the lock, the sound of him wiping his shoes on the mat so as not to stain the recently laid hall carpet. She tried to grieve. She wanted to be upset at the thought of never seeing his face again but every time she tried she pictured him with another woman. If he hadn't had an affair he wouldn't have got himself shot and killed in the first place. This was all his fault. Why should she waste tears on a lying, cheating, piece of shit like Kevin Hardaker?

Jenny entered the kitchen, closing the door behind her. She went to the fridge and brought out a bottle of wine.

'Would you like a glass?' she asked her sister, who was sitting on the leather sofa in the corner of the room.

'I'd like the whole bottle,' she said.

Jenny brought the bottle and two glasses over to the sofa and sat down next to her sister.

The kitchen was a recent add-on to the house. It was less than two years since the extension was built to provide them with a larger kitchen, utility room and conservatory. This had been Alice's dream kitchen with large bi-folding doors to open in the summer so they could have their meals at the table yet feel like they were outside. Unfortunately, this was Sheffield. There weren't many days when the weather was good enough for al fresco dining.

'Thanks for tidying the house up.'

'No problem. Are you OK?'

'No. I don't think I'll ever be OK again.'

'Have you told Warren and Milly about their dad yet?'

'No. I've no idea what I'm going to say. Every time I try I just dry up.'

'Would you like me to be there with you when you do?'

Alice turned to her sister and gave her a smile. 'I'd love that, thank you.'

'What are you going to do about this guy who wants ten thousand pounds by the end of today?'

Alice sighed. 'I haven't got a clue. I've no idea why he thinks he's owed this money. Why now? Kevin is murdered and then this guy shows up begging for money from us. I don't understand it at all.'

'I was thinking about Lucas earlier while I was tidying up. He knows some pretty dodgy people. Maybe he's got himself tangled up in something he can't get out of. Neither of us have seen him in ages; we don't know what he's up to.'

'Maybe we should call him.'

'I tried. I've called his flat and either he's had the phone cut off or taken out but the number wouldn't connect. I called the garage where he worked and his boss had a go at me; said he'd like to know where the bloody hell he is too. Then I called The Red Lion. I know someone who works behind the bar. She said Lucas hasn't been in for weeks.'

'It sounds like he's in hiding or something.'

'But from who? Or what? Alice, we could be talking gangsters here.'

'Oh come off it, Jenny. You've been watching too much *Peaky Blinders*.'

'I'm serious, Alice. You think this ten grand business is down to Kevin, maybe it isn't. Maybe it's all to do with Lucas.'

Alice's face was drawn. If she was on her own, she'd put up with anything from Kevin and Lucas, fight to the death if she had to, but she had two children to worry about. She couldn't allow them to be caught up in all this.

'I heard from Phil today,' Jenny said, sensing her sister would appreciate a change in topic. 'He phoned me while you were out. He wants to come back.'

'What did you say?'

'I told him to piss off. We can't live together. He winds me up and I wind him up and we end up fighting. I told him it's time to move on.'

'What did he say to that?'

'There wasn't much he could say. I'm not having him back. End of story.'

'Good for you.'

'Alice, would you like me to stay here with you for a few days, help with the kids and things around the house?'

'You don't need to do that. You've got your own life.'

'My life sucks. And the plumbing's on the blink again.'

Alice laughed. 'I thought there'd be a catch in it somewhere. Of course you can stay.'

Jenny topped up her glass and took a long swig. They allowed the silence to envelope them.

'Jenny, you know that nice policeman, DC Glass?'

'The tall one with the designer stubble?'

'Yes. Lucas assaulted him. He's in a coma.'

'Shit, Alice. Why didn't you say?'

'I don't know. I can't get my head around any of this.'

'They'll definitely get him now. The police won't rest until he's locked up. You know what they're like when anything happens to one of their own.'

'I know. They want him for these burglaries that are going on too. I didn't know what to tell them. He's our brother but I hardly see him, except when he wants something. When was the last time you actually saw him?'

Jenny blew out her cheeks. 'Blimey, let me think. A good couple of months back. Yes, I was in Bungalows and Bears with Josie. You know, her whose mother faked that fall on the tram to get compensation? Anyway, we were having a few drinks and Lucas walked in with a few of his mates from work. He's put on some weight since I saw him last. He said hello, asked me to lend him twenty quid and tried to chat up Josie.'

'He's not changed then?'

'He'll never change. He'll be back in prison again before too long now.'

Alice slapped her hands down on her lap. 'You know what, sod all this. Sod Lucas and Kevin and Phil and men full stop. We'll tackle anything that comes along and move on. Now, do you fancy something to eat? I'm feeling peckish.'

'I could do with something, yes. What do you fancy?'

'Shall I just put some chips in the oven and we can make a couple of butties?'

Jenny licked her lips. 'I like the sound of that. Plenty of salt and vinegar too.'

They both hoisted themselves up out of the comfortable sofa

and went about making their food. Alice turned on the oven to heat up while Jenny went to the freezer for the oven chips. When Alice turned around she let out a scream that she quickly stifled by slapping a hand to her mouth.

'What's up?' Jenny asked. 'You almost made me pi—' She followed her sister's eyeline and looked out of the large windows, stopping in her tracks when she saw what had frightened Alice.

Standing in front of the window was a man dressed from head to toe in black. His beanie hat came down to his eyebrows and he had a toughened plastic mask over his mouth. He stood there glaring at them through the glass.

'Who is it?' Jenny eventually asked in a whisper.

'I think it's the bloke who came the other night.'

'Oh shit, Alice. What are we going to do?'

'I don't know.'

'Is the door locked?'

'I think so.'

'Right. He can't get in then. I think we should run, get the kids, go upstairs, lock ourselves in the en suite and call the police.'

Jenny edged towards the door while Alice remained rooted to the spot. Her gaze fixed on the huge statue of a man standing at the glass doors.

Jenny was visibly shaking. 'Alice, what are you waiting for?'

From behind him, the intruder produced a gun, which he used to knock loudly on the glass with.

Jenny cried out and dropped the bag of chips she had been gripping. She ran over to Alice and hid behind her.

The intruder banged harder on the glass with the gun and the whole pane shook. Any harder and it would break.

'I'm going to have to let him in,' Alice said.

'No, Alice, don't. Please.'

'He could break the glass.'

'Your kids are in the living room. What if he hurts them?'

'Shit,' she said under her breath. Slowly, Alice held out her hands to show the masked man she wasn't armed, and made her way over to the doors. 'What do you want?' She tried to sound confident and in control but the worry in her voice was evident.

'I want to come in.'

'I'm not opening these doors.'

'I will shoot if I have to.'

Alice smirked. 'The neighbours will hear and call the police. You won't be in here long before they arrive.'

'I'll be in there long enough to cut your daughter open.'

Alice recoiled in horror and Jenny burst into tears.

'You let me in now and we have a chat, just the three of us. If I have to smash my way in, then I'm going to beat you both senseless and make you watch while I slice into your kids. Do you understand?'

Alice turned to look at her sister. Jenny had both hands clasped over her mouth. The tears flowing down her face and she was shaking her head, begging, pleading with Alice not to let him in.

'I have to,' Alice said. She took the key from her back pocket and inserted it into the lock. 'Promise me you won't hurt my children.'

'I have no interest in hurting you or your kids. That's not why I'm here.'

She closed her eyes and turned the key in the lock. The sound it made echoed around the kitchen.

The man quickly entered, closed the door behind him and locked it, removing the key and placing it in his own pocket.

'Go and sit down on the sofa. Now. Both of you.'

Jenny couldn't move. Alice had to practically drag her to the sofa. They sat down and held each other firmly for support.

The masked man looked around the kitchen. He ran his fingers along the oak wooden surfaces, opened cupboard doors and looked inside. He walked over to the sofa, dragging a stool with him which he straddled.

'Now then, where's my money?' His voice was muffled behind the mask.

'Look, I've no idea what you're talking about, honestly I don't. I don't owe anyone any money and I've looked through my husband's things and I can't find anything about him owing anyone money.'

'This has nothing to do with your husband. It's to do with you and your bastard of a brother.'

'Lucas? I've not seen him for ages. He only comes here when he wants something. He's living above a shop in Wincobank, the last I heard.'

'I know. I've been there and there was nobody in. I broke the door down, had a look round, and nothing. He hasn't got anything worth nicking. So I torched the place.'

'Oh my God,' Jenny wailed.

'You must be the other sister,' the masked man said. He turned to her and with a leather-gloved hand he wrenched her hands away from her face. 'Look at me. Come on, look up. Let me see you.'

Slowly, Jenny lifted her head. Her eyes were red and puffy from crying. She tried not to make eye contact with him, just a couple of quick glances before turning away.

'That's better. You're not as good-looking as your sister but I still wouldn't say no.' He leaned in close, his face mere centimetres from hers. She could feel his hot breath on her cheek. 'We could have fun together, you and me. I could make you forget that wanker of a husband of yours.' Jenny's eyes widened in horror. 'Oh yes, I know all about you and Phil. You don't need him: he's a tosser. You need a real man to show you a good time.'

'Leave me alone,' she cried.

'It's up to you bitch. I either fuck you with this,' he grabbed his crotch. 'Or I fuck you with this,' he pressed the gun hard between Jenny's legs. She almost collapsed. She wanted to scream out loud for anyone to hear but the thought of Alice's children in the living room watching television stopped her.

Alice slapped the intruder on the shoulder. 'You promised you wouldn't hurt us. Leave her alone.'

'You're right. I'm sorry. I'm just having a bit of fun. Now, here's my final warning, Alice. Next time I come I won't knock on the door, I won't wait for you to unlock it, I'll just come bursting in and I'll take whatever I can and do whatever damage I can and that includes to your fucking kids. Do you understand me?'

'I have no idea what you're talking about,' Alice cried. She didn't care what happened to her. It was her children she worried about.

'You've got until the end of the month, that's less than a week away, to find your brother and put your heads together and get me the fifteen grand you now both owe me. Capisce?'

Alice nodded. She couldn't think of anything else to say to him. As far as she was concerned she didn't owe him, or anyone else any money. She just wanted him out of her house and away from her children.

'Good girl. I'll be seeing you.'

He glared at them both until he'd had his fun and then left. He unlocked the back door, went out into the garden and locked the door, taking the key with him. He now had a way in whenever he wanted it.

Alice and Jenny collapsed into each other's arms, both of them crying uncontrollably.

THIRTY-FIVE

Matilda wasn't concentrating on the traffic ahead. It was moving slowly at a steady twenty-five miles per hour. She kept a good distance between her own silver Ford Focus and whatever was in front. Leaning back in the driver's seat she had one hand on the steering wheel and the other propping up her head, leaning against the door. Her eyes were forever darting between one wing mirror and the other and the rear-view mirror, searching for any sign of a dark-coloured BMW.

Since leaving Martin Craven's home on Williamson Road she kept thinking of her marriage with James. Would she have been able to forgive him for having an affair? Maybe he had had one and Matilda hadn't known about it. *No.* She shook her head hard, almost veering the car off the road. *Don't think like that.*

She turned into Millhouses Lane and parked neatly in the driveway. She should put the car in the garage, but she didn't like the door closing behind her and plunging her into darkness, especially recently with the anonymous note and phone calls.

Matilda unlocked the front door and walked in. The alarm sounded and she turned it off. The number was the same as her wedding anniversary. She should consider changing it if she was ever going to move on from thinking of James, but wouldn't it feel like trying to forget him?

Her stomach rumbled and she tried to remember the last time she had had something to eat, probably breakfast. She should cook something, even if it was just beans on toast or an omelette, but she wasn't in the mood; cooking for one seemed more like a chore than a necessity.

Matilda kicked her shoes off and walked into the living room, flicking on the light. She was presented with the boxes of books left to her by Jonathan Harkness. Why had he done that? What was she going to do with thousands of hardback and paperback novels? She was surrounded by crime during her working life, why would she want to read about it in the evening?

The living room was a place where she would sit in the evenings, curled up on the sofa, and go through the pages of her wedding album while reminiscing and crying. She'd talk to her husband pictured in the silver frame on top of the mantelpiece and fall asleep on the sofa with him in her arms. With the boxes taking up all of the floor space, and on a few of the armchairs too, how could she be comfortable? It would be like sitting in a warehouse.

She went to the nearest one and picked up the first paperback she could get her hands on – *Eeny Meeny* by M. J. Arlidge. She smiled at the title. Flicking through the book she noticed the chapters were short, a fast-paced read. Turning back to the beginning she started reading. The protagonist, Helen Grace, was a Detective Inspector with as much on her mind as Matilda, though her way of relieving stress was a little more risqué than reciting British Prime Ministers.

Matilda closed the book. For a brief second she wondered if there were any dominators in Sheffield. Of course there would be. No. That was not going to happen. She threw the book back in the box and left the room. She would continue to read it, however, at some point.

She closed the door on the living room and went into the

kitchen. She couldn't tackle Jonathan's obsessive collection on an empty stomach. It was a shame she'd promised Adele she wouldn't drink alone; she could have done with a large glass of vodka poured straight from the freezer.

In the fridge was the remainder of the Carbonnade a la Flamande. Matilda rolled her eyes. She didn't want to eat another portion of it but hated to waste perfectly good food. She threw it in the microwave and went to make herself a black coffee.

The phone rang making her jump. She hoped this wouldn't be another abusive call. She would almost rather it be Rory telling her a body had been found.

'Hello,' she answered. Her tone was uneasy.

There was no reply. She waited for a few long seconds and swore she could hear the distinctive sound of breathing.

'Hello,' she said again, louder this time. 'Is there anyone there?'

'Carl Meagan, Joseph Glass, Scott Andrews. They're dropping like flies around you aren't they?'

'What? Who is this?'

'People don't seem to stay alive long around you do they? Does that remind you of anyone?'

She listened intently. She couldn't make out the voice. It sounded muffled as if the caller was speaking through a mask or handkerchief. 'No. Should it?'

'Jonathan Harkness said the same thing. People who tried to get close to him ended up dead, one way or another. The same thing is happening to you isn't it? Even James only lasted seven years.'

Matilda gripped the phone tight at the mention of her husband's name. 'Who the hell are you? You know absolutely nothing. You're just a sad, sick—'

'No. You're wrong. I know everything about you, Detective Chief Inspector Matilda Darke. You're dangerous. How many more people are going to have unfortunate accidents or die because of your incompetence?'

The caller hung up.

Matilda was left shaking. She dropped the phone and held on to the kitchen worktop to steady herself. She wanted to collapse. She wanted to throw up but she had nothing in her stomach to bring up.

The microwave pinged to signal her dinner was ready. She pulled open the door, grabbed the hot plate and threw the whole lot to the other side of the room releasing a loud scream of anger. The plate shattered against the back wall splattering beef stew on the ceiling, floor, and walls.

Matilda stumbled from the kitchen and into the living room. She wanted to hold her husband. Even though it was just a photograph, looking into those smiling icy blue eyes made things marginally better. As she opened the door she ran into the boxes.

'You bastard, Jonathan Harkness. Why the fuck did you have to inflict all these on me? I'm going to burn the fucking lot of them!'

Matilda opened her eyes. She was surrounded by darkness but there was something piercing the black, something flashing.

'Matilda?'

'James?' she answered.

'Matilda, it's me. Are you all right?' Adele turned on the light in the hallway. She'd used her key to gain entry.

She dropped her bag onto the floor and ran over to Matilda who was on the floor – half in the hallway and half in the lounge.

'What happened? Have you collapsed?' She helped her up and onto the sofa. 'You look shattered.'

'I … I …What time is it?'

'Just after eight o'clock.'

'In the morning?'

'At night,' she laughed. 'Matilda, what happened? You were on the floor.'

'I ran into the boxes and fell over. I couldn't be bothered to get up. I just lay there and I must have nodded off.'

'But you're all right?'

'Yes I'm fine. Well, apart from the phone call.'

'Who from?'

'I don't know. A man. He said I was dangerous. He said I was just like Jonathan Harkness and that people die around me.'

'That's nonsense. Matilda, don't let him get to you. It's just some sick individual with nothing better to do than try to scare people. You can't let them win. Don't let them see that it's getting to you.'

'But he's right,' she said, looking up at her friend. 'Carl Meagan, Joseph Glass, Scott Andrews. Look at what's happened to them.'

'Joseph and Scott are not dead and nobody knows what's happened to Carl.'

'Oh my God,' Matilda said, sitting up straight. 'What if the caller is the kidnapper? Maybe he's making contact, taunting me, telling me he's got Carl. He knows he won't get the ransom money now so he's playing with me, trying to keep the upper hand.'

'I don't think so, Matilda,' Adele said. Like the majority of people, Adele thought Carl Meagan was probably dead. Once the kidnappers fled without their money they would have killed Carl and dumped his body somewhere. It was just a question of where.

'You don't know that.' She stood up. 'There could be … what's happening outside?' She pointed to the window at the reflection of the flashing blue lights.

'Matilda, sit back down.'

'What's happened?'

'What do you know about your neighbours?'

'Very little. I'm never here. Why?'

'The police had a phone call about half an hour ago from a woman saying she had killed her husband.'

'What? Surely not. She's in her eighties.'

'The other side. Jill Carmichael.'

'What? No!'

'She says her husband has been hitting her for years and she just snapped. Matilda, she's stabbed her husband.'

'Oh my God.'

'She's asking to speak to you.'

Matilda had never been in Jill Carmichael's house before, she had no cause to, and, for some reason, expected it to be a mirror image of her own. She was wrong. Adele led her into the living room, which was a buzz of activity: uniformed officers and white-suited scene of crime officers were milling around while DI Christian Brady, looking harassed, was aimlessly looking around.

'Matilda, thank God. I didn't realize you lived next door until Adele mentioned it,' Brady said.

'Christian. What's happened?'

'Jill is asking for you. She won't speak to anyone but she says you'll understand.'

'Understand what? I don't know them. We say hello on the doorstep when we meet, that's about it.'

'Well she won't talk to anyone else.'

'Where is she?'

'In the kitchen.'

'Right. OK.'

Christian led the way into the kitchen at the back of the house, half the size of Matilda's. Jill was sitting on a pine chair. She was visibly shaking and staring into the distance. There was a red stain of blood on her chest. A female uniformed officer was standing next to her with a cup of tea in her hand.

'Jill,' Matilda said quietly to rouse her from her stupor.

She jumped. 'Oh my God, Matilda, thank God you're here.' She was crying, her tears falling freely down her red, stained face. 'I'm so sorry, Matilda. I tried to tell you so many times. I wanted to tell you but I couldn't. I kept thinking of everything you'd

231

been through lately. You wouldn't want to put up with my problems too. I'm so sorry.'

'Jill, calm down. Sit back down and tell me what happened.'

The police officer helped her back into the chair. Jill wiped her nose with her sleeve and tried to compose herself.

'My husband hits me. He has done for years. I haven't taken up kick-boxing again. This is from him,' she pointed to her left eye. 'I thought he'd stop when we had a baby. He didn't touch me at all when I was pregnant so I thought it was all over with. He started again the other week. He called me fat and pathetic. He said I'd be a terrible mother and that maybe I should go back to work, and his mother would move in and look after her. I couldn't have that. I'm the mum.'

Jill became uncontrollable; the sobs and the words mingled to make a heart-wrenching sound. Matilda pulled her close and wrapped her arm around her.

Quietly, Matilda said to DI Brady. 'I did notice a bruise on her eye the other day. She said she'd been kick-boxing. I should have known something was wrong.'

'You weren't to know.'

'I noticed the black eye too,' Adele said. 'I didn't think anything of it.'

'Where's the baby?' Matilda asked.

'Her sister lives in the next road. She came and took her.'

'What happened here tonight?' Matilda turned back to the shaking Jill.

'I was in the kitchen feeding Judi. He came home and asked why I didn't have any dinner ready. I told him I'd do it as soon as I'd finished. He hit me on the back with his briefcase. I screamed. You should have seen Judi's face. She looked so terrified. Her little nose wrinkled and her eyes widened. I thought about what kind of a house she would grow up in if I didn't do something about it. I didn't want her to have the same life I had. I just grabbed the nearest thing I could find and hit him with it. What did I hit him with?'

Brady and Matilda looked at each other with worried glances.

'You stabbed him, Jill,' Matilda said.

'Stabbed him? With a knife?'

'Yes.'

'Is he going to be all right?'

'We don't know yet,' she lied, looking to Christian who just shook his head. 'Look, Jill, I'm going to leave you with DI Brady here. He'll look after you.'

'OK. Will you feed my cat for me?' She looked up. Her tears had stopped but her face was stained and pale.

'Of course.'

'What's going to happen to her?' Matilda asked, pulling Brady to one side.

'I don't know. I'll get a doctor to take a look at her. We'll go from there. A good lawyer will get her off with self-defence.'

'I can't believe this. I cannot believe this was going on right next door and I had no idea.'

'Do you know your neighbours well?'

'Not really. We say hello when we see each other and send Christmas cards. That's about it.'

'Then don't blame yourself.'

'They seemed like such a happy couple. When they were out together they were always smiling, holding hands.'

'That was the husband controlling the wife. She was probably screaming inside.'

'She had looked strange lately. I thought she was suffering from some sort of post-natal depression. She was obviously wanting to tell me about Sebastian, what he was doing to her. How many cases of domestic abuse have I dealt with over the years? I should have noticed it.'

'Christian's right, Mat,' Adele said. 'You can't blame yourself. When you're on the outside looking in you see things a lot differently.'

Matilda moved away and slowly headed for the exit. She

bumped into a scene of crime officer but didn't apologize. Her mind was full of dark thoughts.

'Mat, where are you going?' Adele asked.

'I need a drink.'

THIRTY-SIX

Matilda hadn't been able to sleep much. She didn't fall asleep so much as lose consciousness and woke just three hours later lying face down on top of the duvet, still wearing her clothes from the previous day.

She couldn't get Jill Carmichael out of her head. They seemed like such a happy couple; hard-working, friendly, loving parents – they were the ideal neighbours; like the Cravens and the Hardakers. They never had late-night parties, never made any noise and didn't allow their garden to grow into a wild abandon, unlike Matilda. They didn't stand out in any way, which is why they managed to slip under the radar and the horrific domestic abuse Jill suffered went unnoticed.

'I've taken up kick-boxing again. I'm trying to lose the last few pregnancy pounds.'

Those words echoed around Matilda's mind in the hours of darkness. She should have seen through such an obvious lie. Had Jill been trying to communicate with her on a subconscious level, crying out for help?

Matilda pictured Jill standing next to her car, clutching the baby to her chest. She gave her excuse for the black eye, but was there something else; an underlying statement that should have been obvious to a detective? Did she widen her eyes? Did she mouth something? Was she pleading to Matilda to probe further? It had been dark though and Matilda had other things on her mind. She always had other things on her mind, usually her own worries. She was letting her grief and paranoia flood her mind and stop her from seeing the more important things going on around her. Her neighbour had killed her husband and Matilda should have seen it coming.

Things were going to change. While showering, Matilda made the decision that she would have to put James and Carl Meagan on the back-burner. She had a very disturbing case to try and solve and needed to be one hundred per cent focused. There was no room for error.

After a quick breakfast, and her prescription medication flung into her bag in case she needed an extra kick at some point in the day, she drove to work. For the first time in as long as she could remember, she felt strong, determined, motivated. Today she was going to make a real breakthrough in the case. She knew it. She could feel it.

'Detective Chief Inspector Darke?'

Matilda heard her name being called the second she climbed out of her car at the front of the police station. She turned at the sound of the unfamiliar voice. Standing at the entrance to the station was a casually dressed young man: dark jeans, check shirt and loose tie.

'Yes,' she said.

The man approached holding out his hand for her to shake. 'Alex Winstanley. *Sheffield Star*. It's a pleasure to finally meet you.'

The fake smile Matilda had been wearing suddenly dropped. She refused to shake his hand. Was this the journalist who had been causing all the trouble? He was a child.

'I don't think I have anything to say to you, Mr Winstanley.'

'Alex, please. How's the investigation into the double shooting going?'

'You will receive updates on that as and when we are able to give them,' she said, making her way to the main entrance of the station.

'I hear you've had a problem with some of your officers.'

'I'm sorry?' She stopped on the steps and turned to face her young inquisitor.

'DC Glass and DC Andrews were involved in accidents,' he said, giving stress to 'accidents' as if he was using air quotes.

'DC Glass was injured in the line of duty. DC Andrews suffered minor injuries due to a speeding car.'

'A double shooting. A series of extremely violent burglaries. Two DCs admitted to hospital while on duty. Sheffield appears to be a very dangerous place to live at the moment, wouldn't you agree?'

'No I would not.'

'Look, Detective Chief Inspector, I'll level with you. I'm new to this area. I've only been in Sheffield a few months and I don't intend to spend my entire career working on a local newspaper. I've spent a lot of time researching you and you interest me a great deal. We could help each other out here.'

'How can you help me?' Matilda asked folding her arms.

'It's obvious you need a positive article written about you right now to show people you're perfectly capable of keeping them safe. I could do that. I could write a feature about you: what makes you tick; how you go about solving your cases, etcetera. In return you could give me a few advanced snippets on the double shooting and the burglaries. Give me a heads-up.'

'Do you honestly expect me to feed you information about current cases?'

'You scratch my back.'

'Mr Winstanley—'

'Alex, please.'

'Mr Winstanley, I have absolutely no desire to scratch your back. You can write anything about me in your newspaper and it won't bother me in the slightest. I, and my bosses, know I am capable of performing my duties to the best of my abilities. I chase criminals and I catch them. I don't need someone like you, a boy in a man's world, writing an obvious feature so transparent that the most simple-minded individual could see straight through it. Now, run along, or you'll be late for PE.'

She found it hard to hide her smile as she turned and went into the building. As she disappeared through the doors, she could feel the death rays Alex Winstanley was shooting out of his eyes burning right through her. She couldn't fail to admire his ambition, but he had chosen the wrong person to try and wrap around his grubby little finger.

The atmosphere in the Murder Room seemed lighter. Maybe it was Matilda being in a more confident frame of mind that gave the world around her a brighter tinge.

She went into her office at the back of the room and had just settled into her chair behind the desk when Sian knocked on the door and walked in.

'Morning Matilda, are you OK?'

'Yes I'm fine. Why?'

'I heard about what happened with your neighbour.'

'Bloody hell, this place is like a call centre. Did you want anything specific?' Matilda was keen to get off the subject of what was happening to her outside of working hours.

'I've had George Rainsford's wife on the phone—'

'Who's he?'

'He found Lois and Kevin on Clough Lane,' Matilda nodded her understanding. 'Apparently, George isn't coping well with what he witnessed and she wondered if someone could go around and see him. I remember the counsellor we had working here a couple of years ago left in the budget cuts, but did we replace her?'

Matilda thought for a second. 'I'm not sure.' She opened the top drawer of her desk and looked around for something. Finding it, she handed Sian a business card. 'Tell his wife to give this woman a call. She will definitely be able to help.'

Sian looked at the card. 'Doctor Sheila Warminster, psychotherapist. Is she any good?'

'She is actually,' Matilda said. 'What's wrong with Rory?' Matilda looked past Sian and out into the main office. She didn't want her probing into Matilda's knowledge of psychotherapists.

'Nothing, why?'

'He's got a face like a slapped arse. He's usually so bubbly and annoying. I think this is the first time I've seen him without a gormless grin on his face.'

'Oh. It's nothing. He and Amelia have had a bit of a row. He wants to get married this year; she thinks they should wait. It's a storm in a teacup.'

'Fair enough. Any news from the hospital about DC Glass?'

'No. I called first thing and he's still in a coma. I spoke to his mum and she says the doctors say there's no medical reason why he won't wake up.'

'Strange. Have they said how long he'll be like that?'

'I've no idea.'

'What about brain damage?'

'They don't know yet. I suppose until the brain is active it's difficult to tell. We're holding a whip-round if you want to donate anything.'

Matilda took her purse out of her bag and looked inside. It was the usual mess of screwed up receipts and store cards. She only had two notes in there, both twenty pounds. She handed them over to Sian.

'What are you planning on buying?'

'I don't know. Me and Aaron were talking and, depending on how much we raise, we might just give it to his parents for them to buy anything he may need.'

'Good idea.'

There was a commotion coming from the main incident room. Matilda looked out of her window and saw everyone crowding around DC Scott Andrews who had just walked in. She opened the door and went to join them.

'Scott, nice to see you back. How are you feeling?'

'I'm fine thanks. Glad to be back.' He looked embarrassed to be the centre of attention and his cheeks blushed.

'Have you been to see the ACC?'

'Yes. I've just come from there.'

'Look at that gash on your forehead,' Rory said. 'That's going to leave a great scar. The girls love a scar.'

'Do we?' Sian asked.

'Of course you do. You love it when you know a man's been all heroic and macho. It's a huge turn on.'

Matilda and Sian exchanged glances. 'I don't know what magazines you're reading Rory, but I'd give them up if I were you,' Sian said moving back to her desk.

While the attention was off Scott, he slinked away over to his desk. He made eye contact with Matilda, who gave him a smile and mouthed 'welcome back'. He even blushed at that.

'Right then, that's enough fun for now. Can everyone settle down please?'

Matilda, standing at the top of the room in front of the whiteboards, looked out upon the troop assembled before her. Not exactly a troop, more of a small gathering of concerned parties. Despite the ACC promising to have more officers drafted in to the MIT they seemed conspicuous by their absence.

'Any developments overnight?'

Aaron, swallowing a large bite of a bacon sandwich and licking his fingers said, 'there's still no sight of Lucas Branning. However, his flat was torched yesterday.'

'I thought it was being watched?' Matilda asked.

'Only until yesterday lunchtime.'

'How bad is it?'

'It's been gutted.'

'Deliberate?'

'It looks like it. The fire officers say there are traces of an accelerant on the doormat.'

'Either Lucas has some powerful enemies or there was something in his flat he didn't want us to see and torched it himself,' Matilda said, thinking aloud. 'Are we sure his sisters don't know where he is?'

'That's what they're saying.'

'Right. Sian, go round to Alice's this morning, take Faith with you, tell her about her brother's home being torched and try and get as much out of her about Lucas as possible. This is one loose end we don't need right now and it's starting to really piss me off.'

'Will do.'

'Has anyone been looking into Lucas Branning's background?'

'I have,' Rory said, flicking through his notebook. 'He's been in jail three times. The first was when he was twenty, in 1991, for six months. He burgled his next-door neighbour and his grandmother. The second time was in 1995. He stole his boss's Mercedes and went on a joyride. He crashed into a bus stop, narrowly missing four people. He fled the scene and was later picked up in a bar. He was also banned from driving for three years. His last jail spell was in 2001. He was sentenced to three years for burgling seven properties in a month. He served his full term as the parole board believed him to be a recidivist.'

'Well he sounds like a delight. I bet his family are very proud of him,' Sian commented.

'What's he been up to since his release?' Matilda asked. 'I find it hard to believe a recidivist has kept his nose clean for fifteen years.'

'He's had a few scrapes with the law for fighting while drunk but apart from that, he really does seem to have been a good boy,' Rory said. 'Maybe he has turned over a new leaf.'

'And maybe I'm a size eight. What about the Cravens? Do they have any dodgy family members who could be our killer?'

'No,' Aaron said. 'They're like the Waltons.'

'I must have missed that episode where Ma Walton had multiple affairs and a child with another man,' Sian said, raising a giggle from around the room.

'You know what I mean. There's nothing in their backgrounds to attract the attention of a killer.'

'So what are we saying then, this is a random event? A killer just happened to come across Kevin and Lois and killed them for kicks?' Matilda asked of no one specific.

'Judging by the lack of suspects it would appear so.'

'No. I refuse to believe that,' Matilda was getting riled. 'Like we said before, if this was a random killing Kevin and Lois would have been shot dead where they sat in the car, not subjected to torture. No. The killer was known to them. There must be something in their shared lives that seriously pissed someone off.'

'Well if there is it's so deeply hidden we haven't uncovered it yet,' Sian said. 'We've been through their bank accounts, savings, debts. We've contacted friends, relatives, neighbours, former schoolmates – nobody has a motive to kill them.'

Matilda released a heavy sigh. Her positivity was beginning to wane. She turned and saw the smiling photograph of Gerald Beecham staring back at her. 'And where does Mr Beecham fit into all this?'

When the room remained silent, Rory chimed up, 'Maybe Lois decided to have a taste of a more mature meat.'

'Thanks Rory,' Matilda replied, rolling her eyes. 'So—'

There was a knock on the door and Faith stepped inside. 'Am I all right to interrupt?'

'Of course you are. What can we do for you?'

'There was another robbery last night. This time, one of the victims was killed.'

This revelation stopped everyone in their tracks.

THIRTY-SEVEN

SECRET AFFAIR OF SHOOTING VICTIMS
By Alex Winstanley

The victims of the shooting in Clough Lane were having an illicit affair. Lois Craven and Kevin Hardaker were viciously attacked by a masked assailant in the quiet lane close to the Peak District National Park. Mr Hardaker, 43, was shot twice and died at the scene. Mrs Craven, 41, was shot three times and is currently recovering in the Northern General Hospital.

Friends and family members of the two have since found out about the pair's secret love and commented that both families, and their communities, have been shocked by the news.

Dora Leeves, a neighbour of the Craven family said yesterday: 'I have known the Cravens for years. They always seemed like a loving, happy family. The kids have always been so well behaved. I can't believe Lois was having an affair. It's really knocked me for six. It's shocked everyone in the road.'

Lois, an administrator at the Sheffield College, has had

several previous affairs, according to one of her colleagues. Janet Temple said: 'Lois has been unfaithful in the past. I felt sorry for her husband and the kids, but Lois was just one of those women who enjoyed life and enjoyed having fun. Yes, it was wrong what she's done but she didn't deserve what happened to her.'

Mr Craven was seen with his three children at their home in Williamson Road yesterday but was unavailable for comment.

'Bastards! Complete and utter bastards!' Martin swore, hurling the newspaper across the kitchen. It skidded and came to a stop as it hit the carpet in the hallway.

'I thought you'd want to see it before you left the house.'

Margaret had brought the newspaper round first thing. She didn't usually read the local, believing it to be a waste of money for the amount of adverts that seemed to take over each page; however, since her daughter was in hospital, she wanted to see how the story was being reported. Up until now, she had been pleased by the lack of gossip. It was only a matter of time before Lois's past indiscretions came to light.

'I can't believe this. Who around here's been talking?' Martin was fuming. He paced the kitchen, unable to control himself. 'Have you mentioned her affairs to anyone?'

'Of course I haven't, Martin. What do you take me for? They've been talking to her colleagues by the looks of it. She'll have mentioned it to them. You know what a bunch of women in an office are like.'

'They're all going to be talking aren't they?'

'Who are?'

'The neighbours. Jack used to deliver the local paper around here. Almost everyone in the street has one. They'll all see it. They'll all know that Lois has been having affairs right, left, and centre and I've just put up with it. I should never have taken her back.'

'Martin!' Margaret called out. 'If you hadn't taken her back you wouldn't have Thomas in your life. I know he's not yours but you love him like he is. Who knows what would have become of him if you hadn't been in his life.'

Martin looked up at his mother-in-law. 'You obviously don't think much of Lois either then.'

'What?'

'If I hadn't have taken Lois back she would have had Thomas and brought him up alone. Or don't you think she was capable of raising a child by herself?'

'She's not one for responsibility,' she eventually accepted. 'Oh God. I tried to do right by her. I tried to bring her up to be a responsible adult. I taught her right from wrong, taught her respect and to get a good education and a good job. Where did I go wrong with her, Martin?' Margaret slumped at the kitchen table and put her head in her hands.

'What's going on?' Jack said on entering the kitchen. He picked up the newspaper from the floor and placed it on the table, not looking at its contents.

'Nothing,' Martin lied unconvincingly. 'Shouldn't you be at college now?'

'Free period. What's happened? Is it Mum?'

'No. She's fine. Look, Jack, there are things in the press that are—'

'You mean about Mum having affairs.'

'How do you know?'

'It's all over the Internet.'

'What?'

'*The Star*'s website, Twitter, and Facebook pages.'

'Oh my God,' Martin slumped forward. 'I'm so sorry Jack. I should have realized these things were going to get raked up. I should have prepared you.'

'I don't think you can prepare. Anna's been reading some of the comments people have been saying.'

'Do I want to know?'

'No. You might want to talk to Anna though. She's pretty upset.'

'I'll go and talk to her,' Margaret said, wiping her eyes. She placed a comforting arm on Martin's shoulder as she passed him to show she cared, and hurriedly left the room.

'I'm sorry Jack.'

'Why are you apologizing? It's not your fault.'

'I'd suggest going away for a few days but I think we might need more than a long weekend to get over this.' Martin smiled through the pain.

'It's Easter in a few weeks, we could go to the coast or something.' Jack hinted.

'I don't think I'd want to come back.'

'We don't have to.' Jack leaned forward and placed a hand on top of his father's. 'Me, Anna and Thomas will all come with you wherever you want to go, Dad.'

Jenny Evans had stayed the night but had spent very little of it asleep. The ordeal of being held against her will by a masked intruder was agony and continued to replay itself over and over again in her head. Eventually she gave up on the idea of falling asleep and went downstairs to make a hot drink and find something fattening to eat.

By the time Alice woke up it was daylight and Jenny was on her third Mars Bar. 'How long have you been up?'

'All night practically.'

Jenny turned to face her sister and Alice realized she needn't have asked the question. It was written all over her face. The heavy eyelids and thick bags under the eyes were evidence of a sleepless night.

'What have you been doing all night then?'

'This.' She slid a pad across the coffee table to her sister who picked it up and began reading it.

'What is this?'

'It's as much as I can remember about that bloke last night. I'm going to take it to the police this morning and report him.'

'What? Jenny, you can't do that.'

'Why not? He threatened us. He's demanding money and he threatened to kill your kids. How can you possibly sit there so calmly and say you're not going to report it?'

'You have no idea what we're dealing with here.'

'And neither do you. Whatever it is, it's way out of our depth. We can't cope with it on our own. We need the police,' she said slowly, trying to hammer the point home to her unwavering sister.

'No.'

'Alice. Next time he comes do you think he's just going to issue a few more threats then go away again? No. He'll go further this time. He could maim, rape, kill. Are you willing to risk that on your own sister, on your own kids?'

'And what if the police can't catch him? Then he'll definitely kill us, the kids too. I can't handle any of this right now,' Alice stood up and stormed off into the kitchen. Jenny quickly followed.

'You can't just walk away and hope he decides to try his luck on another family. He will be back. You have to do something.'

'Do what?' Alice exploded. 'I have no idea what's happening. A week ago everything was fine, or rather I thought it was. Then I find out my husband has been having an affair for God knows how long and gets himself killed. Then my brother seems to have gone missing and a bloody cartoon villain comes round demanding money. When did my life become an episode of *The Sopranos*?'

Alice collapsed into the sofa in the kitchen and, with her head in her hands, began to cry a torrent of tears. Jenny sat next to her.

'I'm sorry for what you've had to go through recently, Alice, I really am, but now is not the time to go to pieces. You have to do something about this bloke or he's going to come back and all hell will be let loose.'

'Jenny, my life has been turned upside down—'

Jenny couldn't listen anymore. 'Look, Alice, I'm sorry Kevin's dead, I really am. And I'm sorry he cheated on you. But you're not the first woman in the world to find out her husband has been unfaithful, Alice. So he had an affair; it wasn't the first time for crying out loud. No man is worth tying yourself up in knots about.'

'What?' Alice looked up. Her face deathly pale. 'It wasn't the first time? You mean he's had an affair before? How do you know this?'

Jenny was silent. The look of concentration as she tried to come up with a lie or an excuse was etched on her face. Her eyes darted from left to right. She avoided her sister's glare but could feel her eyes burning into her.

'I don't,' she lied. Her voice was quiet and quivering.

'Jenny, if you lie to me,' Alice suddenly appeared calm but inside she was a seething mass of rage. 'I will throw you out of this house and I'll never want to see you ever again. Now, tell me, has Kevin had an affair before?'

Jenny couldn't speak. She nodded.

'When? Who with?'

'It was a long time ago. Before the kids were born. Remember Carole who used to lived two doors down from me? She had a part-time job at Currys where Kevin worked and they got together. It didn't last long. Only a few weeks.'

'How did you find out?'

'Carole told me she was seeing someone from work. She didn't know I knew Kevin but I worked it out from how she described him. I went to see him and told him to stop or I'd tell you. He did.'

'Why didn't you tell me?'

'You'd just found out you were pregnant with Warren and you were constantly ill with morning sickness. You had enough on your plate. I decided to deal with it myself. I was protecting you.'

'Don't you think I should have known what the father of my children was really like?'

'He promised me he'd end it and he did. I didn't think he'd do it again.'

'Which shows how much you know about men. They're all bastards, Jenny. You should know, you married two of the biggest ones around. I can't believe you didn't tell me. I'll never forgive you for this, Jenny.'

Alice shrugged off her sister's oncoming hug and walked out of the room, heading upstairs. Jenny leaned back into the sofa, cursing herself. She should have kept her mouth shut. There was no reason why Alice should ever have had to find out.

Her eyes fell on the door at the corner of the room where the masked man forced his way in last night and terrorized them both. It wouldn't be long until he was back, and, despite what Alice said, Jenny knew the next time would be a thousand times worse than last night. She had to convince her sister to go to the police. The clock was ticking.

THIRTY-EIGHT

Matilda took Faith into her office so she could fill her in on the details of the latest aggravated burglary to hit Sheffield.

'An elderly couple in Low Edges were asleep when they were woken by a noise. Mr Frank Ackersby got up and went to the top of the stairs to look down. He could see a shadow and heard drawers opening and closing. He went back into the bedroom where his wife, Trudie, was waiting. He closed the door and wedged a chair under the handle. He told her to be quiet and hopefully the robber wouldn't come up the stairs.'

'Was there no phone in the bedroom?' Matilda asked.

'No. They usually take the cordless handset up from the lounge but had forgotten. Anyway, they're in bed when they hear the sound of footsteps on the stairs. The door handle is tried, but he can't get in. They think he's given in when suddenly the door comes crashing open and the chair is literally smashed to pieces. In comes a man dressed from head to toe in black, waving a gun at them. He points it directly at Mrs Ackersby's head. Mr Ackersby sees red and jumps up to attack the gunman. The gunman pushes Mr Ackersby back and he smashes his head on the corner of the dressing table and he's dead before he hits the floor. The burglar, taking no notice of this, then goes and empties the jewellery box and drawers before running off.'

Matilda was shaking her head in disbelief at such a heartless attack. 'How's Mrs Ackersby?'

'The last I heard she had to be sedated.'

'Please tell me she gave a good description first,' Matilda said, hopefully.

'Unfortunately not. However, the bloke over the road had been up all night with chronic wisdom toothache and when he heard a loud noise, which we assume was the bedroom door being kicked in, he had a nosy out of the window.'

'And he got a good look at the bloke?'

Faith turned a page in her notebook. 'About six foot two, broad shoulders, heavy build, light brown or blond hair, pale skin, and a tattoo on his neck but he couldn't make out what it was.'

Matilda frowned while Faith looked on with a beaming smile. 'How did he know all that?'

'The bloke went to his car, opened the boot to put his bag in the back and took off his hat and mask. He was parked directly under a lamppost.'

Matilda joined Faith in a beaming smile. 'God bless the crippling pain that man is in.'

'That's exactly what DI Brady said.'

'Thanks for keeping me informed, Faith. I'm not sure what use it will be to us but it's a step in the right direction. I'll run it past Lois next time I speak to her.'

Rory burst into the office, no knock, no apology for interrupting. 'Ma'am, Lucas Branning has been found.'

'Found' wasn't the word Matilda would have used. Nobody had actually found him at all. Instead, a tired and dirty looking Lucas Branning had walked into Woodseats Police Station and given himself up. He had been arrested on suspicion of assaulting a police officer and taken to South Yorkshire Police

HQ where he was processed then led to an interview room.

The treatment he had received so far was cold and hostile. He had badly injured one of their own and that was unforgiveable. No officer showed Lucas Branning any respect or due care and attention. He was bundled into the back of a car with his hands painfully shackled behind his back and dragged out once he had reached his destination.

Sitting behind the table in interview room three, Lucas Branning looked scared and pathetic. He had several days' worth of stubble on his dirty face and his eyes had dark circles around them. His clothes were stained and creased and he had the odour of a man who had been sleeping among the dustbins for several nights.

Matilda entered the room with Aaron Connolly following. They reacted to the smell and pulled their chairs back from the table. They wanted as much distance between themselves and the interviewee as possible.

Aaron informed Lucas of his rights and told him the interview was being both recorded and videoed. He then introduced them all for the benefit of the recordings. He sat back and folded his arms, waiting for the interview to begin but Matilda remained upright. She sat in her uncomfortable chair and glared at the man sitting opposite her. He looked what he was, a loser, a waste of space, a pathetic excuse for a human. She felt nothing but contempt for the man and hoped her disdainful stare showed it.

'Do you know why you've been sent to me, Lucas?' she eventually asked.

He nodded.

'You're going to have to speak your replies for the benefit of the recordings. I'm guessing you've evolved enough to use words.'

'Yes,' he grunted.

'Yes you've evolved or yes you know why you've been brought here?'

'Yes I know why I've been brought here.'

'And why is that?'

'I coshed that copper.'

'How poetic. Yes, you did indeed cosh a copper. Or, to be more accurate, you assaulted DC Joseph Glass who is currently in Intensive Care following a very serious head injury. He may not even wake up.'

Lucas swallowed hard and the look on his face changed from one of apathy to apprehension. Matilda guessed he probably wasn't concerned for his victim's fate, more for his own.

'Now, you've said you don't want a solicitor present, is that still correct?'

'Yeah.'

'OK. So, why did you run when two of my officers came to see you at your place of work?'

'Because I'm not stupid.'

'You are stupid. Incredibly so, but that still doesn't tell me why you ran.'

'I've seen the news. I know all about these burglaries. I also know you lot are fucking clueless trying to find out who's done them. It's obvious you're going to go after anyone with a record for burgling and that means me.'

'But if you're innocent of those crimes why did you run?'

'You don't give a toss who's innocent. If you can't find who's doing it, you'll finger any poor bastard.'

'Is that what you really think?' Aaron asked.

'It's what I know.'

'Oh come on Lucas. Think it through. If we did finger you for the burglaries do you think they'd have just stopped? Of course they wouldn't have. Your so-called logic makes no sense at all. So come on, out with it, why did you run?'

'I told you.'

'I get the feeling this is going to be a long interview,' Matilda said to Aaron. 'It's a shame the windows in here don't open. Lucas, tell us about your brother-in-law.'

'Which one? Kevin?'

'Yes.'

'He's married to Alice. My sister.'

'We'd worked that one out for ourselves. Do you know what's happened to him?'

'Yes,' he said, laced with heavy sarcasm. 'Don't talk to me like I'm thick. He got himself shot.'

'Do you know anything about it?'

'No.'

'Are you sure?'

'Oh I get it. I've got a criminal record so I must be involved in every crime that happens in Sheffield. Look, I've not been in the nick for over ten years. I've gone straight. I'm clean. I haven't robbed or anything for over a decade. When I did I never used guns. I'm not into any of that.'

'Your sister, Alice, was also burgled the other day. Do you know anything about that?'

'What? No I didn't. What happened?' He genuinely looked surprised by this.

'Apparently she interrupted the burglar before he managed to take anything.'

'Is she all right?'

'As far as we know. Are you sure you don't know anything about them, Lucas?'

'You think I'd rob my own sister?'

'You robbed your own grandmother,' Aaron added. 'Surely you wouldn't bypass a house just because your sister lived there.'

'I didn't do it. I didn't do any of it.'

'We know you didn't do it, Lucas – you're too short and fat. You don't fit the description we have,' Matilda said, enjoying insulting the man opposite. 'However, I'm guessing you know some pretty dodgy people so I'd put money on you knowing who is currently terrorizing Sheffield.'

'I don't know nothing,' he stated loudly and clearly, leaning forward on the table.

254

'We really are going round in circles here. Where have you been hiding since you ran from my officers?'

'I've got an old lock-up in Gleadless. I was sleeping there.'

'Did you know about your flat being burnt down?'

'Yes I did. Look, don't you see, someone is out to get me.'

'I'm sorry?'

'My flat's been torched; you don't think that's some kind of message?'

'Who is out to get you?'

'I've no fucking idea.'

'Oh come on Lucas, you must know if you've pissed someone off enough for them to burn down your home.'

You don't. The dark BMW, the phone calls, the note. Someone is obviously out to get you and you have absolutely no idea who that person is. So, who have you pissed off recently?

'Boss?' Aaron asked when Matilda had fallen silent.

'Sorry. I just thought of something. It's gone now. Where was I? Oh yes, why did you decide to give yourself up?' Matilda asked Lucas, fidgeting in her uncomfortable chair. She tried to block out the thought that, like Lucas, someone may be after her, but she couldn't. She prayed and hoped to God that her home wouldn't get burnt down. James designed that house.

'Because every time I went out I saw you lot. You're all over the fucking place. Like I said, I'm not daft, I knew you'd find me eventually. I thought it best to hand myself over, get time off for coming in by myself, you know?'

Matilda rolled her eyes. This man really was beyond contempt. 'Lucas Branning, we're going to charge you with GBH on a police officer. You'll appear before a magistrate court tomorrow where I hope you will be remanded in custody. I shall certainly be making it known that you're a flight risk. This is not over. I will be questioning you further about the burglaries.'

'Come on, it wasn't GBH. I didn't mean to … Look,' Lucas was becoming restless. He realized he was facing a lengthy term in prison, 'if I tell you something will it help in getting me a lighter sentence?'

'It depends on what you want to tell me.'

The room fell silent while Lucas weighed up his options, not that he had many to choose from.

'I think I know who's doing these burglaries. I'm not certain, but I've got a fair idea.'

'I'm listening,' Matilda said, sitting back and folding her arms.

'And, if I'm right, it's the same bloke who killed my brother-in-law.'

Now it was Lucas's turn to sit back in his chair and fold his arms. He had a pathetic grin on his face, which showed off his brown and yellow stained teeth. Matilda and Aaron looked at each other; could they really trust this lying waste of space?

THIRTY-NINE

Rory was pleased Scott was back at work. He might be shy but when he opened up he had a wicked sense of humour. Together they were undergoing the tedious task of identifying everyone in the block of flats on London Road and Rory was grateful for the banter. It seemed to be taking forever.

'How's the head?' Rory asked, leaning back in his seat and stretching. He'd been bent over his desk for an hour and was beginning to stiffen up.

'It's fine. Bit of a headache but I'm OK,' he replied, not looking up from his paperwork.

'Fancy a few drinks tonight?'

'I can't. I'm not allowed to drink on these painkillers I've got.'

'Oh right. I could come round with a curry if you like. There's a Champion's League match on tonight.'

Scott paused in his deliberations and took a deep breath. Matilda's words from his hospital room echoed in his head. He really should set the record straight with Rory. 'To be honest, I've had to move out of my flat.'

'What? How come?'

'I couldn't afford it. Bills going up, rent, and everything. Plus, we haven't had a pay increase for ages. I've had to move back home.'

'Oh that sucks, man.'

Scott frowned. Was it really this easy? 'Sorry.'

'No don't be. Listen, if we had a spare room I'd let you move in with us.'

'Really?' Scott's face lit up at the very generous offer. He'd only met Amelia once and thought her a bit frosty. He doubted she would allow him to move in but the fact Rory was offering meant a great deal.

'Of course. You're my mate. We help each other out in these situations. At least being back home you'll get your washing done and your meals cooked. I sometimes wish I was still back at home.'

'Do you?'

'Yes. I'm shite at cooking and Amelia's not great either. Between us we're just about managing not to starve. I tell you what, how about we go out for a curry tonight then?'

'OK, sure. I'd like that.'

'Excellent.'

'We could go and see that new Vin Diesel film as well if you like?'

Scott smiled. It wasn't exactly *The Towering Inferno* but it would offer a distraction for a couple of hours.

Scott wasn't the only one lying to cover a personal issue. Rory didn't want to go home as he knew Amelia would have her work spread out all over the living room floor. He admired her ambition and drive, but what about him? When was there time for their relationship? They hadn't been out as a couple since New Year and hadn't had sex since before Christmas.

'So, where are you up to then?' Scott asked, getting back to work.

'Well, out of everyone we've spoken to so far, most of them don't talk to their neighbours. The ones that do only vaguely knew who Gerald Beecham was. Of those, very few actually spoke to him on a regular basis. Those that did only said hello in passing.'

'It sounds like a lovely environment to live in,' Scott said with sarcasm.

'I know. Talk about a suicide block.'

'Did any of them see or hear anything on the night he jumped, fell, was pushed? Delete as appropriate.'

'None at all.'

'I knew this was going to be a boring task when you roped me in on it but I thought we might have got something. Is that everyone covered then?'

'I've identified seven flats where we can't get a reply from the residents. Three are empty, which just leaves,' he flicked through the mess of paperwork on his desk. 'Andrew Parsons, Clayton Fletcher, Colin Theobald, and Fionella Deveraux.'

'What are we going to do about them then?'

'I'll get uniform to keep popping round until they answer. They're probably all old and deaf and never leave their flat anyway.'

'Is it time for a coffee yet?'

'It's always time for a coffee. I'll put the kettle on, you nick a couple of KitKats out of Sian's drawer before she comes back.'

FORTY

'Last time I was in the nick I met this bloke, real headcase, you made sure you never got on the wrong side of him. But, if you got to know him, he was all right. You could have a chat and a laugh with him. The problem was, he'd sometimes just fly off the handle for no reason. He really flipped. When I got out I saw him round Sheffield once or twice, not to talk to or anything, just saw him. I've seen him in pubs as well, only to say hello, not to have a good chat and catch up on old times with. Lately, I've seen him more than usual in the pubs and he's always got a big holdall with him like he's got stuff to flog, you know what I mean?'

Lucas Branning was talking in hushed tones and leaning forward over the interview table as if he was talking about someone within earshot. When he finished he leaned back. He obviously thought he'd said enough.

'Go on,' Matilda prompted.

'That's it.'

'No it isn't. Come on, I want a name and a description.'

'I'm not telling you his name. Weren't you listening? The guy's a psycho. He finds out I've dobbed him up to the pigs and he'll tear me a new one.'

'Lucas, if you don't give me a name you're not going to be around for him to tear you a new one. You're really starting to piss me off now, so spill.'

Matilda was getting agitated. With her hands below the table, she had been tapping her fingers against her thumb and counting them in her head. Now she started digging her nails hard into her skin to give her brain something to focus on: the pain. Without it, her mind would be all over the place.

Aaron looked down and could see Matilda's red hands. 'Do you think we should take a break?'

'No,' Matilda snapped. 'No breaks until this little gobshite gives me something to work with. We've been here nearly an hour and so far he's given us fuck all. Now come on, Lucas, stop playing.'

'In the nick we called him Ronnie,'

'Corbett or Barker?'

'Kray.'

Matilda and Aaron looked at each other. Their facial expressions were identical. This was not going to end well.

'Please don't tell me there's a Reggie out there somewhere.'

Lucas smiled. 'Not that I know of. This guy doesn't need a brother helping him out. He's enough of a psycho all on his own.'

'His name, Lucas.'

'Colin. Colin Theobald.'

FORTY-ONE

Matilda stormed down the corridor to the Murder Room. So much for her new outlook. She didn't know whether Lucas Branning was telling the truth in pointing the finger at a fellow ex-con but it needed investigating. If it turned out he was lying to buy himself more time she would seriously consider using him as target practice.

Aaron Connolly was struggling to keep up with his boss despite there being a massive height difference. He trotted to match her pace.

'You don't believe Branning do you?'

'I've no idea. If a man can burgle his own grandmother I think he's capable of anything. I won't trust a single word he's said until I have it confirmed.'

She threw open the doors to the Murder Room. 'Rory, whatever you're working on put it to one side for the moment.'

'Cool. Are we going out?'

'No. I want you to run a search on a Colin Theobald for me and tell me everything about him from what day he was born to what he had for breakfast this morning and everything in between.'

Rory looked up at his boss and didn't move.

'Would you like me to repeat my request in Welsh?' she asked.

'Did you say Colin Theobald?'

'Yes. Why? Please don't tell me he's a relative.'

'No. He's on my list though.'

'List of what?'

'The residents of the block of flats Gerald Beecham jumped, I mean, was pushed, from. Or maybe he was thrown.'

'Forget the semantics for now. He lives in the same block as Beecham?'

'Yes.'

Matilda looked pensive. 'Right, get me everything you can on him as soon as possible then bring it straight to me. Aaron, you wouldn't fancy fetching me a sausage sandwich would you?'

Matilda sat in her office with the door closed and the aroma of a sausage sandwich in the air. She felt better after having something to eat; the grease, the fat, the meat, the bread and the lashings of tomato ketchup definitely filled a hole. She had her back turned to the rest of the office and was sitting in her chair staring out of the window.

She closed her eyes and leaned her head back and tried to make sense of what was happening. It was a stretch, but say Lucas Branning was telling the truth: Colin Theobald was committing these burglaries and lived in the same building as Gerald Beecham, who had Lois Craven's blood on him. Was Colin Theobald the man behind the double shooting? Branning obviously thought so.

Rory knocked on the glass door and poked his head around. 'Am I all right to come in?'

'If you tell me what I want to hear then you can have my desk.'

'I've done a search on Colin Theobald and he's a very interesting character. Born on 14th September, 1977 in Darnall, Sheffield. He's six foot two and, according to the computer, he's built like a brick shithouse.'

He took a photograph from his folder and handed it to Matilda. It was a police mugshot of a blond shaven-headed young man looking menacingly into the eye of the camera. He had a heavy brow and thick neck with a tattoo of a snake creeping up out of the collar of his polo shirt.

'Blimey, Neanderthal man in all his glory.' She held the photograph closer for a more detailed look. 'What an ugly tattoo. Why would anyone want a snake slithering around their neck? We'll have to get Lois to take a look at this photo, particularly the tattoo, see if she recognizes it. Go on Rory, you were saying.'

'According to the council register he rents a flat in the tower block on London Road and has done for the last fifteen years. His father died when Colin was only five-years-old. His mother died of lung cancer eight years ago. He has no brothers and sisters and no other family at all.'

'I don't like the sound of that. A loner with nothing to lose. Could be dangerous.'

'Funny you should say that.'

She looked up from the photograph. 'Go on.'

'Colin Theobald has been in and out of prison his whole life. I've got a record sheet here as long as the River Don. He started his career in criminality at the age of fifteen when he received a suspended sentence for stealing a car. At the age of nineteen he was banned from driving for two years for drunk-driving, speeding, and having no tax and insurance.'

'Are all his crimes car related?' Matilda interrupted. She would much rather go through the entire history in her own time than have it read out to her like a book at bedtime.

'No,' he scanned down to the bottom of the page and turned over. 'He served eighteen months for GBH in 2000, was given a suspended sentence for burglary in 2003, served eighteen months for burglary the following year, and various other charges and sentences for assault, car theft, and burglary again up until 2014.'

'So, in and out of the nick his whole adult life then?'

'Yes. He's the kind of guy the Sheffield tourist board don't want on the cover of their leaflets.'

'Where is he now?'

'I've no idea. Uniform have been checking on the residents in the tower block. His is one of the flats they've had no response from.'

'No. I mean is he in prison now?'

'No. He served his last sentence in 2014 for assault. He got eighteen months and served five.'

'Right, thanks Rory. Leave me his file.'

Rory closed the file and placed it on her desk. Matilda could see him remain rooted to the spot out of the top of her eyes. He eventually took the hint and left, banging the glass door behind him.

She looked down at the brooding picture of Colin Theobald. He looked a mean bastard. His deep, dark eyes were soulless and penetrating. Matilda imagined even his school photographs had been sinister and frightening. This was not a man to be messed with. This was not a man you took for granted. If he was the aggravated burglar, the perpetrator of the double shooting, and the man who threw Gerald Beecham to his death from a tower block then he was an extremely violent and dangerous man.

FORTY-TWO

The doctor walked down the corridor of the Northern General Hospital with a thick file under her left arm. Life was going on around her. She went relatively unnoticed. As she approached the private room she stopped and peered through the glass. Sitting up, bruised and bandaged, was Lois Craven. She was staring straight ahead, a perplexed look on her face. A single tear escaped from her right eye and fell down her cheek.

The doctor knocked lightly, a tiny rap from a single knuckle. 'May I come in?' She didn't wait for a reply. She entered the room and closed the door behind her.

'Hello. My name is Doctor Sheila Warminster. I'm a Consultant Psychiatrist for the Sheffield Teaching Hospital. Your consultant thought it might be advantageous for me to come and have a word with you.'

Lois quickly wiped her eye. 'A psychiatrist? I really don't think—'

'Don't worry,' Sheila interrupted. She put on her least threatening smile. 'I'm not here to analyse you or write a detailed report on your mental health. I don't even have to write a report at all, just a few lines in your file saying how I think you're coping.'

'I appreciate that, but—'

'Mrs Craven. Lois. You've been through a massive trauma, not just physically but mentally. You mustn't bottle everything up and think you can return home to your usual life. Things have changed.'

Lois finally nodded her consent. She didn't look too happy about it, but Sheila hoped she would see it was for the best to get things off her chest. She smiled and pulled a chair close to the top of the bed.

'So, physically, how are you doing?'

'Well I'm not in as much pain as I was. I'm still on a lot of medication but I'm healing just fine.'

'The doctors are very pleased with your recovery. You've been lucky.'

'Lucky? I don't call watching the man you love getting murdered in front of you then being beaten, raped, and shot lucky.' Another tear fell from her eye. She flicked it away. 'Shit! I never used to cry. I don't know what's wrong with me. The slightest thing sets me off.'

'Crying's good. It's a release. Would you like to talk me through what happened?'

'Not really.' Lois took a handful of tissues from the small box on her bedside table and wiped her eyes and nose. 'I've gone over it in my head so many times it seems to have lost all impact. It's like I'm watching it on film.'

'When you're going through it, how do you feel?'

'Numb. It's like it's not happening. It's not me.'

'You're desensitizing yourself. The more you go over it in your mind the more you're accepting that it really did happen.'

'Accepting?'

'Maybe that's the wrong word. You're not accepting, you're understanding it. You're getting used to the fact that it happened and you can't hide from it.'

'So have I just got to live with seeing it every time I close my eyes or fall asleep?'

'No. Your mind needs to get used to the trauma. Once it has you'll stop thinking about it as much. You'll get the odd trigger but you won't be reliving it over and over.'

'It's all I'm thinking about at the moment and being stuck in here isn't helping. Is there any chance of me being able to go outside, get some fresh air?'

'I'll have a word with your consultant but I don't see why not. I believe your husband has been visiting.'

'Martin, yes.'

'How did he take what happened?'

A tear fell down Lois's face again. 'You mean how did he take to me cheating on him again? Oh he was over the moon. I'm sorry.' She wiped her eyes and bit her bottom lip to hold back more tears. 'I think I may have actually blown it this time. I can't see us making it through this.'

'What makes you say that?'

'He can't even look at me. He's distant. He won't bring the kids to see me.'

'You've had affairs in the past?'

'Yes. More than one.'

'Did he know about them all?'

'I'm not sure. Thomas isn't his, yet he's bringing him up as his own. He's put up with more than any other man would have done.'

'Are you grateful for that?'

'I don't know. At first I was. I was petrified of the thought of bringing a child up alone.'

'And now?'

'I resent him. I know I shouldn't and I hate myself for saying it, but I just wish he wasn't so weak. He should have thrown me out and not taken me back. He'd be happy now. He'd have married again, and chosen someone to love him for the man he is.'

'Don't you think he's happy now?'

'Of course he isn't. Would you be happy married to a serial slut?'

'Why are you being so hard on yourself?'

'It's what I deserve. I've been married to Martin for twenty years next summer and in that time I've slept with six other men. Six. What kind of a wife am I? What kind of a mother am I?'

Lois slumped back on the bed, her head sinking into the pillow. Her tears were flowing freely and she didn't bother to wipe them away.

'I'm in so much pain,' she cried out.

'Emotional? Physical? Mental?' Sheila asked in a soothing monotone.

'All of the above,' she forced a laugh. 'Do you know what the most awful part of it is?'

'What?'

'I'm not sorry. I mean, I'm sorry I've put my kids through all this and Martin, but I'm not sorry I had the affairs. They were fun, they were exciting, they were exhilarating. They were exactly what I needed at the time.'

'And the consequences?'

'Do you mean, were they worth it?'

'Yes.'

'No. I should have been happy. I had stability, a husband, a home, a decent job, a loving family, but I wasn't. I couldn't conform to what was expected of me.'

'When you'd been shot, and you were lying on the ground, what were you thinking about?'

Lois raised her eyebrows as she thought of the answer. 'I don't remember,' she said. After a long pause she continued. 'Yes I do. I thought of myself. I should have been thinking of the kids, and Martin, but I didn't. I thought of how much pain I was in. I thought, I wish he'd killed me.'

'You wish you'd died?' Sheila was expecting to hear that reply.

Lois nodded. She couldn't speak. 'I've ruined so many people's lives. Jesus! Why didn't he just kill me?'

FORTY-THREE

Three cars crawled along the busy roads in rush-hour traffic. In the first, DI Christian Brady was driving with Matilda sitting alongside him. In the second car was Rory Fleming and Scott Andrews with Faith Easter in the back. The third car held four armed uniformed officers. There was a van heading to the scene containing armed response officers but they were coming from a different direction.

The traffic was at a standstill; cars were bumper to bumper, buses were trying to force their way into and out of any gap they could find and the traffic lights pointlessly changed colour without aiding the flow of vehicles at all.

'Why's it so busy?' Matilda moaned, looking in all directions out of the window.

'There's a match at Bramall Lane tonight. I'm supposed to be going,' Christian added under his breath.

Matilda sighed and relaxed back into her seat. She looked through the file on her lap once again. 'Theobald definitely matches the description Lois Craven gave me but does he fit your burglar?'

'I know it's not much to go on; tall bloke, well built, wearing black, but the last witness saw he had a tattoo on his neck and blond hair. Colin Theobald ticks all the boxes.'

'Theobald also has a history of violence.'

'We could solve three major crimes within the next half hour,' Christian smiled.

'Do you honestly think it's going to be that easy?'

'PMA.'

'Is that some kind of new text-speak I'm not up on yet like PMSL?'

'Positive Mental Attitude. If you think positive and with confidence, then good things will happen.'

Matilda rolled her eyes. *Don't tell me he's seeing Dr Warminster as well?*

Matilda spotted a dark-coloured BMW three cars in front. She angled her head to get a glimpse of the registration number. It was a private number plate. It wasn't the car that had been following her. She relaxed. Was that another dark BMW further ahead?

'So Scott, how are you feeling now?' Faith Easter asked from the back seat.

'I'm OK. The headache's finally cleared.'

'Have you seen his scar?' Rory asked from the driver's seat. 'It's his badge of honour.'

'It's going to stand out,' Faith said. 'You have such a smooth face. Any news on Joseph Glass?'

'I called his parents about an hour ago,' Scott said. 'There's no change. He's just lying there. Completely unresponsive.'

'Oh God. You don't realize how dangerous this job is until something like this happens.' Her voice cracked.

Rory looked at Faith through the rear-view mirror. 'You OK Faith?'

'Yes I'm fine. It just puts things into perspective doesn't it? I mean, we come to work and we don't know what we're going to be confronted with. We may not make it to the end of the day.'

'I'm so pleased you decided to come in our car, Faith, and cheer us all up,' Rory said.

'We stop ourselves from doing things because we're afraid of looking foolish but when you think of how precious life is, how fragile it is, you wonder why we don't just take the plunge more often. We're only on this planet about eighty years – that's nothing,' she said, almost to herself.

'Are you getting all philosophical on us?'

'What? No, just thinking aloud, that's all. Ignore me.'

'We're trying.'

'Look, Faith, if you want to go back to the station nobody will think badly of you,' Scott said, turning in his seat.

'God no. I've been after this sodding burglar for months. I want to see it through to the end. Ignore me, I'm just in a reflective mood. It's this business with Joseph, it's getting to me. Bloody hell, I wish someone would do something about this fucking traffic,' she yelled.

Scott and Rory looked at each other with raised eyebrows.

After twenty minutes of wrangling with the traffic, the team of cars eventually made it to the tower block on London Road. The van containing the armed response officers was already waiting. The back doors were open and everyone helped themselves to a ballistic vest. As usual, Matilda struggled into hers. She realized they weren't designed for comfort, but when you carried a few extra pounds and you had an ample bosom they were not the most practical of items to try and squeeze into. Out of the corner of her eye she looked over to Faith who seemed to slip hers on with ease. Typical.

Huddled around so they could be heard over the sound of horns blaring and engines revving, Matilda conducted the short briefing.

'Colin Theobald lives on the twelfth floor. We have no idea if he is in there or not. We also don't know if he's armed. What we do know is that he is a very dangerous man. I want AR in first, secure the scene and Theobald, then the rest of us will go in and turn his place over. Any questions?'

She was met with silence and grave looks as the enormity of the task ahead suddenly hit home.

'Right. Myself and DI Brady will go up in the lift first with the AR. You follow afterwards,' she said to Rory, Scott, Faith and the uniformed officers who weren't carrying a weapon. 'Let's go.'

The foyer to the building was surprisingly bright and clean. There was a faint hint of cheap disinfectant. Matilda pressed the button on the lift, and, even in the silence, the sound of the carriage hitting the ground couldn't be heard.

Squeezed inside, the journey up twelve floors seemed to take a long time. They were packed tightly together; the sound of breathing in through the nose echoed around the tiny space. Someone coughed. Someone hiccupped. Someone burped then apologized, blaming the moussaka he'd had for lunch. The lift juddered to a halt and the doors yawned open and the relief all round was palpable.

Silently, the AR officers led the way. Matilda and Christian held back. Neither of them were armed.

An officer gave a hand signal and another stepped forward and gave the Yale lock a deafening hard kick. The flimsy door flew open and the officers filed in, weapons raised.

'Armed police,' cried one of the officers.

Outside in the corridor, several front doors opened. Matilda raised her warrant card. 'Police. You need to close your doors and stay inside. Now!' she shouted at the gawping neighbours.

The lift beside them pinged and the doors opened to reveal Matilda's team and the uniformed officers.

'Rory broke wind,' Faith said.

'I didn't do it on purpose.'

'All clear ma'am,' one of the armed response officers called out from inside the flat.

Matilda entered to find a grubby and sparse flat. The windows were filthy with years' worth of grime on the inside and out. The net curtains were nicotine yellow. There was an old box-style television set in the corner of the living room and a dark brown corner suite that looked like it came from the 1970s.

'This is not what I wanted to see,' Matilda said to anyone who would listen. 'Don't just stand there, you can still search it.'

The rest of the team set out to search through every drawer and cupboard in every room while Matilda and Christian stood back.

Rory opened a pizza box on the coffee table. There were a couple of slices still inside and they looked relatively fresh. 'Someone's been living in this depressing hole recently then.'

'It looks like someone's been sleeping rough here,' Faith said, her face wrinkled up against the bitter odour that was difficult to trace.

'I honestly thought he'd be here,' Matilda said.

'So where is he then?'

'I don't know,' she snapped, not meaning to. 'Was everything checked; housing register, electoral roll, tax office?'

'Yes. Everything official states that Colin Theobald lives in this shithole.' Rory chimed up from the living room.

'So where is he then?'

'For fuck's sake Christian, I don't know,' she shouted and stormed out of the flat.

'Where are you going?'

'To get some fresh air. Anything of interest I want it bagging and taking to the station. Ring me the minute you find anything of any use.'

Bypassing the lift, Matilda yanked open the door to the stairs and started to run down them. She had no idea where Colin Theobald was right now but as darkness began to fall on the steel city she had a fair idea that he was planning to strike again.

FORTY-FOUR

UNSTABLE DCI PUTS OFFICERS' LIVES AT RISK
By Alex Winstanley

One of South Yorkshire Police's top detectives is mentally unfit for duty, yet is still in charge of an elite team of dedicated officers.

DCI Matilda Darke, who returned to work in December last year following her suspension over the Carl Meagan kidnapping, is suffering with depression and anxiety issues and struggling to cope with the demands of a high-profile job.

An unnamed source within South Yorkshire Police said: 'It's sad to say but Matilda Darke should not be allowed to keep her job. She is a danger to her fellow officers and to the public.'

Earlier this week DC Joseph Glass was injured while pursuing a suspect. He is currently in a critical condition in Northern General Hospital. On the same day, DC Scott Andrews was run off the road late at night after working almost twenty-four hours without a break. Both of these detectives are on DCI Darke's Murder Investigation Team.

The source continued. 'I have worked in various forces throughout my career but it's here at South Yorkshire that has been the most eye-opening. I cannot believe such an emotionally fragile and unpredictable woman is in charge of such a prestigious team. The fault does not lie solely with DCI Darke. It goes much higher than that. Assistant Chief Constable Valerie Masterson appointed her and, to save face, has allowed her to get away with things any other officer would have been fired for.

'In the interest of the public, and her fellow officers, DCI Darke should have done the decent thing and resigned her post as soon as the Carl Meagan case collapsed but she selfishly continued.'

When DCI Darke returned to work four months ago, ACC Masterson said in a statement: 'We all welcome back a hard-working and dedicated officer to South Yorkshire Police. DCI Darke is an exemplary detective who has led the Murder Investigation Team with diligence and passion. Everyone is looking forward to her continuing her successes.'

ACC Masterson refused to comment on the health and well-being of individual officers and asked us not to run this article, believing it to be damaging to the force. However, in the interest of the people of South Yorkshire who put their lives and trust into the police officers under ACC Masterson and DCI Darke's command, we believe the truth should be revealed.

Our source called upon ACC Valerie Masterson and DCI Matilda Darke to resign with immediate effect before somebody tragically lost their life due to an unsound decision.

Matilda didn't go back to the station. She wanted to but the pressure of an oncoming panic attack forced her to drive straight home. She did briefly wonder how Christian Brady was going to get back to the station but she assumed someone would offer him a lift.

By the time she arrived home on Millhouses Lane it was dark. She parked in the driveway, and upon getting out, she looked up at the house next door belonging to Sebastian and Jill Carmichael. It was in total darkness. There was an abandoned look about it. It would be a long time before someone lived here again.

Matilda lowered her head and cursed herself for not knowing what had been going on behind the deep red front door. She should have seen the signs. She had worked domestic violence cases before; she had seen the effects of a battered housewife. Matilda wondered where Jill was right now and how she was feeling. Also, where was the baby? She tried to remember the poor mite's name but couldn't. She knew, deep down, that it wasn't her fault, but something niggling in the back of her mind told her she had failed that entire family. Another stress to add to the ever-growing collection. It was a wonder her mind didn't explode under all the pressure.

She felt a chill as the stiff breeze picked up, and looked around her. The road was quiet, as it always was. Lights were on in people's homes and life was continuing as normal. Normal. What a pointless and pathetic word. What was normal?

The house directly opposite belonged to a large family. Matilda had no idea of their names but knew it was a man and woman and at least five children. Every time she saw them leaving the house as a family unit they seemed happy. The kids were always smiling and talking at that loud volume only children can get away with. The parents looked organized and pleased with their brood and their lives. A week ago, Matilda wouldn't have given them a second thought, now, in the wake of what had happened with Jill Carmichael, she wondered whether their smiles and cheerful persona were a front to something sinister.

She shook her head and chastised herself. Evil did not lie behind every closed door. Nor did evil drive a dark BMW; not that Matilda noticed the car parked a few feet from her own driveway.

Matilda unlocked the front door and entered the house. She expected the alarm to start beeping but nothing happened. She stood in the spacious hallway surrounded by cold and darkness.

The last thing Matilda did when she left the house was to set the alarm. It was something she never forgot to do. The code was the date of her wedding anniversary and it always made her smile when she typed it into the keypad. It was like having James keeping guard over the house while she was at work. So why didn't it start beeping tonight? Had she forgotten to set it this morning? Was the alarm faulty?

And why was it so cold? There was something wrong.

Matilda walked slowly and carefully into the living room. There was nothing out of place here, apart from the stacks of boxes.

There was a large screen door, which separated the living room and dining room. This had been an idea of James's. When they had a party they could pull back the screen and create one large room. When it was just the two of them, the screen would close and the lounge would be a cosy, intimate place for the two of them to snuggle up on the sofa together in front of the fire. Unfortunately, they had never pulled the screen back for a party. James had never used his own beloved house to its full potential.

She pulled open the screen just wide enough to slip through into the dining room. The temperature plunged. This is where the cold was coming from. The veiled curtains were swaying in the breeze; the door to the conservatory was open. She knew for a fact it was closed before she left the house this morning as she hadn't used the conservatory for months.

Sir Robert Walpole, Spencer Compton, Henry Pelham, Thomas Pelham-Holles, William Cavendish.

Matilda didn't mind the Prime Ministers making a return. It would appear that her house had been broken into. This would certainly count as a distressing situation. She needed something comforting to hold on to. She found herself tapping her fingers against her thumb, digging the nail hard against each finger.

Thomas Pelham-Holles, John Stuart, George Grenville, Charles Wentworth, William Pitt the Elder.

She made her way over to the entrance to the conservatory. There was very little light outside coming through the windows but she could make out the silhouette of the objects in what had been James's favourite room; the sofas, the tables, the lamps.

'Good evening, Matilda,' came a voice from a shadow sitting in an armchair in the corner of the room.

'Shit,' Matilda said under her breath. She put both hands in her pockets, looking for her mobile phone. They were empty. She suddenly remembered her phone was still plugged into the dashboard of her car, charging the battery. *Shit.*

Augustus Henry Fitzroy, Frederick North, Charles Wentworth, William Petty, William Bentinck.

The voice was familiar but she couldn't place it.

Matilda found her voice. 'Who are you? How did you get in?' She looked around her for some kind of weapon, something to defend herself with. There was nothing. This was a dining room that was hardly ever used. It was decorated with enough furniture to stop it looking like an abandoned room: a table to seat eight, pictures on the wall, and an empty sideboard.

'When you want something desperately enough you can do anything. By the way, I thought the story in tonight's issue of *The Star* was shocking, completely unfair.'

'I haven't seen it,' she frowned and leaned forward, trying to make out the thin frame of her intruder. He was too slight to be Colin Theobald. 'Who are you?' she asked again.

'I've left a copy of the paper on the sideboard. I can wait while you read it.'

Matilda didn't like leaving a complete stranger alone in her house but she felt this was all part of his game. He wouldn't make a move until she'd read the paper. She knew she should turn and run for the front door, go out into the street and scream for help at the top of her voice to anyone who would listen, but this was her home. This was James's home. Matilda intended to protect it with her life.

The local newspaper was open at page seven where an unflattering photo of her took up a large part of the page. She had spent the past few days wondering if her actions had led to Joseph Glass being attacked and Scott Andrews being driven off the road, and now the whole of Sheffield would be thinking the same.

She didn't read the article. She didn't need to. She knew exactly what was being said about her and every word would be a knife in the back. This would effectively end her career.

'Isn't it sad? The media can be bastards at times can't they?' The voice from the conservatory was dripping with sarcasm.

Matilda closed her eyes. She knew exactly who the man was. 'I know who you are.'

The man laughed. 'It took you longer than I thought it would but then I'm guessing you've not thought much about me in the last four months.'

'Why are you here?'

'This is silly trying to conduct a conversation through the walls. Come and join me. It's a lovely room. It's a shame James didn't get much chance to use it.'

The mention of James was like a slap. Matilda didn't like anyone talking about her husband, especially those whom she despised. She turned the light on, squinting as her eyes adjusted to the brilliant white. She stepped into the conservatory and turned the light on there too.

Former Detective Inspector Ben Hales was a shadow of the man she knew. Just four months ago he had been a tall, well-built man with a neat salt-and-pepper haircut. He had been overweight and solid and commanded a huge presence whenever he entered a room. Now he was thin, gaunt, and haggard. His eyes were drawn, his skin was dull, and his unruly hair was lifeless and completely grey.

Matilda was taken aback. The transformation in just four months was shocking.

DI Ben Hales had been Matilda's replacement in leading the Murder Investigation Team while she was on her enforced sabbatical following James's death and her handling of the Carl Meagan kidnapping.

To say he had been annoyed at her return would be an understatement. He had tried everything in his power to make sure Matilda didn't retake command but had failed at every turning. ACC Masterson believed in Matilda and made sure Ben knew his place.

Ben had been craving a top position within the police force since he first put on the uniform. He thought the best way would be through nepotism and had married the daughter of a Chief Superintendent in the hope of ingratiating himself with the top brass. Unfortunately, the opposite happened, and Ben was constantly overlooked when it came to promotion. His one chance was when Matilda was absent. Those nine months were bliss for Ben and he had shone in her role. He had a one hundred per cent success rate and there was no way he was going to give it up so readily.

However, the force of the ACC and the Teflon coating of Matilda Darke soon had him playing dirty tricks. They had backfired, and he found himself out of a job, his career and his future shattered, and his life practically over.

'Did you do this?' she asked, holding the newspaper aloft.

He put his hand up like a child in a classroom and gave a sly, sneaky grin. 'Guilty.'

'You do realize you've killed my career.'

'Have I? Oh no. I'm so sorry. That wasn't my intention at all.' He was thoroughly enjoying himself.

'Why have you done this?'

The sinister smile dropped. 'Don't do that. Don't pretend you've no idea what you've done.'

'Have you been following me too? Making phone calls?'

He frowned. 'I've called you a few times, yes. I've no need to follow you, I know exactly what you've been up to.'

'What's happened to you?'

'This is what happens after four months of humiliation. This is four months of torture. I've been through hell since you got me sacked.'

'No. Oh no, I'm not taking the blame for that. What happened to you was of your own making. I had nothing to do with it. I didn't kidnap a leading witness. I didn't threaten your wife with a knife. I didn't conduct an illegal interview. Everything that happened was down to you and I won't have you sitting there trying to make me feel guilty because of your own failings.'

She turned and left the conservatory, taking large strides into the dining room. 'I want you out of my house right now,' she called out behind her.

Ben Hales followed her. In the brightness of the hallway Matilda could see him more clearly. His clothes were hanging off him, his cheek bones were prominent. She almost felt sorry for him.

'Go home to your wife, Ben,' she said, her voice no longer angry.

'Sara left me just after New Year. She took the girls and moved in with her dad.'

'Oh. I had no idea, Ben. I'm sorry.'

'Sorry? No you're not. If you even considered other people and their feelings I would still have a job and Carl Meagan would still be with his parents.'

That was a blow to Matilda. He obviously knew her Achilles heel.

'Ben, I want you to leave. Get on with your life and please don't come back to my home ever again,' she said firmly.

She moved to the front door to open it when Ben's right arm pushed the door from her grasp and slammed it closed.

'Did you honestly think I was going to leave quietly?'

Matilda was noticeably frightened, though she fought hard to hide it. 'Ben, please—'

'You have ruined my life. You took my career and you wiped your feet all over it. Do you think I'd just go home, take up golf, and get a part-time job as a night watchman? No. You've fucked up my entire life and I'm not going to let you continue as if nothing's happened.'

Ben had backed Matilda into a corner of the hallway. His eyes were wide and staring. Up close he looked wild and determined. His jaw was clenched and he was visibly shaking.

Matilda raised her hands pleadingly. 'Ben, whatever you're considering doing I strongly advise against it. This is no way to go about things.'

'I don't care what happens to me. I've nothing left to lose; you've seen to that. If I'm going, I'm taking you with me.'

Ben and Matilda were nose to nose. She could feel his warm breath on her face. Slowly, he raised his hands and aimed them at her throat.

'Do you have any idea how long I've waited to do this?'

His knees almost buckled as he touched her bare skin; it was warm and soft against his chapped, gnarled fingers. He wrapped them around her throat. He felt the rapidly beating pulse in her neck, the contours of muscles and bone. The closer he stood the more he could smell his adversary: her perfume, her fear, her deodorant, her sweat. The enjoyment was evident on his face; the eyes brightened and a small smile crept along his thin lips. He gently applied pressure and watched as Matilda struggled to breathe. Her face turned red and she gasped as the life was slowly squeezed out of her.

FORTY-FIVE

'Thank God you're here. I thought you'd have gone home by now,' Faith Easter said as she barged into the Murder Room.

'No. I was just about to though. What's happened?' Sian asked. She was tidying up her desk while waiting for her computer to shut down.

'Nothing. You know what we forgot to do today?'

'No. What?'

'Go and see Alice Hardaker.'

'Shit!' Sian cursed herself. She prided herself on having a good memory. How could she have forgotten? She had even written it down on her notepad. She looked at her watch. 'Well, it's only seven o'clock now. We could pop along and see her if you've got time.'

'Yes. I've no plans for tonight apart from a cat to feed and a pathetic ready meal. What about you? Won't your husband be expecting you home?'

'Stuart? No. There's plenty of food and lager in the fridge. He'll not even notice. We'll go in my car and then I can drop you back off here on my way home.'

'You don't mind?'

'No. Come on. Let's see if Alice will give us all the gory details on her family.'

Alice Hardaker was in the kitchen preparing a meal for the children. She hadn't left the house all day. She called her sister in the morning to ask if she would take the kids to school as she couldn't face leaving the house, and she'd apologized profusely for her behaviour at finding out Jenny knew about her husband's affairs.

When Jenny returned to Broad Elms Lane just after 9.30 they sat down with a mug of tea each and a large supply of biscuits and had a heart-to-heart lasting several hours. Jenny apologized for not telling her sister what Kevin was really like. Alice apologized for never trying to get on with Jenny's husbands and they both apologized for putting men before each other.

'At the end of the day we're much better off on our own,' Alice had said as she opened a second packet of Jammie Dodgers. 'Don't get me wrong, I love Warren and Milly to bits and wouldn't swap them for the world, but men are complete bastards. They're ruled by what's between their legs and listen to that before they listen to what's up top,' she said, tapping her head.

'Well I'm perfectly happy with being single now,' Jenny replied. 'Men are only useful for having kids, and seeing as I can't have any there's no point in having a bloke is there?'

Alice placed a comforting hand on Jenny's knee. 'I think it's awful you can't have children. You'd have made a great mum.'

'I know I would,' she smiled through the pain. 'Still, I can be a great aunt to Warren and Milly instead.'

'You are a great aunt. The kids love you.'

'Look, if you need any help getting through all this with the funeral and everything I'm here for you. I'll take the kids to school, I'll pick them up again, and when you need time on your own I'll take them to the park or the cinema.'

Alice leaned forward on the sofa and pulled her sister into a hug. 'Thank you, Jenny. I don't deserve you.'

'You know what we both deserve?'

'What?'

'Some of that vanilla cheesecake you've got in the fridge.'

Jenny came into the kitchen and closed the door behind her.

'Warren's done his homework and Milly's finished learning her times table. They're watching *SpongeBob SquarePants* now.'

'God I hate that programme. That bloody sponge's laugh cuts straight through me.'

'The one that lives next door to him with the big nose reminds me of my first boyfriend, Terry. Remember him?'

Alice laughed. 'God yes, the miserable sod. What you saw in him I've no idea. Two years you went out with him; I don't think I saw him smile once.'

'Neither did I and I slept with him.'

They both laughed.

'Tea will be ready in about fifteen minutes. Do you want to open a bottle of wine?'

'What a silly question. Of course I want to open a bottle of wine.'

Alice screamed.

'What the hell?' Jenny asked, startled. She looked over to her sister, thinking she'd burnt herself on the cooker but she hadn't. Once again she saw Alice staring straight ahead out of the window. Jenny followed her gaze and saw the masked man who had threatened them two nights before.

'Oh God Alice, he's come back. Call the police.'

Alice stood still, frozen to the spot.

'Alice, do something.'

Alice was just about to move when the intruder used the key and unlocked the door. He stepped in, locked the door behind him and held a gun aloft, pointing it directly at Alice.

'Don't even think about it,' he said, his voice deep and menacing.

He was dressed from head to toe in black like last time. The same wrap-around goggles and the elaborate face mask covering his nose and mouth. It muffled his voice but the accent was distinctly Yorkshire. He took huge strides forward to the stricken sisters, his solid, muscular build making heavy footfalls on the wooden floor.

'I've come back for my money. I know I gave you until the end of the month but things are happening and it needs to be now. This time I'm not pissing about. I either leave with cash or one of your kids. Which is it to be?'

Alice was shaking. 'Look, I told you, I don't know what you're talking about. I don't owe you any money. Kevin didn't owe anybody any money and I haven't seen Lucas for months.'

The intruder stared into Alice's eyes, watching as the pupils danced wildly back and forth. She was scared. He turned and moved over to Jenny.

'Do you watch horror films?'

'What?' The heavy frown on her face showed she wasn't expecting to be asked that.

'Horror films. Do you like them?'

'Some. Not all.' Jenny was petrified. She was clutching the bottle of wine as if her life depended on it.

'Do you know what I hate about horror films? You've got the killer who spends most of the film going around killing people then at the end when he's trapped his main victim he spends about twenty minutes chatting to her, giving the police plenty of time to come and save the day. Why not just kill her as soon as he gets there instead of all that chatting? Doesn't that piss you off?'

'Erm, yes, I suppose it does.'

'What about you Alice?' He looked over to Alice who was still standing by the cooker, unable to move.

'I guess so.'

'The killer should just walk up to his victim and put a bullet between her eyes. Like this.'

He placed the gun directly onto Jenny's forehead and pulled the trigger. She didn't have time to scream or beg or plead. The back of her head exploded and splattered on the cupboard doors behind her before she dropped to the floor with a dead thud.

Alice buckled. She almost fell to the ground at the horror of what she had just witnessed. She tried to scream but nothing would come out. She fell against the built-in cupboards behind her and tried, but failed, to keep herself standing. She slipped to the floor and began to cry. All she could think about were her children innocently watching *SpongeBob SquarePants* in the next room. The contrast in events in the space of a few feet was too sickening to contemplate.

The intruder walked towards her and crouched down to her level.

'I bet you thought I'd get bored and leave you alone. Wrong. I want my fucking money.'

Alice was about to start pleading again before the attacker held up a hand to silence her.

'I've been doing some ringing round since my last visit. I've got contacts. I know people; bad people. Either I get my money or I take your daughter and I hand her over to men who love nothing better than fucking little girls.'

The doorbell rang.

Sian and Faith were standing on the doorstep of the Hardaker home in Broad Elms Lane. It was coming up to 7.30. The surrounding houses were all lit up; the everyday routine of a weekday evening was continuing as normal.

'Nice area,' Faith said.

'Yes. I like this front door,' Sian replied looking at the Victorian wooden door with its symmetrical stained glass window in the centre. 'I wonder how much something like this would cost.'

'Maybe she's gone out,' Faith said looking up at the house.

'Well her car is there and there's a light on in the living room. Ring again.'

Faith pressed the doorbell and stepped back to look up at the upstairs rooms.

'Answer the door.'

Alice was shaking. Her hands were covering her mouth and her eyes were wide. She was in shock and couldn't stop looking down at her sister's body. Her face was a distorted mess. Jenny was pretty, her hair neatly styled, make-up always applied, understated and never too much, just enough to accentuate her natural beauty. She was no supermodel, and could maybe stand to lose a few pounds, but she was attractive in a simple and discreet way.

'Answer the door,' the intruder said through gritted teeth. His voice low and deep.

'I can't. I can't move,' she eventually said.

The doorbell rang again.

'I'll get it,' the sing-song voice of the eldest child, Warren, said.

Alice gasped and brought her hands up to her mouth again to stop herself from crying out.

The intruder grabbed her by the collar and dragged her over to the kitchen door. He held her firm in the crook of his arm and placed his leather-gloved hand over her mouth to keep her quiet. He was hurting her and she was struggling to breathe. He leaned in to the door, straining to listen. He could hear the security chain being removed and the door opening.

'Oh. Hello. Is your mummy in?'

'Yes. She's making us tea.'

'Could we talk to her?'

'Who are you?'

'My name is Sian and my friend here is Faith. We're from the police. We'd just like to have a few words with your mum before you have your tea.'

'Can I have a look at your badges?'

'Of course you can. Here you go.'

There was a long silence while the small boy was looking at the identification cards.

'They are so cool. I want to be a policeman when I grow up.'

'Do you? That's good. Well, you need to be a good boy and work hard at school.'

'I do. Mrs Bishop says I'm good at maths and I always listen.'

'You are a good boy. Can we come in and see your mummy?'

'Yes. Me and my sister are watching *SpongeBob SquarePants*. Mummy is in the kitchen.'

'OK. Well you go back and watch your cartoon and I'll come in and see you before we leave.'

The front door was closed. The intruder pulled Alice to the other side of the kitchen and pushed her down on the leather sofa. He stood at the side of the fridge, out of sight of the door, his gun pointing at Alice.

There was a slight knock on the door and it opened quickly. 'Mrs Hardaker, I'm Detective Sergeant Sian Mills. This is—'

She stopped dead in her tracks as she saw a stricken looking Alice with uncontrollable tears rolling down her cheeks. Her eyes followed Alice's as she looked from Sian to the floor behind the worktop where Jenny's body was.

'Alice. What's happened?'

The intruder waited until Sian and Faith were fully in the kitchen before he jumped out from behind the fridge, ran over to the door, slammed it closed, locked it and pocketed the key. He held the gun aloft.

'None of you move. Not a single step.'

'Oh my God!' Faith cried out and immediate fell onto the sofa next to Alice. Sian remained stoic and eyed the intruder.

'Colin Theobald?' she asked.

There was no reply.

'We've been looking for you all day,' she continued. 'You're not an easy man to track down. Why don't you take off the mask? We know who you are, you may as well.'

Sian and Colin remained locked in a stand-off. Neither of them was going to move first, giving the other the upper hand. Eventually Colin removed his glasses to reveal deep-set dark eyes sunken beneath a heavy, threatening brow. Slowly, he unhooked the mask from the back of his head and removed it from his face. He had several days' worth of stubble and his jawline was firm and rigid with angry tension. His nostrils flared rapidly. He was standing on a knifepoint. He was ready to snap.

'Shit,' Sian said under her breath, so quiet that only she heard it.

'So what happens now?' Colin asked.

'Why don't you tell me what you're doing here?' Sian placed her hands in the pockets of her jacket to hide the fact they were shaking.

'That's between me and Mrs Hardaker.'

'And what about …' Sian nodded towards Jenny.

'Well, nobody seemed to be taking what I was saying seriously. I think they needed a warning. They're not very bright these Hardakers.'

'You know the family then?'

'I know the brother; a complete loser. I've only just become acquainted with Alice and Jenny.' He looked past Sian and winked at Alice who winced under the power of his stare.

'So why are you here?'

'I'm owed some money. I've come to collect.'

'Who owes you money?'

'Alice does.'

Alice shook her head but couldn't open her mouth to talk. Her emotions were running high. She was afraid that if she tried to speak a torrent of tears would pour out, alerting her children, and putting them in mortal danger.

'How much?' Sian asked.

'It started out at ten thousand pounds. It's twenty now.'

'That's a lot of money. Why would she owe you twenty thousand pounds?'

'Because she paid me to kill her husband.'

FORTY-SIX

The black BMW drove at speed down Dobcroft Road. With cars parked on both sides of the narrow road traffic flow was restricted to a single lane. Ben Hales swerved close to parked cars as he ignored the twenty miles per hour speed limit. Cars coming in the opposite direction had to pull over, if they could find a space, or risk having their wing mirror whipped off. Drivers beeped and swore at Hales but he continued regardless.

He turned onto Whirlowdale Road, much wider than Dobcroft, so he hit the accelerator hard and charged up the road. The road was in darkness with Ecclesall Wood on either side of it. Hales was lucky he didn't run anyone down.

His vision blurred through the tears and panic. He slammed down onto the brakes, the tyre screech echoing around the quiet road. He pulled off his seat belt, jumped out, and headed into the woods.

Hales was breathing heavily. He fought against the strong wind and fine rain. The terrain was soft and awkward underfoot and he was soon out of the range of his headlights and plunged into darkness. What was happening to him?

He fell against a gnarled oak tree and crouched among its mighty roots. His intention was to frighten Matilda, to warn her, to tell her that he would always be watching her. Even if it took the rest of his life he would be keeping a close eye on her, waiting for her to slip up and then he would pounce, rub her nose in her failure, and tell the world that he had been right all along: Matilda Darke was unfit to work for the police. He knew it before everyone else and he would have the last laugh. That was his plan. He had been building up to it for months. So why hadn't it worked?

When he cornered her in the hallway and he inched closer he saw the look of terror etched on her pale face, the fear in her wide eyes. He could hear her breathing quickly, see her chest rising and falling, feel her warm breath on his face as he leaned in. He raised his hands and placed them on her throat. He was going to strangle her, squeeze every last ounce of life out of her body and drop her to the floor. Except … when he touched her, when his cold shaking fingers made contact with her neck, the anger he felt dissipated. The feel of her skin ignited something within him. She was smooth and soft. He felt a stirring in his stomach, like butterflies. He instantly began to relax and the sensation of warmth spread down to his groin and up to his lips. He felt himself smile. He locked eyes with Matilda and the world stopped turning. Neither of them blinked. The unknown had become known. Matilda's fear escalated. Ben's determination to kill waned. Something else was about to happen. Ben Hales was going to force himself onto her. He was going to rape Matilda Darke.

He let go; backed off. He turned and left the house without looking back. He couldn't look at her. He didn't want her to see the tears streaming down his face.

Now, crouching in the damp woods by the trunk of a several hundred-year-old tree he vomited. The disgust he felt for himself, for what he had turned into, rose up inside him and he ejected it all over the soggy ground. When his stomach was empty he kept retching. He wanted every drop of evil inside him to come out.

Through the tears and the hacking he screamed his apologies to Matilda – but they were lost in the wind.

Ben Hales had reached the point of no return. He had become everything he had ever hated.

Matilda stood in the shower as the skin-dissolving hot water rained down on her. The strength of the jets and the heat had numbed her body long ago. She no longer felt the pain and the burning, yet she still felt the sensation of Ben Hales' fingers lightly tracing her neck before his grip took hold. The second he touched her his entire persona had changed. He turned from a pathetic, angry, bitter man into a vicious predator. He was going to inflict the worse possible crime a woman could endure. He was going to rape her. She saw it in his eyes: the brief glimpse of violence and lust. She knew he wanted to hurt her – something long-lasting that would live with her for the rest of her life. She had no idea he was capable of such barbarity.

She braced herself. The last man who had touched her was her husband. She had never thought of being physical with another man. Matilda didn't want anyone else touching her. She had no idea her next form of physical contact was going to be a violation of her body. Her mind immediately brought up the conversation she'd had with Rory in the hospital canteen after interviewing Lois Craven: *If a bloke tried to rape me I'd kick him so hard between his legs he'd need surgery to have his balls removed from his throat.* That hadn't happened. She'd frozen. Fight or flight? Like Lois, she did neither.

Matilda stared deep into Ben's eyes and saw the hatred and the anger looking back at her. And then, it was over before it could even begin. He let go of her neck. He swallowed hard and blinked and when he opened his eyes the monster was gone. He was back to the sad, pathetic Ben Hales. He turned and left without looking back.

She waited in the hallway and listened for the sound of his

car starting. She strained to hear it disappear down the road at speed. As soon as the house fell into silence once more Matilda ran to the front door, slammed it closed, and locked it with the bolts at the top and bottom before securing the safety chain. She ran upstairs and made it to the bathroom just in time to be sick.

Ben Hales was wet, cold, and covered in dried vomit. He was frightened by what he was turning into. Did he really have the potential to become a rapist? He wondered what had stopped him and, more importantly, what would happen if there was a next time?

He staggered out of the woods and, surprisingly, his car was still waiting for him at the side of the road. He had left the driver's door open and the key in the ignition. People were obviously very honest in Whirlow. He slumped in behind the wheel, turned on the engine, and slammed his foot down hard on the accelerator. He didn't bother putting on his seat belt.

From Whirlowdale Road he turned left onto Abbey Lane. At the junction, the lights were in his favour, not that he was planning to stop, so turned left onto Abbeydale Road. There was very little traffic about so he roared along at sixty, seventy miles per hour. As he reached the bright lights of the Tesco petrol station the traffic started to build up. He swerved to get around an ancient Fiat Punto and drove into the path of a single decker bus. The driver slammed on the brakes and sounded his horn but Ben paid no attention.

The lights ahead were on red. He pressed his foot down harder on the accelerator and closed his eyes. Something hit him. He had no idea what it was but he felt his entire body shift in the car. His head hit something hard and the life was knocked out of him. Before he lost consciousness Ben thought of the driver who had rammed into him. He thanked them for saving his life by taking it away from him.

FORTY-SEVEN

DC Rory Fleming drove like a man possessed. He had tried to call Matilda's mobile several times but she wasn't picking up. He'd managed to get through to the ACC who was on her way back into the station but Matilda seemed to be off the grid.

The traffic was shocking as he approached Abbeydale Road. He assumed there had been an accident or a break down, so he took the back roads. He pulled up outside Matilda's house and ran to the front door, simultaneously knocking hard and ringing the bell. Her car was in the driveway so she was obviously home.

He looked up at the house but it was in darkness. He knocked again, harder this time.

'I'm coming,' he heard an exasperated voice from inside call out but he still continued with his knocking.

The door opened and a very red-faced Matilda stood in the doorway wrapped in a pink towelling dressing gown.

'Rory, what the hell do you think you're doing?'

'I've been ringing and ringing for ages. You've not picked up.'

'There's a reason for that. Phones don't work in the shower. What's going on?'

'You need to get dressed. We think Colin Theobald is at Alice

Hardaker's house. Sian and Faith are there and from what we can gather, he's armed and he's holding them hostage.'

Matilda told Rory to wait in the kitchen while she ran upstairs to get dressed. She closed the door to the living room before he could see the mass of boxes and books she had recently inherited. After a few minutes she ran into the kitchen where she found Rory eating an apple.

'Sorry,' he said. 'I hope you don't mind. I was feeling a bit sick. I haven't eaten since lunchtime.'

She smiled. 'Let's go. You can fill me in on the way there.'

Once Sian had realized they were in a hostage situation she had put her hand in her pocket where her mobile phone was and dialled the last number she had called – Rory's. He had been in Meadowhall at the time trying to find something cheap but expensive looking for Amelia's birthday when his phone rang.

Above the din of chattering shoppers he couldn't make out much of what Sian was saying but he was under no illusion she was in trouble.

'How do you know she's being held hostage?' Matilda asked as they made their way quickly, but cautiously, along the back roads of Sheffield.

'She told him to stop pointing the gun at her. I called the station and the sergeant on the front desk with the lazy eye told me he saw Sian and Faith head out about half an hour earlier. I looked on the tracking device on Sian's car and it's in the vicinity of Alice's home.'

'Sian has a tracking device on her car?'

'We all have?'

'Do we? Have I?'

'Yes.'

'Oh. I don't know if I like that.'

'I'll ask you the next time you're being held hostage,' Rory said through gritted teeth as he tried to squeeze his car around a slow moving people carrier towing a caravan. 'I fucking hate caravans.'

'You should have taken Abbeydale.'

'It's gridlocked, probably a broken-down bus or something.'

'So what's happening now?'

'The ACC said she was going to the station and she's going to organize the Firearms Unit to meet us at the scene. She asked where you were and I said I'd already called and you were on your way back in.'

'Thanks Rory,' she said. She looked across at him and smiled but his eyes were fixed on the road ahead. 'I hope Alice's kids aren't at home.'

'Where else are they going to be?'

'Didn't someone say her sister's been having them a bit since her husband died?'

'Yes. Let's hope they're there tonight.'

They turned onto Broad Elms Lane and parked several doors up from the Hardaker house. They looked at each other with worried faces when they both saw Sian's car.

The road was in darkness, save for the useless solar street lights. It was difficult to think that among these perfectly set houses, neatly trimmed bushes, freshly mown lawns, and quaint hanging baskets, an armed siege was taking place.

They stepped out of the car as the rest of the team arrived. The ACC, in a crisp uniform, jumped out before the car came to a halt.

'Matilda, what the hell is going on?'

'We've just arrived ourselves, ma'am,' she said, holding herself to keep warm against the stiff breeze. Thankfully it had stopped raining.

'Who's in there?'

'As far as we know Sian and Faith. We think the gunman is Colin Theobald and I'm guessing Alice Hardaker is there too. No idea if the kids are at home.'

'I bloody hope not. Right,' she said, clapping her leather-gloved hands together, 'the Firearms Unit are delayed. There was more unrest at Page Hall this evening. In the meantime, we need to proceed with caution.'

'What do you suggest?'

'To be perfectly honest, Matilda, I haven't a bloody clue.'

Twenty minutes went by with everyone standing around waiting for something, anything, to happen. The only difference was everyone was now wearing a ballistic vest. A white van came around the corner and a team of officers carrying automatic weapons jumped out of the back. Superintendent Edmund Hasselbank stepped out of the front and joined the ACC and Matilda. They shook hands.

'Nice to see you again, Valerie,' Hasselbank said. He had the stance of a drill sergeant, the crew cut of an Action Man, and the mixed accent of a Scotsman who's been living in Yorkshire too long.

'You too. Look, this is all yours. Anything you want or need you've got it. As far as we know there are four adults in there; two of them are my police officers. There are two children who live at the property but we don't know if they're in there.'

'Until we know for certain, we'll assume they are. Has the gunman made contact?'

'As far as we know he isn't even aware we're here.'

'Even better. Is there a back way into the house?'

The ACC looked to Matilda for the answer.

'There is but it's not easy. I've been on Google Earth and if you go to the next street there are some flats. Between the two properties is a small woodland area. You can get through there to the back garden of the property,' Matilda said.

'Excellent. I'll send a few men round. In the meantime, make sure nobody leaves their homes or looks out of the windows. Don't do anything until I get back,' he said, looking at Valerie, Matilda, and Rory in turn.

'You heard the man,' Valerie said. She looked out of her depth and was obviously pleased Edmund Hasselbank had turned up. She knew him of old and his capability for the job. He was a natural leader and maintained a cool and calm approach under stress. He was born for tasks like this.

Valerie returned to her car to make a call to the Chief Constable, while Rory assembled a team of uniformed officers to make door-to-door enquiries, to find out who was actually in the Hardaker house and to tell them to remain indoors and away from their windows. He also needed to call Aaron and Scott; every man was needed.

Matilda remained rooted to the spot. She was on the pavement directly opposite 101 Broad Elms Lane and kept her eyes firmly on the house. She strained, refusing to blink, as if she was using X-ray vision to see through brick. Eventually, something caught her eyes and she snapped out of her reverie.

There was a gap in the living room curtains where they failed to meet in the middle. Through this gap Matilda could see there was a light on, and now, someone had just moved across it. The living room was occupied. Is this where the gunman was?

She went to the Armed Response Vehicle and asked for a pair of binoculars. Going back to her spot she lifted them up and adjusted the settings to get a clear image. It wasn't perfect but she was sure she could make out colours dancing on a television screen, and— Matilda lowered the binoculars.

Matilda ran to the car where Valerie was ending a call on her mobile. She didn't look too happy.

'Ma'am, the kids are in the house.'

'Shit!'

Valerie climbed out of the car and looked around for Edmund but he wasn't there. He had gone to the next street to instruct his officers to find a safe position among the undergrowth and focus on the Hardaker's house.

'Are you sure?'

'Positive.'

'Any sign of the gunman?'

'No. I wasn't looking for long enough but it looks like the kids are just watching television.'

'Then maybe Theobald is holding his hostages in another part of the house,' Valerie guessed.

'Or maybe he's left already. We've put these cars through the ANPR and they're all registered to people in this road. Either Colin Theobald is clever enough to park in another street or he's been and gone.'

'But Sian's car's still here.'

'I know,' Matilda said, not wanting to think the inevitable. Had Colin Theobald left the house with whatever he came for and shot his hostages? It would not look good for Valerie or Matilda if two police officers had been shot dead while they had stood outside in the cold waiting for nothing to happen.

'Keep watching the living room until Edmund comes back. It's his call.'

Matilda went back to her observation point and looked through the binoculars, focusing on the living room once again. There was definitely a television switched on: she could see the reflection of images against the back wall. Nobody seemed to be moving about. She remained engrossed, gripping the binoculars hard, not daring to blink in case she missed even the slightest hint of movement.

There it was. Someone was coming to the window. The curtains were opening a little. A young face popped through. It was a boy.

Matilda's heart raced. She didn't look about her in case she drew attention to herself. She walked slowly, but with determination, across the road and onto the Hardaker's drive. The young boy at the window saw her and gave a little wave. She smiled and ducked under the view from the glass in the front door and crouched the rest of the distance to the living room window. She instructed the boy to open it.

'Hello,' she said in her best sing-song voice. 'Is your mummy in there with you?'

'No. Just me and my sister,' he said in his usual volume. Matilda wanted to ask him to lower his voice but didn't want to frighten him.

'OK. Where is your mum?'

'She's in the kitchen with Auntie Jenny making the tea. And two women policemen.'

'Oh right. What are you having for tea?'

'Pasta and meatballs I think.'

'Yummy. My name's Matilda. What's yours?'

'Warren.'

'And what's your sister called?'

'Milly.'

'Warren, I'm a police officer too. I really need to speak to your mum. Do you think you could let me in?'

'How do I know you're a police officer?'

Matilda struggled for her warrant card from the pocket under her ballistic vest. She eventually wrestled it free and showed it to the boy. His eyes lit up.

'The other lady showed me hers but yours is better,' he said, taking it from her. 'I really want to be a policeman when I grow up.'

'That's great. I think you'd be a good policeman.'

'Do you think so?'

'Definitely,' she smiled. 'Warren, will you do me a favour?'

'What?'

'I need you and your sister to come to the front door for me. Don't let your mum know. Just come and open the door. Will you do that?'

'Why?'

Matilda thought for a few long seconds. She wasn't good with children and had no idea how she was supposed to placate them during times of stress. 'Well, I'm not supposed to tell you but me and your mum are playing a game and I want to surprise her.'

'Can we play?'

'Not right now. In a little while you can. But first I need you and Milly to open the front door and step outside and then I'll pop in and get your mum. Will you do that?'

He frowned while he weighed up his options. 'OK,' he said. He trotted away from the window and over to the door leading into the hallway.

Matilda moved to the front door. She looked behind her and saw Rory standing on the pavement opposite the driveway. His face was pale and the look of stricken horror was evident.

'What the fuck are you doing?' he mouthed at her.

Before she could reply the front door opened and shrouded in the light of the hallway stood Warren and Milly in their school uniform, oblivious to the events going on somewhere in the house. Matilda breathed a sigh of relief.

'Do you see that man behind me?' Matilda asked them turning and pointing at Rory. 'He's a really good friend of mine and he knows some really funny jokes too. I want you to run over to him right now, OK?'

It was only now that Warren and Milly appeared sceptical about what was happening.

'I don't know. I should probably go and ask Mum.'

Matilda turned around and beckoned Rory towards her. Grudgingly, he went, crouched down.

'Take the kids,' she said to him.

She pulled Warren and Milly out of the house. Rory placed his arm around them both and ran up the drive and across the road. Matilda could hear their protestations but ignored them. She waited until they were safely across the road before entering the house and closing the front door firmly behind her.

FORTY-EIGHT

Matilda stood in the hallway; the silence enveloping her. She could only imagine the scene of chaos outside as ACC Masterson and Superintendent Hasselbank learned of her unprofessional conduct. She knew she would face serious repercussions for her actions – providing she survived them. After what she had been through tonight, however, she didn't care what was thrown at her. She had saved the lives of two innocent children. If she had to take a bullet to save the lives of two of her colleagues, then so be it.

There were four doors leading off the hallway: the toilet, the dining room, the living room, and the kitchen. They were all closed. Taking slow and careful steps she listened intently to what was going on in each room.

'How many people are going to have to die tonight, Alice?'

'I … I … please. I don't know what you're talking about.'

'Are you going to keep this up all night? I've just killed your sister. Who do I have to kill for you to tell the truth? Do you want me to bring your kids in here?'

'No!'

'Then hand over the money. Look, this is a nice house, I don't mind taking goods to the value you owe. I'm sure you've got some expensive jewellery. You've got two minutes to make up your mind or I'll bring one of your kids in here.'

Matilda stepped back from the kitchen door. The exchange between Colin and Alice was terrifying. Alice was obviously in an emotional state. She was sobbing uncontrollably and refusing to give in to Colin's demands. He sounded determined. His voice was full of rage and venom. He meant business. Had he really killed her sister? Matilda couldn't hear anyone else's voice so didn't know if Sian and Faith were in there. She had two minutes to do something or he would open the door and go for one of the kids. When he found them missing, who knew what he would do.

It seemed to take ages but she grabbed the cold doorknob and turned it slowly and gently. The door didn't open. It was locked from the inside.

There was a small faux-antique desk in the hallway that screamed veneer. She pulled open the drawers and rummaged around among the pens, batteries, odd gloves, and little packets of tissues until she came across a small bunch of keys. They were all identical but she guessed they had to be to the locks of the internal doors. All the doors matched so it seemed obvious the keys would match.

She went back to the kitchen door and inserted the key in the centre of the lock. She turned it slowly, listening for a click but it stuck halfway. It was the wrong key. It took another two attempts before she found the correct one. As the door unlocked, Matilda realized she had been holding her breath and she let out a huge sigh of relief.

Walpole, Compton, Pelham, Pelham-Holles, Cavendish, Pelham-Holles, Stuart, Grenville, Wentworth.

Now was not the time for an anxiety attack to set in. She needed to have a clear mind in order to take control of the situation. She almost scoffed. She hadn't had a clear mind for over a year, why should right now be any different?

Pitt the Elder, Fitzroy, North, Wentworth, Petty, Bentinck, Pitt the Younger, Addington.

'Fuck it,' she said to herself. She counted to three and pushed the door wide open and entered the kitchen.

'Why don't we all just calm down and talk about this like sensible adults?'

Matilda stopped dead in her tracks as Colin Theobald turned quickly and aimed his gun at her. Her eyes darted to Sian who was standing by a leather sofa with a tearful Alice Hardaker and Faith Easter sitting down. Sian proffered a small smile of relief at seeing her boss.

'Who the fuck are you?'

'I'm Detective Chief Inspector Matilda Darke from South Yorkshire Police.'

'Darke?' Colin started laughing. 'Oh my God, they've sent you? This is brilliant. I know South Yorkshire Police are struggling at the moment but are they really so desperate that they've sent you into a hostage situation?'

Matilda tried not to look hurt but it wasn't easy.

'You're the equivalent to the canary they sent down the mines to make sure it was safe.' He turned to his three hostages. 'I hope you realize that you're all going to end up dead before this is over. This woman is to a successful case what I am to a nine-to-five job.'

'I heard you saying something about money you're owed,' Matilda said. Her voice was shaking. The tiny piece of confidence she had managed to muster out in the hallway had disappeared. Did everyone who read the local newspaper think the same way about her? Was she a joke?

'I'm not going through all this again,' he waved the gun to the leather sofa. 'Go and join your fellow bitches.'

'Mr Theobald, you don't seem to understand the seriousness of the situation. There are armed police surrounding this entire house. You won't be going anywhere. So put the gun down and let's talk about this down at the station.'

He laughed. 'You sound like a tough bitch copper, you've got the words and everything, but I'm not feeling it. I bet if I put the end of this gun in your mouth you'd just stand there and piss yourself. Now, I'm owed twenty grand. I don't care how I get it, or who gives it to me, but I'm not leaving this house until I get it. And if that means you four slags end up with bullets in your heads, and those two kids get cut up, then so be it.'

'Oh God,' Alice broke down once again. Faith put a comforting arm around her but the gesture was hollow. She was just as petrified.

'Alice, your children are safe. I led them out of the house myself.'

'What?' she asked, a smile of relief spreading across her face.

'What?' Colin asked. 'You took the kids out of the house?'

'Yes. You're running out of options Mr Theobald. Now put down the gun.'

Colin stormed over to the sofa and dragged Alice to her feet by her hair. She screamed as he wrapped her shoulder-length hair around his free hand. He placed the gun to her temple.

Matilda and Sian exchanged glances. A message was passed between the two. They had been working together for many years – they knew a glance and a slightly raised eyebrow meant more than a nervous tick.

'Colin,' Matilda shouted. 'Let go of Alice. She's been through enough. If you want to hurt someone come and hurt me.'

He stopped in his tracks and looked up at Matilda.

'You've been in and out of prison your whole life; you know the score. Say you do walk out of here with twenty grand, maybe killing one or all of us, sooner or later you're going to end up in prison. Now, how good do you want to look inside? Do you want the death of a housewife on your hands, or the murder of a Detective Chief Inspector? Which one will make you the big man?'

'Matilda, don't,' Sian pleaded.

He seemed to be weighing up the options. 'You've got a point there. A cop killer is definitely going to get me on the front pages.'

'If you plead not guilty then there'll be a full trial. That will be on the front pages for months. Leave Alice alone.'

He finally relented and let go of Alice's hair. She almost collapsed and was caught by Faith just in time.

Colin stepped forward. 'Come on bitch, how about I send you to meet your husband?'

The rage building inside Matilda blurred her vision and she almost missed her opportunity. Seeing Sian move made her jump into action.

Sian stepped forward, picked up a glass bottle of olive oil and smashed it over Colin's head. As he screamed and ducked in pain, Matilda picked up the marble rolling pin from the counter and brought it down on Colin's right arm that was holding the gun. He screamed again and fell to the floor. Matilda reached for the gun and kicked it out of the way. Sian jumped and landed on Colin's back so he couldn't get up. He was crying out in pain.

Matilda leaned down and whispered into his ear. 'Men like you are pathetic. You sound like a tough bastard, you've got the words and everything, but I'm just not feeling it.'

FORTY-NINE

Alice was inconsolable. As armed police and uniformed officers burst into her house she cried and screamed for her children. Aaron restrained her and led her out of the house with his arms around her shoulders. The second she saw her two terrified kids she shrugged out of Aaron's hold and ran towards them and refused to let go. All three went into the ambulance as one.

Faith was also having a hard time dealing with what she had just gone through. It was the first time she had been on the receiving end of a gun and it was not what she had expected. She thought she was cool and calm under pressure. Her brief sojourn in the Murder Room last year had made her lose a great deal of confidence; however, four months on, Faith believed she was back to her usual self. She was wrong.

Being the victim in a hostage situation was surreal, horrifying, and traumatic. She smiled at her fellow officers and watched Sian out of the corner of her eye to see how she was dealing with it all, but she seemed unfazed. How was that possible?

She made her way through the hectic crowd, avoided questions about how she was feeling and practically fell out of the house and into the cold night air. The fine rain had started up again and the wind was brisk. She could feel the naked elements against her skin. Her hair was whipped up by the breeze and the cold cut through her but she didn't care. She was alive. That was what mattered. She had survived.

'Are you all right?' Matilda asked Sian quietly in the corner of the kitchen.

'Yes I'm fine. You?'

'I think so.'

'I didn't think you were going to hit him after I clocked him with that bottle. I saw you just standing there. My heart was in my mouth.'

'I know. It was him mentioning James; it was like a slap in the face. I just froze. Then James popped into my head and I knew he'd want me to beat the crap out of him.'

'I think you may have broken his wrist,' Sian said, looking over to the sofa where Colin Theobald was sitting on the floor, leaning against the units, and holding his wrist. The agony on his face was satisfying for the two detectives. His suffering wasn't enough though. Not for everything he had put them all through.

A team of paramedics pushed their way through the crowd and began to tend to Colin who was now under arrest. His good arm was handcuffed to a uniformed officer. There was no chance he was going to be allowed anywhere on his own. Not for a long time.

'Sian, I want you to do me a favour,' Matilda said, lowering her voice even more. 'Give Scott Andrews a call. I know it's late but this is vital. Ask him what make of BMW ran him off the road.'

'What? Is that relevant?'

'Depending on what answer I get from him, it could be very relevant.'

Sian saw the ACC heading towards them. Her stony face and pinched lips were evidence this was not going to be a slap on the back and a cheery 'well done'. Sian made her excuses and left.

'I don't even know where to begin,' Valerie said. 'You broke every single rule in the book. You put the lives of two officers, Alice, her two children, and yourself in the most serious danger.'

'I know. I'm sorry. As soon as I saw the two kids through the gap in the curtains I knew I couldn't stand by. I had to do something.'

'Do you have any idea what kind of a nightmare you've caused? I should suspend you on the spot for what you've done.'

'Ma'am, I understand where you're coming from and I really am sorry for the headache I've caused you but look around you, we've got a result.'

'It could so easily have gone the other way.'

'But it didn't. And that's my point. If this had turned into a bloodbath I would have given you my ID right now. I would have handed myself in and told you to charge me with manslaughter because I would have deserved that. But what I did here tonight worked out for the best.'

'There will be an inquiry,' Valerie said after a while.

'I'm aware of that.'

'And there is a dead woman over there.'

'That happened before even Sian and Faith got here.'

Valerie took a deep breath and let out a long sigh. 'One of these days, Matilda, your luck is going to run out and I won't be able to protect you.'

She didn't wait for a reply. She turned and left the room, not giving a second glance to Matilda or the scene of chaos that lay on the kitchen floor around her.

Superintendent Hasselbank had been eavesdropping and came over to speak to Matilda. 'If you tell anyone I said what I'm about to say I will strenuously deny it. If I were in your position, I would have done exactly the same thing. You saw two kids in peril and you saved them. Well done, Mat.'

He didn't wait for a response. He patted her on the shoulder and then left the room. Matilda stood, her back to the wall, and inwardly smiled. She had received a bollocking, but it could have been worse. She had received praise, and that made up for the inquiry and the questions and the finger-pointing that was to come.

Matilda didn't want to let Colin Theobald out of her sight so asked Rory to drive her to the Northern General Hospital, following the ambulance.

There seemed to be more uniformed officers milling about the hospital than there were back at HQ. They had been assigned to look after Alice and the children, and Colin needed an armed guard. He may be incapacitated with cuts to the head and a broken wrist, but he was still a highly dangerous man.

Matilda was shocked to find Faith sitting in a chair in a cubicle, a red blanket wrapped around her shoulders.

'Faith, what happened? I thought you weren't injured.'

'I'm not. Apparently I'm in shock,' she smiled.

'Was that your first time staring down the barrel of a gun?'

She nodded, holding back the tears.

Matilda sat on the edge of the bed. She was relieved to take the weight off her feet. 'The first time is always the hardest. You're trained for it and you think you'll be able to cope when it happens but it's never the same as when you're in a classroom.'

'Sian seemed to handle it OK.'

'During Sian's first week on the force she attended a robbery in a bookmakers' on London Road. She and another uniformed officer were first on the scene. They entered the shop to find the robber still on the premises. He had two handguns and he pointed them both at Sian. She froze. She had no idea what to do and couldn't remember any of her training. Later she told me that she looked at the kid holding the guns and saw he was more scared than she was. There's nothing more dangerous than a scared man holding a gun. She talked to him, and after about twenty minutes, he put the guns down.'

'Colin Theobald isn't a scared kid though.'

'No he's not. But he isn't the norm. The man is a psycho. Thankfully the majority of those only exist in films. We rarely meet one in our work. Use what you went through tonight, don't try and forget it or feel embarrassed by it, remember it, then, next time you face something like this you'll know exactly what to do.'

'When Colin pointed that gun at you, what did you think?'

'I'll be perfectly honest with you Faith, and if you tell anyone, I'll kill you: when he pointed that gun at me, I wet myself a little. I was terrified.'

'Thank you.'

'What for?'

'Your honesty.'

'I know we haven't worked together much Faith, but there's one thing you should know about me, I will never lie to you.'

Matilda left Faith to her thoughts and went in search of Rory. There was nothing more she could do here tonight. Once Colin had had his wrist tended to and his head patched up he would be transferred to a police cell. She would interview him in the morning after everyone had had a good night's sleep.

As soon as she stepped into the corridor she was greeted by a stern-looking Adele Kean.

'Give me one good reason why I shouldn't slap you across the face.'

'Because I make a great beef stew?'

'What the hell were you thinking tonight?'

'Who's been talking?'

'Rory phoned and told me everything.'

Matilda rolled her eyes. 'Thanks for the loyalty, Rory.'

'Don't you dare have a go at him. He's looking out for you. He's got your best interests at heart, though God only knows why. You could have got yourself killed tonight.'

'But I didn't.'

Adele, put her arm around her friend and took her to one side. She lowered her voice. 'I know you're going through hell right now with what's been written in the newspapers and the anniversaries and everything, but are things really so bad that you're playing Russian roulette every time you leave the house?'

'Adele, you weren't there. You didn't see the kids in that house. If you had, you'd have done exactly the same thing.'

Adele didn't reply. The thought of two innocent young children in danger would have made anyone put their own life at risk. She couldn't deny that. 'Just don't do it ever again, do you understand that?'

'I'll try.'

'Good. Anyway, how are you feeling?'

'I'm fine.'

'No, really?'

Matilda laughed. 'Really, Adele. I'm fine.'

Adele frowned. 'You haven't heard, have you?'

'Heard what?'

'About Ben Hales.'

Matilda's heart sank. She didn't want to hear that man's name again, not after what had happened tonight. 'What about him?' Her question lacked sincerity.

'He's in Intensive Care. He drove through a red light and was hit by a car. According to witnesses, it looked deliberate.'

Matilda swallowed hard and the prickly sensation of anxiety crawled up her back. Was this another man's death she was going to have on her conscience?

'Is he going to be all right?'

'He'll be lucky if he makes it to morning.'

FIFTY

Matilda didn't sleep much after the excitement of the hostage situation. Fuelled by adrenaline, anger, and stress she eventually fell asleep around three o'clock, only to wake less than two hours later.

Come on bitch, how about I send you to meet your husband?

She woke with Colin's words echoing around the room. Given his character he would have pulled the trigger and shot Matilda. Is that what she wanted? Did his words ignite something in her that made her realize she wanted to be reunited with James? Is that why she risked her life as soon as she realized the situation was fraught with danger?

On her bedside table was a wooden framed photograph of her husband. She took it just after they had become a couple on a weekend away to the Lake District. He was leaning against the railing outside the cottage and looked straight into the lens of the camera. His hair was windswept, his blue eyes bright and intense, his smile beaming, his teeth chattering as the cold tore through him. But he was happy.

Matilda wiped away the tears and pushed back the duvet. She knew sleep was lost to her now.

Sitting up in bed, she picked up her mobile and dialled a familiar number. It took a while for the call to be answered.

'Hello?' a sleepy voice asked.

'Hello Mum, it's me.'

'Matilda? What is it? What's the matter?'

'Nothing. Why?'

'Well it's … it's still dark out. What are you doing ringing at this hour?'

Matilda looked at the alarm clock on the bedside table. It wasn't quite five o'clock yet. 'I'm sorry, Mum, I thought it was later. Do you want me to call you back another time?'

'No it's all right. I'm awake now. Are you OK?'

'I'm fine. I just wanted to ring for a chat, see how you are.' Matilda's voice was breaking and she had to swallow hard a few times to keep her emotions under control.

'I'm doing OK, thank you, Matilda. How are things with you?' The worry in her mother's voice was palpable. She had never been comfortable with her daughter being in the police force.

'They're OK. I'm sorry I haven't called recently. Things have been a bit … well I've been busy.'

'I understand.'

'What have you been up to lately?'

'Your dad took me to Bakewell yesterday. He bought me a lovely antique necklace. I think he's feeling guilty over inviting his brother to stay without asking me.' She half-laughed. 'We had a great meal too. Then we went to feed the ducks and some of them got a bit over-excited and your dad panicked. I wish I'd had a camera on me, Matilda, you should have seen his face. He's standing there with a full loaf of bread and the ducks are literally jumping out of the water. He ended up emptying whole slices into the river. Everyone was laughing.'

Matilda leaned back in bed and began to relax. She could picture her father standing by the river's edge battling with the ducks. It made her smile. She listened while her mother regaled her with more tales from Bakewell, including her father standing in a cowpat (it wasn't his day yesterday), and how they bought a real Bakewell pudding and ate it all last night, something her mother was now regretting (but loved every mouthful).

Eventually Matilda ended the call. She promised she would visit at the weekend and it was a promise she intended to keep.

She made herself a strong black coffee and took it into the living room. She turned on the light and saw the mass of boxes that, somehow, she had forgotten about. She opened the nearest one to her and pulled out the first book: *No Night is Too Long* by Barbara Vine. She laughed at the irony of the title. Every night spent alone was too long.

Matilda sat among the boxes and began to look through them. Jonathan Harkness seemed to own every printed word by Michael Robotham, Mark Billingham, Simon Kernick, P. D. James, Agatha Christie, Susan Hill … the list was endless. Had he really read them all? She wondered how many books he'd read in a year; did he read as soon as he came home from work in the early evening until the early hours of the morning? He had immersed himself in fiction. When Matilda considered what reality contained, she could understand why he'd done it.

At the bottom of one of the boxes, Matilda found a hardback notebook. It was Jonathan's book of books: the journal he used to write a list of books he wanted to buy from his favourite authors and the date they were published. She flicked to the last page with writing on it and saw several novels he had wanted but hadn't got around to buying. There were three: Elly Griffiths, Sarah Hilary, and James Oswald. Books were important to Jonathan, owning them as well as reading them. He'd wanted these to complete his collection.

Matilda put the notebook to one side. She'd buy the books once the shops were open. She was happy to act as caretaker to Jonathan's collection, and she was determined to make sure it was a complete collection.

Matilda arrived at South Yorkshire Police HQ for eight o'clock. She wanted to prepare the interview with Colin Theobald. She had called DI Christian Brady while it was still dark and he had agreed to go over the burglaries with her so she could hit Colin with everything they had. There was no way he was escaping justice.

'Good morning Matilda,' Sian said. 'You look tired; didn't you sleep much?'

'Not really.'

'I was out as soon as my head hit the pillow. I couldn't keep my eyes open.'

Matilda smiled. Did nothing faze this woman?

'I spoke to Scott last night about the kind of car that ran him off the road.'

'Go on.'

'It was a BMW 3 Series convertible.'

'Oh.'

'He got part of the number plate too. It began YP and ended KKE or it could have been KKD.'

'Right.'

'Not what you wanted to hear?'

'Not really.'

'Colin Theobald drives a BMW series 1.'

'I know, Sian. Lucas Branning works for a garage; get on to them and ask if they've had any BMW convertibles in recently. Check the reg number. If it's a match to the one that ran Scott off the road then charge Branning with endangering lives, driving without due care and attention, assaulting a police officer and anything else you can think of.'

'Will do. Oh, by the way, Colin has changed his mind about not wanting a solicitor present so we've had to request one as he doesn't have one. There'll be a bit of a delay on the interview.'

'He's doing this on purpose.'

'Well he doesn't have any cards left to play so he's playing the "piss the police off" card. Very effectively too judging by the vein throbbing on your forehead.'

Following a lengthy chat with DI Brady in which Matilda was told everything she needed to know about the aggravated burglaries, and a great deal of information she had no interest in, she found a note on her desk informing her the ACC needed to see her immediately. She had been waiting for this all morning.

Valerie held up a copy of last night's newspaper. Matilda winced as it brought back memories of what happened in her house with Ben Hales.

'Neither of us come off well in this.'

'I'm aware,' Matilda said, head down, eyes fixed on the carpet.

'I've spent most of the morning getting a dressing-down from the Chief Constable. I've been threatened with suspension.'

'Bloody hell.'

'Fortunately, I know the editor on *The Star* and I was able to do a bit of a quid-pro-quo. Do you know who the source for the article is?'

'No,' she lied.

'Former DI Ben Hales.'

'Oh.'

'He called up Alex Winstanley specifically with a red hot story about the unfit running of South Yorkshire Police. I've listened to a recording of the conversation. Fortunately, Alex isn't a big fan of yours so he was only interested in the juicy bits about you. If he'd been a more qualified journalist this whole station would have been under the microscope.'

'What else did Ben have to say?'

'That's not important. What is important is that Alex Winstanley is no longer working on *The Star* and the editor, God love him, is going to be running a retraction article in this evening's edition.'

Matilda visibly relaxed. 'Well that's good.'

'Matilda, you don't look at all surprised that Ben Hales double-crossed us like this.'

'Sorry, I'm just tired,' she said, struggling for an excuse. 'To be honest, I've been half expecting something like this since he was forced out of the police. He's not the type of person to walk away quietly.'

'Did you hear he tried to kill himself last night?'

'Yes. Adele told me.'

'Remorse do you think; for what he'd said to Alex?'

'I don't think Ben Hales has much remorse.'

'He's made it through the night. I've got the doctor at the hospital going to call me as soon as he's in a fit enough state to talk to. I'm going to be having a serious word with that man.'

You're not the only one.

'So, fill me in on this Colin Theobald; is he responsible for the double shooting?'

'It would appear so.'

'And the burglaries?'

'Again, it would appear so.'

'Get him interviewed. Get him charged and get him out of here, Matilda. Do you understand? I know we're getting a retraction in the local paper but I'd love for there to be a genuine good news story about the force in the not too distant future.'

'I'll do my best.'

FIFTY-ONE

Matilda Darke and Christian Brady were to conduct the interview together. They spent almost half an hour in the CID suite going through who was going to lead and what direction they were going to take, but mostly it was to make Colin Theobald sweat just that little bit longer.

The smell in interview room one was an assault on all the senses; the pine disinfectant coming from the floor, the stale odour of sweat coming from the interviewee, and the bitter tang of an expensive cologne that even Rory Fleming would refuse to wear emanating from the duty solicitor, Francis Evans.

Evans was a tall imposing figure who had obviously been otherwise engaged when looks were being handed out. His eyes were too far apart and sunk deep into his skull. His large nose was almost a caricature, and he had the complexion of a man who enjoyed a drink or three in the evenings (and the mornings and afternoons). He sat behind the desk looking awkward; his lanky hulking frame too big for the chairs. When he held his hand out to shake it with the two detectives the sleeve of his jacket retracted up his arm, exposing a skeletal wrist.

Faux pleasantries exchanged, formalities made for the benefit of the recording and video equipment, it was time to begin the interview. However, before Matilda could even open her mouth, the nasal tones of the solicitor, trying to sound like an Oxford graduate but with the definite twang of true Yorkshireman, cut through the atmosphere.

'My client is considering taking legal action against South Yorkshire Police and you personally, Detective Chief Inspector Darke, for the injuries he sustained during his arrest.'

Matilda did not look surprised. She had clocked the smug expression on Colin's face as soon as she walked into the room. She knew the slimy solicitor would try this tactic. She sat back in her chair and folded her arms.

'Well if that's the road you want to go down Mr Evans, I'll instruct Alice Hardaker, DC Faith Easter, and DS Sian Mills to do the same for the emotional distress they were put through at being held hostage at the hand of your client. They will all need counselling and therapists aren't cheap. Mrs Hardaker will also be needing a new kitchen as the current one is stained with the blood of her dead sister – again at the hand of your client.'

The smirk had left Colin's face. He turned to his solicitor who gave the briefest of nods before turning back to face his interviewer.

'Now,' Matilda continued, 'shall we stop pissing about and get down to the real reason why we're all here?'

Round one to the police.

Francis Evans shifted uncomfortably in his seat and cleared his throat several times. He fingered the collar on his shirt and scratched at his neck where the tightness of the collar was interfering with his prominent Adam's apple.

'My client would like to make a confession,' he said in a matter-of-fact tone.

Now it was Colin's turn to adjust himself in his seat. He looked tired after a sleepless night in hospital and then the cells in the bowels of South Yorkshire Police HQ. His eyes drooped and his skin was dry and pale. The designer stubble he usually sported was growing thicker and unkempt. It would be a long time before he could spend hours in front of the bathroom mirror carefully neatening his beard.

'It's about the burglaries,' he began.

'You're going to have to speak up Colin, for the benefit of the recording equipment.'

He coughed, the phlegm rattling around in his throat, which he swallowed. 'The burglaries. I did them. I did them all.'

Matilda and Christian exchanged glances. Matilda could almost see the relief on the DI's face. He had been trying to solve this case for the best part of nine months. To get a confession, and so quickly, was music to his ears. There was even a hint of a smile.

'We know,' Christian said. He sat back. He was going to enjoy this. 'From the snippets of description we've managed to obtain from each of your victims there was no doubt in my mind, the second I walked into the room, that you were the perpetrator. Not to mention the fact that at your last robbery you removed your hat and mask before getting into your car and were seen by a neighbour. However, thanks for your confession. You've saved me weeks of preparing a case for the CPS and trying to convince all your petrified victims to be witnesses. You've saved me a real nightmare of a task.'

Round two to the police.

'I'd like to have a word with my client,' Francis Evans said.

Matilda smiled. 'I think that's probably wise.' She terminated the interview and both she and Christian left the room. In the corridor they resisted a high-five.

'You two look smug,' Sian said as she walked towards Matilda and Christian.

'We feel smug,' she replied.

'I've been onto the garage where Branning works. They have had a BMW 3 Series convertible in for the past few days and it matched the partial registration number Scott was able to supply us with.'

'Excellent. Have you spoken to Branning yet?'

'No. I'm going to do that now. Thought I'd give you some good news to cheer you up but you don't look like you need it.'

'Sian, the more good news the merrier. Just keep it coming.'

Sian walked on but turned back and called out, 'Oh, by the way, your lottery numbers came up at the weekend. Eight million.'

'You know, I think I prefer a confession.' She turned to Brady as Sian disappeared around a corner laughing to herself. 'Oh God, how sad does that sound? I'd rather take the confession of a murderer over having eight million in the bank.'

'You've been doing this job too long.'

'You're not kidding. Let's go for a coffee.'

'Are you treating me out of your winnings?' Christian smiled.

'I might even treat you to a bag of peanut M&Ms.'

'The last of the big spenders.'

Colin Theobald must have realized all hope was lost as when the interview resumed he could not talk fast enough. Matilda had heard plenty of statements and confessions in her time but what Colin told her made her blood run cold.

'I shared a cell, years ago, with Lucas Branning. I can't remember what he was in for, assault or something. I'd been caught robbing a paper shop in Doncaster and they got me for two more in Barnsley so I got a bit of a stretch that time. Anyway, me and Lucas got chatting, well, you do don't you, and we hit it off. Both support United, like the same music, same favourite curry. We had a laugh. Lucas got out before me but we said we'd keep in touch. We did at first but you know how it is, you go your separate ways. Lucas was going straight, last I heard. Good on him. I tried that and couldn't do it. I'm not one for routine, staying in the same place, settling down, getting a shit office job. It'd do my nut in.'

While he had a captive audience, Colin was using his statement as an excuse for his actions over the years. Was this an attempt at getting a lighter sentence if he had mitigating circumstances?

'Anyway, the years go by and suddenly I see Lucas again in the Penny Black. I thought it was just one of those things at first, you know, a coincidence. We had a few jars, a bit of a grin, a few games of pool, but by the end of the night he said he wanted a favour. He'd obviously been looking for me.

'Now, you've seen Lucas, he's not the tallest bloke in the world. He's not a threat to anyone. Now me, well, I can scare the shit out of anyone if I have to. That's what Lucas wanted me for. His sister's husband had been cheating on her and Lucas wanted me to have a word with him. Well, more than a word really, he wanted me to put the frighteners on him, slap him about a bit. He said he'd pay me a grand. Well, I wasn't going to turn that down was I?'

It was at this point Colin stopped and asked if he could have a cup of tea. Confessing to murder, rape, and attempted murder was thirsty work. Grudgingly, Matilda acquiesced. The four of them sat in relative silence while waiting for the tea to arrive. Matilda tried to prompt him to continue but he wouldn't. He was enjoying himself.

When the tea arrived he made a show out of blowing on it to cool the orange liquid, and taking the first sip. He exaggerated a sigh and had another drink. Judging by the drumming of the fingers on the table, even Francis Evans was beginning to get pissed off.

'Is that nice?'

'Lovely. There's nothing like a nice cup of tea is there?'

'So, you were saying,' Matilda pressed.

'Oh yes. Where was I?'

'Colin!' Matilda warned, her face reddening.

'All right.' He grinned. 'Don't get your under-crackers in a knot. I'm just having a bit of fun with you. You want to lighten up, love. You'll give yourself a stroke one of these days.'

'I'll lighten up when you've finished.'

'All right then. So, Lucas offers me a grand to give his brother-in-law a few slaps and teach him a lesson. Easiest grand ever I thought. He said we'd meet up a few days later to go over the details, when and where, that kind of thing. A couple of days go by and I get a call from Lucas. We meet up in that park near the Children's Hospital. He tells me his name, Kevin Hardaker, what kind of car he drives, where he works, and what he usually does after work. He gave me five hundred notes in an envelope and says he'll give me the rest when it's done. Fine by me.

'Now, here comes the interesting part. Lucas left the park first. I'm just sitting there pretending to enjoy myself when this bloke comes up to me, all posh in a suit, and sits down on the bench next to me. He said he's got a message from Alice Hardaker, Kevin's wife, and she doesn't want Lucas knowing about it. I'm to follow Kevin and wait until he picks up his fancy piece and jump them both. I'm to kill Kevin and have as much fun as I want with his tart but make sure she's still alive at the end of it. And, get this, he's going to give me ten fucking grand. Can you believe that?'

Colin jumped back in his seat, excited at the prospect of having ten thousand pounds in cash to do with whatever he wanted. The joy on his face, the smile on his lips, the glint in his eyes – he was loving it.

'He gave me a grand and Alice's address and told me when's it done, I'm to leave it a couple of days as the police'll be round and then I'm to go and collect my money. So I'm sat there in the park with fifteen hundred quid in my pocket and I've done fuck all. This is mint.

'I leave it a couple of days and I follow Kevin from work, watch his routine, and I see him pick up his tart. She's not bad to look at; I've had better and I've had worse. On the third time of following they park up in this out of the way lane and I'm like "this is going to be so fucking easy" so I just went for it.'

He leaned back as if that was the end of his story.

'This man in the park, who was he?' Matilda asked.

'Fuck knows.'

'Did he give you his name?'

'No.'

'A number to contact him on?'

'No.'

'An address?'

'No. He just said that I was to collect my money from Alice and he gave me her address. I guessed that if there were any problems I could have gone to her.'

'What did he look like?'

'I don't know.'

'What do you mean you don't know?'

'Well he didn't really look like anything really,' he shrugged. 'He was just a bloke. You know, brown hair, not tall, not short, not fat, not thin. He was just an ordinary bloke.'

'Did he speak with an accent?'

'Yes. Sheffield.'

'Would you recognize him again if you saw him?'

'Of course I would. I'm not senile. If someone offers you ten grand, you'll know him again when you see him. It's just that he looked plain, ordinary.'

'Where did you get the gun from?' Christian Brady asked.

'I've got a mate.'

'And his name?'

'Oh no, I'm not dobbing him in.'

'So you beat and shoot Kevin Hardaker,' Matilda said. 'That didn't bother you?'

'I was just doing my job.'

'Beating, shooting and raping Lois Craven – that was just a job too was it?'

Colin looked down at the table. The beaming pride of a job well done slipped away.

'What's the matter Colin?'

'Is that was she was called, Lois Craven?'

'Yes. Why?'

'I didn't know her name.'

Matilda opened the folder in front of her and removed a photograph of a smiling Lois Craven. She held it up and leaned forward. 'It makes it more real now you know her name and see what she looks like doesn't it? Let me guess, you're picturing it over and over again when you close your eyes aren't you? You're a burglar and you beat people up, but you're not a rapist. You got carried away that night and you couldn't help yourself. Afterwards, I bet you couldn't even remember what you'd done. Then it came back to you. You'd forced a woman to have sex with you. You've raped an innocent woman.'

Colin looked Matilda in the eyes, the tough exterior had crumbled. His shoulders were hunched. He looked like he was about to burst into tears. He turned away and Matilda placed the photo on the desk facing Colin. She wasn't going to let him forget the face of the woman whose life he had ruined.

'At first you told yourself it didn't matter, you're hardly likely to bump into her again. So you avoid the papers and the news on TV and you don't know anything about her. You're shocked that you're capable of raping a woman but you tell yourself it doesn't matter, that she was just an object. You can live with that, can't you? But now you know her name. Lois Craven. She's a person, a woman, a mother of three children. When you close your eyes at night now, you'll see her for who she really is. I'm right aren't I?'

Colin looked up once more. His face was stained with tears. His granite face was soft and flushed. He was full of remorse. 'Yes.'

'Interview terminated 13.27,' Matilda said. She turned off the recording equipment and left the room without looking back at Colin Theobald.

FIFTY-TWO

'Do you believe him?' Christian Brady asked following Matilda into the Murder Room.

'I'm not sure. If he was lying we'd find out eventually so it's only buying himself more time.'

'What are you going to do?'

Matilda looked pensive. She ignored the rest of the room, not that there was much going on to distract her, and went into her office. 'I don't know. I mean his description was certainly lacking in detail wasn't it?'

Christian scoffed. 'Not tall but not short. Not fat but not thin. I'd love to see how a court artist would draw that.'

'It's a shame he wasn't approached by Francis Evans. You could write a thesis on how he looks. I'm sure his nose gets bigger every time I see him.'

'Well, I'm going to get some lunch. I missed breakfast. You want anything?'

'Not yet. We'll have another go at Colin in an hour or so.'

'No problem. I'll be back by then.'

Christian left Matilda's office, closing the door quietly behind him. He left the DCI to her thoughts. She turned in her chair and looked out of the window overlooking the depressing image of a city in decay. The clouds were heavy with the threat of rain pushing down on the steel city. Grey offices built in the sixties and seventies, some of them long since abandoned and left to the elements; soulless new apartment buildings and hotels designed by the same architect with no imagination, all built at speed to save money but wouldn't last twenty years. There was so much wrong with Sheffield.

Matilda sighed. The longer she remained alone in her office the likelier her mind would fester. She should be concentrating on the double shooting and Colin Theobald's surprising interview but her mind kept changing direction. The anniversary of James's death was just a few days away. Carl Meagan has been missing for exactly a year – where was the little boy? Was he still in Sheffield being held against his will? There were plenty of abandoned buildings that hadn't been touched for decades, could he be trapped in one of those? Or was his body in one of those buildings? Slowly rotting away as time slipped by.

'Get a grip, Matilda,' she said to herself. She eased herself up and went into the main part of the office.

'Rory, I need a man,' she said.

The young DC looked up with a worried expression on his face. 'It's a nice thought ma'am, but I'm engaged.'

Matilda laughed. 'The look on your face was priceless, Rory. Thank you for that. No, I need you to get me some photos of men. Not mug shots, just happy family snaps.'

'Where from?'

'The Internet. Just print me off five or six photos.'

'Do I dare ask why?'

'Call it a social experiment.'

Sian entered the office carrying a large takeaway coffee and balancing a sandwich on top. 'Glad I found you,' she said to Matilda. 'I've checked with the garage and they did have a convertible BMW in. According to the bloke who runs the place the car needed a tune-up. Lucas took it for a test drive and was pranged by another driver, apparently, so they're doing the repair free of charge for the owner.'

'Please don't tell me it's all fixed and ready to go.'

'No. They've not even started it yet. I'm having it impounded for forensics to take a look at it. I saw the state of the car; it's definitely been involved in a scrape. Let's hope it matches Scott's car.'

'I'm sure of it.'

'I'm letting Lucas stew while I have my lunch. My stomach thinks my throat's been cut.'

'That coffee smells nice, what is it?'

'A peppermint latte.'

'What's wrong with the tea and coffee here?'

'I'm guessing you've not had a coffee this morning. It was Rory's turn to buy and he's bought the cheap crap.'

'I'm skint this month,' Rory chimed up. 'I've had to buy my season ticket. They're not cheap you know.'

'Has anyone seen Scott?' Matilda asked, suddenly remembering she hadn't seen him since morning.

'He's gone to the Northern General on his lunch to see how Joseph Glass is doing,' Sian said.

'Any news?'

'None. He's just not waking up. If he does I bet he'll have brain damage. I can't see him making a full recovery.'

'As optimistic as ever, Sian. Can I help myself to a bar of chocolate?'

''Course you can. I just think, the longer he's unconscious the less likely it'll be for him to wake up and actually get back to normal.'

'Poor sod. How's the whip-round going?'

'Very well. Got a few hundred already. I'm telling people notes only, no coins.' Sian smiled.

'Here are your photos,' Rory said slapping six images printed on photo paper in front of the DCI.

Matilda picked them up and flicked through them. 'These are

great, Rory, thanks. Hang on a minute. Isn't that Jonathan Ross with his family?'

'Yes. I couldn't find any others. You said you wanted a family man photo.'

'How many family men do you know attend film premieres? I sometimes wonder what's in that head of yours, Rory.'

As Matilda made her way down to the holding cells she came across Colin's solicitor in reception.

'Are you leaving?' Matilda asked.

'Just going to grab a bite to eat. No offence but your canteen doesn't offer anything appetizing today.'

'It never does. You are coming back though aren't you?'

'I most certainly am.'

'I'm just off to see Mr Theobald now.'

'Anything I should be privy to?'

'It depends on the answer I get from him. I'll see you later, Francis.'

'You certainly will, my dear.' He threw a flat cap on his large head and headed out of the double doors into the rapidly darkening afternoon.

Matilda watched him walk away before heading down to the cells.

Colin had just eaten lunch and had practically licked his plate clean. Facing a long sentence for murder, rape, attempted murder, aggravated burglary, and manslaughter had not affected his appetite at all.

'I could eat that again,' he told Matilda. 'You don't give large portions in here, do you?'

'I'm sorry about that Mr Theobald. I'll inform the chef. Look, Colin, about this bloke you said offered you ten grand to kill Kevin Hardaker ...'

'I know my description of him was shit but he really was an ordinary looking bloke.'

'I've got some photographs I want you to look at.' From the file she had under her arm, Matilda took out the photographs Rory had printed from the Internet for her, not including the one of Jonathan Ross, but definitely including the one from the files she was interested in. It was just a hunch and she really hoped she was wrong, but it was a question niggling at her brain and she needed it answered.

'Well it's definitely not him,' he said handing back one of the pictures.

'You seem sure.'

'I don't think Gordon Ramsay goes in for hiring hitmen.'

Matilda snatched it from him and looked at it. *Bloody Rory Fleming, I'll kill him.*

'This is him,' Colin said, sitting up straight on his bed. 'This is definitely the bloke.'

'You're sure?'

'Absolutely positive. Look, I know I said he was an ordinary bloke but you don't forget the face of the man who offers you ten thousand quid to kill a man, do you?'

'I suppose not.' Matilda looked at the photo of the family man with his arms draped around two children. The look on his face was one of happiness: his smile was wide and beaming as he looked up to the camera. It was a snap from a warm summer's day and everything seemed right with the world. Matilda was looking at him in a completely different light now. His smile no longer seemed innocent and dedicated to the upbringing of his children. He looked sinister and had the expression of a man with a miasma of dark thoughts running around his head.

'Do you know him?' Colin asked.

'I'm afraid I do.'

FIFTY-THREE

'Right everyone, listen up please.'

Matilda called the Murder Investigation Team to attention. Team. That was an understatement. It appeared that the 'team' was already being wound down and sent to different departments. Where were the uniformed officers who had been handling door-to-door enquiries? Where were the civilian support staff who had been answering the phones?

'The good news is that Colin Theobald has admitted to the burglaries. That will help free up some members of CID so maybe we can have a couple of their officers in here. He has also admitted to the double shooting of Kevin Hardaker and Lois Craven. However, he has stated that he didn't act alone. He was paid to kill.'

'Hired killers in Sheffield?' Sian asked.

'Originally he was asked by Lucas Branning to have a word with Kevin and stop him from having an affair and hurting his sister—'

'Wait,' Sian interrupted, 'that doesn't make any sense. How did Lucas know about the affair? Alice didn't know until after Kevin was killed. So if Lucas paid Colin who told Lucas?'

'Maybe Alice has been lying to us the whole time,' Rory suggested.

The room fell silent. It was a very interesting question.

*

'Lucas, how did you know about your sister's affair?'

Lucas was sitting in his prison cell waiting to be processed and sent to magistrate's court. He didn't seem to be enjoying the experience as much as Colin Theobald was. He looked depressed and tired. His head was slumped on his chest and the red eyes and nose were evidence he had been crying. He had tried to go straight but circumstance hadn't allowed it.

'I was told.'

'Who by?'

'A man.'

'Who?'

'I've no idea. I just got home from work and this bloke came up to me. I got the feeling he'd been waiting. He told me Kevin had been having an affair with some bird and it had been going on for a while. I didn't believe him at first. I mean, I didn't really know Kevin all that well but Alice always seemed happy and everything. Then this bloke showed me a photo of Kevin and the woman he was seeing. They were in their car, kissing.'

'So what did this man say to you?' Matilda asked. She was growing impatient.

'He said that Kevin needed someone to have a word with him, you know, sort him out.'

'Why was he telling you all this?'

'He said he knew I'd been in the nick and I must know people.'

'And did you?'

Lucas looked down and played with his shaking fingers. He nodded. 'There's this bloke I used to share a cell with in Doncaster. I paid him a grand to give Kevin a bit of a hiding.'

'Where did you get a thousand pounds from?'

'I've been saving up for a better flat. I've not got much saved for a deposit but I could spare a grand and I knew Colin wouldn't do it for free.'

'Colin Theobald?'

'Yes.'

'Did you speak to Colin after Kevin had been killed?'

'No. When I found out what had happened I got scared. I told him just to give Kevin a bit of a slap, you know? I didn't think he'd kill him and I definitely didn't think he'd shoot him. Then he went and raped that woman. That wasn't part of the plan.'

'Why did you hide?'

'I thought Colin would come and look for me, say he'd done the job proper, like, and ask for more money. I haven't got any more money. I didn't ask him to do this. I swear I didn't. I just wanted Kevin to stop hurting my sister.' Lucas lost his grip on his emotions and out poured a torrent of tears.

From the file under her arm Matilda produced the same photograph that Colin had identified in his cells.

'Lucas, is this the man who told you about Alice's affair?'

He looked up, sniffled, wiped his nose with his sleeve, and looked at the photo. He didn't need long to make up his mind. He nodded. 'That's him. That's the bloke.'

For a split second, Matilda almost felt sorry for him. Then she remembered that Lucas was the one responsible for putting Joseph Glass in hospital and the anger she felt towards him returned.

'Lucas, why did you run Scott Andrews off the road?'

'I wasn't thinking straight. After what I'd done to that copper I knew you'd be after me. I watched while the ambulance came for him and that other copper, the blond one, followed in his car. I followed too. I waited all day for him to come out and when he did I just thought maybe if I could scare him he wouldn't identify me to the police. I thought he wouldn't have said anything yet as he'd been at the hospital all afternoon.'

'So you ran him off the road?'

He nodded, shaking the tears from his face. 'Is he all right?'

'Why do you care?'

'I'm sorry.'

'No you're not, Lucas,' Matilda leaned in close, her face just

337

inches away from the prisoner's. 'I'm going to make sure you're jailed for a very long time.'

'Are you sitting comfortably people?'

Matilda breezed into the Murder Room with a satisfied smile on her face. Her head was held high; her back was straight. She seemed ten feet tall in the wake of her triumph. Flicking through the file she extracted the photograph and placed it at the top of the whiteboard.

'This is the man who orchestrated the killing of Kevin Hardaker and the attack on Lois Craven.'

Everyone leaned forward to get a good look at the family snap.

'But that's Martin Craven,' Sian said.

'Correct.' Matilda stood to one side, arms folded.

'He has a cast-iron alibi,' Aaron commented.

'Ah, I didn't say he committed the crime. I said he orchestrated it.'

'You're going to have to talk us through this, boss.'

'Which is why I asked if you were all sitting comfortably.'

Matilda filled them in on what she had found out from Colin and Lucas. Unfortunately, it was only their side of the story. She needed to hear it from Martin's own lips. She wanted to know what turned a mild-mannered family man into a twisted manipulator. Lois may have treated him badly, but she didn't deserve that. And neither did Kevin.

'So where do we go from here?' Sian asked.

'We're going to talk to Martin. However, if this is all true, then he's a bit of a loose cannon. I don't want to go in there not knowing what to expect. So, Sian, you come with me. Aaron, you, Scott and Rory stay in the background until we need you. Understand?'

Heads were nodded. Then coats were gathered. As they were leaving the Murder Room, Matilda almost ran into Christian Brady as she strode along the corridor.

'Christian, will you do me a favour?'

'You've saved me a massive headache with these burglaries, I'll do anything you want,' he smiled.

'Well, we'll talk about you donating your sperm at a later date.' Christian's smile dropped and a look of horror swept across his face. 'I'm joking Christian, but thanks for hiding your repulsion so well. I want you to interview Colin Theobald again for me. Ask him about Gerald Beecham. Find out if he had anything to do with his death.'

'Will do.' The look of shock was still on his face as he headed past her down the corridor.

Over her shoulder, Matilda called out. 'Maybe have a strong coffee first to calm your nerves.'

She laughed as she trotted to join the rest of her team. This was what Matilda enjoyed most about policing; when everything seemed to be going in the right direction and she knew what she had to do to reach the finishing line. If only she knew how much would change before she reached it.

FIFTY-FOUR

'I didn't think you were coming until tonight.'

'I've had my compassionate leave extended. I thought I'd come and take you out.'

Lois's eyes lit up. 'Really?'

'Yes. I've had a word with the nurses and they say a touch of fresh air may do you good. They've given me a wheelchair. Fancy a spin around the grounds?'

Martin smiled as he looked down on his wife who had been sitting up in bed and staring out of the window between the dust-covered slats of the ancient venetian blind.

Martin's face was red and his eyes were bulging. He looked exhausted and downtrodden, yet determined and poised. His body was rigid. He could feel the ticks of emotion beating away in his face and neck, which he struggled to keep under control. He held on to the wheelchair tightly, his knuckles white with tension.

'You're going to have to help me out of bed; I'm still in a lot of pain,' Lois said as she tried, but failed, to get out on her own.

Martin walked around the bed. He didn't know how to hold his wife. He had seen her in the hospital gown – her entire body was covered in bruises. Now in pink pyjamas brought from home she looked fragile and timid. She put her arms around his neck and lifted herself up off the bed. He felt nothing as he touched her. Any last vestiges of love had been destroyed. The pain was evident from the excruciating look on her face. Carefully, Martin placed her in the wheelchair and covered her up with a blanket over her knees.

'Are you comfortable?'

'Despite being in agony, yes.' She smiled through the pain.

'Come on then, I've got a surprise for you outside.'

Colin Theobald said he didn't want his solicitor present this time. 'What's the point? I'm going down anyway.' The cold interview room was occupied by DI Christian Brady and DC Faith Easter on one side of the table and a self-satisfied Colin Theobald on the other. Despite confessing to the burglaries, his part in the double shooting, and facing a lengthy stretch in prison, he was full of bravado. Or was he still playing a part? Would the real Colin Theobald ever stand up?

'Colin, you live on the twelfth floor of Tower B on London Road don't you?'

'I certainly do: flat 86.'

'On the night of the double shooting, where did you go afterwards?'

A light turned on in Colin's head: he knew where this conversation was heading. He sat back and smiled. 'I went home.'

'Straight home?'

'Yep. I went to get changed.'

'Then what did you do?'

'I went out again. I needed to get rid of the clothes I'd been wearing. They were filthy and covered in blood,' he said, savouring the last sentence and glancing at Faith Easter's poker face.

'Where did you go to get rid of your clothes?'

'I went up to the roof. I was going to burn them.'

'And did you?'

'Yes … eventually.'

'Why eventually?'

'Well I set fire to my trainers first and they took a while to burn as they were soaked so I just sat back and watched, when this old bloke came out from the stairs.'

'Old bloke?'

'Yes. Some old bastard. I've heard him moaning before about people going up to the roof to mess about, drinking, dealing, kids on their scooters. I mean, what's it got to do with him? He doesn't own the bloody building.'

'Do you know who this old bloke is?'

'No. Just know him by sight. He looked like a joyless bastard.'

'So what happened?'

'He came out onto the roof and asked me what the fuck I thought I was playing at. They were his exact words too. He swore at me. I told him to mind his own business, nosy old twat. He said it was his business as I could send the whole building up in flames. I told him, it wouldn't be a huge loss. They need pulling down anyway. I'd be doing everyone a favour. He said if I didn't put the fire out he was going to call the police.'

'What did you say?'

'Well, I said that if he wanted the fire to go out then he would have to put it out himself. I stood back, you know, inviting him over.'

'And did he?'

'Yes, he came over to where the trainers were burning. Then he looked behind me and saw my clothes with the blood on them. To be honest, I'd actually forgotten they were there for a minute. He asked me what I'd been up to. I told him to keep his fucking nose out. So he said he had a right to know if my actions were going to interfere with his life. So I told him.' Colin shrugged. His nonchalance was frightening. He had no regard for anyone else's life. Other people were expendable: an obstacle he needed to climb over in order to achieve his aim.

'What exactly did you tell him?' Christian asked.

'I said I'd just been out killing a bloke and raping his bitch girlfriend.'

Christian swallowed hard. It was difficult to listen to Colin talk about his crimes so casually, as if they were a day at the seaside. 'Did he believe you?'

'Dunno. He looked a bit white so I'm guessing he did. He started to back up then. He said I should be locked up.'

'What happened then?'

'He walked away. I knew he was going to phone the fire brigade and the filth. I couldn't have that. I picked the trainers up and threw them at his back.' Colin laughed. 'You should have heard the sound he made when he thought he'd caught fire. I nearly pissed myself laughing. I told him if he called the police I'd break into his flat while he was sleeping, tie him to his bed, and set fire to him. Do you know what he did then?'

'Go on,' Christian was dreading the answer. He could picture the photograph of Gerald Beecham he had in the incident room. He looked like a kind, elderly gent, who didn't deserve to live out his days in the soulless box of a tower block.

'He started to cry. Can you believe that? A grown man and he was fucking crying. He walked away then. I wasn't having him ring you lot on me. So I grabbed him – he was light for an old bloke – picked him up and lobbed him over the side.'

The room fell silent. Colin folded his arms. His story was over. He told the story of Gerald Beecham's death like it was a fairytale: a bedtime story for a small child, not the murder of an innocent man.

Faith looked away as she swept away a tear. Christian ran through the preliminaries and turned off the recording equipment.

'When you're in prison,' Christian began, voice lowered. 'I'm going to make sure people know exactly what you've done, and if there is any justice in this world, your death will be as painful as Gerald Beecham's.'

This time the real Colin Theobald did stand up. His face dropped. The smile vanished and he began to twitch as if he didn't know where to look. The realization of what awaited him inside prison had suddenly hit home.

'I want to see my lawyer,' he said, voice quivering.

'Too late,' Christian said. He turned to leave the interview room with Faith Easter following. He slammed the door hard, leaving Colin alone in the room with only his dark imagination and twisted thoughts for company.

FIFTY-FIVE

As usual, parking on Williamson Road was a nightmare. There was a nursery school at one end and an NHS building for the treatment of people with mental health issues at the other. The narrow road was clogged with parking on both sides. Matilda eventually found a space several doors down from Martin Craven's home, while in the second car, Aaron, Rory, and Scott continued to drive and ended up parking in the next street.

Matilda and Sian waited for the others to join them.

'Right, you three wait here. We're going to go in for a nice wee chat. If we're not out in ten minutes, come and find us.'

They nodded in agreement.

'Don't be long, it's cold out here,' Rory said.

'Oh man up,' Sian replied as she and Matilda made their way down the drive.

Sian knocked on the door and stepped back, looking up at the house. Matilda, on tiptoes, looked into the kitchen window, but couldn't see any sign of life.

'Knock again.'

Sian did, louder this time, but there was still no reply. She tried the handle. The door was unlocked.

'I don't like the look of this,' Sian said.

'Come on.'

Matilda took the lead and headed into the house. The heat from the kitchen was comforting – Rory would love to have been in Sian's position – but the room looked like it hadn't been used all morning.

'Hello? Mr Craven? It's DCI Matilda Darke from the police again. I've got a couple more questions I'd like to ask.'

They stood stock-still while they waited for a reply from upstairs, or any sign of life. Nothing happened.

'Hello? Mr Craven? Jack? Anna? Anyone?'

'Thomas?' Sian called out.

Matilda looked at her and rolled her eyes. 'Thomas is deaf, remember?'

'Oh God, yes, of course he is. Sorry.'

They moved into the hallway. Matilda peeked into the dining room – empty. The door to the living room was closed. She pushed it open and signalled to Sian that this was where they needed to be. The room was a wreck. The coffee table was over-turned, the TV tipped off its stand, books pulled from the bookcase, and in the centre of the room was the motionless body of an elderly woman.

'Get the others,' Matilda shouted as she made her way to the stricken body.

All Matilda could see was a mass of blood on the back of the woman's head. The hair was matted around the wound. From this angle, Matilda couldn't see who it was. The last time she was here, Martin Craven mentioned his mother-in-law had been coming round often to help with the kids. Is that who this was? Was this Lois's mother?

Matilda felt for a pulse and found one. It was strong. She tried to rouse her by shaking her slightly by the shoulder but nothing happened. She turned her over carefully. Her face was free from injury and her eyes were closed.

'Can you hear me?'

346

Matilda looked up as Sian entered with Aaron, Scott, and Rory in tow. When she looked back down at the woman, she was slowly opening her eyes.

'What's happened? What's going on? Thomas?' She called out, growing more and more panicked as she came to. She started shaking.

'She's in shock.'

'Scott, try and find a brandy or a whisky or something. Then put the kettle on and make a hot, sweet tea. Rory, call for an ambulance.'

Between them Matilda and Sian carefully lifted her off the floor and onto the sofa. 'Can you tell me your name?'

'Margaret. I'm Lois's mother.'

'OK, Margaret. What happened here?'

Scott ran in with a large whisky and handed it to Sian who passed it to Margaret. She gave her thanks and took a large sip. She winced at the taste then had another drink.

'Martin saw the article in the newspaper about Lois having had several affairs in the past. Before it was only us who knew about it, now everybody did. He thought the neighbours would start talking about him for putting up with it all over the years. I told him not to be so silly. They wouldn't think like that at all. They'd admire him for not abandoning his children. Then he just flipped.'

Aaron had found a first aid kit in the kitchen. He pulled out some padding and passed it to Sian for her to hold against the wound on Margaret's head. The bleeding had stopped but it was still an open, angry-looking wound.

'He said some horrible, hurtful things about Lois. I know she's not been the best wife in the world, and he's overlooked so much, but there was no need for any of that. He went mad. Well, you can see what he did in here. I tried to stop him but he kept pushing me away.'

'Did he hit you?'

'No. I fell. I must have slipped on a book or something that

347

he'd thrown to the floor and banged my head on the coffee table. He wouldn't hit me. If he ever tried to raise a hand to me I'd kick him where it hurts.'

Matilda smiled. 'We're going to get you to hospital, Margaret. Have you checked out. You may need a few stitches though.'

'Oh God, do you think so? I've a birthday do coming up next month.'

'Margaret, was there anyone else in the house while Martin was kicking off?'

Margaret suddenly jumped up. 'Thomas. Oh my God, Thomas. Where is he?'

'Rory, look upstairs.'

Rory flew out of the room. The sound of his heavy footsteps on the stairs echoed around the house as everyone downstairs waited with bated breath for confirmation that Thomas was upstairs playing quietly in his room.

'There's nobody up here,' Rory shouted.

'Oh my God, Thomas,' Margaret began to cry. 'Where's he taken him?'

'Margaret, calm down. We don't know if he's taken him anywhere. Nothing bad is going to happen.'

Matilda and Sian exchanged glances – neither of them believed that.

The ambulance arrived within five minutes. As Margaret was being loaded into the back she told Matilda to find the children and keep them safe. She said that the look in Martin's eyes was petrifying. She had never seen him look so wild before.

Matilda tried to fit that image with the one she had seen last time she was at the house. Martin had looked tired, worried for his wife, and his children. He was doing his best to keep the kids happy and content while their lives were being dragged through the mire of the local newspapers, and the gossips were making up their own stories of the Cravens' home life. To Matilda, Martin looked every bit the broken man trying to piece back together his life and make some sense out of the rubble. Had it all been an act? If so, he had certainly fooled her. This begged the question, how much danger were the people around him in?

'Scott, go in the ambulance with Margaret.' He wasn't happy about being assigned to babysitting duties, but he nodded and climbed in behind the trolley.

'Aaron, we need to find the kids—' Matilda began.

Aaron interrupted. 'Margaret gave me her mobile before she was put into the ambulance. I've called Anna and Jack; they're in town doing some shopping. I've not gone into any details but I've told them to go to HQ straightaway and ask for Faith. I've just got off the phone to her; she's going to keep them safe until she's heard from us.'

'Excellent work, Aaron, thank you. Do they know where Thomas is?'

'I didn't ask. I didn't want them to be worried.'

'OK. Go to the Northern General and make your presence known around Lois, but don't make it look like you're there for her protection.'

'Will do.'

'Take Rory with you. And, if Martin does turn up, give me a shout straightaway.'

'What the hell has happened now?'

Sian turned around to see an elderly woman struggling under the weight of two shopping bags in each hand trundling up the road. She wasn't more than five foot in sensible heels and the bags were scraping along the ground. Her face was ruddy as the bitter spring wind nipped at her exposed nose and cheeks.

'You are?'

'I'm Jennifer Nash. I live next door. Don't tell me something else has happened to that poor family. They've had enough bad luck lately.'

'It's nothing like that. Lois's mother, Margaret, she's had a fall.'

'I'm not surprised in those shoes she wears. At her age she should go for flats. For a minute I thought you were going to tell me Martin had done himself in.'

'Is he the type?'

'They're all the type, mark my words. My brother jumped in front of a train in 1972 over some woman. Men! They haven't got the staying power of us women. Mind you, I read the paper this morning. It sounds like Martin's put up with a lot over the years. Is it true what they're saying about Lois having affairs right, left, and centre?' Sian didn't reply, not that she was given the chance. 'I wouldn't put it past her. She looks the type. That Martin's a saint though. He's practically brought those three kiddies up on his own. It's them I feel sorry for. If I were that Martin, I'd have knocked her into touch years ago. Anyway, I can't stand here gabbing, I've got stuff for the freezer in these bags. Ta-ra love.'

Sian smiled. The gossip of neighbours never ceased to amaze her.

'You look worried,' Sian said as she joined Matilda in the middle of the road to watch the ambulance drive away at speed followed by Aaron and Rory.

'I am. I spoke to Martin only yesterday. He didn't look like he was about to fly off the handle.'

'Maybe he reached breaking point.'

'I think he reached breaking point the second he hired a hitman. The question is, has he finally lost control? From the state of the house, I'd say yes. That's years' worth of pent-up aggression about to burst out. If Thomas is with him, then he's in serious trouble.'

FIFTY-SIX

There was a new unit being built at the Northern General, complete with helipad, so the car parks were more congested than usual. Parking wardens were directing people carefully around the building site and traffic was held up while diggers and heavy machinery were brought in. Aaron and Rory waited patiently.

'If your Katrina said she was having another man's baby, what would you do?' Rory asked from the front passenger seat.

'I'd find out who it was then I'd kill him,' he replied in his usual deadpan tone.

'Would you stay with her though, bring the kid up as your own?'

'Piss off. Do I look like a mug? What about you with Amelia?'

Rory rolled his eyes and sighed. 'There's no chance of that happening. Until she's qualified the subject of marriage, kids, and sex is completely off the table. She's even started wearing a nightie to bed. At this rate we'll have separate beds by Christmas.'

'How long until she qualifies?'

'God knows. I can hardly get two words out of her. Every evening she's got her face in some law book. Still, at least I can watch Sheffield United in peace.'

Aaron looked out of the side window as a large crane made its way noisily and slowly down the road. As his view cleared, he cast his eye over the impressive sight of the hospital grounds and their various buildings and units. Something caught his eye and he looked up at the roof of the Hadfield Wing – a six storey recent addition to the Northern General site, named after Sir Robert Hadfield, discoverer of manganese steel. On the roof he saw three figures moving about, one of whom was wearing a dressing gown.

'Shit,' Aaron said under his breath.

'What's up?'

'Look up there, on the roof.'

'Where?'

'On the roof! Is that who I think it is?'

Rory leaned over to the driver's side of the car and was almost on Aaron's lap, straining to see out of the window. 'Jesus Christ. Is that Lois Craven?'

'If it is then that's her husband with her. And, by the look of it, little Thomas.'

'What are they doing on the roof?'

'I doubt they're up there for a picnic and to admire the view. Phone Matilda.'

Aaron climbed out of the car while Rory made the call. He didn't want to draw attention to himself, or to whatever was happening on the roof, but he needed to keep an eye on any development. He looked around to see if anyone else had noticed, but, thankfully, the disruption from the building work was more interesting to visitors to the hospital.

'Matilda's on her way,' Rory said as he appeared next to Aaron. 'What are we going to do?'

'I've no idea until Matilda gets here,' he thought for a moment. 'Right, go into the Hadfield Wing and discreetly ask how you get up onto the roof. Show your ID and tell whoever you ask to keep it to themselves. I'm guessing Matilda will want to go up there when she arrives.'

They both looked up at the imposing building. Judging by how wildly Lois's hair was flying about in the breeze, it looked mighty dangerous up there.

It didn't take Matilda and Sian long to arrive at the hospital. They didn't bother looking for a parking space, they just pulled up. As Matilda jumped out of the car and approached Aaron, she looked up at the roof.

'How long have they been up there?'

'I've no idea. I've been keeping an eye on them. It looks like they're just talking.'

'Anyone else up there with them?'

'No. Well, there's a young child who I'm guessing is Thomas.'

'Shit.'

'Rory's in the building trying to find out how to get up to the roof.'

'Right, OK,' she said, thinking aloud. 'Aaron, get on to the fire brigade and tell them what's happening. I don't want them coming with sirens blaring though. Also, try and keep people away from the building. Don't draw attention to it. Fingers crossed we can stop this from escalating any further than it already has.'

'What are you going to do?'

'I'm going to go up there and have a word.'

'What are you going to say?'

'I haven't the foggiest. Come on Sian.'

'Me?'

'Yes.'

'I don't like heights.'

'Neither do I. Come on, we can be scared together.'

They met Rory as they were entering the building. Rory told Matilda he had secured the confidence of a security guard who was going to take Matilda up to the roof.

The journey in the lift was smooth but seemed to take an age. Matilda and Sian stared straight ahead, their concentration firmly attached to the doors. The unnecessarily tall security guard tried to make small talk but he soon gave up when he realized he was being ignored.

There was a ping. They had reached their destination. Matilda took a deep breath as the doors opened and a gust of wind hit them all in the face. Fighting back the elements, Matilda and Sian struggled to leave the lift.

'Keep this lift free,' Matilda shouted to the security guard. Her words were blown away by the wind and she was sure he hadn't heard her. He smiled and nodded as the doors closed.

Matilda and Sian looked like a comedy double act as they held on to each other for dear life. They made their way around to the front of the building and stopped as soon as they saw the Cravens.

Thomas was sitting on the ground, back against the ledge of the building, sheltering from the worst of the wind. Lois was leaning against the ledge. She was shivering with cold and struggling to keep her dressing gown closed. The pain she was in was etched on her face. It was difficult to tell whether it was pain from her injuries or pain from the situation she had found herself in. Martin was looking out over the city. He looked lost, his face a map of anger, frustration, betrayal, and despair. The wind blew away his tears before they had a chance to fall down his face.

Matilda, with Sian keeping her distance (her fear of heights was almost chronic), managed to get quite close before she was noticed.

'Stay back,' shouted Martin, though his words were little more than a whisper by the time they reached Matilda's ears.

Matilda stopped and held her hands up. 'What are you doing, Martin?'

'What does it look like I'm doing? I'm teaching this … this … thing a lesson,' he said. He pointed at his wife. He was unable to call her a woman, by her name, or his wife. The hatred he felt for his wife was of volcanic proportions. This was not going to end well.

'Martin, I know you're angry. I would be too, but there's no need to drag Thomas into this.'

Martin looked down at the child shivering at the corner of the roof. 'Did you know this bastard isn't even mine?'

Matilda closed her eyes. *It's a good job he's deaf. He doesn't deserve to hear any of this.*

'I know, Martin. Look, it's bloody freezing up here. Why don't we all go down and have a coffee, warm up, and have a good chat. You can air your views.'

'I don't want to chat. I'm fed up chatting, of listening to this bitch's lies. She's lied from day one.'

'I haven't, Martin,' Lois cried. 'I love you.'

That's the last thing he wants to hear.

'Love? You don't know the meaning of the word. You're selfish. You've thought of nobody but yourself your entire life.' He turned to Matilda, 'do you know, she was the last of us to learn sign language? Do you know why? Because she was never at fucking home. She was constantly out, probably sleeping with any bloke who smiled at her.'

'That's not true!'

'No? I may look stupid but I'm not. You've cheated on me our entire marriage and I've just sat back and taken it. I've let you get away with so much and what have you done for me in return? Nothing.'

'Martin, please, let's go down. I'm in a lot of pain,' Lois said, holding firmly onto her stomach.

'Pain? I'll tell you what pain is. Pain is having to talk to your daughter about periods while you were fuck knows where; watching a child who isn't even your son in the Christmas nativity; explaining to Jack why his mother wasn't at his tenth birthday party. You think you're in pain? You haven't got the first idea.' He lunged forward and punched his wife hard in the stomach. She screamed and staggered backwards. She held onto her stomach and bent double.

Thomas flinched as he saw his mother's pain. There were tears in his eyes. He had no idea what was going on.

'Martin, stop,' Matilda called out. She started edging forward again. 'This is not going to solve anything.'

Lois took her hand away from her stomach. It was covered in blood. The punch had torn the stitches and opened up a healing wound.

'I'm bleeding. You have to do something,' she pleaded with Matilda.

'Martin, calm down. Come on, let's talk. Tell me about meeting Lucas Branning.'

Matilda turned back to Sian and nodded for her to edge closer so she could attend to Lois and her injuries while she distracted Martin. Unfortunately, fear had gripped Sian and she was rendered stuck against the back of the lift shaft. Matilda was alone.

'Lucas? That loser. I knew him for what he was the second I set eyes on him. I'm good at reading people. I have to be. After this bitch cheated on me and promised never to do it again I knew the signs. I knew there'd be a second time. And a third. And a fourth.'

'Martin, what did you say to Lucas?' She needed to get him back on track, take his attention away from his wife and on to her.

'I told him that his brother-in-law was making his sister's life a living hell and he should do something about it. He looked gullible so I knew he'd fall for whatever I told him. Pillock. He did too. He went straight round to that … whatever his name is.'

'Colin Theobald.'

'Whatever. Now, he was a bloke I could do business with. Have you seen him? Built like a tank. I could picture him teaching that bastard Kevin Hardaker a lesson and I knew he'd scare the shit out of this little bitch.'

'How much did you offer him?'

'Ten grand. I didn't tell him I'd pay him. I said Kevin's wife would. He believed me too. Can you believe that? Another gullible twat.'

'You asked him to rape me?' Lois cried through the tears and the pain.

'No,' he leaned in close to her face. 'I told him to have some fun with you. I told him to do whatever he wanted but to keep you alive.'

'Oh my God.'

'What are you crying for? Knowing you, you probably enjoyed it.'

'Martin—' Matilda began but he interrupted her.

'Have you seen the paper today? They know. Everybody knows what a lying, cheating, dirty, sex-mad whore this piece of filth is. They're all talking about me. They'll all be laughing. "Oh look, there's Martin the doormat. Did you know his wife screws every man she meets and he just lets her? What a mug! He stays at home every night looking after the kids, one of them isn't even his, while she's out shagging anyone in sight".'

'Nobody is saying that, Martin. We've just come from your house. I spoke to your neighbour. She doesn't think like that at all.'

'Of course not, not to your face. But behind your back they'll be saying all sorts of things. No, I'm not putting up with it anymore. Come here.'

Martin grabbed his wife by the shoulders and dragged her up from the roof. She screamed in pain. The front of her dressing gown was soaked in blood. He clamped his arm around her neck and held on to her tight. She pulled at his arm as her face reddened. She was struggling to breathe. With his free arm he grabbed the collar of Thomas's jumper and lifted him up.

'Martin, wait,' Matilda screamed. 'What about Jack and Anna?' She edged ever closer. She could almost reach out and touch them.

'What about them?'

'They need you. They need their mother. They need their brother.'

'No they don't. They're old enough to look after themselves. Besides, she's not been a mother to them.' His voice was calm. He had made up his mind.

Matilda looked directly into his eyes and all she saw was sadness. There was no stopping him. There was nothing else she could do.

Martin took a step back, all the time keeping his eyes locked on Matilda. Lois struggled but the life was being choked out of her. Thomas, scared, crying and clinging to his father, was oblivious to what was about to happen next.

Matilda jumped forward.

Sian, struck with terror, let out a glass-shattering scream. She raised her hands to cover her face. The last thing she saw was four people disappearing over the edge of a tall building.

EPILOGUE

Music began. *Beautiful Day* by U2. By the first chorus, the curtain slowly closed around the coffin. Sobs from the congregation were heard, growing louder as the dark blue heavy curtains met in the middle, drowning out the song.

The front row was packed out with family; mother and father inconsolable, sister equally devastated at the side of her grieving parents. The second, third, and fourth rows were taken up with cousins, aunties, uncles, distant relatives, close friends, and neighbours.

Towards the back of the hall sat the work colleagues; Sian Mills cried a torrent of tears into a rapidly disintegrating tissue, Faith Easter was fighting a losing battle and searched her bag for one more hanky. Aaron Connolly was his usual stony-faced self but he kept swallowing hard, choked with emotion. Rory Fleming wasn't afraid to shed a tear or two, but he swiftly wiped them away, and Scott Andrews looked down at the floor. His tears ran freely down his face. Valerie Masterson was the picture of professionalism. She sniffled several times but managed to keep her emotions in check. At the end of the row sat Adele Kean. She was hidden behind a pair of large sunglasses but her face was stained with the tracks of dried tears. This was a genuine tragedy.

Outside, the clouds were heavy and threatened rain. So far it had stayed dry but the wind was blowing strong and the dark clouds were thickening. It was only a matter of time before the heavens opened and released a deluge of rain.

It was to be Matilda Darke's first funeral since her husband's exactly one year ago to the day and she could not face going inside the crematorium. Making sure she was at the back of the crowd, she waited until everyone had entered before she turned on her heel and headed in the direction of the graves.

She visited Jonathan Harkness first and thanked him for the collection of crime fiction novels. She promised to look after them and said she would continue adding to it with new releases from his favourite authors.

'I phoned a carpenter last week. They've measured up one of my spare rooms and I'm turning it into a library. It's going to be floor to ceiling shelves. I'm changing the glass in the windows too so the sunlight won't bleach the books. I know you'll approve.'

She touched the headstone with a gloved hand and turned away. She would be visiting him again. He may have been a murderer, but there was something about Jonathan Harkness that would always have a hold over her. Next time, she would make a point of bringing flowers.

As she made her way to her husband's grave she heard the sound of the last verse coming from the hall. The service was coming to an end. Was it fate that said she should return exactly one year later to witness a funeral of someone taken long before their time?

JAMES MATHEW DARKE
OCTOBER 6TH 1970 – MARCH 28TH 2015
LOVING HUSBAND, SON, BROTHER & UNCLE

'Hello James,' she said to the marble headstone. 'One year ago today we were lowering you into the ground. Sometimes it feels like only yesterday and other times it seems like a lifetime ago. Some days I think I can't carry on without you. But I know that I have to, I can't let myself or my team down. I think about you all the time, day and night. You're the only person I've ever loved and being without you is agony. I … I can't … I don't … I—' She couldn't finish. She searched in her pockets for a tissue.

'Matilda.' Adele put a hand on Matilda's shoulder and stirred her from her reverie.

'Adele. Is it over already?'

'Yes.'

'How was it?'

'It was horrible. A beautiful send-off though. His family said some lovely things about him, especially his sister.'

'How are his parents?'

'I have no idea how they're going to get through this.'

They both looked over to where Grahame and Sandra Glass were being escorted by their surviving child. Grahame looked numb, his face expressionless. Sandra needed supporting. So struck with grief she could hardly walk. It had been a difficult decision to choose whether to turn Joseph Glass's life support machine off. In the end they couldn't bear to see their son lying comatose in a strange bed, knowing he would never wake up.

'How are you?' Adele said, rubbing Matilda's back.

'I'm OK. Exactly a year ago today since we buried him.'

'I know.'

'I couldn't go in there. I'm sorry …'

'Don't worry about it. Everyone will understand,' Adele quickly placated. 'There's a bit of a do at the Beauchief. Are you coming?'

'Yes. I want to offer my condolences to Mr and Mrs Glass. Today is about them, not me.'

Matilda looked down at the grave of her husband, said a quiet goodbye, and turned away. She linked arms with Adele as they made their way to the car park.

'It was Lois Craven's funeral yesterday,' Matilda said.

'Yes. I saw it in the paper this morning. When's Martin's?'

'I'm not sure. Sometime this week.'

'It must be hell for those kids. Who's going to be looking after Thomas?'

'Jack is being very responsible. He's deferring his A-levels for a year and will take them part-time while he works to support Thomas. Anna isn't interested in going to college so she's going to get a job too when she's finished her GCSEs.'

'It's a bit of an undertaking though.'

'What else can they do? There's no other family to take care of him. It's either that or put him up for adoption.'

'By the way, Sian finally told me everything that happened on the roof of that building. She says you were almost taken over yourself.'

'Not quite.'

'Your feet left the ground as you grabbed for Thomas.'

'Well, yes, but only for a short—'

'You could have died, Matilda. You took a massive risk. Again.'

'You didn't see him, Adele. Thomas was sitting in the corner of the roof, just waiting there. His mum and dad were going through all sorts and he was completely oblivious. He was an innocent victim in all of this. You should have seen his face when Martin grabbed him; he looked so confused: terrified and yet trusting of his father at the same time. I couldn't let Martin kill a defenceless child. You'd have done exactly the same thing if you were in my position and don't try and tell me otherwise.'

'But still ... You should have waited for backup before going up to the roof. What was going through your mind when you leapt forward like that?'

Matilda thought for a second. *I would have been reunited with James.* 'I've no idea. I didn't want Thomas's death on my conscience though. If Martin had been up there with Lois, I wouldn't have put myself in such a position. A child should not suffer for the actions of their parents.'

'If you'd gone over—'

'No ifs, Adele,' Matilda interrupted.

They walked on slowly towards the exit. 'Any news on Ben Hales?' Adele asked.

'He's been discharged from hospital. Apparently his wife's returned and is taking care of him. He was lucky he wasn't killed.'

'I wonder what happened to him to just suddenly make him want to kill himself like that.'

Matilda opened and closed her mouth. She hadn't told anyone of the confrontation in her hallway – the angry, faraway look Ben had as he gripped her throat. She genuinely believed he was going to rape her. She hoped she would never have to see him again.

'What is it?'

At the edge of the car park, Matilda stopped dead in her tracks. Her lower jaw dropped and her eyes widened.

'Matilda? What's wrong?'

'That car. That black BMW. That's the one that's been following me.'

'Are you sure?'

'I'd know that registration number anywhere.'

The driver's door opened but nobody stepped out. First, Matilda thought she was being followed by Colin Theobald, then Lucas Branning, but neither of them had access to the same model of BMW that had been following her. She then assumed it was Ben Hales. He had been driving a black BMW, though he had only admitted to the phone calls, not to following her. Now, she had found them. Or rather, they had found her.

Matilda swallowed hard. She was about to face her stalker.

Out of the car, dressed from head to toe in black, stepped Sally Meagan, Carl Meagan's mother.

'Oh my God.'

'Is that who I think it is?' Adele asked.

363

'I'm afraid so.'

Their eyes locked. Matilda couldn't blink, the wind was stinging her eyes and her vision was blurring. She could feel the onset of a panic attack, but nothing could tear her away.

Eventually, Sally closed the door of the car and headed towards Matilda, taking long, slow strides. They didn't break eye contact.

Adele's grip on Matilda tightened in solidarity. Matilda was unable to move, so rooted was she to the spot. She would love to turn heel and run off into the distance, but her legs wouldn't allow it.

'I'm not going to make a scene,' Sally spoke quietly. 'This is hardly the time or the place. I've come here to give you a warning.'

Matilda swallowed hard.

'I've been watching you and I will continue to watch you every day of your life so that you never forget me or Carl. I blame you 100 per cent for not returning him to me and I will not rest until I know what happened to him. Do you understand me?'

She didn't wait for a reply. Her voice was breaking, the raw emotion difficult to contain.

'I can't continue with my life while I don't know where Carl is. I will campaign, I will do interviews and I will keep him alive in everyone's mind until someone tells me where he is. Until that day arrives I don't have a life. And neither will you.' Sally turned and walked away, her head held high, her strides strong and determined.

Matilda and Adele waited until she had driven away, before any of them dared move or speak.

'Are you OK?' Adele asked pointlessly.

'No I'm not. She blames me.'

'She's angry. She's still grieving. I read in the paper the other day she's writing a book.'

'What?'

'She signed a six-figure deal to write a book about her ordeal and the treatment she received at the hands of the press and police.'

'Oh my God. It's going to be a hatchet job.'

'Not necessarily.'

'The woman hates me, Adele. It's hardly going to be a love letter is it?'

'Come on. Let's go and have a drink.' Adele grabbed her arm and tried to get her into the car.

'No. I don't want to. I want to be on my own.'

'Matilda, that's the last thing you should be.'

'I'll call you later.'

Matilda turned and headed back towards the graveyard. She needed someone to talk to, someone who wouldn't judge her, someone who would understand exactly how she was feeling right now. James or Jonathan?

ACKNOWLEDGEMENTS

It may take one person to create a story, but it takes a whole team to put the words in the correct order. I would like to thank Lucy Dauman, Kate Stephenson and all the team at Killer Reads and HarperCollins, and Janette Currie, my brilliant copyeditor.

Claire Walker of iGene London Ltd. who gave me a detailed insight into digital autopsies and answered my many questions. I hope I wasn't too much of an inconvenience. Alex Curran who supplied me with some excellent legal advice. Unfortunately, the plot didn't make the final version of this book but I am very grateful to you, and to Chris Ratcliff for the author photographs.

The advice given to me by members of the police, who wish not to be named, has been invaluable. Any mistakes are my own and for the purposes of fiction.

I have been given some sensible advice, great reviews and encouragement by established writers in the crime fiction community: Alex Marwood, Elly Griffiths, Ben Cheetham, Chris Simms, M. H. Hall – thank you all. I owe you a drink.

I am also indebted to the reviewers and bloggers who helped to make my first book a success. There are too many to name but you know who you are. A special shout out to Kate, Noelle (and Buster), Joseph, Amanda, Liz, Karen, David, Sarah, Vicki, Kelly and Fiona.

The usual suspects to thank are: Jonas, Chris, Kevin, Chris, and most importantly, the encouragement of my family, specifically my mum (who supplied cake to keep me writing and spread the word about my book to most of Sheffield) and the devotion of and motivation from Woody (best writing companion ever).

KILLER READS

DISCOVER THE BEST IN CRIME AND THRILLER

Follow us on social media to get to know the team behind the books, enter exclusive giveaways, learn about the latest competitions, hear from our authors, and lots more:

 /KillerReads

 /KillerReads